DREAMER

TALES OF THE OUTLAW MAGES
Book Three

AMY CAMPBELL

Legend
Has It LLC

DREAMER

Copyright © 2022 Amy Campbell

Published in the United States by Amy Campbell

Publisher's Cataloging-in-Publication data

Names: Campbell, Amy D., author.

Title: Dreamer : tales of the outlaw mages , book 3 / Amy Campbell.

Series: Tales of the Outlaw Mages

Description: Houston, TX: Amy Campbell, 2022.

Identifiers: LCCN: 2022902957 | ISBN: 978-1-7361418-4-7 (paperback) | 978-1-7361418-5-4 (ebook) | 979-8-7655276-2-7 (paperback)

Subjects: Magic--Fiction. | Animals, Mythical--Fiction. | Pegasus (Greek mythology)--Fiction. | Alchemy--Fiction. | Asexual people--Fiction. | Outlaws--Fiction. | Fantasy fiction. | BISAC FICTION / Fantasy / Action & Adventure | FICTION / Fantasy / Dragons & Mythical Creatures | FICTION / Fantasy / Historical | FICTION / LGBTQ+ / General

Classification: LCC PS3603.A4685 D74 2022 | DDC 813.6--dc23

Cover design by Anna Spies, Atra Luna Cover & Logo Art

Edited by Vicky Brewster

Author photograph by Kim Routon Photography

Map by Amy Campbell, designed in Wonderdraft

Pegasus chapter heading art © Depositphotos.com

ISBN-13: 978-1-7361418-4-7 (paperback), 978-1-7361418-5-4 (ebook), 979-8-7655276-2-7 (paperback)

First edition: June 2022

10 9 8 7 6 5 4 3 2 1

www.amycampbell.info

v05252022

For my boys - always dare to dream.

Author's Note

As in reality, sometimes our beloved characters encounter circumstances that cause deep emotional wounds. I don't want any of my readers to have adverse reactions to these scenes, so please be aware that *Dreamer* includes animal injury, blood, death, drinking, forced captivity, guns, kidnapping, murder, PTSD, violence, and weapons.

Previously...

In *Effigest*, Breaker Blaise Hawthorne is imprisoned at the mercy of the Salt-Iron Confederation, slated to become a theurgist against his will. His only ally is a man he no longer trusts—Doyen Malcolm Wells, also known as entrepreneur Jefferson Cole.

Despite Blaise's mistrust, Malcolm is determined to help Blaise any way he can. When his wealth and political power fail him, he decides he has little choice but to forge a path that will change him forever. With the help of half-knocker Flora, he secretly hires an Inker to apply the geasa tattoo that will bind him to Blaise as a handler, preventing anyone else from claiming the Breaker.

Meanwhile, in the town of Fortitude (formerly Itude), outlaw mage Jack Dewitt learns that his teenage daughter Emmaline has run off. He suspects that she's hared off to free Blaise. With his trusty pegasus, he sets off on her trail. When he reaches the Confederation city of Izhadell, he seeks the only person who might help him: Doyen Malcolm Wells.

The outlaw uncovers Malcolm's plot to bind Blaise and is furious, believing that the Doyen seeks to use the young man. Only Flora's intervention and Malcolm's sudden illness keep the scene from turning into a bloodbath.

On the hunt to help her employer, Flora locates Blaise's mother, Marian Hawthorne, who's also held by the Confederation. Marian reveals Blaise wasn't born a mage. The dark alchemy that transmuted Blaise is the likely culprit for Malcolm's illness—and his newfound magic. The alchemist coerces Flora to find the rest of the Hawthorne family and help them flee the Confederation, in exchange for a potion that will stabilize Malcolm.

Jack and Malcolm reach an uneasy agreement to free Blaise. Their strategy nearly collapses when Flora reveals that she's conscripted Commander Lamar Gaitwood—Jack's bitter enemy—to aid them in the rescue. Unbeknownst to them, Lamar has learned Malcolm's dual nature, and he's prepared to weaponize the information if necessary.

All goes according to plan until they discover Blaise's cell is empty. Lamar suspects that Doyen Gregor Gaitwood has sent the Breaker to take out the Salt-Iron Council. Malcolm and Flora head out to find Blaise, with Jack assuring them he'll catch up. With no one around to stop him, the outlaw ends Lamar once and for all.

Malcolm and Flora catch up to the wagon bearing Blaise. Malcolm uses his new magic to neutralize the guards. Blaise is ultimately freed, but an alchemical potion granting him an overwhelming amount of magic almost destroys them all. With Malcolm's help, Blaise bleeds off the excess power.

When they return to Malcolm's home, they learn Jack killed Lamar Gaitwood. Flora is livid—with Lamar's death, all of Malcolm's secrets unravel. Unrepentant, the outlaw storms out to continue on the trail of his daughter, leaving Malcolm, Flora, and Blaise to pick up the pieces.

Malcolm's political life fractures, and he gambles on the only way that he and Blaise might make it out of this. He calls for an Inquiry against the Golden Citadel.

Malcolm's gambit seems to succeed, but during the Inquiry he and Blaise discover Jack has been captured by Gregor Gaitwood.

The outlaw is under the sway of the geasa again, and they have no way of knowing what the sinister Doyen has planned for them.

On the eve of the Inquiry's end, Jack kidnaps Malcolm and Blaise. After Blaise takes a chance to send Flora to track down Emmaline for help, they find themselves on a train bound for Ganland.

When they reach Ganland, Malcolm is forced to face the past he'd desperately hoped to leave behind. Gregor hands them over to Stafford Wells—Malcolm's father, a man who values wealth over his own family ties.

Disgusted by his son, Stafford Wells uses an alchemical potion to shatter the geasa binding Malcolm to Blaise. He and Gregor hatch a plot to send Malcolm back to Izhadell, coercing him to undo all the beneficial legislations that he'd fought for through the years.

Malcolm's Dream magic proves to be their ace in the hole. He uses it to find Flora and tell the half-knocker where they are. Flora tells them she's on her way—and she's bringing along Emmaline, Marian Hawthorne, and Jack's long-missing wife, Kittie.

A fight breaks out as soon as the women arrive at the Wells estate. Kittie's fire ravages the grounds as she faces off against her geasa-bound husband in a showdown.

While Kittie distracts Jack, Blaise frees himself and searches for Malcolm. With Emrys's help, he discovers Malcolm in a second-floor room and breaks in through the window. But Stafford Wells is there, too, and he's intent on fleeing the scene with his son. Malcolm refuses to go with him, and Stafford attempts to shoot Blaise. But Flora is faster, stabbing the elder Wells.

Malcolm declares that he's no longer a Wells. He uses his enchanted ring to return to his preferred visage—Jefferson Cole. In their moment of inattention, Stafford Wells takes the opening, this time to murder Jefferson. Blaise uses his magic to shatter the bullet while Malcolm's drug-addled mother kills Stafford before tottering away.

Blaise and Jefferson join in the struggle against Jack. Marian uses an alchemical potion to sever the geasa, and the outlaw regains control of himself. The ragtag group heads to Jefferson's Ganland home, where Blaise ultimately learns that not only is he an alchemical mage, but an orphaned experiment.

Ultimately, they return to Fortitude, though Blaise's family has settled in Rainbow Flat. Jefferson surprises Blaise with the gift of the bakery, fulfilling the Breaker's lifelong desire. But that's not the only dream that the Dreamer is trying to realize. With the blessing of the Fortitude Ringleaders, he's pushing for the Gutter to be recognized as a nation.

Will their dreams come true, or will nightmares consume them?

Pronunciation Guide

Argor – ARR-gor
Blaise – BLAY-z
Canen – KAY-nun
Chupacabra – CHOO-puh-cah-bruh
Desina – Dess-EE-nuh
Effigest – Eff-IH-jest
Emmaline – Em-uh-LINE
Emrys – Em-RISS
Faedra – FAY-druh
Faedran – FAY-drun
Ganland – Gan-LUND
Garus – Gair-USS
Geasa – GESH-uh
Hospitalier — Hoss-pih-tal-yer
Itude – Ih-TOOD
Izhadell – Iz-UH-dell

Knossan – NOSS-uhn
Knossas – NOSS-us
Kur Agur – Kur Ah-GRR
Leonora – LEE-oh-nor-uh
Leorus — LEE-oh-russ
Lucienne – Loo-SEE-ann
Marian – Mayr-EE-uhn
Marta – Mahr-tuh
Mella – Mell-UH
Mellan – Mell-UHN
Nadine – Nay-DEEN
Nera – NEER-uh
Nexarae – Nex-UH-ray
Oberidon – Oh-BEAR-uh-don (alternate: Oby – Oh-BEE)
Oscen – Oss-KIN
Petria – Pet-RIA
Phinora – Fin-OR-uh
Ravance – Ruh-VAN-s
Ravanchen – Ruh-VAN-chen
Reuben – Roo-ben
Seledora – Sel-uh-DOR-uh
Seward – SOO-urd
Tabris – Tab-RISS
Tabrisian – Tab-REE-shen
Theilia – Thee-LEE-uh
Theilian – Thee-LEE-uhn
Theurgist – THEE-ur-jest
Zepheus – Zeff-EE-us

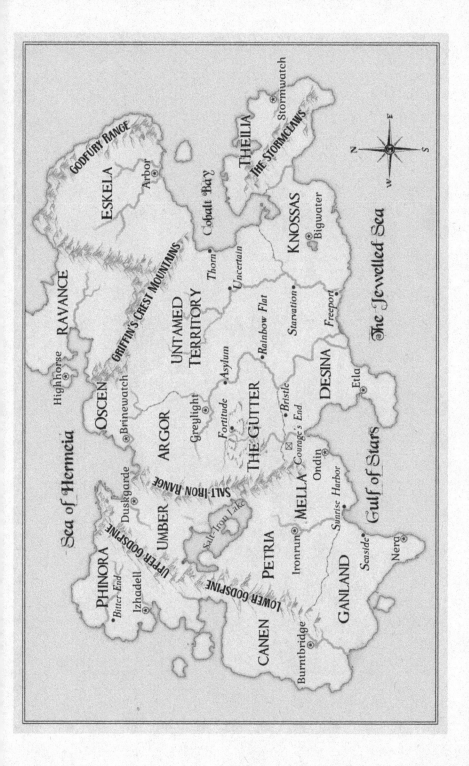

CHAPTER ONE
The Herald

Gregor

Gregor had known they would come for him. It was only a matter of *when*. Trapped in an unceasing web of nightmares, he often lost track of time—a circumstance that had never happened to him before. He didn't know if it had been days, weeks, or months since Jefferson Cole had cursed him to this horrifying existence. But he knew, even in the depths of despair, that the Quiet Ones would come for him.

The mage they sent was as thin as a rail, with spidery limbs and a severe face. She said nothing as she entered his study, flowing into it through the floral wallpaper like an alligator breaking the surface of a bayou. Gregor had encountered the Herald before, and while her entrance was disconcerting, at least it wasn't as terrifying as it had been the first time he'd witnessed her foul magic.

"You are summoned," the Herald said, void of inflection. Her voice was always monotone, as if any joy she held in life had long since bled away. Idly, Gregor wondered if she'd ever had a day of free will. From what he understood, the geasa did not bind her as a true theurgist. But he knew well that control over a person could be attained in other ways.

"I don't wish to go. I'm still healing." Gregor crossed his arms as he spoke. That had been his reasoning the first time a summons had gone out for him, and it had been accurate enough. He was better now, but still not himself—no, far from it. It was difficult to concentrate on anything. Impossible to keep the terrors that were waiting behind his closed eyelids at bay.

"That was your excuse two months ago. It no longer suffices."

Two months? Had it truly been that long? Gregor sighed, shakily rising from his favorite chair. To delay the inevitable would only risk further angering the Quiet Ones, and their favor was tenuous at best.

The Herald extended her hand, as pale as a fish's belly. Gregor reached out to take it and discovered it was just as cold and clammy. He grimaced as she tightened her fingers around his hand, her nails digging crescents into his skin, and led him to the wall.

He hated this, hated this blasted Walker and her freakish ability to spirit herself from one wall to another, from building to building like a specter. She tugged him *through* the wall, and for far too long, he existed in a yawning emptiness that was a nightmare all its own. Though now, after *living* in nightmares, he knew the difference. This would end. The others might not.

There was a sensation like the shattering of ice, and then they were in an ornate room far from Gregor's plantation home. Mage-lights flanked the walls, bathing the room in their brilliance. Well-dressed men and women sat at an oval table, the cherry wood agleam with a freshly polished shine. Behind each of the seated Quiet Ones, a mage stood vigil, so still they reminded Gregor of human statuary.

So unjust. Gregor should have been seated there with a Breaker at his back. Or, barring that, that blasted Effigest outlaw. Having the Scourge of the Untamed Territory at his beck and call would have been a coup. But no, they had denied him. Everything had gone wrong, and now he was being called on it.

"Doyen Gaitwood, how kind of you to *finally* join us," a voice rang out with false cheer. The speaker sat at the far side of the room, elbows on the table with fingers steepled in front of him. The Herald parted ways with Gregor, slipping behind the man who had spoken as if she were his shadow.

Gregor did his best to compose himself, crossing the short distance to claim a seat at the table. "With all due respect, Phillip, you *are* aware I nearly lost my life in the fire that claimed Stafford Wells." He hadn't spoken to anyone about the nightmares, not yet. Part of Gregor wasn't certain that Jefferson Cole had been the one to imprison him in a never-ending world of terror. How could it even be possible? But then again, Jefferson Cole had *also* been Malcolm Wells.

A tepid smile slid onto Phillip Dillon's face. He was a classically handsome man, though his once dark hair was more salt than pepper. His sharp eyes shifted to the only other empty chair at the table—the seat that belonged to the late Stafford Wells. The seat that Gregor desperately wanted; if only he could show them he was worthy. "You seem to be faring well enough now. And we need answers." He leaned forward, and the lithe woman at his back mimicked him, lending the movement a predatory air. "You had the Breaker in hand."

"He couldn't be bound," Gregor started, then realized that was untrue and wouldn't stand up to scrutiny. Not with all the Quiet Ones, who knew better, staring at him. Anyone with any connections had heard the tale of his failure with the Breaker. "He couldn't be bound to *me*. Doyen Wells snagged him first."

"We heard of this." A raven-haired woman, who appeared bored by the entire affair, reclined in her chair. She wore trousers like a man, which suited her. She casually slung one leg over the arm of her chair. Tara was one of the more *unusual* Quiet Ones, from what Gregor had seen. "And my darling *pet* even gave you the means to fulfill your end of our dealings." She jerked a meaningful thumb toward the man at her shoulder. Tara was the only Quiet One who hadn't laid claim to a mage. But she had nabbed something almost as good. She had seduced and married a talented alchemist, one of the best. Her handsome alchemist had the gall to flash a brilliant smile at Gregor, a taunt.

Gregor's jaw clenched, and he felt a headache swarm in the base of his skull. Headaches plagued him often. Lack of sleep, according to his physician. "We nearly got the Breaker to the council chambers, as you asked me to do. But his allies thwarted me."

"*Nearly* isn't good enough." Tara cocked her head, winking at him. "And besides, you act as if *we* were too stupid to figure out your play after it all went wrong."

Gregor went still. It should have been impossible for them to —wait. He scanned the others at the table, eyes roving over the array of mages. Not all of the magic types present were known to him. He knew of Dillon's Herald and her Wall Walking magic, of course. And Tara's alchemist, who wasn't a mage at all. But he didn't know the others. Such information was on a need-to-know basis, and he hadn't needed to know. Did they have a Scryer? Or had Stafford Wells simply sold him out, hoping to benefit from both sides of the deal?

Phillip Dillon chuckled. "You thought we wouldn't figure it out." Around the table, no one else joined in the laughter. Their gazes fell on him like hunting wolves, assessing him for weakness. "Tell us why we should not only let you walk out of here alive, Gregor, but remain a Doyen."

He swallowed, blinking. In the split second of darkness, another nightmare found him. His lips curled in momentary horror at the sensation of phantom blood running down his arm, and he panted for breath. Gregor hated this. It made him look weak and vulnerable, all because of—*wait*. He might have currency for them after all. True, his gambit may lose him any chance for a seat, but he was a patient man.

"You still want the Breaker, correct? And…" His gaze skated to the empty seat. "You need a successor for Stafford Wells."

Dillon narrowed his eyes. "I hope you're not suggesting the position for yourself."

Gregor waved a hand, dismissing the notion. No, he knew that the Quiet One positions were usually hereditary. When there were no available heirs, the Quiet Ones selected someone new. Gregor knew at the moment he was a longshot until he made amends. So, why not offer them someone else?

"No. I'm suggesting Malcolm Wells."

Around the table, the Quiet Ones scoffed at his audacious words. Tara lazily slouched forward. "You know he's *dead*, right?"

"I know he's *not*. He just wants everyone to believe that."

They stared at him, silence reigning for a dozen heartbeats before Phillip dared to speak. "And how did he manage *that* little trick?"

"Magic of some sort, I assume," Gregor said with a shrug. He wondered if he should offer information about the man's magic— but no, he needed to keep some of his cards to himself. "He masquerades as Jefferson Cole."

Recognition lit the eyes of the Quiet Ones. Cole was a known commodity, and the allegation startled them. "How…?" Everett Duncan, a magnate from Phinora, shook his head like a wet dog. "Impossible. I saw them both attend the Ganland Derby ball two years ago!"

Gregor crossed his arms. "I don't know how he does it. I only know that he does. He's maintained this charade for Garus knows how many years."

Phillip frowned. "And you suggest we bring him in for his father's seat? This sounds like a foolish endeavor on our part. He made it quite clear that he doesn't condone the shadow work we do."

Gregor shook his head. "You're not looking far enough. Malcolm Wells can give you access to the Breaker. And he'll play right into your hands if you let him know you're aware of his little secret."

Tara gave him a dubious look. "Why are you interested in Malcolm Wells becoming a Quiet One? We're not stupid, no matter what you may think. We know you weren't on the best terms."

Gregor held up his hands, placating. "I'm not firing a cannonball in your plans. Quite the opposite. Malcolm wants to hide from his birthright—from the power he was born into." Gregor smiled. "He needs to own it. And you have the leverage to make it happen now."

Dillon steepled his fingers. "You believe it will be enough to make him comply?"

Gregor smiled. "Any man desperate enough to hide the truth about himself will go to great lengths to make sure it doesn't come out."

"And what do you get out of it?" Tara asked.

When Gregor blinked, renewed nightmares danced across the canvas of his mind. He shuddered, banishing them and regaining his composure. "Revenge."

CHAPTER TWO
The Thing About Salt-Iron

Blaise

*B*laise licked his dry lips, staring at the tiny chunk of salt-iron resting on the silver tray before him. Nadine, the town Healer, stood across the clinic from where Blaise sat on a cot, eyeing the nefarious metal. She didn't desire to be anywhere near the salt-iron, reluctant to let it drain her magic. The only reason she allowed it in her presence was because of Blaise.

"Well?" Nadine asked, scrutinizing him. "Do you feel it leeching your magic?"

Frowning thoughtfully, Blaise gave a small nod. "A little. Not enough to be a concern, though." It was true. There was the sluggish drip of his magic wisping to the chunk, but as quickly as it ebbed away, his internal well of power refilled like a lake fed by a rain-swollen river. It was different from what he'd felt with salt-iron in the past. Like the time he had been on the deck of the salt-iron-reinforced airship, in the struggle of his life as he pitted magic against the metal. His exertion and the inexorable pull of the salt-iron had emptied him completely.

"Hmm." Nadine tapped a pen against the notebook she held, jotting down a note. "What happens if you pick it up?"

Blaise cocked his head, considering. He usually handled the chunk while wearing a pair of sturdy leather gloves. Really, they weren't supposed to even have the piece of salt-iron, but after Jefferson's loyal half-knocker confidant Flora had admitted she was attuned to the foul metal, Jefferson had made it a point to squirrel away the nub in the bakery's loft. Under normal circumstances, they kept it swaddled in a layer of cotton, locked inside a small wooden chest. Anything less, and Jefferson, the newest—and most secretive—mage in town, was prone to headaches as it leeched his magic.

"Guess we'll find out," Blaise said with a shrug. It wouldn't be the first time he'd touched salt-iron with his bare skin on purpose.

Blaise reached out and gingerly picked up the glob. Just because he *could*, didn't mean he wanted to do it. He winced, expecting the sharp bite of it lacing through his skin. The sensation differed from before—in the past, it had been like touching a hot stove. A flash fire of pain. This was…tolerable? Maybe that wasn't exactly right, but he could grasp it with only mild discomfort. More like carefully holding jagged shards of glass than anything else.

Nadine stared at him. "How does it feel?"

"Um." Blaise had never been eloquent. "It hurts, but not that bad, I guess?"

"Is it leeching your power more than before or the same?"

Blaise took a moment to consider the question. "The same." He knew it should have been worse with direct contact. Blaise set the block back down on the tray, wiggling his fingers. His skin had reddened but hadn't developed the characteristic welts associated with touching salt-iron. On the one hand, that was a relief because the welts *hurt*. Tiny scars dimpled the undersides of his wrists, courtesy of the salt-iron shackles used on him in the Golden Citadel. But this new resistance to salt-iron? It made him different from other mages—and Blaise didn't like being different. Maybe he should have been used to it by now, but it was something that would always bother him.

Nadine's eyebrows lifted high, furrowing the pocked skin on her forehead. Even with all her power, she'd never fully recovered from the assault on Itude. "When did this start?"

Blaise edged away from the salt-iron. "It bothered me less after..." He faltered, heart racing as phantom memories reared up. The sickening sensation of a wooden deck plunging beneath his feet. The helpless feeling of *falling, falling, falling* and then hitting Lamar Gaitwood's magical trap. *Darkness.*

"You're not there. Think of something happy. Go there instead." Nadine's voice was soft but insistent.

He swallowed, summoning up his happy place in his mind's eye. *My bakery, golden in the early morning sunrise. Jefferson drowsily climbing down from the loft, hair tousled. Scents of yeast and sugar riding the air currents, drawing Emrys to the open window.* Blaise nodded, opening eyes he hadn't realized he'd closed.

"Thanks." He rubbed the ridge of his jaw, scuffing his beard. He had appointments with Nadine weekly for this very reason. Physically, he had recovered. But memories of the things he had endured plagued him, giving him nightmares. Jefferson used his magic to hold them off at night, but when Blaise was awake, the Dreamer was helpless against the bouts of panic that came and went. Out of desperation, he had sought the Healer, who had known of his oldest emotional wounds but never forced him to speak about them unless he wanted to.

"Blaise?" Nadine prompted, a reminder that she still expected an answer.

Right. Blaise could do this. It was only three words. He swallowed. "After the airship."

Nadine nodded in understanding, waiting for him to expand on the topic. That hadn't been the only time, though. Salt-iron had still affected him after that. *Until...* He swallowed, concentrating on the feel of dough in his hands, companionable conversation with Emmaline and Reuben. "And after they dosed me with the potion."

Nadine didn't know the specifics of this potion. He had mentioned it in passing during a previous session while explaining the circumstances of his rescue. Blaise had left it at that since discussion of the potion could lead down a dangerous path, one littered with painful memories of betrayal, of a life that he had thought was his.

The Healer studied him with her cool eyes, unflinching as she waited to see if he would continue. Blaise shivered. He didn't want to speak more on the topic, too afraid he would stumble onward and reveal the awful secret. The information that was far more problematic than the fact that he was a Breaker. How could he tell her that alchemy had *transmuted* him into a mage? That he had been born normal? That was dangerous information, and the less people who knew, the better.

When it became clear Blaise wouldn't speak further, Nadine tapped the point of her pen against her notebook. "And you think the potion that nearly killed you had something to do with this?"

He nodded. "It's hard to explain." Blaise swallowed, aware of her keen interest once again. His resistance to salt-iron intrigued Nadine. "You ever seen a pond get dredged?"

Nadine raised her brows at the analogy. "I have."

"It's like that." Blaise looked down at the floor, wondering if he should even say that much. But it wasn't as if anyone here had easy access to such a potion. "The potion...I think it did something like that to me. It dug so deep into me. Almost hollowed me out." He shivered at the memory, taking a gasping breath as he summoned up a happy thought to chase it away. *Emrys shoving his head against Blaise, nearly knocking him over as he laughed at the stallion's exuberance.* "And I just keep filling up, almost as fast as it's drained. It doesn't matter."

The Healer watched him, lips pursed as she weighed his words. "There're a lot of mages who'd be very interested in that."

Blaise nodded, shoulders hunching. "It's *alchemy*."

"There is that," Nadine agreed. Mages had a troublesome relationship with alchemy. The Salt-Iron Confederation employed it as a tool to control the mages in their domain. She massaged her forehead. "Doesn't matter, though. I'm not telling another soul of this. Healer-patient confidentiality, as always."

He relaxed at her words. She had mentioned it before, but Blaise couldn't help but wonder what might be the tipping point. What would be the piece of information that might be too tempting to share? He rubbed his hands together, staring down at them.

"Put it away," Nadine said, jerking her chin toward the salt-iron. As Blaise pulled out his gloves, she added, "And how are you handling Jefferson's upcoming departure?"

I should have known she would ask. He tugged at the leather gloves, focusing on the task as he spoke. "I'm thinking of taking a trip of my own." She raised a single silver brow, inquisitive. "Not to Ganland, if that's what you're wondering." *Not with Jefferson.* It was ridiculous, the very thought that he didn't *want* to be apart from Jefferson. But there it was.

"Oh?" Nadine prodded as Blaise picked up the salt-iron lump and wrapped it in a layer of cotton before slipping it into a carry sack. "Where are you going?"

He tightened the drawstrings on the sack and placed it on a nearby cot. "I said I was *thinking* of taking a trip. I'm not sure where yet." That part was a lie, and he suspected she knew. But there were some things he didn't want to talk about.

Her light grey eyes narrowed. "A change of scenery might be what you need."

He wrinkled his nose. "Nadine, I know you mean well, but I've had enough changes of scenery to last me a lifetime."

The Healer scowled. "There's a difference between *that* and traveling because you can. Because you *want* to."

But I don't know if I want to. Blaise rubbed his forehead, well aware that when Nadine had an idea in her head, she would keep at it. She was a lot like Jack in that way, though both the outlaws would be mightily offended if he told them as much. He frowned, deciding in this case, he might do better to throw her a bone. "The truth is, I'm thinking of going to Rainbow Flat to see my family."

Nadine nodded at his words. Blaise hadn't told her everything, but the Healer wasn't stupid. She knew his mother was an alchemist and that something had happened in relation to her. Something that had hurt him on a deep, emotional level.

"That I can understand." She stepped closer and laid a hand on his shoulder, meeting his eyes. "I've had bad blood with my family. Sometimes it can't be helped. But if there's a chance whatever's happened can be fixed, you should try." Nadine squeezed his shoulder for a second before releasing it. "But that's up to you. Only you know how to cure what ails you in that regard."

Blaise reached up to touch his shoulder in the spot she'd gripped. It tingled for a heartbeat, as if she'd left a trace of her magic behind. "I'll think about it."

"You do that," Nadine said, stepping over to her desk to check the time as they heard the approach of hooves. "We're at the end of our session. Come see me again if you need."

"Thanks," Blaise told her, picking up the salt-iron parcel and heading for the door. When he stepped out into the late afternoon sunshine, Emrys trotted up to greet him.

The pegasus nearly knocked him over as he rammed his head into Blaise's chest, blowing out a snotty breath. <Took you long enough.>

"This shirt *was* clean," Blaise grumbled, tottering beneath the enthusiastic greeting. He braced a hand against Emrys's neck to steady himself, pulling back enough to give his shirt a critical look. Equine hair clung to the fabric, and a streak of glinting mucus shone in the sunlight. "You know Jefferson's going to make me change, right?"

<Oh no, how terrible.> Emrys didn't sound in the least contrite. In fact, his dark eyes danced with amusement.

"Did he put you up to this?" That would have been a very Jefferson thing to do. Jefferson had *opinions* about Blaise's selection of clothing. Sometimes Blaise had taken to dressing in his most mismatched or threadbare garments just to see how Jefferson would react. It had almost become a strange game between the pair.

<I imagine he does like you with your shirt off,> Emrys said.

"Now I *really* think he put you up to this. Did he offer you a slice of apple pie? Whatever he's offered, I'll double it," Blaise said as he dug into a pocket for a handkerchief. He mopped up the trail of pegasus snot.

<He didn't, but now I wish he had,> Emrys admitted, his mental tone wistful.

"I saved some for you anyway," Blaise told the stallion, tucking the handkerchief away and rubbing Emrys's broad forehead. "Let's go get you a treat."

<Those are my favorite words.> Emrys fell into step beside him as they strode up the dusty street the short distance to the bakery.

The building was dark as Blaise entered. He tapped a mage-light on, then moved to open the window at the back so Emrys could thrust his head inside. "I suppose Jefferson is still meeting with the Ringleaders and the representatives from Asylum and Rainbow Flat?"

Emrys bobbed his head with enthusiasm, nostrils distended, as Blaise uncovered a tin with the leftover remnants of the promised pie. <Yes. Seledora was still outside HQ when I went to the clinic to wait for you.>

"Gotcha." Blaise slid the pie onto the counter, though he held the tin in place so it wouldn't slide around as the pegasus dug in.

In the past, Nadine would have attended the meeting, too. But as the population of Fortitude expanded with more mages and their families seeking a home out of the Confederation's clutches, she had resigned as a Ringleader to see to the demands of her profession. Mindy, the Hospitalier mage who co-owned the Jitterbug, had stepped up for the position and been voted in. Their meeting couldn't run much later, though, or it would affect the Jitterbug's dinner service. "I imagine they'll finish soon."

Emrys's velvety lips and pink tongue quested after the last dregs of sweetness in the tin. <You're stuck with me in the meantime.>

Blaise couldn't help but smile. "I'm glad to be stuck with you."

CHAPTER THREE

Impostor Syndrome

Kittie

Kittie felt like an impostor. There was no other way around it. Everyone else gathered in the meeting room at Ringleader HQ knew what they were about, and they seemed secure in who they were and what they were doing. Kittie was a pretender, struggling to be something she had once been, but didn't feel like she was any longer.

She hadn't realized how hard this would be, and a part of her wondered how long it would take for Jack to figure out that she wasn't the same woman he'd married so many years ago. Most days, Kittie didn't feel like the Firebrand, the notorious young woman who had once sought to rally the mages of the Confederation. She was trying to find that part of her again, those embers buried deep down, but Kittie feared it was forever doused.

Kittie blinked when Jack nudged her with his elbow. She winced, realizing he'd noticed she was busy wool-gathering and not focusing on the logistics of their delegation. They were planning to travel to Ganland to gain support to recognize the Gutter as its own country.

"—still plan to leave later this week?" The question was posed by Eileen Harker, the mayor of Asylum. Eileen was dubious about their gambit to make a nation of outlaws. She crossed her arms, the corners of her lips down-turned.

"Yes, we do," Jefferson replied. The well-dressed would-be ambassador sat beside Ringleader Vixen Valerie, which placed him across from Kittie. Jack always grumbled that Jefferson was a dandy or a peacock, but Kittie wondered if the younger man intimidated her husband. Jefferson was handsome and knew it. He wore the finest clothes and was clean-shaven, with golden-brown hair sculpted to rakish perfection. He wasn't overly large or muscular, but the power that came with self-assurance and wealth cloaked him. "And both Asylum and Rainbow Flat are welcome to send along anyone you'd like to join our delegation."

Wesley Slen, the mayor of Rainbow Flat, shook his head. "You know I'm not willing to risk my people with that, Jefferson. Nations are born from battle and blood, not diplomacy and words."

Beside Kittie, Jack made a soft grunt of agreement. Her husband had similar concerns, though, in a surprising turn, he actually thought their diplomatic mission stood a chance.

Jefferson's eyes glittered at the challenge presented by Slen. "You're welcome to your opinion. But this wouldn't be the first time I've been a player in a radical shift."

"We're seeing this through regardless," Kittie finally said, drawing the attention of the others in the room. Of the mages in attendance, she knew she was one of the most powerful as a Pyromancer. Fortitude boasted three other Pyromancers, but their magics were mere sparks compared to the inferno she could command. Her words had weight simply because of who and what she was.

"We would look better with at least one more outlaw along." This from Ringleader Raven Dawson, who leaned back in his seat, the skin around his dark eyes crinkling with concern. "I could—"

"*No.*" Vixen's voice was sharp as she scowled at her beau through the smoky lenses of her glasses. "We only..." The redhead trailed off, shaking her head. She was reluctant to finish her sentence, but Kittie knew where she was going. The Confederation had stripped Vixen and Raven's magic, and only recently had the Breaker restored it. Kittie didn't know the details beyond the fact that he'd done the same for Jack.

"I can join the delegation, if you'll have me." The assertion pulled everyone's attention away from Kittie, which was welcome. Kittie raised her brows at the newest member of the Fortitude Ringleaders, the Hospitalier Mindy Carman. The young woman didn't wilt beneath their gazes, instead straightening her spine. "You'll need more than just the pair of you."

"And Flora," Jefferson reminded them gently. Kittie noted the pucker in his brow, a sign that it bothered him when the half-knocker wasn't in attendance. "If she's back in time, anyway." He cleared his throat, smiling at Mindy. "You're welcome, of course, if you like."

"I think I'm *needed,*" Mindy clarified. "I'm invested in Fortitude —in the Gutter. I want us to succeed, and if that means I need to tag along, then so be it." Her gaze slid over to Kittie.

"Didn't know Hospitaliers were also Seers," Jack murmured so softly only Kittie could hear. But he didn't seem opposed to the idea—Kittie knew he would have objected aloud if he had strong feelings. Which meant her husband thought Mindy had value in coming along, too. *Interesting.*

They hashed out further details for their delegation's departure before adjourning for the day. Jefferson slipped over to Mindy, stepping aside with her to discuss something out of earshot. Kittie headed to the door with Jack, though Vixen ghosted over to them as soon as they made it outside.

"Mindy's a solid addition," Vixen told them, keeping her voice low. Jack cocked his head but didn't ask for specifics. "Just trust her, okay?" She lifted a finger to reposition her glasses on her nose.

Jack tensed when Vixen touched her glasses, then settled. "You know more about her than I do, Vix?"

The Persuader shrugged with one shoulder. "I know some stuff she's had to keep quiet, is all." Then she poked an index finger into Jack's chest. "And I didn't want you scaring her off by huffing and puffing that she shouldn't go."

"I wouldn't do that," Jack grumbled. Vixen and Kittie both scoffed. The Effigest grunted. "Maybe I would. But I didn't object in there. I was *reasonable*. Kept my trap shut."

"A surprise to everyone," Vixen said with a grin before sobering. "Yeah, you behaved in there. But I know how you can be, going behind someone to intimidate them." To his credit, Jack didn't deny it. Vixen nodded to Kittie. "Just wanted you to know. We're counting on this."

"Everyone is," Kittie agreed, watching as Vixen strode off. When she was gone, Kittie rubbed her forehead. Jack stepped closer, snugging an arm around her. "Can we go to the Broken Horn?"

He glanced at her, lips pursed. "You want a drink for nerves or because you can't do without?"

Both. Can't it be both? Kittie gritted her teeth. "I'm worried about this mission, is all. One little drink. Then I can stop."

"We both know that's a lie." His voice was whisper-soft, full of disapproval. And that was unfair, since Jack enjoyed a good whiskey as much as the next outlaw. But the difference was he didn't *need* it the way she did. "I thought you were going dry."

"Dry brush burns so easily," Kittie muttered. That was how she felt about all this, at any rate. She was trying to lose her dependency on alcohol—and failing miserably. Like she was burning up from the inside with all of her inadequacies and the shadow of what she had been before.

"If you won't do it for me, then at *least* do it for our daughter."

Oh, that hurt. Kittie's hackles raised as she jerked out from under his arm. "You think it's so easy? Like I can just snap my fingers and, poof, I don't *need* it anymore?" As she spoke, she snapped her fingers, and a tongue of flame appeared in her palm. Kittie curled her hand, extinguishing it into nothingness. Not even a wisp of smoke. "It's not *magic*, Jack."

His lovely eyes bored into hers, intense and full of so much passion for her it was almost painful. "I never said it was easy. But you have to *want* it." Jack tilted his head. "And I don't think you do."

It was damned annoying how right he was. She wanted to stop. But she also *wanted* a drink, which ran counter to this entire conversation. She didn't like the idea of leaving her husband and daughter. Didn't want to travel to Confederation lands, even if she was going as a diplomat. Kittie balled her fists, nails biting into the palms. "Could say the same for how well you and Emmaline get along."

Jack twitched, almost as if she'd moved to slap him. That was a sore spot, and maybe unfair that she'd gone for it. His relationship with their daughter was still on the mend, and lately, he'd been lax. He squared his shoulders, eyes glinting as if he were about to pull his ace in the hole. "Yeah? Well, I've got plans."

"Do you?" Kittie asked, surprised. "Want to tell me over a drink?"

He snorted. "I'll treat you to dinner at the Jitterbug. Deal?"

Kittie wrinkled her nose. "They're going to suggest the strawberry ginger switchel for me again, I bet."

Jack chuckled. "Can't be that bad. Blaise swears by the stuff." He cleared his throat. "I'll try some with you. How about that?"

Kittie sighed. He would not relent, and she both loved and hated him for it. "It's a date."

CHAPTER FOUR
Nightmare Fuel

Jefferson

The bell above the bakery door jingled as Jefferson opened it. Blaise glanced back, his shoulders taut with tension. *Odd. He's not usually worked up when he's baking.* Jefferson gave an appreciative sniff as he moved inside and shut the door behind him.

"Is that pork pie I smell?" Jefferson asked, his stomach rumbling at the savory scents wafting through the air.

"Yes and no," Blaise said, which wasn't an answer at all. He glanced over his shoulder, the hardness around his eyes easing. "Trying a new recipe. They're more like rolls stuffed with meat and cheese." He shifted to the side, pointing to a tray where a set of tawny brown orbs rested.

"Whatever they are, they smell amazing." Jefferson studied Blaise as he moved closer, searching for clues as to what had him on edge. *Oh. Wait. Today's the day he...yes.* "How did things go with Nadine?"

Blaise slid a pair of meat rolls onto a tin plate and handed it to Jefferson. He didn't answer until he had similarly loaded a plate for himself and moved over to the small table in the corner. "It was okay."

Jefferson bit into the savory bun to buy himself time as he waited for Blaise to expand on the topic, but the Breaker never did. Blaise's new recipe was just as delectable as it smelled—tangy bits of honey ham mixed with one of the sharp white cheeses brought in from the outlying ranches. Jefferson made an appreciative noise as he chewed. When he finished, he pressed on. "I can tell something is bothering you."

Blaise looked up from his plate, a frown creasing his face for a moment before it melted into a wince. "She thinks I should go to Rainbow Flat, too."

Ah-ha. Jefferson gave a small nod. He and Blaise had spoken about this before. Blaise was torn—he loved his family, but the recent truths revealed by his mother had cut him to the core. Jefferson had mixed thoughts on Marian Hawthorne. From what he had seen, she truly loved Blaise. But he also understood Blaise's feelings of betrayal and hurt. Oh, he understood those only too well from his own family history.

All the same, Blaise *wasn't* Jefferson. And the Hawthornes were *not* the Wellses, thank the gods. Blaise was more likely to forgive someone once he overcame the hurt—but for that, he needed to reconcile with his mother. Jefferson had suggested that he at least try. It wasn't only to make Blaise feel better—the young man needed answers, too.

"That would be a good thing for you to do while I'm away," Jefferson agreed, licking his lips. He had briefly entertained the idea of Blaise traveling to Ganland with him. Well, not just entertained. Fantasized about it, more like. He wanted to show Blaise everything, to share the world with him. But that was a flight of fancy—Blaise had too many damaging memories to overcome.

"I'm considering it," Blaise said. He rubbed his cheek. "It would keep my mind off of you."

"I'll pretend that sentence doesn't wound my pride."

"I meant it would keep me from worrying about you."

Jefferson chuckled. Oh, he'd known. "I'll be *fine*. It's my home turf."

Blaise huffed at that, and he seemed to shake off some of his nerves. His voice was more certain when he spoke. "No, it's the home turf of entrepreneur Jefferson Cole. Not *mage* Jefferson Cole."

"Same thing." Jefferson shrugged, then realized he'd misspoken by the way Blaise's eyebrows slanted. *Time for a change of topic.* "I certainly hope Flora will return from your *errand* soon."

Jefferson knew very well that Blaise was up to *something* with Flora. The Breaker wasn't practiced in getting away with intrigue. The statement disarmed Blaise's previous argument, and he stumbled over his words before he found his proverbial footing. "I... probably?" Blaise scowled at him, annoyed at the change of topic but unable to combat it.

You're so bad at being sneaky, but at least you're cute. Jefferson grinned. "Anyway, enough of that. Our time together is limited. We should do something fun."

Blaise relaxed, though he gave Jefferson a dubious look. "Define *fun*."

Do I suggest something scandalous or mundane? Jefferson finished the last of his bun, deciding to err on the side of caution. "What do *you* think is fun?"

Blaise's expression softened. "A game. We can play a game— after you do the dishes."

My staff back home would absolutely have kittens to hear that. Jefferson chuckled. He enjoyed these simple things with Blaise. "Fine. I'll wash if you dry."

ONE STACK OF DISHES AND A CARD GAME LATER, JEFFERSON CURLED up facing Blaise. The Breaker twitched as he dropped into slumber, his previously slack face twisting into a grimace. Jefferson's power was especially sensitive to Blaise, and he felt the night-mares rising to greet the young man. *No. Leave him be. I have someone else to feed you to.* Jefferson snared the nightmares with his magic, tugging them away from Blaise.

Jefferson's hand rested on Blaise's bicep, listening as his breath evened out in the darkness. Muscles relaxed beneath his touch. Jefferson was tempted to allow the nightmares to coalesce, so he could see for himself what was bothering Blaise. But there was no guarantee that whatever manifested was the actual problem. The subconscious, Jefferson had learned, was fickle. No, it was better to keep the nightmares away from Blaise and be done with it.

He leaned over and gave the Breaker a gentle kiss on the cheek, running a finger along his jawline, savoring his well-kempt beard. This was what Jefferson would miss most on his trip to Ganland. Blaise and everything about him. *I'm being ridiculous. I have an advantage no one else has. The dreamscape. We won't always be apart.*

"And I've delayed it too long," Jefferson murmured as a thought occurred to him. He settled alongside Blaise, fingers tracing the fading tattoo on the Breaker's arm. The geasa tattoo was dead, though for a while, it had been the bond between Jefferson as handler and Blaise as theurgist. They were neither of those now. In fact, with his magic, Jefferson was now the furthest thing from a handler. And Blaise was free of the geasa—a true outlaw mage. But there was still someone who had to *pay* for that. "I'll see you soon, Blaise. Until then, sweet dreams."

Jefferson burrowed into the mattress. The bed left much to be desired—the mattress was lumpy and not as soft as those Jefferson liked. And because of the size of the loft over the bakery, it was barely large enough to fit the pair. Well, perhaps Jefferson didn't object to *that* part too much. He enjoyed being nestled close to Blaise, and the Breaker had made it clear the feeling was mutual.

He closed his eyes, summoning up a wisp of his Dreamer magic to ease himself into the dreamscape. It was an odd thing, but for someone who commanded dreams, he was finding it harder and harder to fall asleep at night. Though he had a lot on his mind, and none of that helped.

Jefferson practiced breathing exercises to relax his body—a suggestion that had come from Vixen. It helped, and before long, he was in the grey expanse that led to the dreamscape.

He was still unclear on exactly what the dreamscape was. Jefferson didn't know if it was some sort of magical plane, an overlay of the waking world, or something beyond his comprehension. All he knew without a doubt was that it was real and that, as a Dreamer, he could exert his will on it. Mold it into a thing of *his* design.

He could pull others into it, though that was sometimes difficult. Bringing Blaise there had become second nature. Jefferson had brought others there, too. Jack. Flora.

And Gregor Gaitwood.

Gaitwood was the one he needed to attend to. Jefferson called up his magic, and before him, stone grated as a floor rose from nothing, the blocks coming together like the pieces of a puzzle. Walls reared up, lit by phantom mage-lights. Jefferson strode down the newly created corridor, his footfalls echoing.

He didn't like this place, but it was a necessity. It was a shadow of the Golden Citadel, the prison where the Confederation had held Blaise. Tormented him. Abused him. Jefferson released a resentful breath, old anger burning in his heart. He hadn't told Blaise he allowed a version of the Cit to exist in the dreamscape. The dreamscape was supposed to be a safe place, and Jefferson made certain that, for Blaise, this was always the case.

Jefferson's steps slowed as he neared his destination. Around him, the walls bore signs of strain. Spider web cracks ran from floor to ceiling, the lumber reinforcing the damaged wall doing very little. Salt-iron reinforced the wall, too, though in the dream-scape, the metal was inert. Little more than set dressing.

He frowned. Though this resembled Blaise's cell in the Cit, it wasn't supposed to be so damaged. Jefferson wondered if he had weakened the walls without intending to, merely because his subconscious knew what Blaise had done to them. Licking his lips, Jefferson sent his magic into the substance of the walls, strengthening them. The cracks receded as the stone sealed itself.

"I was wondering when you'd show your face again."

The voice put Jefferson on edge, fury boiling through him. He crossed his arms and released a tendril of power, causing the door to the cell to swing open with a creak. Gregor Gaitwood stood inches from the threshold. The enemy Doyen had learned from past visits that although the door appeared open, Jefferson wouldn't allow him to cross the invisible barrier. Jefferson had promised Gregor a life of nightmares every time his eyes closed, and he was a man of his word.

He met Gregor's gaze, staring back at him. It was like old times, when he had been Doyen Malcolm Wells, going toe-to-toe against this man. Neither of them backed down for what felt like an eternity. Gregor finally averted his gaze with a frustrated hiss.

This was how it went every time Jefferson came to reinforce the magic he used to keep Gregor ensnared—and to infuse him with more nightmares. Gregor always tried to get him to speak, to offer information that the Doyen no doubt hoped to use. Jefferson still couldn't believe that Phinora allowed the man to sit on the Council. The newspapers that had slowly made their way to Fortitude declared the Doyen had suffered a "mental collapse over the loss of fellow Doyen Malcolm Wells" and convalesced on his estate for a time.

"You can't keep me here forever, Cole!"

Jefferson raised his brows. He was tempted to reply to the challenge, but that would play into Gaitwood's hands. The trapped Doyen had slowly become more lucid in the dreamscape, and Jefferson couldn't figure out how. Was he developing a resistance to Jefferson's influence? Blaise hadn't, but then again, the Breaker *wanted* Jefferson's help. Gregor actively fought against it.

"I brought you something," Jefferson said, a self-righteous thrill shivering through him when Gregor's eyes widened in alarm. "More fuel for the fire."

"No!" Gregor howled as Jefferson pulled on the freshly culled nightmares, forcing them into the Doyen's psyche. Gaitwood collapsed to his knees with a pathetic whimper. Jefferson didn't have a shred of compassion for the man. Every terror he fed to Gregor came directly from Blaise, from the traumas of his past. Gregor had been responsible for more than his fair share of them.

"Sleep tight," Jefferson called, turning his back on the prisoner. It was time to join Blaise. He raised a hand, the cell door slamming shut with the final click of a lock falling into place. Gregor made a choked half-sob, followed by the thud of the man ramming his body against the door in frustration. In desperation. Jefferson tucked his chin. Gregor wanted him to cave, to feel sorry for him. But he wouldn't. Not after what Blaise had endured.

He headed up the stone hallway, and as he walked, it shifted into a black and white patterned floor. The same sort of design as the floorboards of Blaise's Bakery. The yellow-painted walls of the bakery swooped in around Jefferson as he appeared beside Blaise. Then he raised his brows, realizing he had spent perhaps a bit too long with Gaitwood. Blaise's slumbering mind had wandered into ridiculousness.

The bakery itself was normal, though the new sink (with running water) Jefferson had paid to have installed had…a tree in it? Leaves littered the interior of the sink, and Blaise was shaking his head as he cleared the debris into a bucket.

"Why would a tree grow in your bakery?" Jefferson asked, eyes roving up the length of the trunk that somehow pierced the ceiling without damaging it. Dreams were strange that way.

Blaise shrugged. "Because you took too long to get here, and my brain is weird."

"Your brain is *not* weird. Everyone has odd dreams," Jefferson said. "You're just spoiled because I can make your dreams whatever we'd like them to be."

Blaise scoffed, setting down the leaf-filled bucket. He poked his chest with a thumb. "*I'm* the spoiled one?"

"I bought you a very expensive sink, complete with the plumbing for running water. I stand by what I said."

Blaise chuckled, his mood much improved from earlier in the evening. "Fair enough." He gestured to the tree. "Can you make this not be here?"

Jefferson grinned. He touched a finger to a bough. The tree misted away from existence, taking the leaf remnants with it. "As you wish."

"Show off."

This banter...this was *good*. Jefferson breathed a sigh of relief, pleased that Blaise was feeling more like himself in the dreamscape. "Yes, I've been called a peacock often enough. It goes with the territory." Jack had taken to calling him that. *I suppose it's better than* dandy. Jefferson didn't mind it. Peacocks were territorial, which seemed fitting.

"Did you have trouble falling asleep?" Blaise asked, moving closer to Jefferson until they were shoulder to shoulder.

Jefferson couldn't help looping an arm around Blaise's lower back, pulling him closer. "A little. And I had to take care of something before I could join you."

Blaise glanced at him, the unasked question on his lips. Jefferson didn't want to keep secrets from him—but he didn't want to hurt him, either. He knew that eventually, he needed to tell the Breaker about Gregor. Not anytime soon, though. Not while he was still learning how to cope with his trauma.

"A few simple things related to the dreamscape," Jefferson said, resting his head against Blaise's shoulder. "I had to keep parts of it stabilized." That was the truth, at least.

Blaise nodded, accepting the answer. "Thanks for fixing the tree." He shifted beneath Jefferson. "I have a special request for tonight."

"Oh?" Blaise's idea of a special request rarely aligned with his own—as evidenced by the card game. That was also what made the younger man so *interesting*. And honestly, Jefferson savored every moment he spent with Blaise. The Breaker made him feel whole. Blaise accepted him for who he was, not caring a lick for his wealth or influence.

"You've traveled a lot more than I have. Show me some of the places you've been?"

Jefferson blinked. That was a good idea. He smiled. "I doubt I can show you *all* the places I've been in one night without expending an immense amount of magic. But we could take a tour. A different destination each night? All without the fuss of having to pack your bags and go anywhere." *Though, I hope to do that with you. Some day.*

Blaise sighed with contentment. "I'd like that a lot."

CHAPTER FIVE

I Don't Fret. I Brood.

Jack

"Jack!"

The Effigest paused mid-stride at the voice, pivoting to face the speaker. When Nadine called, he knew it was in his best interest to listen. There was an urgency in the single word that made him frown. She stood outside her clinic, framed by the bright mid-morning sunshine, glowering at him as if something was his fault. Maybe that was the case. A lot of things were Jack's fault. But this time, he honestly didn't know what he might have done to earn her ire.

"Yeah?" he asked, crossing his arms to meet her surliness with his own.

"Get over here. It's rude to have a conversation shouting across the town square."

He snorted at her hypocrisy but ambled over nonetheless. Nadine wasn't one to trifle with. Not only could she use her magic to suck the life out of someone if she so chose, but as the most skilled Healer in town, for the sake of his long-term health, it was important to be on her good side. Or at least as good as he could get. A couple of new mages with Healing power had joined their town recently, but none of them were on a par with Nadine. One of them was a Beast Healer anyhow, which would do little good for Jack.

When he was closer, Nadine retreated into the clinic, and he followed. That was curious. Whatever she wanted to discuss, it was something she sought to keep private. As Nadine shut the door, he claimed the chair she usually had her patients sit in. The Healer raised an eyebrow at him, then climbed atop her stool with a shrug.

"What's got you hollering across the town at me?" Jack asked.

She pursed her lips. "Two things. First, Blaise."

Jack cocked his head. "What's *he* got to do with me?" He almost regretted the sting in his voice, but not really. Wouldn't do to have people think he actually *liked* the Breaker.

Nadine made a soft snort. "Not that you'll ever say as much, but I think you know more about what's happened to him than he'll even tell me." Jack met her eyes at the assertion, dipping his chin in silent agreement. "His physical wounds have healed as much as they can. But he's hurt on the inside, and that's not something I can fix."

Jack shrugged. "We all have those wounds." While that was true, he knew that few outlaws in Fortitude had been hurt as deeply as their Breaker. And if Blaise had kept that from Nadine... well, it wasn't Jack's place to inform her.

Nadine scowled. "All I know is, it's something to do with his family. He's thinking of going to Rainbow Flat."

Rainbow Flat. Jack tensed at the town's name. So Blaise was thinking of confronting his mother on the bitter truth. That was his right—but Nadine's worry was justified. The young man was so emotionally wounded that Jack wasn't sure how he'd stand up to facing the issue head-on. There was only so much a person could take before they unraveled.

He met her silver eyes. "Why are you telling *me* this? You should tell the peacock."

"Don't be daft. Jefferson Cole is leaving for Ganland. I won't breathe a word of this to him because we *need* him to go with the delegation." There was a sharp desperation in her voice that drew Jack's interest. Nadine wanted this for the Gutter, and badly. "This is something Blaise needs, too, but I don't think Emrys is enough to keep him stable."

Jack crossed his arms. "Are you insinuating that I should go with him? Because we're...partners or some such?" He uttered a derisive snort. "You forgetting I punched him in the face the first time we met?"

Nadine pinned him with a knowing look. She saw through his dragonshit. Jack made a face at her, annoyed. He had a reputation to maintain, after all. Couldn't have people thinking Wildfire Jack, Scourge of the Untamed Territory, was cuddly and lovable as a jackalope.

"Maybe I think it would be good for *you*," she said.

His brows knit at her new ploy. "What?"

The Healer crossed her arms. "You forget this place is a rumor mill? I heard you intend to spend more time with your daughter. This is the perfect chance." Then she leaned closer to him. "And your wife is about to travel to Confederation territory, and you need a worthwhile distraction. I can't imagine what it's going to do to you when your brain catches up with the fact that she's not here, and you have to wait and fret about her."

"I don't fret," Jack grumbled. "I brood."

"Fine, *brood*. When you brood, you tend to get violent."

He shrugged. "Ain't nothing wrong with that."

Nadine heaved a pained sigh. She was the one who healed him when his tendencies put him on the receiving end of a beat-down. "What I'm saying is, Blaise needs someone he can trust. Emmaline is one of his closest friends. And you? You're going to need a distraction, even if you don't think you do right now. You've worked with him before, and you know him. Blaise is comfortable around you, no matter how much of an ornery cuss you are."

"Did he tell you that?" Jack was genuinely curious.

"In not so many words," Nadine said. She licked her lips. "Consider going with him, that's all I ask. Fortitude will be fine. More mages arrive every week. We're not as soft a target as we once were."

She was right, but he would still worry about his town. He rubbed the back of his neck. "I'll think about it. You said there were two things. What's the second?"

Nadine crossed her arms, pinning him with another of her no-nonsense looks. "Your wife."

Jack went rigid. He'd approached Nadine about Kittie's problem, and the Healer had taken pains to speak to the Pyromancer. Kittie hadn't appreciated it at all. "Yeah?"

"Mindy's going along for several reasons. Kittie is one of 'em," Nadine started. Jack couldn't hide his surprise at the revelation, but the Healer didn't give him room to comment before plowing on. "She won't listen to me, but she might listen to Mindy. At any rate, a Hospitalier will have good instincts about what to shovel into her body to keep her healthy. And that ain't liquor." Nadine snorted with disdain.

Jack relaxed. That wasn't a bad idea. He liked Mindy—he'd go so far as to say he trusted her, which wasn't true of most people. Jack cocked his head. He wasn't used to people doing thoughtful things for those he cared about, not like that. "Thanks."

The Healer gave him a rare smile. "Don't mention it. And I mean that literally. Don't mention it, because I'm not sure I could heal myself if she took offense and barbecued me."

CHAPTER SIX
The One and Only Flora Strop

Blaise

B laise smiled, reminiscing on the previous night. Asking Jefferson to show him new places in the dreamscape had been the diversion he needed. Jefferson's enthusiasm for travel was downright infectious, and they had both awoken in a pleasant mood. Well, Blaise had, anyway. As usual, Jefferson had languished in bed for another hour while Blaise readied the bakery for the day's work. Jefferson didn't get up before the sun if he could help it.

Now Jefferson was off at another meeting, and Blaise was preparing a baker's dozen of the meat-filled buns that they had enjoyed the previous evening. He lost himself to the familiar work of kneading the dough, his mind drifting to Jefferson. And how in a few short days, Jefferson would leave him.

No, that was the wrong way to think of it. Blaise wrinkled his nose as he reconsidered. Jefferson wasn't leaving because he *wanted* to, but because it was *necessary*. *And he's not leaving* me—*not leaving this...whatever we have.* That was noteworthy. A small part of Blaise wanted to be selfish and keep Jefferson here for himself.

If he asked Jefferson to stay, Blaise had no doubt that he would. But the thing Jefferson was going to do was bigger than the both of them. It was important, and Jefferson's political savvy and deep ties to Ganland would help their cause. Didn't mean that Blaise had to be happy he was leaving, though.

Someone poked his shoulder, and he spun, heart racing as he found Emmaline giving him a squinty-eyed look that would have made her father proud. "What?"

"I asked you a question three times, and you're standing there gathering wool. What's going on?" Her hands were on her hips, her blonde ponytail swinging at her back.

He winced, glancing around the bakery. *His* bakery. It was one of the few places he could always stay on track—though apparently not today. Sheepishly, he turned back to the dough. "Oh, I guess this is ready to be rolled out so we can add the meat and cheese. Sorry. I was thinking."

Emmaline's face softened. She understood the traumas of his past in her own way. He still didn't know what had happened to her at Fort Courage, but he knew it wasn't good. In the time between her rescue and the gambit that had freed him from the Golden Citadel, she had changed. She'd become a little harder, like her father. Jaded. Sometimes angry. Blaise understood that, too.

"The diced ham is ready." She nodded to a nearby ceramic bowl. "Sometimes you think too much."

"I *have* to think about the people I care about." Blaise laid out a sphere of dough before taking a rolling pin to it. "I'm not about to stop doing that."

"I don't think that's what she's saying," Reuben piped up quietly from across the small bakery, where he had been decorating a tray of cookies while he waited for customers. It was late morning, and they weren't busy. "You latch onto things and worry them to shreds."

"I do *not*," Blaise muttered, feeling the back of his neck warm at the good-natured accusation. A part of him realized they were probably right. But it wasn't like he knew how to change that part of himself. Not without losing the ability to care about people. Or to just *care*.

Emmaline opened her mouth to say something, but the jingle of the bell over the door cut her off. Reuben straightened, setting down his piping bag to see to the customer, when they saw it was Jack. The outlaw swaggered into the bakery, all business, and by the way he draped an arm atop the glass display case, Blaise figured he hadn't come for a donut.

But it didn't hurt to coddle the Effigest's sweet tooth. And it would take the focus off himself, which was a bonus. Blaise set aside his rolling pin. "Morning, Jack. Want a donut? On the house."

Emmaline huffed out a breath, seeing through his plot. Amusement flickered in her father's eyes, as if he knew he had interrupted something with his entrance. "I'm not fool enough to turn down a donut."

"I got it, Reuben," Blaise called, slipping over to snag a piece of waxed paper so that he could retrieve a donut.

The outlaw watched his every move like a hawk preparing to stoop on prey. "Word is you're going to Rainbow Flat."

Blaise froze for a beat, then forced himself to finish the task. He straightened, handing the donut over to Jack. "Might be. Not sure if I want to leave the bakery, though." That was always a worthwhile excuse. And truth be told, Blaise *didn't* want to leave it. He loved every inch of the place.

That was the wrong thing to say, though. Reuben bounced on his heels, his face suddenly animated. "You can go if you need to, Blaise. We can make the basics. Did it before, and we're so much better at it now."

Blaise blinked, stymied by the teenager's words. It was true, too. Reuben and Emmaline had run the bakery when he and Jack had taken a previous ill-fated trip into Desina. And while he had been...never mind. Best not to think of that.

"Won't be a *we* thing because Emmaline won't be here," Jack said, interrupting Blaise's train of thought. Emmaline shot a look at her father that was half glare and half amazement at his audacity. "'Cause she'll be going to Rainbow Flat with me." The outlaw punctuated the statement with a bite of his donut, ignoring the motes of powdered sugar that fell to his chest.

At that, Emmaline's expression shifted yet again. This time, excitement reigned. "Wait, Rainbow Flat? We're going to Rainbow Flat?" She nearly squealed the question.

"Yep." Jack was gloating, his frosty eyes falling on Blaise in what was almost a dare.

Blaise's lower lip jutted out in consternation. He hadn't even decided that he was going, and Jack had the nerve to bluster into the bakery and all but demand it happen. "Well, I hope you have a good time."

Jack tilted his head. "I think we will. I heard that fancy musical *Breaker* is going to make its debut there next week. Bet I can finagle some tickets." He grinned.

"Go lick salt-iron," Blaise growled, earning a bark of laughter from Jack.

"C'mon, Blaise," Emmaline said. "You should go! Have a little adventure. Take your mind off your worries."

This would be the exact opposite of that. By the way Jack's gaze cut over to him, the outlaw knew. Blaise rubbed the back of his neck, glancing at Reuben. It was getting harder and harder to say no without bursting Emmaline's bubble. And the blasted outlaw knew it. "We'd have to close the bakery if I went. This place is too much for a single person to run." *Please tell them what a bad idea that is, Reuben.*

Instead, Reuben's face lit up. "I know exactly who I can ask to help! Hannah's back in town, working at the Jitterbug. But I think she and her sister are about to have it out again. I could ask if she'd like to help here?"

Oh gods, Hannah. Blaise had so many mixed emotions over the young woman who had been one of the first to befriend him in the outlaw town. Looking back, he realized that she'd *liked* him —in ways that he would never be comfortable reciprocating. And that was complicated because she was nice and kind and...*argh. Maybe there's a cave I can crawl into until Jefferson gets back.*

Reuben was watching him, waiting for an answer. Blaise wasn't about to unleash any of his confusing thoughts on his current audience. "Um, I guess it wouldn't hurt to ask."

Reuben punched a fist into the air. "I'll ask her this afternoon!"

Emmaline clapped her hands. "This is so exciting! When do we leave?"

Jack tipped his head. "That's entirely up to Blaise."

———

BLAISE GLANCED AT THE SADDLEBAG DRAPED ACROSS THE FOOT OF the bed, a neat assortment of clothing nestled beside it. Jefferson's things, ready to be slipped into the compartments for his journey. He couldn't help but grin at the cobalt blue bottle nestled amidst the garments. *Of course, he would pack cologne.*

He shifted his focus from Jefferson's luggage to himself. Blaise had put on one of the crisp, button-down shirts that Jefferson had given him, pairing it with a blue greatcoat. If it was to be their last evening together for a while, Blaise had decided to make it memorable. No games over proper attire tonight.

But I really wish he wouldn't leave until Flora was back. As much as Jefferson had evaded the discussion, Blaise worried about him traveling to Ganland. He would feel slightly better if Flora were along to accompany him from the start. The wily half-knocker would be able to catch up to Jefferson on her own, but Blaise hoped that wouldn't be necessary. Especially since it would complicate the entire reason he had sent her off on this little errand in the first place.

Blaise heard the soft pop of displaced air, freezing as he reached down to pull out his least scuffed pair of boots. "Flora? That you?"

"The one and only!" she called back. "You coming down or want me to come up? If you're not decent, I'm more than happy to come up." A raucous laugh followed her bold words.

Blaise snorted. "Sorry to disappoint you, but I'm fully clothed. You can come up."

"You're no fun at all." The thud of feet on the perilously steep stairs that led to the small loft room heralded her arrival.

"Not that kind of fun, no," Blaise agreed. He had grown accustomed to Flora's filter-free conversational style. "Did you get it?"

Flora grinned at him as she mounted the top of the stairs. In reply, she pulled a small, velvet-covered box out of a pouch at her side. "Of course I did. This was a good idea you had. Expensive, but a good idea."

Blaise winced at the reminder. Jefferson didn't know it yet, but Blaise had sunk his full inheritance from Malcolm Wells into the contents of this box. "Did the Enchanter tell you how it works?"

Flora tossed the box into the air and caught it, ignoring Blaise's moment of panic at her flippant treatment of the pricey investment. "Similar to the one he has, 'cause I went to the same Enchanter. Top of the line, that one." Then she paused, tilting her head. "There're instructions inside the box. I peeked, since I wanted to make sure we weren't getting cheated."

"How do we know it'll work?" Blaise asked, extending his hand.

Flora dropped the velvet box into his palm. "You won't know until it's on. But that's also why I went to the best. Better odds it'll do what you need it to do."

"Hmm." The box rested in Blaise's palm, small and unassuming. He unleashed a tendril of his magic, sending it into the box—

careful to only quest and prod with it, not allowing it to exert its true power. He'd learned he could use his magic to assess things, to an extent. Sort of like groping for something in the dark. Blaise knew by touching a glass exactly how much magic he had to spend to shatter it; where the most vulnerable parts were. And when he encountered something magical, he gained a sense about that, too.

His magic raced along the circle of metal nestled within the box. Blaise didn't even have to open it to confirm that it was a ring. He could almost feel the cool smoothness of the metal and the tiny chasms of the sigils engraved in the band. At first, nothing about the ring felt remarkable to him, as if it were completely ordinary. Flora was right. This Enchanter was a master at their work.

"Well?" Flora asked, watching him expectantly.

"Gimme a moment," he murmured, continuing his exploration. He was tempted to open the box, but he would have to withdraw his magic and start anew. And it took a lot of effort to keep his power in line, assessing rather than destroying.

Ah. He was suddenly glad he had continued on. There it was. The Enchanter had folded whatever spell they'd used back on itself, making it almost imperceptible unless someone knew to look for it. *Jefferson's cabochon ring is probably similar. That one never felt magical to me, either.*

Blaise pulled back his power. "There's definitely a spell enhancing it. Now we'll see if it works when I give it to him."

Flora eyed him appreciatively. "Hot date tonight?"

"Something like that," Blaise agreed, slipping the velvet box into the pocket concealed beneath his greatcoat.

Blaise was certain she would needle him about it, but to his surprise, she let it go. Something like happiness sparked in her violet eyes for a moment before she yawned. "Well, have fun. Tell Jefferson I'll be ready in the morning. I'm gonna get some shut-eye since I used a lot of magic hustling back here."

"Hey, Flora?" She paused, looking back at him. "Thanks. I mean, for getting this. And for…everything."

Flora waved over her shoulder. "No thanks needed. Aside from maybe some sugar cookies for the road. And cinnamon rolls to start the day tomorrow would hit the spot. Notice I said cinnamon *rolls*. More than one. I wouldn't turn down an entire pan."

Blaise chuckled. "I can do that."

CHAPTER SEVEN

Socially Awkward

Jefferson

efferson hesitated, clutching the bakery's door knob. This would be the last time he'd come home to Blaise for...well, he didn't know how long. He felt a little guilty—he was excited about the prospect of going to Ganland and dabbling in politics to help the Gutter. It was a good thing he was doing, a *necessary* thing. But by the same token, he didn't want to leave Blaise.

"Howdy."

He couldn't help the grin that slid onto his face at the sight of Blaise leaning against the bakery counter, waiting for him. Blaise did that sometimes—waited downstairs until Jefferson arrived. A pair of saddlebags rested against the wall near the door, an unpleasant reminder that they would soon part ways, if only temporarily. Jefferson shoved those thoughts aside, focusing instead on the young man watching him. "What's that? Did you finish packing for me?"

"I thought you might not have enough time tonight," Blaise replied. "Though you're welcome to make sure I got everything you need. I left your grooming supplies alone, since I figured you'd want to use them in the morning."

"I'll check later," Jefferson said, touched by Blaise's gesture. Then he paused, taking in Blaise's attire. "Did someone die? Why are you dressed up?"

"Oh my *gods*," Blaise mumbled, pushing off from the counter and inadvertently displaying the amount of care he'd taken to look good. "Why is that the first place you go with that question?"

Because you're not one to dress up fancy. It's not you, although, sweet Tabris, you look good. Wait, focus. Jefferson cleared his throat as he cycled through a proper response. "Ahem, forgive me. You took me by surprise." Then he allowed an edge of roughness into his voice. "But very *appealingly*, I assure you."

The apology soothed the Breaker. "I was hoping we could enjoy the evening together." His voice was soft. Wistful.

"I would like that *very* much," Jefferson said immediately. Really, he wanted nothing more than to spend the rest of the night curled up beside Blaise, memorizing the planes of his face and the rightness that accompanied just being with him. "What are you thinking?"

"Maybe we could go eat at the Jitterbug."

The suggestion gave Jefferson cause to raise his eyebrows. Most evenings, Blaise was content to whip up a simple meal for them to share or dine with Clover at the Broken Horn. They seldom ate at the Jitterbug, though Blaise still provided bread to the diner daily. "Is this a *date*?"

A smile curled Blaise's lips. Whatever he was thinking, it made him happy. Jefferson liked to see that. "You tell me."

"You're trying to play coy, so it must be." Jefferson chuckled. "It's not working, is it?"

Jefferson stepped closer until only a hand span separated them. "No, but it's endearing and very *you*. And I mean that in all the best ways."

A shy smile returned to Blaise's face, making Jefferson glad he had offered the compliment. One day, he hoped Blaise would truly understand how much Jefferson treasured him for being exactly who he was. Something flickered in the Breaker's eyes, as if a stray thought had interrupted his plans. "Oh. Flora is back."

Jefferson blinked. "Wait, really?" He hadn't been aware—but then again, he had been in meetings all afternoon. No doubt Blaise had told her as much, and Flora knew better than to interrupt him in a meeting unless it was dire. "Where is she?"

"Resting. And getting ready to eat an entire pan of cinnamon rolls, if she's to be believed." Blaise stepped away, heading for the door. "She's still planning to go with you tomorrow."

"I certainly hope she'll save a cinnamon roll for me." Jefferson moved to follow. "She arrived just in time, then."

"I'll make you anything you want tomorrow," Blaise promised. "Now, let's get over to the Jitterbug before they get too busy."

The Jitterbug was only half-full, with most of the evening crowd over at the Broken Horn Saloon or not yet arrived. Mindy waved to them as they seated themselves at a table, swooping over. "Evening. You planning to chance the menu or leave it to me?" She grinned. Mindy's Hospitalier magic helped her to perceive the best food and drink for those around her. She was never wrong.

"The usual," Blaise said, meaning that Mindy could pick for him.

"Likewise," Jefferson echoed, nodding to her.

"Got it!" the Hospitalier replied, rubbing her hands together. "Hmm. Something special is going to be required tonight!" She sounded pleased with herself, and as she spun on her heel, she nearly glowed with excitement at the challenge they presented.

Blaise rubbed his cheek, seeming to have second thoughts. "Maybe we *should* have gone to the saloon."

Jefferson chuckled. Blaise hated being fussed over, and he felt awkward at fancy dinners. Jefferson loved both of those things. It meant a lot that Blaise was doing this. "What, you don't want a romantic dinner with me?"

Blaise shook his head. "It's not that. I don't like being reminded it's our last night together."

Jefferson reached over and placed a hand atop Blaise's, lightly, in case the Breaker would rather not be touched. He didn't shrink away, instead, relaxing beneath his hand. "It's *not* our last night together. And it will take more than distance to keep us apart." Jefferson didn't dare expand on that. Very few people knew he was a mage, and it was critical that it stayed that way—for both their sakes.

Blaise rubbed the back of his neck with his free hand. Worry reflected in his blue eyes, fears that he seemed unable or unwilling to express at the moment. He shook his head, releasing a soft sigh. "Something you said earlier stuck with me."

Jefferson raised his brows. "What was it?"

The corners of Blaise's eyes wrinkled. "When you asked why I dressed this way. If someone had died." He paused, reluctant to finish the thought, though he seemed to decide to plow onward. "You're going to Malcolm's funeral when you go to Nera."

Oh. Jefferson winced. Honestly, that was something he'd given little thought to. Seledora had acted on his behalf to put everything in motion for a proper service to bid goodbye forever to Malcolm Wells. The least he could do was attend his own funeral.

"Well, yes, but *I* haven't thought about it very much," Jefferson admitted.

"Doesn't it bother you?" Blaise asked, pulling his hand away. He made a circular gesture, as if attempting to explain and failing. "It's..." Blaise pointed an index finger at Jefferson meaningfully.

Jefferson sighed inwardly. Blaise had a very confusing relationship with Malcolm—which was odd since Jefferson and Malcolm were one and the same. It had taken time for Blaise to reconcile his dual identities, and now it clearly bothered him that Malcolm was, for all purposes, dead. Jefferson idly rubbed the scarlet-stoned cabochon ring that made his preferred visage possible.

"It would be a lie to say it doesn't bother me." Jefferson kept his voice soft, the words for Blaise alone. "But you also know how I feel about Malcolm." *And you know why I'm trying so hard to separate myself from the Wells name.*

Blaise relaxed, offering a small nod and the hint of a smile. "He wasn't such a bad guy in the end."

"I *told* you so," Jefferson said, chuckling.

"He was just a little arrogant, is all."

And now he's teasing me. Good. That means he feels a little better about things. "If that's his greatest flaw in your eyes, then I believe he would be quite happy with that." Jefferson didn't know if Blaise was being flippant or if that was truly what he saw as Malcolm's biggest flaw.

Blaise's gaze flicked toward the kitchen area, his forehead crinkling. A young woman bustled out, carrying plates in their direction. Hmm, something about her was familiar. Jefferson hadn't seen her in town recently, but...oh yes, now he remembered. She was the one who had asked Blaise to dance ages ago at the Feast of Flight. The pretty brunette he had shied away from in a panic when no one else had understood that he didn't want to be touched. Jefferson glanced at Blaise, expecting that her approach might alarm him, but to Jefferson's surprise, he discovered that his beau didn't seem any more tense than usual.

"Howdy, Blaise, it's been a while," she greeted him, the smile in her voice extending to the shine in her eyes. She nodded to Jefferson, but her focus was fully on Blaise.

"Howdy, Hannah," Blaise said, shifting to make room for her to slip a plate in front of him. "You remember Jefferson Cole?"

Hannah set a plate before Jefferson, too. Like Blaise's, it was loaded with wine-braised beef and mushrooms, buttered peas, and fresh rolls. "I do recall Mr. Cole. It's a pleasure to see you again." She flashed a smile at Jefferson.

"Likewise," Jefferson replied, though, in truth, he was watching for the slightest hint that Blaise was uncomfortable. Hannah seemed innocent enough, and the Breaker had come a long way from the insecure young man he had been. But he had also been through so much since then.

Hannah clasped her hands behind her back. "I appreciate the opportunity to work at your bakery."

What? That was new. Jefferson knew nothing of this, and it was either a recent development or Blaise had forgotten to tell him. Small wonder, though. Jefferson had been in so many meetings lately. He caught Blaise's eye and mouthed the words, "Work at the bakery?"

"It'll be a big help to Reuben when I'm traveling," Blaise said in response to both Hannah and Jefferson. "I appreciate it."

Ah. That makes sense. Hmm, but what about Emmaline? Though it was promising to hear Blaise was seriously considering a trip to Rainbow Flat.

Hannah beamed, tilting her head. "I tried my hand at the rolls today." She shifted her weight from one foot to the other. "Thought it was worth a shot."

The Breaker raised his eyebrows, tapping the still-warm roll. There was a soft, hollow sound. "The top is firm. Sounds good." He inhaled deeply, the corners of his lips lifting. "Smells good, too."

Hannah nearly blushed at his comments. Then she straightened, remembering her current task. "Be right back. Need to get your drinks."

Jefferson watched her go. "Where's Celeste?"

"Hannah doesn't get on well with her sister. Celeste is probably lying low." Blaise picked up the roll, breaking it open.

"And so you invited her to work at the bakery?" Jefferson asked, keeping his tone neutral.

"It was Reuben's idea, actually. He asked for permission, and I told him to go ahead. He'll need help," Blaise replied, though he didn't sound happy with the arrangement. The Breaker slathered a pat of butter on one side of the roll.

Before Jefferson could ask any further questions, Hannah returned with their drinks, no doubt suggested by Mindy. She placed a glass of wine before Jefferson—Knossan dandelion wine, one of his favorites—and something that Jefferson was willing to bet was a switchel for Blaise. "Thank you."

Hannah nodded to him, then licked her lips. "I just wanted to tell you…I'm glad you found someone, Blaise."

A momentary look of surprise flashed across Blaise's face. The Breaker stiffened as all of his anxiety about awkward social situations no doubt came to a head. Beneath the table, Jefferson nudged his foot against Blaise's, a reminder that he wasn't alone. That he had no reason to be nervous.

"Me, too," Blaise said after a moment. "Um, thanks."

Ah, she was sweet on him. Jefferson watched as Hannah drifted off to see to another table, then glanced back at Blaise. "Nothing about that was awkward in the least."

"Not at all," Blaise muttered, making a face. "But I sort of figured that conversation was going to happen, eventually. Better now than later."

They ate in companionable silence, speaking occasionally but mostly focusing on the food laid out before them. Mindy was right—it was delicious, a worthy meal for his last evening with Blaise for the foreseeable future.

Blaise sighed with contentment as he finished eating, setting his knife and fork on his plate with a clatter. His blue eyes flicked up to Jefferson, and Blaise's lips pursed as if he were uncertain about something. "Want to go for a walk with me?"

A walk? Jefferson canted his head, wondering what this was about. Blaise was definitely not the sort who took romantic walks. "I would love to."

A small smile lit Blaise's face, and together they rose from the table. Jefferson paid for the meal before stepping out to join Blaise on the porch. The Breaker was staring at the western horizon, where the clouds were afire with brilliant hues of scarlet and gold. They headed toward the rim of the canyon overlooking the Deadwood River. Overhead, the stars slowly became visible as the sun sank lower on the horizon. Sleepy birds called in the distance, and Jefferson heard the thunder of wings as a sentry pegasus flew nearby on a round. The river rumbled in the depths below them as Blaise found a chunk of sandstone that had been formed into a rudimentary bench by one of Fortitude's new Earthshaper mages.

Jefferson sat down beside him, hazarding a glance at Blaise. He looked brilliant with the sunset making his hair gleam like copper, his face bathed in the glow. Jefferson tried to commit this moment to memory, this fleeting time when Blaise looked like the legend many said he was.

"There're no views like this in Ganland," Jefferson murmured, nudging Blaise with his shoulder.

At the mention of Ganland, Blaise's expression cooled. He licked his lips, shifting to better face Jefferson. "Speaking of that. I, ah, got you something." The Breaker fumbled in his pocket and pulled out the box, holding it lightly in his hand.

"Oh." Jefferson didn't know what else to say. Should he have gotten Blaise a present? He thought about asking, but he saw Blaise was gathering the courage to speak.

"It's...well, let me show you." The younger man's fingers fluttered against the edges of the box as he pulled it open. Something glinted in the waning light.

A ring? Jefferson inhaled a sharp breath. Is he proposing? His traitorous tongue almost asked, but he pulled it back at the last second, coughing instead. He knew Blaise better than that, but his enthusiasm sometimes got away from him. Jefferson laced his fingers together, resting them atop one knee as he bit his lower lip to keep any potential comments at bay.

Apparently, Blaise knew how things looked. His cheeks

flamed, and he shook his head as the box flipped closed. "It's not...
I mean..." The Breaker made a frustrated sound.

"Whatever it is, it's only you and I here," Jefferson reminded
him. "You have no reason to be embarrassed." At least he hoped
Blaise never had reason to be embarrassed with him.

Blaise rubbed the back of his neck, though his shoulders lost
some of their tension. "This conversation was a lot easier in my
head."

Jefferson laughed. "That, I can understand." He eyed the box,
unable to help his curiosity.

Blaise opened the box again. "It's for your trip."

"Oh." Jefferson watched as Blaise pulled the silver ring out
from where it nestled in the cushion. What sort of ring would
Blaise get him for his trip? "Is it for good luck?"

"Better," Blaise said, holding it in his palm. He had mastered
himself, regaining his lost confidence. "It's supposed to prevent
your magic from being detected."

At that, Jefferson pursed his lips. "You got me an enchanted
ring? Blaise...how? They're so expensive. Especially *good* ones."
And even without touching it, Jefferson saw it was a quality ring,
on a par with his cabochon.

"I'm not as wealthy as you, but I'm not *poor*." Blaise's brow
furrowed with indignation.

Jefferson sighed. "Sorry, that came out wrong. I'm just
surprised. And honored. I know how costly things like this
can be."

"Try it on," Blaise said, brushing away the apology.

Jefferson accepted the proffered ring, sliding it onto his left
ring finger. It fit well, which led him to believe whoever had
crafted it knew his size. Flora had had a hand in this, no doubt. As
the silver loop settled against his skin, he felt whatever magic was
within it activate, as his cabochon ring did. Only this was different. He gasped as something seared through him. He felt as if he'd
suddenly been cut off from something. *Something important...oh.*

"What's wrong?" Blaise asked, noticing his discomfort.

Jefferson swallowed. "Ah, this ring seems to *cut off* my magic."

Blaise's eyes widened, and he flipped open the lid of the velvet box, pulling out a small piece of paper. He unfolded and read it, dismay crossing his face. "Oh. That's part of how it conceals your magic."

Jefferson studied the ring. It was a thing of beauty, a line of sigils engraved along the band. Something that gleamed like a fire opal blazed in the setting—no, it wasn't quite a fire opal. It was different but somehow familiar. He swallowed when he realized what he was looking at. "This ring has *ivory* from a unicorn's horn."

"I wondered what that was. Not sure I like that they had to use part of a unicorn for this. But I guess that makes sense." Blaise sighed, disappointment lining his face. "I didn't know it would lock out your magic. I only want you to be safe."

He was so earnest that Jefferson immediately put an arm around him, leaning over to give him a gentle kiss. "This is an incredibly thoughtful gift. And if it makes you feel better, I promise to wear it when I'm traveling with the delegation."

Blaise leaned against him. "It *would* make me feel better." His voice quavered, and he rested his head against Jefferson's shoulder.

The Breaker's worry reminded Jefferson of how delicate his situation was. If anyone found out Jefferson had magic, they would no doubt want to know what kind he had. And how he'd *gotten* it. *Your secret is safe with me. I promise.* But… "It will mean I can't visit you at night."

Blaise swallowed a lump in his throat. "It won't be forever."

"No, it won't," Jefferson agreed. He slipped the ring off, relief suffusing him as he felt the connection to his power return. Blaise held out the box, and Jefferson took it, nestling the ring inside. "I'll always think of you when I look at it."

Blaise glanced at him. "Did you think I was proposing?"

Yes. No. I don't know. I wish you would, but I know you won't. Not yet, anyway. I know you need time. All of those thoughts raced through Jefferson's mind in a blur. "I know you too well."

"That's not an answer."

"It is," Jefferson insisted. Blaise puffed out a breath. "Look, I know most things between us aren't easy for you. They don't come naturally, but you try. You're cautious and want to understand what something will cost you before you commit." He chuckled at the grudging look Blaise gave him. "What? You can't be mad that I'm right."

"I'm annoyed that you're accurate," Blaise grumbled, "which is another thing entirely."

Jefferson cocked his head. "You do realize the way I've survived this long is by figuring people out, yes? That's like ninety-five percent of my life as a politician and entrepreneur."

"And here I thought more of it would have to do with knowing who to sweet talk and where to invest your money."

Jefferson grinned. He rather enjoyed it when Blaise sassed back. "Obviously, that's the other five percent."

Blaise relaxed. "I guess I'll be glad for that, then. You'll probably need that with the delegation."

"No doubt," Jefferson agreed. He turned the box over in his hands, still charmed by all the effort Blaise had gone through on his behalf. "I'd rather not speak of that now, though. Better to focus on this moment."

Blaise took Jefferson's hand and gave it a light tug as he rose from the stone. "Come on. Let's go home."

"Already? I wouldn't mind watching the stars." Jefferson was reluctant to leave. The sooner they reached the bakery, the sooner dawn would come. A soft sound of amusement from Blaise caught his attention. "What?"

In answer, the Breaker merely raised his eyebrows.

"Let me guess. You expect me to use my amazing powers to figure you out, hmm?" Jefferson asked with a laugh.

"Something like that."

Jefferson rubbed his chin, suspecting what Blaise hinted at. "Forgive me, but in this, you lead and I follow. You're too important for me to risk misunderstanding."

Blaise's eyes softened, as if Jefferson had offered him something he hadn't known he needed. "You. I want you."

The Breaker's soft words sent a jolt of anticipation through Jefferson, his breath hitching. Blaise had firm boundaries. It had taken them time to reach an agreement to satisfy both of their needs. Jefferson craved the physical closeness that Blaise had never sought in his adult life. By all rights, that should have made them incompatible, but Jefferson had learned there was more to a relationship than lust.

A victorious rush of heat flooded through Jefferson's veins. "Do you, now?"

"I do," Blaise murmured, leaning in to capture his mouth in a kiss.

Oh yes, these unexpected moments were far better than any Jefferson had experienced in the past. He enjoyed the sugar-sweet taste of Blaise on his lips before pulling away. "Home?"

Blaise released a soft breath. "Home."

CHAPTER EIGHT
Break the Cycle

Blaise

*J*efferson was warm beside him. Blaise didn't want to get up, didn't want to relinquish Jefferson to his responsibilities. Didn't want what they had to end. He was quite willing to ignore the incessant ring of the expensive, new-fangled alarm clock perched on the bedside table.

"Ugh, make it stop," Jefferson mumbled beside him, rolling over.

The blasted clock was closest to Blaise. He reached out to turn it off but missed, instead knocking it to the floor, where it continued to chime aggressively. Under normal circumstances, Blaise wouldn't mind the clock. But today? He considered using his magic on it, but it wasn't the clock's fault. He slung an arm over the side of the bed, fumbling until he found it. Blaise hauled it up and turned it off, then deposited it back on the bedside table.

Jefferson stirred, grumbling something as he came to wakefulness. The bare skin of his chest nestled snug against Blaise's back. Blaise shifted to face him, placing a hand against the other man's chest, contented by the rhythmic beat of the heart within.

"Getting handsy, are we?" Jefferson murmured, amusement in his voice.

"Don't ruin this," Blaise whispered.

Jefferson chuckled. "Nothing could ruin this. You're here with me, and there's *nothing* better." He placed a hand over Blaise's. "And we're opposites this way. As much as you shy away from touch, you know I crave it. I'll miss this, so thank you."

Blaise knew. And while it was true he disliked most touch, he didn't mind Jefferson as much as others. Jefferson was safe. And complicated. And sometimes not complicated at all. "I thought about breaking the clock."

Jefferson withdrew his hand, undaunted by Blaise's odd change of topic. "Better the clock wake us than Flora."

Flora. He owed her cinnamon rolls, plus whatever Jefferson wanted. Blaise glanced at the window. It was still dark, with no sign that the sun had any intention of coming up soon.

"We could stay curled up and warm here for another hour," Jefferson suggested with a yawn.

"I would, but cinnamon rolls don't bake themselves." Blaise leaned over to kiss him. "And I need to have the oven warm before Reuben arrives."

"Mmm, the demands of a small business owner," Jefferson marveled, satisfied. "I love the sound of free enterprise in the morning."

Blaise snorted a laugh. "Wait until I tell you I have to do the inventory later."

"Just when I thought you couldn't possibly be any more attractive to me..." Jefferson propped himself up on one elbow, grinning.

Blaise's cheeks warmed with pleasure. He ducked his head and pulled away, sitting up and swinging his legs over the side of the bed. The sudden draft was a stark reminder of his lack of clothing. He rose and crossed to the trunk that contained his limited wardrobe, dragging the lid open. Blaise even picked out clothing that matched, declaring a truce in their ongoing style battle.

When he looked up, Jefferson was watching him intently, as if the other man were trying to commit him to memory. "Last night, you told me that when I got up, you needed to get ready, too," Blaise commented, nodding at the nearby selection of clothing Jefferson had laid out the previous evening.

"The Jefferson of last night has no appreciation for the fact that Present Jefferson would like to stay curled up in the blankets. Preferably with you."

Blaise snorted. "Past Jefferson told me to tell you that you can't stay in bed. If you do, you'll never be ready in time, and you don't want to be late."

"I dislike Past Jefferson." Though, despite his complaint, Jefferson sat up, raking a hand through his hair. It was unfair that even disheveled, he still looked *good*.

"Future Jefferson will like the cinnamon rolls that will be waiting for him later, though," Blaise said as he buttoned his shirt. "So, you've got that going for you."

With a yawn and a stretch, Jefferson lumbered up from the bed, collecting his clothing. "Would you like a hand in the bakery until Reuben arrives?"

The question distracted Blaise, and he misjudged the next button, forcing it out of alignment. He glanced down to fix it. "I wouldn't say no." Jefferson's offer made him feel warm and squishy. And loved.

Blaise finished dressing first, heading down to start the fire. Jefferson joined him a short time later, and together they set to work. While the dough rose, they shared a quiet breakfast. By the time the cinnamon rolls were ready, Reuben had arrived to start his workday. Flora bowled in a short time later, eager for her promised pastries.

Then, before they knew it, Jefferson had to head to the stables to meet the rest of the small delegation. Blaise picked up Jefferson's saddlebag, impressed by how much clothing he had stuffed into it.

"I could get that," Jefferson said.

Blaise smiled. "You could, but I want to." He hefted it in one hand. "You have clothes in Nera, don't you?"

"Well, yes, but I needed some for on the road, too," Jefferson pointed out as they strode out the door.

"He wouldn't be caught dead wearing the same clothing twice in a row!" Flora called to their backs.

Jefferson sighed. "I have a certain reputation to uphold." He tucked a hand inside his coat pocket, as if checking for something. The telltale dark blue velvet of the ring box was visible for a heartbeat before the Dreamer eased it back inside. Jefferson caught Blaise's eye and winked.

They drew to a stop outside the stables. Seledora and the other pegasi who would travel with the delegation were already outside, saddled and waiting for their riders. Their coats gleamed in the early morning sunlight, their sleek wings tucked against their sides.

Blaise didn't like goodbyes—they were awkward and uncomfortable. Often heart-wrenching. He wanted to kiss Jefferson, to taste him one more time. But he was painfully aware that they had an audience, so he shifted his weight and rubbed the back of his neck as he tried to figure out how to make this *right*.

"Why are you frowning?" Jefferson asked.

Blaise sighed. "Because the last time I kissed you and we parted ways, things didn't go so well for me."

At his admission, Jefferson stepped closer, warmth in his eyes. "This is *not* like that. But if you want to break the cycle, *I'll* kiss *you*."

Break the cycle. Blaise liked that idea—he was a Breaker, after all. He gave an almost imperceptible nod, but Jefferson was watching for it. The other man swooped in, tugging Blaise into a proprietary embrace. Jefferson paused, aiming a saucy grin at him, lifting a hand to trace the line of Blaise's jaw.

"Remember this." Jefferson's voice was husky with emotion.

Then their lips met. For the moment, Blaise's world contracted to only him and Jefferson. He focused on the feel of Jefferson's lean frame against him, the citrus tang of the cologne wafting from his neck.

Someone nearby whooped encouragement, distracting Blaise. *Flora.* Of course, it was Flora. Other voices chimed in, a clamor of appreciation for their show of affection.

"Well, that's mortifying," Blaise muttered, close against Jefferson.

"No, it's not. They're happy for you," Jefferson whispered, gently placing his forehead against Blaise's. He held on to Blaise like he didn't want to let go, though after a moment, he loosened his grip.

Blaise stepped back, ducking his head shyly. He would never be used to being the center of attention, not the way Jefferson was. But Jefferson was right—when he hazarded a glance, those still looking his way were smiling, joy on their faces. Happiness had been in short supply for many of the recent settlers in Fortitude. Blaise supposed he gave them hope.

"Don't forget: this isn't *goodbye.* It's *see you later.*" Jefferson touched Blaise's chin, thumb brushing against beard. Then he drew his hand away, moving toward Seledora.

Blaise nodded, though the other man couldn't see it. He allowed a smile to reach his lips. He rubbed his chin where Jefferson had touched him, then pivoted to look for Emrys. Blaise didn't have to go far. The black stallion had come to see the delegation off as well, though he was most interested in Seledora.

<Did you slip sugar cookies into Jefferson's saddlebags like you promised?> Emrys asked, nostrils fluttering.

Blaise reached up and smoothed the stallion's wild forelock. "Yes, and I even left him a note, so he'll know that he's supposed to share with Seledora."

Emrys blew out a contented breath. <She will like that, I

hope.> He flicked his ears in Seledora's direction. Blaise smiled. His pegasus was trying very hard to court Jefferson's attorney.

"I haven't met a pegasus yet who dislikes a good sugar cookie," Blaise said with a chuckle. He knew for a fact Seledora enjoyed them, though as with most things, she liked to hide her pleasure. All the same, he had taken notice of the way she peered out of her stall office when she thought he might come around with cookies or some other baked treat.

With one hand on Emrys's neck, Blaise turned to take in the rest of the people gathered. He found Jack there, the outlaw watching his wife with smoldering intensity as she swung into the saddle. Blaise was still getting used to the man Wildfire Jack Dewitt turned into under the influence of his wife. The Effigest lost some of the serrated sharpness that made him prickly to deal with. *Some*—not all. Blaise wondered how Jack was going to cope with his wife gone for weeks, possibly months.

And how am I going to deal with Jefferson being gone that long?

Blaise pushed the thought away, wincing as he recalled Jack's suggestion to travel to Rainbow Flat with him. He wasn't sure he wanted to have the outlaw along for company if he devolved into the snarly, difficult man he often was without Kittie around. But Emmaline was supposed to accompany them, and if he would get his act together for anyone, it was her.

"Daddy, stop making stupid cow-eyes at Mom so she can go," Blaise heard Emmaline say nearby.

Her comment stirred Jack, and the outlaw swung his gaze to her, scowling. "That's *not* what I was doing."

Blaise ambled over, deciding that maybe he should get involved before Jack said something stupid that set back all the progress he'd made with Emmaline. Not that the outlaw would even remotely see it that way. "She has a point. It's either that or it's the same look you have when you're figuring out how to murder someone."

"None of your sass," the Effigest growled, though there was a hint of amusement in his voice. "Besides, not as if you can talk after all your canoodling with that peacock."

"Pot, meet kettle," Kittie called from the back of a chestnut pegasus, looming over them. "He's not the *only* one that's been canoodling, and you know it."

Jack narrowed his eyes, attempting to glare at his wife, who only met his look with a playful grin. "Making me feel outnumbered here."

"You know you love it when the odds are stacked against you," Kittie said, and there was a depth of fondness in her voice that made Blaise smile. "You behave while I'm gone, *Wildfire* Jack Dewitt."

"Not making any promises I can't keep," the outlaw said, which was probably the most truthful response he could make.

"I expect nothing less." Kittie blew a kiss to her husband and daughter, then waved as her pegasus joined the others.

A few moments later, Blaise stood beside Emrys, Jack, and Emmaline as the small delegation receded into tiny specks before they were lost to the horizon. A profound feeling of loneliness tugged at Blaise's heart, as if Jefferson's absence were a physical malady. Emrys bumped his shoulder with his velvet-soft nose, a silent reminder that Blaise wasn't alone.

Boots crunched on the dirt as Jack and Emmaline turned. The Effigest's eyes glinted with a mix of…was that sadness and worry? Jack brushed at one eye, his mouth deepening into a scowl when he realized Blaise was watching.

"So, when are we going to Rainbow Flat?" Emmaline asked, as if she sensed that both Blaise and her father needed a distraction from their messy emotions.

Rainbow Flat. Maybe a trip really would be good for him. And it seemed that no matter what, they were going to encourage him to go. Blaise exhaled a soft breath. "In a couple of days. That'll give us time to pack and get things settled with the bakery and…whatever it is Jack actually does around here."

The outlaw snorted. "What I do around here is more useful than you, cookie."

Blaise hid a smile. He knew exactly what Jack did. Even though the outlaw put on a show that his biggest contribution to Fortitude was the occasional heist he pulled off on Confederation stagecoaches or pack-trains, Blaise knew that he was so much more. Jack was the spider who tended to the web of information that kept them all safe. He was in charge of the sentries, their first line of defense. Jack was *important* to their growing town, even if he pretended to be nothing more than a bandit.

"But yeah, a few days to get things settled is good," Jack murmured.

CHAPTER NINE
A Lack of Hospitality

Jefferson

Flying astride a pegasus was one of Jefferson's great pleasures. He loved every moment, though he would have enjoyed it even more with Blaise and Emrys nearby. He glanced over his shoulder, hoping to see the black stallion bobbing through the air. It was nothing more than a flight of fancy but one Jefferson couldn't help but continue to entertain.

<You have other things to focus on,> Seledora reminded him as they soared through the last of the red rock ravines that gave the Gutter its name.

Jefferson sighed. All of this had seemed more tolerable when he was talking about doing it. Now that it had him apart from Blaise, though? Never had he expected to become so spellbound by someone. In the past, he would have relished this task. It would have given him life. Now? He didn't mind it, but it didn't thrill him as it once might have.

Seledora flew in the lead. Kittie's chestnut pegasus stayed on the grey's right flank, while Mindy's pegasus was on the left. Flora, on the white pegasus, Tylos, who she had flown with before, brought up the rear. Tylos wasn't as robust as the other pegasi, and they had to stop every hour to allow the small stallion a break. Jefferson didn't mind, though. Like Kittie and Mindy, he wasn't accustomed to the demands of a sustained pegasus flight, and the opportunities to stretch were welcome.

During one of the breaks, Seledora caught him fidgeting with the velvet box. <What is that?>

He glanced at her. Of their group, only Flora and Seledora knew about his magic. "Blaise gave it to me." When he was certain no prying ears were near, he explained what the ring did.

Seledora snorted. <That was a good idea. Knowledge of your magic would no doubt endanger this delegation.>

She was right. He knew it in his heart, but he still disliked it. It was a little frightening how quickly he felt like his magic was an intrinsic part of him. Jefferson wasn't looking forward to being cut off from it.

"How much further to the first town?" Kittie called, striding over and interrupting his thoughts.

Jefferson pulled the map out of his saddlebag at her question. This part of their travel was easy—it was simply a matter of following the Deadwood River out of the Gutter. But their evening accommodations weren't something he was looking forward to. The most suitable lodgings he could locate were at Courage's End, a town in the country of Mella that had cropped up in the shadow of Fort Courage. It was that or go well out of their way to a town in Desina, and they would lose too much time doing that.

"At our current pace, we should be there by midafternoon," Jefferson said, tracing his fingers along the blue ribbon of river.

She nodded and went back to her mount. Moments later, their group was airborne again, and Jefferson's thoughts turned to their destination. Of their group, only Flora had been present at the assault that had destroyed the fort. But Kittie's daughter had been held there. And Jefferson's tie to the disaster was more personal than he liked.

As they flew in, the ruins of the fort were like the hulking skeleton of a slain beast. The massive stones of toppled towers and the metal ribs that had enclosed the mighty hull of the *Retribution* grappled as if frozen in the throes of death. Jefferson's breath caught. How had Blaise survived that? By all rights, he should have been crushed, as so many others had been. *I should never have asked him to break the* Retribution. *I could have lost him.*

"Land here, please," Jefferson called to Seledora over the rush of wind.

The grey pegasus alighted near the ruins, the other pegasi following her lead. Flora peered at him, brows arched. Kittie and Mindy studied the destroyed fort. The Pyromancer's mouth was a grim line, her eyes narrow.

"Blaise did that?" Mindy's question was a whisper on the breeze.

"He had to." Jefferson swallowed, thinking of the disasters that Blaise had averted with his magic. And the price the Breaker had paid to do so.

"I know," Mindy agreed, placing a hand on his arm. "I was there when the Salties attacked Itude." Her yellow eyes narrowed, bitter memories no doubt rising to mind. "Maybe I'm only wishing he could have done it sooner." Then she exhaled a whistling breath, shaking her head. "Sorry, that's probably not a thing someone in this delegation should say."

"Don't confuse Ganland with the Salt-Iron Confederation," Jefferson said, smiling as both Kittie and Mindy turned to pin him with sharp looks.

"How can we not?" Kittie asked, gesturing to the battered airship. "Ganland is *part* of the Confederation."

"Let's continue on, and I'll explain," Jefferson said. He had wanted to see the carcass of his airship, and he had. It was a reminder that he had made mistakes in the past, and they'd had consequences. Even though, at the time, he thought it was the right thing to do. And maybe it had been the right thing. The *only* thing.

He shook his head, banishing the unpleasant thoughts. Jefferson was more than happy to explain the intricacies of the Confederation, if only to take his mind off his own guilt. "Think of the Salt-Iron Confederation like a family. United by name and perhaps blood ties, but still full of individuals."

"But the Salt-Iron Council passes on most of the same laws to all of them," Mindy pointed out. "So, it's as if they're no different at all. And Confederation soldiers represent *every* nation."

The Hospitalier was delightfully astute. Jefferson nodded. "Those are both true—to an extent. As far as the soldiers go, each nation also has its own separate military. Some, like Ganland, boast a navy as well. And while the laws are often passed down to all the nations, there is still wiggle room for differences at a national level. Which is why Ganland is overall more friendly to mages." He made a face. "They still must be registered and tattooed, but it's more difficult to force them into an indenture." Difficult, but not impossible. And Jefferson knew only too well that there was a thriving, seedy underbelly of those who would snag mages and traffic them.

"Doesn't spare them if a Saltie Tracker and unicorn come across them, though," Kittie said quietly. "They can overrule the local laws."

"Yes, they can," Jefferson agreed, pressing a hand against the pocket where his new ring nestled. Guilt pulled at him. He would need to put it on soon. He cleared his throat. "Ah, and here's the town where we'll spend the night."

Courage's End was composed of buildings cobbled together from the ruined timber and stone of the fort. Townsfolk silently edged out of their homes and businesses as the delegation entered the outskirts, their expressions grudging. The pegasi had hidden their wings as soon as they approached the town, but the suspicious eyes spoke volumes. They knew who had come to town, and none of the citizens appreciated their appearance. Jefferson was going to have to smooth things over as he normally did: with money. Doubling someone's income could ease mistrust and anger better than words.

The mistrust wouldn't die, though. That would likely never be fully erased from those who had seen the fort fall. Those who had loved ones smashed beneath the fallen airship or crushed by stone. Shot by outlaws. Jefferson wouldn't begrudge them those feelings.

"Someone should stay with the pegasi tonight. Just in case," Kittie suggested, as they bowed their heads close over a table in the town's diner. Mindy had pronounced their food fit for eating. That didn't mean it *tasted* good—it only meant it wouldn't kill them.

"I will," Flora volunteered with a nonchalant wave. "I'll take the last watch."

"I'll take the second," Kittie said.

Jefferson yawned. "I suppose that leaves me with the first."

Flora eyed him. "You're going to fall asleep, aren't you?"

"No." Jefferson crossed his arms, rather offended by her lack of faith in his ability to stay up into the wee hours. "It's waking up that I have a problem with."

"I can take the watch," Mindy offered with a shrug. "I'm not tired yet."

Though the afternoon had taken more out of Jefferson than he cared to admit, he still wanted to contribute to their group. "Are you certain? I'd be happy to take the watch."

The Hospitalier read the bald-faced lie in his words. She waved a hand. "I insist."

Jefferson wasn't going to argue any further. With that decided, he excused himself and found their room. They had to sleep four in a single room. The hosteler claimed he had no other accommodations, although there seemed to be no one else staying at the inn. As much as Jefferson had wanted to argue, he hadn't. Not after the way some of the citizens had stared at their group, hatred burning in their eyes.

The room only had one bed, though simple sleeping mats provided small comfort. Not much, though. As Jefferson undressed, he glanced wistfully at the bed but decided he should cede it to one of the ladies. He doubted even the bed would prove to be that comfortable.

He laid down on a mat, huffing in annoyance at how stiff it was. Even the extra pillow was one big lump, like resting one's head on week-old bread. *Actually, week-old bread is probably softer.*

Fortunately, riding a pegasus all day was tiring, and it wasn't long before his muscles relaxed and his mind drifted to sleep. The dreamscape opened around him like the petals of a flower. Jefferson stretched out his awareness, searching for Blaise. He had never been so physically far away from the Breaker, but he'd decided that if he could still cage Gregor Gaitwood from such a distance, he could locate Blaise.

There. Jefferson found a hint of Blaise, but he wasn't asleep. He had lulled his beau to sleep before, but only when they were close and Jefferson knew Blaise wanted to sleep. So far away, Jefferson didn't want to risk pulling him into slumber during an awkward moment. He would wait and try again later.

He took the time to renew Gregor's dream prison. Jefferson heard the Doyen's angry shouts as he approached. "*Sorcerer!* Let me go!" Something rattled. Hands against the bars on the door.

Jefferson walked up, standing a foot away from the cell. He narrowed his eyes, the carnage of Fort Courage fresh on his mind. *I may have asked Blaise to break the airship, but he wouldn't have had to do it if not for the Gaitwoods.* "No. This is what you deserve. Death is the only other escape, and that's too easy." Jefferson clenched his jaw, silently adding, *I want you to suffer.*

Gregor stared at him, his eyes glazed like a feral beast. "*Deserve? I* don't deserve this. I'm not the *filthy magelover* here. No."

The Doyen paused, wheezing. "I'm going to make sure *you* get what *you* deserve."

"Best of luck with that," Jefferson said, finishing his renewal. "Pleasant dreams." Okay, perhaps it was cruel to taunt the nightmare-plagued Doyen—wait, never mind. It absolutely wasn't cruel. Not after all he had done to Blaise. Jefferson turned and stalked away, ignoring Gregor's indignant demands.

That task done, he reached out for the Breaker again, this time relieved to discover that he was asleep. Jefferson was always careful when approaching Blaise in his dreams, as deliberate as he would treat his beau if they were together. Jefferson made the equivalent of a knock at the door, though there was no door. It was difficult to describe, but that was how he thought of it. The way between him and Blaise opened as the other man let him in.

Blaise cocked his head, eyeing Jefferson. "What part of promising to wear that ring did you not understand?"

"*How was your flight, Jefferson? Oh, it wasn't bad, thank you for asking,*" Jefferson parroted, hoping to finagle his way into Blaise's good graces with a reminder of etiquette. "You can berate me after pleasantries."

The corners of the Breaker's mouth twisted up in amusement he failed to hide. "Fine. How was your flight?"

"Missing you," Jefferson admitted, gratified when a genuine smile spread across Blaise's face. "And before you start on your spiel about how disappointed you are that I'm not wearing the ring—I promise I *will*. Tomorrow. You can't fault me for wanting to see you again."

Blaise's shoulders relaxed. "I miss you, too." He glanced around as Jefferson called on his magic, weaving the dreamscape into something new. "What's this?"

Jefferson smiled. "You wanted me to show you places I've been, right? Allow me to show you where I'm going. You've seen my estate outside Nera but not much else. Since you can't be there with me, let me show it to you tonight."

Blaise licked his lips, crossing his arms. "And then tomorrow you'll wear the ring?"

"And then tomorrow I'll wear the ring," Jefferson agreed, though it stung to know it would muzzle his power. He didn't want to be cut off from Blaise.

Blaise smiled. "Show me."

TO SAY THE HOSPITALITY WAS LACKING WAS TO SUGGEST THERE HAD been hospitality at all. None of them had slept well that night—but they had slept, and the pegasi were unbothered, which Jefferson considered a victory.

The straw in the pegasi's box stalls had the musty smell of mold, and when Flora asked after it, she was told it was all that was available. For their evening meal, the pegasi had to settle for oats—none of the sweet feed that the equines loved so dearly was anywhere to be found. At least the oats weren't fouled, according to Mindy, whose magic seemed to work for the pegasi as well. Jefferson consoled their steeds by splitting the treasure trove of precious cookies from Blaise that he'd found packed in his saddlebags.

At breakfast, the staff conveniently *forgot* to bring their meals, and by the time their food arrived, it was cold. The scrambled eggs tasted like runny boot leather (or so Jefferson imagined), and the bacon would have made fine shingles, but Mindy whispered they were otherwise fine.

"I don't recall the Mellans being so petty," Mindy commented as they led their fully tacked pegasi out of the stables. None of them had trusted the stable hands to tack up the equines, so had done it themselves.

"It doesn't excuse them, but they have a reason for their poor behavior," Jefferson reminded them softly, casting a meaningful look over his shoulder toward the fallen fort. It wasn't visible from their current location, blocked by the nearby trees, but they understood.

Kittie set her jaw, eyes narrowed, as she laid a hand against the neck of her chestnut mare. She looked as if she wanted to say something, but she kept it to herself. Jefferson found he liked Kittie Dewitt for her spirit and drive. He only knew bits and pieces of her story, much of it gleaned from Blaise. He didn't know what she had endured. From Flora, he'd learned Kittie had once been seen as a threat to the Confederation, called the Firebrand. A fiery woman who spoke out against the oppression of mages. Something had dampened her fire, but she seemed to be slowly regaining it.

<Our tack is secure, and we are ready to be under way,> Seledora informed him.

Jefferson nodded to her. "Very good. I'll settle our bill at the inn, and we'll be off."

He strode into the building, one hand over his coin purse. He wouldn't put it past someone to cut it free. It would be a setback, though nothing insurmountable. The bill he was about to pay was highway robbery as it was. The hosteler watched him approach, face impassive as he leaned against a table.

"I've brought the rest of the agreed-upon payment," Jefferson said as he opened the pouch, drawing out a handful of gold coins. They glittered in the low light.

"You won't be paying in coin," a dangerous voice growled behind him.

Jefferson swallowed, slipping the coins back into the purse and snugging the laces. He turned slowly, dismayed by the trio of burly men edging in to block his escape. They were built like bulls, their arms muscular and chests broad. Former Confederation soldiers? Veterans from Fort Courage with a bone to pick? That was the most likely answer.

"We know who you're traveling with, *magelover*," one of the other men sneered.

"Really? You're using tired old insults like that?" Jefferson asked to buy time. He took a half-step back, though there wasn't much room to maneuver with the wall behind him. "I'm sure you gentlemen can do better than that. Perhaps we should behave like civilized men, since this is a place of business." Jefferson hazarded a glance at the hosteler. The man was watching them with little enthusiasm, though Jefferson didn't miss the plump bag of coins resting on the counter beside him.

His gut clenched. The hosteler was being paid to look the other way. This was a set-up. No doubt they had pegged him as the weakest member of the group. The non-mage. The dandy. They were ready to make an example of him. But he wasn't without options—he only had to buy time, or so he hoped. *Seledora, I hope you're listening. A little help would be welcome.*

Jefferson lifted his chin, drawing on every bit of arrogance he possessed—which, honestly, was bloody hard when he was mere inches from being stomped by this nefarious trio. "I'll ask you gentlemen to step aside one more time so that I can settle my bill, and I'll be on my way."

"You can settle your bill with blood," the stocky man in the middle said, pounding his knuckles into the meat of his palm.

Then they were in motion, flying at him with murder in their eyes. Jefferson barely had time to dodge a beefy fist, though it grazed his cheek, throwing him off balance. A heavy body slammed into him, knocking him against the wall with such force the air whooshed from his lungs. Jefferson's vision wavered as his attacker smashed him against the wall as if he were a ragdoll.

A memory of a time in the past seized him, a time when he thought Jack was about to kill him. The only difference was, to the outlaw, it had been a game, a ruse to test Jefferson's magic. Now it was real. He pulled on his magic with all his might, shoving it at his attacker. *Sleepsleepsleep, please! Sleep, damn it!*

His cast slipped around the brute like a lasso, though it was sloppy, and the man evaded it. Desperate, Jefferson sent out another coil of magic, pulling it taut. He dragged the unwilling man into slumber. Into a blank dreamscape that Jefferson didn't have the time or presence of mind to populate with anything.

The man slumped to the floor with a resounding thud. Jefferson groaned, then tensed when he felt new hands grasp his upper arms, holding tight. Panic rose again, and he flung out his magic, prepared to use it against his new assailants. But just as quickly, he called it back as he recognized Flora and Kittie peering at him with worry in their eyes.

Blood spatter peppered Flora's cheek, though Jefferson presumed it didn't belong to her. The half-knocker's lips pursed as she considered the downed man.

"Are you hurt?" Kittie asked. She reeked of smoke, as if she had spontaneously combusted someone. Jefferson couldn't see any nearby piles of ash.

Jefferson took a gasping breath and nodded, not trusting his voice immediately. He straightened, smoothing the lapels of his mussed greatcoat and brushing a clod of dirt from one sleeve. Let them think he was a preening peacock. He didn't care. In truth, he was shaken up, but he knew from his many years as a Doyen that this wasn't the time to show weakness.

"Who do these goons belong to?" Flora asked, hiking a thumb at the sleeping man. The other two were down as well—one of them was nursing a long gash down the length of one thigh and whimpering, while the other appeared unharmed but was staring at Kittie with wide, white-rimmed eyes.

"Never seen them before in my life!" the hosteler said, holding his hands up. Jefferson noted that the money bag had vanished, secreted away, no doubt.

Jefferson rolled his shoulders. *Ugh, I'm going to have some bruises, but at least I have my life.* "Unbelievable. Such a shame that I can travel to the Gutter and Untamed Territory without so much as a hair on my head bothered, and here I am, attacked on Confederation ground!" Never mind that he had outlaws in

Rainbow Flat on his payroll to make certain nothing happened to him. And he had Blaise. They didn't know that. He shook his head and tut-tutted, arrowing a look at the hosteler. "How unfortunate that I'll have to spread the word in Ganland that this part of Mella is *inhospitable*."

The hosteler swallowed, realizing that the threat was financial more than anything else. *Hit them where it hurts: in the coin purse.* It was an adage that had worked well for him in the past. "Now, don't be hasty, Mr. Cole. All's well that ends well, you know. As I said, I've never seen 'em before." His beady eyes cut to the thugs.

Never seen them before, indeed. But I'll play your game. Jefferson inclined his head. "Then you won't be opposed to us calling our bill fair and settled before I pay the rest. Seeing as they attacked me in *your* establishment, and no one but my companions lifted a hand in my defense."

This demand pained the hosteler, but he knew he was on tricky footing. Requiring full payment now, after this, would only drive home their lack of care and hospitality for guests. He licked his lips as he weighed the options, then ducked his head in agreement. "There's a Healer up the road. Visit her before you leave town. Tell her Ivan sent you and to tend to you at no charge."

"Thank you for the offer, but I'll be fine," Jefferson replied. He wouldn't trust a Healer, not in this town. A Healer could do just as much harm with their magic as they could good.

He strode out of the inn, proud that he didn't limp or move too stiffly, though his body complained every step of the way. Flying would not be fun today, not at all.

Seledora was waiting outside, ears pricked. Her nostrils flared as she read his scent. <I sent the powerful ones in when I picked up the threads of danger in your thoughts.>

"It's appreciated," Jefferson murmured, rubbing her forehead. He hated to consider how it might have turned out if not for that saving grace.

Flora sheathed her blades, gathering up Tylos's reins. "What was that about?"

"I'm not sure. They may be Confederation veterans who have a bone to pick with outlaws," Jefferson answered, wiggling his fingers and toes to be sure everything was intact. Nothing seemed broken, though he had skinned areas beneath his clothing that were going to chafe in flight. And too many bruises to even catalog. All in all, he had been lucky, and he knew it.

Mindy frowned, her pale eyes flicking over him. "I'll figure something out that'll help you feel a little better once we're out of this town."

"Thank you," Jefferson murmured.

"Is this sort of reception going to be an ongoing problem for us?" Kittie asked.

Jefferson winced. It was a valid question. "I don't know," he said, rubbing Seledora's muzzle as he thought. "It may. But we won't let that stop us." *We can't let it stop us because then they'll get exactly what they want.*

Kittie nodded. "Good. We'll have to be more vigilant."

"I let you out of my sight for *two minutes*," Flora huffed.

"I was paying the bill. Completely normal transaction." Jefferson sighed. "Let's put this town behind us, shall we?"

CHAPTER TEN

Grave Dancing

Jefferson

ortunately, after the dust-up with the thugs in Courage's End, nothing else unusual cropped up to interrupt their journey. Jefferson supposed it helped that on the second night, they stayed in Ondin, the capital of Mella. As soon as they approached the city, he slipped on his ring—as he had promised Blaise he would.

They spent the following evening in Sunrise Harbor, the last major town before they would briefly cross into Petria, and then on to Ganland. Jefferson had mixed feelings about their lodging for the fourth evening of their trip.

Seaside. The pegasi landed a few miles outside the town, and Seledora jigged as she sensed his unease. Flora was watching him closely, too. She knew his long history as a Wells around Seaside. Kittie and Mindy didn't, though luckily, neither of them knew enough to ask. He suspected Kittie knew of his double life, but she was savvy enough to not bring it up. Mindy had no idea, and as much as Jefferson liked the Hospitalier, he was happy to keep her in the dark. The more people who knew his secrets, the harder they became to conceal.

"We'll be staying in the finest hotel Seaside has to offer," Jefferson told them, feigning false cheer as they rode to the town. "It's on the beach, and the sunrise will be absolutely splendid. If you're the sort to wake up that early."

"I will," Mindy said, her eyes bright at the prospect. The Hospitalier had relaxed once they put Courage's End behind them. "I'll have time to go to the beach, right? How many days are we staying here?"

Jefferson smiled at her eagerness. He was glad their excursion would be pleasant for someone, at least. "Three days, and then we'll be on the road again." He glanced at Kittie. "You're welcome to enjoy the beach as well. The afternoons are often balmy in the autumn, and I think you'll find it refreshing. There are swimming outfits we can buy in town."

Kittie had a dubious expression on her face. "I've never gone swimming before. I don't know how."

"You can wade, too," Mindy pointed out.

The two women immersed themselves in a conversation about beach activities. Jefferson fed them additional information when asked but otherwise left them to it. The pegasi hid their wings as they entered the town at Jefferson's request. Overall, he didn't mind people knowing that the Gutter delegation of outlaws and pegasi was coming through. But right here, right now, he didn't want to draw any undue attention to himself.

They found the hotel on the beach, a beautiful stable next to it. The pegasi were enthusiastic about their accommodations, too—especially when Jefferson suggested they might enjoy playing on the beach. Seledora declined, however. He wasn't sure if it was because she was too straight-laced to romp on the beach or because she was worried about him. While he suspected the latter, the grey mare wouldn't admit to such a thing.

Their group settled for the night. The pegasi happily munched on the finest sweet feed they'd had for several days while their riders had a veritable feast at the hotel. Jefferson felt as if something was right in his world again, at least. A good meal in a beautiful setting always did wonders. *The only thing missing is Blaise.*

The next morning, Flora wandered off to *look into some things* while Jefferson showed Kittie and Mindy to the swim shop. Not only did the shop boast an array of outfits designed for the water, but also rubber bladders filled with air, fishing poles, buckets, and sundry items for anyone seeking a day of fun.

Jefferson eyed the swimsuits with appreciation. It had been years since he'd hit the beach in Seaside, and the last time he'd had the chance, full-body wool swimsuits had been the rage. Now... well. Times had changed, and so had fashion, it seemed. The women's swimwear boasted shorter skirts that clung to just above the knee, and bare shoulders were a common theme. The men's swimsuits had pants that ended at the knee as well, with form-fitting, short-sleeved shirts. Jefferson considered a purchase of his own as the ladies shopped.

Kittie held up a sapphire swimsuit while Mindy grinned. The Pyromancer seemed torn, though.

"If it's the price that's stopping you, that's not a problem at all," Jefferson said.

She shook her head. "It's not that. I've never worn something like this before."

"Ah." Jefferson considered the problem. It hadn't occurred to him that Kittie might prefer modesty. Like the other women of Fortitude, she favored trousers over skirts. Jefferson assumed it was because trousers were so much more versatile for the hard life in the Gutter. Perhaps there was more at play, though. "Keep looking. Maybe you'll see something else you like."

But Kittie seemed drawn to the sapphire. While Mindy selected a floral number, Kittie hemmed and hawed over her decision. At last, she nodded and brought it to the counter, though she and Mindy only grudgingly allowed Jefferson to pay since they didn't have enough funds to cover the outfits.

"There, now you'll be properly attired for a day of relaxation," Jefferson said as they walked up the street, heading back to the hotel.

Kittie stared down at the folded swimsuit in her arms. She said nothing, but her eyes narrowed as if she were thinking. Jefferson wondered what was on her mind.

When they made it back to the floor where their rooms were located, Jefferson caught Kittie's attention while Mindy hurried off to change. The Pyromancer frowned, though she followed him into his room when he beckoned.

"Is something bothering you?" Jefferson asked.

Kittie drew her bottom lip into her mouth, chewing it for a moment before sighing. "I don't know if you'll understand."

He shrugged. "I can certainly try. But if you'd rather not…"

Kittie shook her head. "Do you ever feel like…you're trying to be someone you're not? As if you're trying to reinvent yourself?"

Jefferson's brow arched. For a moment, he wondered if she was prodding at his dual identities in a roundabout way, but she seemed…distracted. No, she was thinking this about herself. That was interesting. "I have some understanding of that, yes."

She lifted her gaze to meet his, momentary humor on her face. "I suppose you do. The fact is, I'm trying to figure out who I am now." Kittie rubbed her cheek. "When I was young, I was the Firebrand. Then I lost everyone I cared about, and…well, I can't be that woman anymore. I'm a husk of who I was." Kittie swallowed. "Then I got Jack and Emmaline back. And now I'm trying to reconcile the spirit of the Firebrand with a charred husk."

That is some vivid imagery. I think I see why she was the Firebrand. Jefferson offered her a sympathetic smile. "Can't you be something new?"

"But I have to be the *Firebrand*," Kittie said. "I don't think I'm strong enough to be what I was before."

Jefferson cocked his head, trying to think of a metaphor that would work. "Have you ever seen a forest fire?"

Kittie snorted a laugh. "I've *caused* one. It was an accident, but…" She shrugged and didn't elaborate.

Well, that's concerning. He cleared his throat. "Right. Understand the cycle of the forest. The pines live, they burn, and though the fire destroys, it also makes new life. New trees replace the old."

Kittie opened her mouth to respond, then snapped it shut as if his words had hit her between the eyes. She blinked at him in surprise. "You're a lot smarter than Jack gives you credit for."

Jefferson chuckled. "Thank you. I think. Do you feel better now?"

Kittie smiled, nodding. She glanced down at the sapphire swimsuit. "I do. And now I think I'll see how this looks on me and then head down to the beach."

Jefferson watched as she headed out the door. The irony wasn't lost on him. Kittie was reinventing herself while Jefferson was burying an old part of himself.

FLORA RETURNED THAT EVENING, HOLING UP WITH JEFFERSON TO give him the rundown on what she'd learned. "I made the rounds, and I have a pretty good idea of who's in town for the big shindig."

"It's a *funeral*, not a party," Jefferson muttered, watching as Flora helped herself to the wet bar.

The half-knocker snorted. "You say that, but you wouldn't know it, judging by the so-called mourners. I swear, half of them are here to dance on your—on Malcolm's grave."

Now her errand made a lot more sense. Jefferson hadn't even stopped to consider who might show up for the funeral. No, his mind had been on other things. Which was another point that made him glad for Flora. "Oh?"

"Your Doyen buddies are here. Leonora, Aaron, and Seward. Oh, and Seward's wife, Lizzie." Flora ticked off the count on her fingers, listing several other Doyens before narrowing her eyes. "And Gregor Gaitwood."

Jefferson's mouth went dry at that. He reached over and picked up the glass of wine he'd ordered to enjoy for the evening, taking a restorative sip. "Oh? And how is dear Gregor?" *Was he screaming incoherently? Babbling mindless gibberish?*

Flora tapped a finger to her temple. "Something squirrelly going on with him. I guess a remnant from when you shoved him into the dreamscape and whisked his brains like they were cracked eggs."

Jefferson nodded, not bothering to correct her. The only one who knew even half of what Jefferson had done to Gregor was Blaise. "And yet he maintains his position?"

"Somehow," she agreed, though she was bothered by that, too. "I thought there was a clause that Doyens could be forced to resign if they were unfit for duty?"

"There was," Jefferson said. He pulled his lips taut. "Though sometimes the Doyens have ways of sidestepping rules like that." Odd that the other Doyens hadn't pushed at it. Perhaps it came down to the power of the Mossbacks, the political group headed by Gregor and his ilk. They were likely to band together to oppose the Faedran faction who fought for the mages. They would be reluctant to lose any of their number. Even if one of their number was unwell. "Anything else?"

The half-knocker pushed her red-rimmed glasses up her nose. "Yeah. A bunch of the Wells family *friends* are here, too, if you catch my meaning."

Jefferson rubbed his chin. "I do." That wasn't unexpected. Funerals among the elite were events—even if the elite in question was someone that had been at odds with others among the high echelons of society. Oh, certainly, many of them were there to gloat and metaphorically dance on his grave. That was fine. In his own way, Malcolm still had the last laugh. "I suspected as much, which is why I've been hanging around the hotel and not making any social calls."

Flora's face was grim. "And Alice is here."

Alice. He froze at the name. Jefferson hadn't heard his sister's— Malcolm's sister's—name uttered in years. But he thought of her often, and the way he hadn't stood up for her at the time she'd been traded off as if she were livestock. All because she had developed magic. "I see. How did you find that out?" He had to ask because Flora had never met Alice. His sister had been sent away before he'd ever crossed paths with the half-knocker.

"The usual. I'm incredibly nosy." Flora shrugged. While it was true that she was, in fact, nosy, Jefferson knew there had to be more to it than that. He crossed his arms, pinning her with an expectant look. "Okay, okay. I saw a woman with the... ahem...*Wells look* about her, and when I had time to peruse the hotel registry, I confirmed the name."

The Wells look. Jefferson knew it intimately after staring at it for too many years. Chiseled cheekbones, strong chin, and glossy dark brown hair that gleamed with indigo in the right light. "I see. It's not unexpected that she would come."

"Yeah, but I'd rather you know the lay of the land, so you don't do or say anything stupid," Flora said.

He snorted. "You have such little faith in me."

Flora shook her head. "Nah. It's not that." Suddenly, her violet eyes were the most serious he'd seen them in ages. "You're going to a funeral tomorrow. *Your* funeral. If ever there were a time you might get overwhelmed and slip up, that's it."

"*Malcolm's* funeral," Jefferson corrected stiffly. "Honestly, I've kept up the charade for so long. I know what I'm doing." He took another sip of wine before continuing. "And I don't have to do it anymore. I can just be *me*. The person I *want* to be." His mind drifted to Kittie for a moment, and he hoped she had discovered who she wanted to be, too. And that she could do it. Sometimes, that was the hardest part.

Flora eyed him. "I know. I just hope it will be as easy as you think to be who you are tomorrow."

CHAPTER ELEVEN

Family Matters

Blaise

*B*laise smiled as he finished organizing the pantry. It was the last task he had to complete, and only because he wouldn't be there to help Reuben or Hannah rummage around to find whatever they might need inside its depths. He kept the kitchen in an overall orderly condition. The exception was the pantry, and it had sorely needed attention. It was satisfying to see the spice tins standing side by side like flavorful soldiers ready to be deployed.

But with that done, he couldn't procrastinate any longer. He was supposed to leave for Rainbow Flat in the morning, and even though he wanted to go, he also *didn't* want to go. Blaise took a moment to pull out a flat, stiff-sided carrier he had devised for packing small baked goods in saddlebags. The leather of the carrier was more flexible than a tin, which let it fit into the compartment more easily. He stuffed it with as many leftover cookies and pastries as he could, then set it aside for the next day.

Now I really need to pack. He rubbed his chin, climbing up to the loft. Part of the problem was that he missed Jefferson—gods, why did he miss that man as much as if he'd lost a limb? The loft was a constant reminder of his absence. Blaise shook his head. This was exactly why he needed to go to Rainbow Flat. It would take his mind off things, ease the time away from his Dreamer.

He set about his task, pulling out the few clothing items he figured would fit in the saddlebags. All the while, he wondered what Jefferson would have thought of his choices. Blaise chuckled to himself, suspecting he would have been appalled since Blaise was mostly selecting older shirts and trousers. *This is so last season. Wait, not even last season. Probably last three years.* The teasing mental conversation made him smile.

A solid knock on the door downstairs startled him. The bakery door wasn't locked—Blaise only did that at night. Hinges creaked as the door opened. "Blaise?"

Jack? Something in the outlaw's tone put Blaise on edge. "Upstairs."

"You need to come down. Now."

The Effigest's words brooked no argument. He wasn't being surly or pushy—no, he was being urgent and matter-of-fact, and that was *scary*. Jack became all business when something bad was afoot. Blaise set aside the shirt he'd been about to fold, hurrying down the steep stairs so fast he almost lost his footing.

Jack didn't even comment on his lack of grace. The man's blue eyes were troubled. "Message for you at the post office. You need to talk to Hank."

What? The first place Blaise's mind went was Jefferson. Something had happened to the delegation. Tears stung his eyes, but he shook his head to dismiss them. No use borrowing trouble until he knew what was going on. "Okay." The sound that came out of his mouth was husky and broken. It didn't sound like it even belonged to him.

"C'mon." Jack nodded to the door and led the way, more solicitous than normal. That worried Blaise even more.

The post office was a short distance from the bakery, but it felt like the longest walk of Blaise's life. A handful of citizens were about to enter the building when Jack approached with Blaise in tow. Blaise couldn't see the outlaw's face, and Jack said nothing at all, but the townspeople took one look at him and decided they would visit the post office later. The Effigest shoved the door open and held it for Blaise.

Hank Walker, Fortitude's postmaster, leaned against the counter. He looked pale and tired, as if he'd exerted his magic quickly to travel a great distance. Blaise didn't know the details of his job, though he knew the man traveled to other outlaw towns— and a handful of Confederation ones—to pick up and deliver mail. A burlap sack full of envelopes and boxes lolled nearby. An envelope rested on the counter in front of him.

"Would have come for you myself, but I'm bushed," Hank said, apologetic. He had a difficult time getting around. He'd lost a leg —a parting gift from Lamar Gaitwood. Nadine and a tinker had worked together to create a contraption that served in place of the missing limb, but Hank was still adjusting to it. "I just came back from Rainbow Flat. Stopped my rounds because I needed to get back to tell you."

Rainbow Flat. It wasn't about Jefferson, then. Momentary relief flooded through Blaise until he realized—*Rainbow Flat.* Gooseflesh crawled across his body. "Tell me what?"

Hank tapped the envelope. "This tells you some, but I thought you might want to hear it from me." Something flickered in his eyes. Compassion. Sadness. "Your family there…they got attacked."

Time stood still. Blaise forgot to breathe until his lungs demanded it. He reached a hand out, clawing the envelope over. Didn't even realize he used his magic on it, shredding the envelope to reveal the letter within. Barely registered Jack's sharp intake of breath at the trick. Blaise unfolded the paper, hands trembling so badly that the words jumbled on the page, impossible to read.

"Give it here." Jack's voice was the softest he'd ever heard it. Blaise released the letter. Jack read it aloud, but the things he said made little sense at first. It was like being submerged underwater and hearing someone speak. Garbled. Blaise had to ask him to read it twice more before any of it took hold in his mind.

"The Hawthorne residence was attacked through the night. Daniel Hawthorne was killed in the struggle. Marian Hawthorne is missing, presumed taken. The children hid and are being cared for by a neighbor." The paper crackled in Jack's hand, suddenly the loudest thing in the post office.

Blaise squeezed his eyes closed. Hank spoke, but he didn't hear. Blaise's magic rose, defensive at the bitter grief welling up. There was nothing to guard against, though. Nothing could stop the hurt he felt.

The next few minutes—maybe hours, he wasn't sure—were a blur. He sat behind the bakery in the growing darkness, leaning against Emrys's warm bulk. The stallion was down, legs tucked neatly beneath him. A wing curled against Blaise like a blanket. Emmaline crouched nearby, her face illuminated by a mage-light.

Blaise swallowed. Maybe it had been a nightmare. Jefferson wasn't around to chase them away, after all. But the stricken look on Emmaline's face told him the truth. The awful letter Jack had read was real. A dry sob racked his chest, and Emrys adjusted, craning his head around to nuzzle Blaise. The stallion said nothing, but he didn't need to. There wasn't anything that could be said to make this better.

Emmaline was silent, too. Questions gleamed in her eyes, but she didn't utter them. Instead, she sat down, placing the mage-light between them.

"You don't have to stay," Blaise croaked when he finally found his voice.

"'Course I do," Emmaline said, whisper-soft. "You're hurting, and I'm not about to leave you alone to suffer. That's not what family does."

Family? Her words confused him. His family—they were in Rainbow Flat. They'd been attacked, and he hadn't been there. He blinked as he decoded her meaning. Blaise's breath caught again, but now because of the precious thing she was offering him. He almost couldn't believe he hadn't seen it before. "Family?"

"Yeah," she agreed. "How could you not be like family to me? We're friends. And you...you sacrificed everything to free me." Her voice cracked. They hadn't talked about Fort Courage much. Or at all, really. The memories were too difficult for both of them. "So, what're we going to do?"

"Cry for a while, probably." He was already accomplishing that. His nose was runny, and it took him a moment to find a handkerchief to blow it.

"That stands to reason. I mean after that."

Blaise shoved the soggy handkerchief back in a pocket, not caring about its lack of cleanliness. He looked at her blankly. His mind hadn't gotten that far, not yet. He was still processing the knife's edge of pain that came with the news. But she had a valid question. Blaise mopped his forehead with one hand, brushing his hair back. Lucienne and Brody were all alone. And his mother...

Blaise drew in a deep breath. "I...I suppose I need to get my sister and brother. Make sure they're okay. Get them somewhere safe." Yes, that sounded like the start of a coherent plan. Then, within, something cold and calculating arose like a dragon from slumber. Anger. "Then...then I need to figure out who did this. Who killed my father? Where's my mother?" He pulled away from Emrys, back ramrod straight. "Find whoever did this and make them regret it." The steel in his voice surprised him, and a distant part of his mind boggled that he was the one who'd spoken. No time to think of that now.

He struggled to his feet. "I should go. Now. Emrys, let's go."

The stallion nickered in surprise. <Now?>

"*No*," Emmaline said, firm but soft. She lifted a hand, no doubt seeing the uncharacteristic rage flit across Blaise's face at the denial. "It's night, and it's cloudy. Not safe for traveling. And you're too upset. You shouldn't do that right now."

He shook his head. "I need to *help* them."

"I know." She took a chance, laying a hand on his arm. "But like this, you won't do anyone any good. Emrys loves you, and if you want to go, you know he'll fly in the dark, his own safety be damned." The stallion snorted in agreement. "Look, Blaise. I'm not saying don't go. Just don't go right this instant." She blew out a breath. "Go to bed. Get some rest, and I promise we'll leave first thing in the morning."

"We?" There she went again, confusing him with simple words. He was tired. He hadn't known grief could be so exhausting.

"Yes, *we*," Emmaline said, exasperated. "You think Daddy and I are gonna let you hare off to Rainbow Flat on your own? No way in Perdition. Daddy's finishing preparations."

Blaise closed his eyes. Relief washed over him. He wouldn't be alone. But still... "I couldn't bear it if something happened to you or Jack. This is about my family. It's for me to handle."

Emmaline scoffed. "I know you don't have cotton in your ears. You heard what I said earlier. You're *our* family, too. Even if you try to leave us behind, we'll be hot on your heels."

<I will not leave Fortitude without them, if this is the case,> Emrys said, bumping Blaise with his head. <Because *I* could not bear if something happened to you. Again.>

Blaise sighed, rubbing the bridge of his nose. He couldn't argue anymore. He just couldn't. "Okay. But we leave tomorrow."

Emmaline nodded. "I'll help you upstairs. Do you need someone to stay with you tonight?"

"Emrys can sleep in the bakery," Blaise murmured. It was something the pegasus had suggested before, promising that he would be careful and that he would go outside if he needed to relieve himself.

<I can?> Momentary excitement laced the stallion's voice,

though it was quickly dampened. <I mean, I will, if you like. So that someone is close.>

Emmaline pursed her lips. "Guess I'll leave a note for Reuben to mop in the morning. But fine, if that's what you want, your pegasus can bunk in the bakery."

A few moments later, Emrys's hooves clopped as he carefully followed Blaise and Emmaline inside. The pegasus had banished his wings, so only had to be mindful of his bulk and his swishing tail. Emmaline shoved a table out of the way, shooting a glance at Blaise before urging him up the stairs.

Blaise fell into the bed, once again painfully aware of the Jefferson-sized hole in his heart. He squeezed his eyes closed, fearing the nightmares that would come. But thankfully, only dreamless sleep found him.

WHEN BLAISE AWOKE, GROGGY AND STIFF, FOR A FEW FLEETING moments, he hoped that the previous day was a nightmare. But the hollow thump of hooves on the floorboards below was all the validation he needed. He rubbed his eyes with the heels of his hands, struggling against the surge of heartache.

No. He couldn't function like this, locked down by grief. He had been through difficult times before. Survived horrors that others could only imagine. *I can get through this, too. I just have to take it moment by moment. Even if it's hard.* Slowly, he sat up, fighting off the urge to collapse back onto the bed, into the mindless comfort of sleep.

<Blaise? Are you coming down? I'm hungry. And someone left a tin of cookies on the counter, but I can't get it open.>

Emrys. Right, he was downstairs. Because last night, in the depths of his agony, Blaise had suggested the stallion spend the night in the bakery. He hadn't been thinking straight. "You're *always* hungry," Blaise called, reaching over to flick the mage-light

on. Gentle blue light washed across the small room as he tottered
out of bed and found a change of clothes.

<I'm an equine. We're designed to eat a lot. And besides, if I
were in my stall, I would have sweet hay to snack on.>

Suddenly, Blaise felt a wave of guilt. Did Emrys even have
water through the night? He shoved his feet into boots, then made
his way down. To his relief, he discovered that someone—probably Emmaline—had filled a bucket of water from the sink and
left it for Emrys. The pegasus carefully trod over, snuffling at
Blaise's chest to assess his rider.

"Sorry. I should take better care of you," Blaise whispered,
leaning his forehead against Emrys's.

<Sometimes it's my job to take care of you,> Emrys said
simply. <Now, about those cookies...>

Blaise chuckled, though it came out as a half-sob. He wiped at
one eye. He almost wished he were totally alone, like he had been
in the Golden Citadel. That time in his life had been terrible, but
he had blocked out the trauma and hurt by mentally distancing
himself from it. Pretending that things weren't happening to him.
Somehow, he didn't think any of his friends were going to let him
get away with that.

"Yeah, let me get them for you." Blaise moved over to the
counter. Telltale teeth marks dented the metal, and one side was
sticky and wet with saliva. He arched his brows. "I see you already
tried."

<I was hungry, and I didn't want to bother you while you were
sleeping.> Emrys was apologetic, though he moved over to sniff at
the tin hopefully.

Blaise opened the container, then held it out to allow the stallion to nibble on the butterscotch cookies and almond pinwheels
within. Emrys ate with enthusiasm, licking the last crumbs from
the container when he was finished. <Thank you. Are there any
more by chance?>

There were. Blaise kept stock on hand from the previous days, and before long, Emrys had made another two dozen cookies vanish. If he were a horse, that might have been problematic, but pegasi thrived on sugar. And if they were to set out for Rainbow Flat, Emrys needed all the fuel he could get.

With that thought, Blaise pulled out additional tins to carry to the stable. Then he threw together a simple breakfast for himself while Emrys hovered nearby. Was it odd to have a pegasus lumbering around the bakery? Most definitely. But there was a warm bliss in it, and Emrys was as much a comfort as Jefferson would have been.

Reuben and Hannah arrived a short time later to start work for the day. They greeted Blaise gently, neither of them asking after the news he'd received. He could tell by the pitying looks on their faces that they knew, though. Reuben didn't even say a word about a pegasus in the bakery. He glanced at the note Emmaline had left on the display case, then pulled out another bucket and the mop, ready for when the stallion departed.

Blaise went up to retrieve his saddlebags from the loft, pausing in front of the mirror on the wall. His eyelids were puffy, and his hair stuck up in wild hanks. Not to mention his beard needed a trim—that had been his intent, to take care of before he'd received the soul-shattering news. Releasing a soft sigh, he set about the simple self-care tasks, if only because he knew Jefferson would have urged him to do so.

When he was finished, he looked presentable. Like someone who hadn't had life ambush him once again. Blaise studied his reflection, noting the new hardness of his eyes. Then he shook his head, glancing around to see if he'd forgotten anything before snagging his saddlebags and going downstairs.

"Good luck, Blaise. Take care of yourself," Hannah said as he started for the door.

He paused, turning to look back at her and Reuben. "I'll try."

Reuben offered a grim smile. "Don't worry about the bakery. We'll take good care of it while you're gone."

A lump formed in Blaise's throat. "I know you will. Thank you."

With those goodbyes said, he and Emrys exited the bakery. A pair of gawking children squealed with glee when they saw the ebony stallion emerge from the building, clapping their hands in delight as his wings shimmered back into existence in the early morning sun. When Blaise and Emrys reached the stable, they found Oberidon and Zepheus saddled and ready, their riders lounging nearby. More surprising, however, was the presence of Nadine and her strawberry roan stallion, Leorus.

<Cookies!> Oberidon declared as soon as he spied the familiar tins Blaise carried. Ears pricked with anticipation, the spotted stallion sidled over. <Did you bring us cookies?>

"I did," Blaise agreed, though he handed a tin to Emmaline rather than her pegasus. Then he did the same for Jack, the outlaw giving a curt nod of approval. Blaise glanced uncertainly at Leorus, who was eyeing the last of the tins with a great deal of desire.

"We're coming along," Nadine said, matter-of-fact.

Blaise rubbed the back of his head. "But aren't you needed here?"

"I'm not the only Healer in town anymore. The best, but not the *only*," she answered. Nadine held out a hand, demanding the cookie tin without words. "And the way I see it, you'll want someone you trust to bring your sister and brother to Fortitude while you figure out what to do."

Blaise blinked. He hadn't thought through the logistics of that. And Nadine was a Healer—and she hadn't exaggerated about her ability. She was the best in Fortitude. Maybe in all the Untamed Territory. If Lucienne or Brody were hurt, she could help. And if any threat cropped up with Nadine around...well, she might *look* like a woman approaching her golden years, but she was a force to be reckoned with.

"Thank you," he whispered, handing her the tin.

Nadine popped the lid off, holding it out for her pegasus. Leorus's pink tongue swiped a currant cookie. While the trio of pegasi enjoyed their sugary snacks, Blaise took Emrys into the barn, setting to the familiar task of tacking him up. There was something calming in the simple actions. Over the past few months, Blaise had worked on becoming more comfortable on the stallion's back. And in the air. He didn't think he'd ever be as good at it as Jack, nor as enthusiastic as Jefferson, but he was much better. And this was something he could *do*. Right now, he needed to be *doing*, so this was good. A relief.

With Emrys ready, they came back out to meet the others. Blaise found Emmaline had already returned the empty tins to the bakery to be washed and stored for future use. Jack studied Blaise. The outlaw had been unusually quiet until that moment. "You ready for this?"

No. But I have to do it, anyway. He nodded, hiding the lie. Blaise figured Jack saw it in his eyes, though. "Yeah. Let's go."

CHAPTER TWELVE
Send a Casserole Next Time

Jefferson

The Good Fortune Sacellum was shoulder to shoulder with mourners, all dressed in traditional charcoal grey edged with gold thread. The women in attendance wore outrageous hats of varying sizes, many of them with gauzy, gilded veils that swept over their faces at an angle. Most of the hats had a daunting amount of decoration. Stuffed birds, fruit, and flowers perched above the bobbing heads gave the appearance of a gaudy parade.

"Did they mistake the funeral for the Ganland Derby?" Flora asked, peering up at a hat that indeed had a prancing horse statue atop it.

Jefferson stifled a chuckle at her observation. She wasn't wrong. If not for the mourning colors, the service could be mistaken for the clubhouse at Aspenpoint Downs. True to Flora's assessment, everyone who was anyone had come out for Doyen Malcolm Wells's funeral. *I suppose I should be honored.*

He kept to the outskirts, for once trying to keep a low profile. Jefferson scanned the gathered elite. His former fellow Doyens sat in a cluster near the front, as was their due. A smattering of Confederation leaders were there as well—Madame Boss Clayton of Ganland flanked by underlings from Phinora and Petria. So, Malcolm Wells hadn't warranted the Luminary of Phinora coming herself, but at least she'd sent a representative. That was something.

With Flora at his side, Jefferson slipped into a pew near the rear. Oh, he could have sat at the front, in the rows reserved for friends and family. But he'd rather not. The old family friends who had claimed the seats were people who had written him off when he'd turned his back on their ways. The powerful elite in Ganland who supported trafficking and other illicit activities. He was loath to rub elbows with any of them.

But he saw a single person who might have been enough to lure him to the front. There was no mistaking the sweep of dark hair, so like their mother's had been in her youth. The woman's back was to him, but Jefferson would have recognized his sister anywhere.

My sister. Unlike the rest of his family in his—Malcolm's—old life, Jefferson couldn't set his sister aside as someone who no longer belonged to him. A surge of anticipation snaked through him at the sight of her. He hadn't seen her in years. She was a woman grown now, so unlike the betrayed teenager she had been. But he would know her anywhere.

Flora elbowed him. "Stop staring."

He frowned. "I'm not."

"You are. Knock it off. It's creepy."

I am not being creepy. He crossed his arms, instead directing his attention to the gold-robed Tabrisian acolyte who strode down the aisle bearing a gleaming copper urn. Soft choral music floated through the Sacellum as the service began.

The acolyte hefted the urn, setting it atop a marble dais at the front. For obvious reasons, there had been no body to bury, only the mishmash of ashes and charred bone in a fire-gutted bedroom. Jefferson heard someone nearby murmur, "Doyen Wells's lapel pin is inside." He set his jaw at the grim gossip, though he knew it was true.

Jefferson leaned into the uncomfortable wood of the pew, listening as the priest led the service. People he had known came up to speak about the things Malcolm had done in his *short, brilliant life*, as one of them put it. Most of the speakers were people he had worked closely with during his time as a Doyen. It was disconcerting to hear about himself in the past tense. But at least he had been well-regarded. *Though I am certain my father was lauded at his funeral, as well.*

When the service ended, the crowd slowly filtered out of the Sacellum. By that time, he was recognized by some of the attendees, and he politely answered questions and bandied about compliments—all the idle chatter one had to endure for the sake of social obligations. Flora stayed nearby, as close as a burr stuck to a pegasus tail, though she was mostly ignored.

"You okay?" Flora asked when Jefferson finally caught a break from social niceties.

"It's been an experience," Jefferson murmured, though he really wanted to say more. Never in his life had he imagined he might attend his own funeral. Disconcerting. "I want to speak to my—to *Malcolm's* sister." *Sloppy.* He couldn't be sloppy here. He was off his game, faced with his own mortality. *To be fair, I think that would rattle anyone.*

Flora cocked a pink eyebrow at him. "You sure about that?"

No. "Yes." He cleared his throat. "I should offer my condolences."

Flora snorted. She wasn't an idiot. Of course, she saw through his schemes as if they were a scarf concealing a draft horse. Jefferson didn't care, though. He had so many regrets—he would not let this opportunity pass him by.

A knot of guests blocked his path to her. Just as well. He sidled up against a wall, waiting for more of the mourners to clear out.

Flora sighed and turned to scrutinize the stained glass window to their side, tilting her head as she regarded it. Jagged angles of colorful glass depicted the ruby-haired god Tabris from one of the old tales. "What is this?"

Jefferson glanced at the window. "That? Tabris relaxing in his swimming hole filled with gold in Paradise."

Flora whistled. "Maybe I need to find me some religion. No wonder you follow the guy."

Jefferson shook his head at her insight. "You make it sound rather shallow that way."

"Isn't it, though?"

He crossed his arms. "It's how I was raised." Jefferson knew that wasn't much of a defense—it wasn't a defense at all. No time to debate theology with Flora, though. The last of the mourners trailed away, leaving his sister alone in front of the dais.

Flora cocked her head, noticing the direction of his gaze. "I'll give you a few minutes with her. Don't say anything stupid."

Jefferson grimaced, though he was thankful for the illusion of privacy. The sight of his sister was almost enough to make him turn and run. Oh, how she had grown from girl to woman. Her obsidian hair, which had been straight as an arrow in her youth, had been tamed into waves that framed her face and gave her an aristocratic air.

She caught sight of him, her caramel-colored eyes puzzled. "Do I know you?"

Oh, gods. Yes. Yes, you do. I'm so sorry. For everything.

Jefferson swallowed the words, removing his hat as he strode over to her. "No, I don't believe you do. But I was very close to Malcolm." His gaze drifted to the urn, the last physical remnant of Malcolm's existence in this world. Jefferson cleared his throat. "My name is Jefferson Cole."

Recognition flared in her eyes at the name. She cocked her head. "It's a pleasure, Mr. Cole. My name is Alice Dillon."

Dillon. He focused on her surname. She'd been married—

sold, really—into the wealthy Dillon family. Jefferson hadn't
paid much attention to Phillip Dillon, aside from a rumor that
the railroad baron wanted to dabble in airships. Then he realized he hadn't responded yet, and he dipped his head politely.
"The pleasure is all mine, I assure you. You're welcome to call
me Jefferson." He sighed. "It's what Malcolm would have
wanted."

She considered him, weighing the invitation for familiarity.
"You were *that* close to him?"

You have no idea. He offered her a smile and a disarming
chuckle. "We were friends, nothing more than that. He was..."
Jefferson trailed off, suddenly unsure what to say. All the words
that clung to his throat felt like lies. There was nothing he could
say that would make amends for the wrong that had been done to
her. Malcolm would always be a villain to her, even if she
pretended otherwise in the public eye. Unable to form the rest of
his sentence, he shrugged. "I seem to be overcome with emotion.
Words escape me."

Alice nodded. "Understandable, given the circumstances." Her
sharp brown eyes analyzed him. "Unfortunately, I can't be as
mournful as you. Good riddance, the way I see it."

As much as he thought he had expected it, her words *stung*. He
blinked in surprise, the beginnings of tears prickling the corners
of his eyes. *What is wrong with me? Did I honestly think this would be
some sort of happy reunion? Well, I suppose that's what I was hoping for.*
Jefferson swallowed. "I'm sorry you feel that way. Though I
suppose we all cope with loss differently."

Alice narrowed her eyes, shooting a look over her shoulder at
the urn. "No loss to me. Only gain. I'm the sole heir of the Wells
fortune. This will give me the chance to do exactly what I've
wanted to do all along."

Jefferson's mouth went dry. He had known from Seledora that
there was a very large inheritance at stake. It wasn't something he
needed. Not when any attempt to go after it would lead to suspi-

cion. Anyway, he didn't want that ill-begotten money. He nodded politely. "And what's that?"

His sister huffed out a soft breath, as if she couldn't believe she was having this conversation with someone she just met. For a long moment, Jefferson thought she wouldn't answer. Alice shifted her weight from one foot to the other. "Leave this gods-forsaken wasteland of corruption while I have the chance."

Leave? Oh. Suddenly, he understood. She was a mage—unregistered because their parents had worked the system, but still a mage. She had a spouse among the elite, and no doubt he would try to sink his claws into the inheritance if he had the chance. Alice had never been free. And now she was going to take the money and run.

There was nothing he could say that wouldn't lead down a potential rabbit hole of danger for him. Jefferson settled for an encouraging smile. "Good for you. I hear the Untamed Territory is lovely this time of year."

She gave him a wary look. "That's what I'm counting on." Alice turned to leave. "It's been...interesting, Mr. Cole. I appreciate your condolences, despite my feelings about the deceased."

"Of course," Jefferson murmured. One of the hardest things he'd ever done in his life was walk away from the sister he desperately wanted to repair things with—all without telling her who he was.

He whirled on his heel—and almost ran face-first into the single person he most definitely did not want to cross paths with. Gregor Gaitwood stared at him, though there was a wild gleam in his eyes, like someone being harried to the breaking point. Jefferson took a quick step back, hoping that Flora was nearby if he needed a hand. He didn't think Gregor would try to murder him outright, but...well, there was no telling what the unstable Doyen might do.

"Why, Doyen Gaitwood, I wouldn't have expected you to come

to the funeral of a Faedran," Jefferson said, hoping to catch the politician off balance.

Gregor smiled, but it was too wide. Unhinged and wicked. "I would hardly miss it. Not when it would give me a chance to speak with *you*."

Jefferson frowned. "I regret to inform you the feeling is *not* mutual. I suggest you simply send a casserole next time. Now, if you'll excuse me—"

Gregor grabbed his sleeve as he tried to slip away, fingernails digging into the fabric. "No, Cole. You think you've won—that you can get away with these things you've done. That you've taken some sort of gods-damned high road." The Doyen spoke through clenched teeth. "You think you're better—different—from the rest of the elite simply because you think you're right. But you're not. You use others just as much as any of the elite. You *lie*. You *cheat*. Tell me, Cole—does your Breaker know all your deceptions? How you've used him?"

Jefferson's temper flared as soon as Gregor mentioned Blaise. If not for the blasted ring on his finger, he would have drop-kicked Gregor into the dreamscape, consequences be damned. He was taller than Gregor, so he took a step closer, glowering down at the Doyen. "I am *not* using him."

Gregor's smile widened. "Not now, maybe. But I know you. Know what you've *done*." The Doyen took a step back, smug and self-assured, as if he were no longer plagued by nightmares. Jefferson wanted to ask if that was the case, but there was no way he would inquire that of Gregor. He settled for glaring as Gregor chuckled. "You can't escape what you were born to be, Malcolm."

"Malcolm Wells is dead," Jefferson said, voice soft with warning.

Gregor turned on his heel. "We'll see about that." The Doyen cast a withering look over his shoulder before vanishing around a corner.

Flora ghosted up next to Jefferson. He glanced down at her. "Where were you?"

"Watching." Jefferson didn't miss the fact that she had a knife clutched in one hand, as if she'd considered using it. Flora twirled it, then slipped it back in the sheath at her belt. "I didn't like him threatening you, but I figured slitting his throat in a church might be frowned upon."

"More than that, the problem would be a member of the Gutter delegation attacking a Doyen," Jefferson murmured.

Flora snorted. "Wouldn't be an *attack*. It would be straight-up murder. If I go after him, he's dead. No other way around it."

Her words sent a chill through him, and not for the first time, Jefferson was glad she was on his side. He blew out a breath. "Fortunately for us, we can be on our way and put that snake and his venom behind us."

CHAPTER THIRTEEN
He's Tougher Than You Think

Blaise

Blaise wanted to push the pegasi to cover as much ground as they could, but Jack quickly put a damper on the idea.

"You wanna exhaust Emrys and have it take twice as long to get there? That's how you do it," the outlaw said, though there was no rancor in his voice. Only facts. Reluctantly, Blaise bent to the years of experience Jack had in traversing the Untamed Territory.

A chill autumn wind buffeted the pegasi and their riders as they made the final approach to Rainbow Flat at the end of their second full day of flight. The weather had been in their favor—this time of year a freak snowstorm was just as likely to crop up as a heatwave, according to Jack. Blaise was simply thankful that the worst they'd had to contend with was cloudy skies and a stiff breeze.

Rainbow Flat was exactly as he remembered it, an idyllic town overlooking the unfortunately named Tombstone River. Everything about the town was orderly. Its prim and proper appearance brought Jefferson to mind, and for a moment, Blaise almost felt his beau's presence as Emrys's hooves kissed the ground.

The ebony stallion glanced back, his head bare of hackamore. There was no need for the farce that the pegasi were normal horses while they were in the Gutter. Blaise had the sense Emrys wanted to say something or check on him, but the telepath had no doubt been monitoring him as they traveled. Sometimes words weren't necessary. He reached down and ruffled the pegasus's mane to let him know he appreciated the thought.

Oberidon trotted alongside Emrys, Emmaline peering at Blaise. "How're you doing?"

He blew out a breath. All things considered, he was a lot calmer than he would have expected to be at this point. But he'd had so many hours in the saddle—time to mull over his own thoughts and feelings. He had felt so *much*; it was as if he were tapped out. "That'll be a better question to ask later."

She nodded, understanding. Jack and Zepheus moved to take the lead, with Nadine bringing up the rear. The Effigest had a deep scowl twisting his face. "No sentries. I've suggested it before, and still *no sentries*." He shook his head. "That's going to change if we become a nation. Sloppy. That's what this is." He spat in the dirt to fully express his disgust.

Blaise swallowed as he realized what Jack meant. The sentries in Fortitude were the town's first line of defense, a warning system for impending danger. From what Blaise had gleaned, the sentries existed mostly to keep tabs on any potential Saltie incursions. But maybe they could have helped prevent this, too.

"That's something to look into later," Nadine said, keeping them on track. "Dusk is coming, and the priority should be to find the children."

Zepheus drew to a stop as a thoughtful look spread across the outlaw's face. "We have two priorities. Find the children *and* figure out who might have taken Marian Hawthorne. There's enough of us here to do both." His cool eyes flicked to Blaise. "Daylight's burning."

Blaise sighed. "But there's only one of me."

Annoyance slid across Jack's face, but he relented with a nod. Blaise understood what the Effigest had been trying to do. He was concerned about Blaise going to the scene where it had all happened, and…what? Breaking down again, probably. And as tempting as that was, he didn't think he could cry anymore. Icy resolve had replaced the tears. A part of him wondered if this was what had forged Jack into who he was. Had he been so damaged by the circumstances in his life that the only choice had been to become hardened and dangerous?

"Nadine's right. Let's find Luci and Brody first. They can probably tell us more about what happened, too," Blaise said.

Jack's shoulders hunched. "*That's* what I was trying to avoid." He urged Zepheus back into a trot, the palomino springing along with ease. "Kids don't deserve to relive that sort of thing."

Oh. Blaise felt like a heel for the suggestion, but he also knew his sister. Or he thought he did, anyway. "Luci's tough, and she would want us to know." He swallowed. *And talking about it might help.* He knew a thing or two about trauma.

After a few inquiries, they got directions to the Hawthorne home, as well as the neighbor who had taken in Blaise's siblings. The sun was setting as their pegasi trotted to the neighbor's house. Blaise hazarded a look over his shoulder at the home he figured belonged to his family, crouched a quarter-mile away.

A woman with grey hair pulled into a bun peered at them through a screen door. A moment later, two smaller faces appeared, accompanied by a wail of recognition. The door flew open, crashing against the exterior wall as Brody exploded out as only a six-year-old could. His face was red as he raced over to them, yelling Blaise's name.

Blaise didn't even realize he was dismounting until the shock of his heels hitting the dirt ricocheted through him. Brody jumped at him, wrapping his slender arms around Blaise's abdomen with such ferocity it would have knocked him over had Emrys not been at his back.

"I want my Mama," Brody whimpered, his face buried against Blaise's chest.

Carefully, Blaise adjusted to crouch down and hug his little brother. Brody clung to him like he never wanted to let go, and Blaise let him. He looked up as the scuff of feet announced a new arrival: Lucienne, her face pale and void of the spark that had characterized her before. She held something cuddled in her arms, and it took Blaise a moment to realize it was the family dog, Chester. The terrier's face was dark with dried blood, and Blaise's stomach dropped as he saw Chester was missing an eye.

Jack had moved to intercept the neighbor, no doubt hoping to mine her for information as he exchanged what passed for pleasantries from him. Nadine and Emmaline remained on their pegasi, though Blaise knew they were ready to dismount if needed.

Lucienne glanced down at the injured dog. "You're *too late*."

Emmaline made a sound of displeasure at the vitriol in Lucienne's voice, but Blaise only nodded. He felt the same way. If he had been there, maybe he could have stopped whatever had happened. "I know. But I'm here now."

Lucienne sighed heavily, tears welling in her eyes. But she didn't allow them to fall. She jostled Chester so she could lift a hand, brushing them away. "And what are you going to do about it? Daddy's dead. Mom is *gone*." She glanced back toward their house. "What are *we* going to do?"

Brody sobbed all the harder as Lucienne spoke. Blaise was quiet for a moment, slowly digesting that his sister wasn't mad at him but at the situation. That it had even happened. That their illusion of safety, of happiness, had been shattered. He knew all about that awful feeling.

Blaise rubbed Brody's back. The child quieted, as if he were exhausted from crying. Blaise's shirt was wet and probably snotty, but he didn't care. "You're going to go somewhere..." He hesitated. *Safe* wasn't a good word right now, not when he had no assurances that such a thing existed. "Somewhere full of people who will do everything in their power to protect you." He lifted his eyes to Nadine. The Healer nodded, expression grim. Blaise decided to have Nadine ask Clover to house Lucienne and Brody. The Broken Horn Saloon had empty rooms, and the Knossan would be a stalwart protector, too.

"You'll take us there?" Brody's voice was so small, Blaise almost missed the question.

"No," Blaise whispered, shaking his head.

Lucienne turned her baleful glare on him again. "Then what *are* you going to do?"

"Everything in my power." Blaise met her haunted gaze. "I'm going to find Mom. And find the people who did this."

At his words, Brody squeaked, burrowing his head against Blaise again, trembling with fear. Lucienne shook her head. "They'll kill you. It's a miracle we survived." Her mouth was a thin line, and somehow she had paled another shade at his declaration.

"They're not gonna kill him 'cause he ain't gonna be alone," Jack announced, swaggering over. Somehow, he managed a combination of self-assured menace that promised doom to whoever had done this while also attempting to not frighten the Hawthorne children. "But even if he *was* alone, give 'im some credit. He's tougher than you think." His eyes glinted. "A real outlaw."

I'm pretty sure Jack just complimented me, and I'm not sure how I feel about that. Blaise ignored it for the present. "Let's go into town and get settled in a hotel. Grab some dinner." He didn't know enough about this neighbor to trust them to extend their hospitality any further. And besides, Blaise now lived in a weird world where all he had to do was mention Jefferson, and he knew he would be well taken care of in Rainbow Flat.

"Then we need to hear what happened," Jack added. Apparently, he had decided they may as well fish for whatever information they could.

Blaise nodded, rising out of his crouch. He glanced from Emrys to his siblings. "Do you want to ride a pegasus?"

Brody's eyes widened, and for a beat, he seemed to forget all about his current circumstance. The question even distracted Lucienne. "We can ride a *pegasus?*" Brody asked.

Emrys lowered his head until his muzzle was at the same height as Brody's head. <You may ride on my back with your brother. Oby has offered a ride to your sister.>

Blaise scratched Emrys's neck in appreciation, glad the pegasi were agreeable. He knew it wasn't good for their backs to bear a double burden for an extended length of time, but they would stay on the ground, and Rainbow Flat was only a mile and a half away. Blaise hadn't known how else they would get to town, aside from on foot, which seemed unreasonable after everything.

"Give me the dog," Nadine said, brooking no argument. Lucienne offered Chester to her, and before long, the terrier was curled up against the Healer's bosom. The dog looked a little more comfortable, leaving Blaise to wonder if Nadine had a knack for animals she didn't advertise.

A few moments later, Brody perched in front of Blaise while Lucienne sat behind Emmaline, hands around the older girl's waist. Brody reached down and stroked Emrys's mane, and for a short time as their procession rode to town, the Hawthorne children had a bright spot in their overwhelming day.

CHAPTER FOURTEEN

Unicorns Again

Blaise

Blaise gave silent thanks for Jefferson and his connections. No one so much as batted an eye when they entered the Starlight Hotel and Blaise asked for rooms. In fact, the clerk at the desk inclined his head, full of reverence. "Of course, Mr. Hawthorne. You'll be staying in the suite Mr. Cole has reserved for you. The staff will ensure that your companions are housed nearby."

"I want to sleep with *you* tonight," Brody whined, tugging at Blaise's hand. There was no way he could deny his scared little brother, so he only nodded. Nadine had the mind to ask the clerk to have someone send along additional appropriate clothing, as well.

"I'll stay with you, too. If there's room," Lucienne said.

Their group followed a concierge to the upper floor where they would be staying, promising to bring the clothing soon. Blaise pushed open the door to his suite, the familiarity making him smile. It was the same room Jefferson had put him up in the last time he'd been in Rainbow Flat. The bed was enormous and would easily fit him and Brody. There was a comfortable chaise lounge that would work in a pinch. "Oh, there's definitely room."

Jack and Emmaline had the suite across the way. Blaise decided not to tell Jack that it was Jefferson's personal suite. That fact might annoy the outlaw. Nadine had the room next to theirs. They settled their meager belongings in their rooms.

The concierge returned a short time later with clothes for Lucienne and Brody. She aimed a sympathetic smile at the Hawthorne siblings as she handed the clothing to Blaise. "My children have outgrown these. They're a little threadbare, but they'll serve for the moment, I hope."

No wonder she had been so quick. Blaise's heart warmed at her thoughtfulness. "Thank you, um...I didn't catch your name."

She gave him a surprised look, as if guests seldom asked her name. "Trudy," the concierge said, voice soft. "You're quite welcome, Mr. Hawthorne. Now, if you like, I'll have you and your friends seated for dinner."

To Blaise's surprise, they were led to a private dining room. Another perk courtesy of Jefferson, no doubt. It wasn't long before they'd placed their orders, and all they had to do was wait for the food to arrive.

That meant they had time for unpleasant conversations. Blaise rubbed his cheek. "Can you tell us what happened, Luci?"

She stiffened at the question, then nodded. "Yes."

Lucienne

FRANTIC YAPPING, FOLLOWED BY A YELP AND WHIMPERING. *CHESTER?* Luci's eyes flashed open. It might have been a nightmare, but no. It was too real. And too close. She froze beneath her blankets, straining all of her senses to gain some understanding of what she had heard.

Crash. A shout. The sound of breaking glass, of metal instruments hitting the floor. Maybe silverware, it was hard to say. Downstairs. Definitely downstairs. Luci shot upright in her bed, casting around in the darkness for whatever was close at hand. Boots below her bed. Trousers slung over the nearby chair. She pulled them on, trying to stay as quiet as possible.

Once she was dressed, she edged closer to her door and paused by it, listening. She heard people downstairs. More shouting. The percussion of fists hitting flesh. The hiss and sizzle of what was probably an alchemical potion, accompanied by a male shriek. Luci swallowed, nudging her door open enough to peer out. Not far, another door opened, and in the wan light, she saw the gleam of her little brother's frightened eyes.

Brody. She had to get to him. Had to get him clear of whatever this was. Her mother had warned her, instructed her what to do if this ever happened. She—

"No!" Luci heard her father's voice ring out, a strident command. A gun roared in response, followed by his sharp, pain-tinged cry.

"Stop! You're killing him!" Panic filled her mother's voice. "You can have whatever you want. Money, jewelry. But don't—"

Indistinct noises drowned out her words. More chaos, more struggling. A final, gasping shout from their father before he was silenced. Luci trembled. Mama was fighting, that much she knew. She would always fight. Marian Hawthorne had explained to her daughter there was no other option at this point. She was a dangerous—and desired—commodity. An alchemist.

Nearby, Brody whimpered. She refocused her attention, sneaking up the short hallway to him. Luci knelt down to his level, relieved to see that he had remembered the plan. He wore clothing suitable for a quick escape, though his shoulders heaved with every breath, as if he were about to break into a howling tantrum.

"*Daddy*," he whispered, his small face crumpled in despair.

Luci nodded. She wanted to join him in mourning, to curl up with him and cry and cry. But that might end up with them dead or captured again. Neither were options she wanted, especially not when her mother had given her a plan to follow. "I know. I heard. But we gotta go. We can't stay here." His shoulders racked with pent-up sobs. She hustled him to the window at the end of the hallway, propping it open as the sounds of struggle continued downstairs. Their father had nailed wooden pegs into the side of the house below this window to allow them an avenue of escape if it was needed. Luci and Brody had practiced climbing up and down. Luci had hated every minute of it. Splinters bit into her hands, and there were a thousand other things she'd rather be doing. But now, she was grateful for it.

She went first, under the theory that she might catch Brody if he fell. Luckily, it didn't come to that, and they both reached the bottom safely. Luci shivered, glancing up at the setting sickle of moon in the distance. There wasn't much light, but that was good for them. It would provide them with cover that was sorely needed. Her only regret was that it gave her no clue who had attacked them in the middle of the night.

"I want Mama," Brody whined as Luci grabbed his hand.

Me, too. "We can't go to her. The plan. We have to go with the plan." Luci tugged him along, and he reluctantly followed.

Their home was on the far outskirts of Rainbow Flat, and Luci wondered if that had been a mistake. If they lived in town, would they have been a more difficult target? She had no way to know. Luci peered around the side of the house, heart pounding so loudly she feared it might give them away. She heard a pathetic whimpering nearby. Chester. The terrier had limped behind a rain barrel. He turned his head in their direction, whining softly.

"We have to get him," Brody pleaded, pointing at the dog.

"We will." Luci glanced from Chester's position to the closest bush that might mask their escape. "Go over behind that bush and wait for me."

Brody didn't argue. He rubbed one eye, then nodded and scurried across the shadow-pocked ground, diving behind the bush. Once he was safe, Luci slipped closer to Chester. As she moved, she caught sight of their attackers' mounts. Unicorns. Their horns caught the moonlight, gleaming with brilliant malevolence. Luci had no love for unicorns. The last time she'd seen one, it had been the harbinger of their capture by the Salt-Iron Confederation.

Swallowing, she picked up Chester, gasping softly when sticky blood oozed against her. Gore dribbled from one of his eyes. The terrier shivered in her arms, and she cuddled him against her chest. "I've got you. You're going to be okay. We're all going to be okay." It was a lie, but she had to say it.

Luci slunk over to Brody's hiding place. He opened his mouth when he saw Chester, but Luci shook her head urgently, making a shushing sound. She wrapped one hand around Chester's muzzle, afraid the injured dog might bark and give them away.

She didn't know how long they stayed there, too afraid to go any further for fear of being seen. Eventually, the assailants filed out of the house, laughing and joking. Luci couldn't hear what they said, but their growling voices promised nothing good. She studied their profiles in the dim light, trying to figure out who they were. They didn't look like Confederation. The outlines of their clothing were all wrong, as well as their hats. No, they wore the broad-brimmed slouch hats she associated with the outlaw mages who called Rainbow Flat home. But the few outlaws she had seen rode pegasi, not unicorns. One of the men mounted, and something on his hat gleamed like fire.

"They have Mama," Brody whispered. He rose and probably would have run out, spoiling their position, if Luci hadn't grabbed his shirt.

"No," she hissed. "Stay put." *They killed Daddy. No telling what they would do to us.*

The marauders rode off. Luci and Brody stayed where they were, too afraid to move for fear the attackers would return. When dawn tinged the sky with rosy light, Luci gingerly rose.

"C'mon. Let's go to the neighbors and get help."

CHAPTER FIFTEEN

A Man Who's Really Good at Breaking Things

Blaise

Jack tented his fingers before him. Their food had come during Lucienne's tale, but none of them had touched it yet. Brody cried again. Blaise pulled his little brother onto his lap, though his focus was on the outlaw. "What do you know, Jack?"

"Nothing good," the Effigest admitted with a shrug. Blaise had figured as much from his stony look. "Sounds to me like it's the Copperheads, though they sometimes get called the Unicorn Desperadoes. The hatband gave it away."

"How's that?" Blaise asked.

Disgust crossed Jack's face. "It's the reason they're called Copperheads. Those bands are fashioned from the scales of copper dragons. When they're buffed, they shine like fire in even the dimmest light."

"So, they're outlaw mages?"

"Yep."

Blaise gently put Brody back in the seat beside him, leaning forward with sudden eagerness. "Then that means we can find them and reason with them."

Jack gave him a pitying look. "Not all outlaw mages are the same." He shook his head. "There're outlaws like me and Nadine... and then there're *desperadoes*. They make me look like a choirboy." At Blaise's puzzled look, Jack sighed. "Okay, you know the pegasi are allied with the outlaw mages, right?" Everyone nodded. "Ask yourself why they're riding unicorns, then."

Blaise's frazzled mind was too tired to figure it out, but Emmaline slapped the flat of her hand against the table as it came to her. "The same reason they have the dragon scales on their hats. They don't respect the mystic creatures one bit."

Jack aimed a finger at her. "Got it in one. The Copperheads are more like the Salties than they'll ever admit. They got magic, they're gonna use it to dominate." Then he chuckled. "Though they're a fair bit jealous of us and our pegasi. One of the Copperheads got a pegasus once. Didn't live to regret that choice, though." He reached over and picked up his drink, taking a sip. "Now they got a healthy respect for heights, at least."

"So they're land-bound. We should be able to catch up to them in no time, even with the head start they have," Blaise said, though his optimism waned at the way Jack dropped his gaze to study the untouched plate in front of him. "What?"

"We're hunting a gang of ruthless outlaw mages. They're gonna be guarding against pursuit." Jack looked as if he wanted to say more, but he clammed up on the topic, nodding to their meal. "We should eat. Talk later."

They were subdued as they finished eating. Although the food was no doubt the finest around, it didn't sit well in Blaise's stomach, and it wasn't long before he begged off, heading for his room. Brody and Lucienne tagged along, unwilling to be parted from him now that he was there. He understood their clinginess.

Brody fell asleep almost as soon as Blaise and Lucienne got him settled on one side of the king-sized bed. Chester dozed atop a cozy rug in the corner, dosed with medicine and fresh magic from a local Beast Healer Nadine knew. Blaise dimmed the lights until only a single mage-light illuminated the room. "I'm sorry I wasn't there when you needed me, Luci."

She rubbed one eye, shaking her head at his apology. "I shouldn't have said that earlier. What could you have done against all of them?" Then, as if reconsidering her question, she asked, "Did you really bring down an airship with your magic?"

Blaise sat down on the edge of the bed. "Yes. But it didn't go well." Absently, he rubbed at the pale scar that ran the length of the sensitive underside of his left arm.

Lucienne's eyes went wide as she saw the scar, roving up to the divot on his cheek where a rock had left a mark. "So, you really *are* powerful."

He shook his head. "No. I'm just a man who's really good at breaking things. You're right—I might not have been able to do anything. Bullets can still hurt me." He bore a scar on his arm as a reminder. He didn't mention he'd figured out a way to protect against bullets. Maybe that had only been luck. The fact of the matter was, if he wasn't careful, a bullet could kill him as dead as anyone else. "I bleed, same as you."

She swallowed, worry shadowing her eyes. "And you're going to go after these desperadoes?"

"I have to."

Lucienne frowned. "I don't think Mom would want you to."

Blaise didn't bother to point out that Marian Hawthorne wasn't really his mother. He doubted Lucienne knew a thing about that. And yes, he was still upset over the lifelong deception, but he *loved* the woman he considered his mother. He could still be mad at someone and love them. And want to do everything he could to save them. "Yeah, well, she's not around to stop me." Blaise raked a hand through his hair. "Tomorrow, Nadine is going to take you and Brody to Fortitude. I have a friend there—Clover.

She's a Knossan, and she'll look out for y'all until I get back with Mom."

"A Knossan?" Lucienne's mouth hung open in a small O of surprise.

"Yeah. You'll like her." Blaise blew out a breath. There was a question he needed to ask but hadn't had the nerve to utter yet. But he was tired and needed to sleep soon. So did Lucienne. "What happened to our father? His body, I mean." He shuddered at the question. Didn't like to think about someone he loved as no longer there. The man who had taught him how to cook. How to *bake*.

Tears welled in Lucienne's eyes again. "Some of the neighbors came around and helped bury him." She scrubbed a tear away. "Under the oak tree behind the house. It's a nice spot. Peaceful."

"Nobody in town looked into the attack?"

She shook her head. "This is the *Gutter*, Blaise. There's no *law* here. No sheriff, no deputy. Nothing."

Lucienne was wrong on part of her statement, but Blaise left it. Fortitude, it seemed, differed from the other Gutter towns. It made him think more about how Jack had said he wasn't the same as the Copperheads. Fortitude didn't have set laws, but there were basic rules that were silently enforced. If something bad happened, it was investigated by one of the Ringleaders—usually Jack or Kur Agur. No wonder Jack had been annoyed by the sentry oversight.

"Time to hit the hay," Blaise said after a moment, reaching over to give her a brief hug. Lucienne clung to him even as he drew away, and though he had hit his limit with touch, he didn't have the heart to shrink back. She heaved a deep sigh and then, at last, pulled back.

"Goodnight, Blaise."

"Goodnight, Luci."

THE NEXT MORNING, THEY BREAKFASTED IN THE SAME PRIVATE dining area. Afterward, Blaise worked with Nadine to make arrangements for the trek back to Fortitude. Emrys had secured the help of two additional pegasi, though Blaise had concerns about Brody flying alone. In the end, they settled for the largest stallion, who assured them he could carry a teenage girl and a child with no issue. Chester was still drugged, and according to Nadine, would do well in her saddlebag.

Nadine, Lucienne, and Brody were on their way by mid-morning, and Blaise felt better with that taken care of. *Now for the part I'm really not looking forward to.*

"Ready?" Jack asked, looking at him from his seat aboard Zepheus.

"Let's go," Blaise said, patting Emrys's neck.

"That ain't an answer." Zepheus and Oberidon's hooves clopped after Emrys. Blaise studiously ignored Jack watching him.

"It's the only one you're getting right now," Blaise replied, shaking his head.

"Fair," Jack murmured.

Truth be told, he was glad to have Jack and Emmaline along. They were quiet as they made their way to the Hawthorne house. The fair weather had receded, and dark clouds hung overhead, as if mirroring Blaise's mood. A light mist fell—not enough to hamper their progress, fortunately.

From the outside, the home looked as if nothing were awry. Their trio of pegasi halted out front, allowing the riders to dismount. Zepheus lowered his head, inspecting tracks that had torn up the grass. <Cloven hooves and unicorn droppings.>

Blaise walked closer, noting that the tracks were, in fact, cloven, like a goat or cow's hoof. Or, he supposed, a unicorn. The tracks were larger than a goat's, certainly. A pile of manure pebbled the ground near the tracks, though the brown was shot through with brilliant hues—vivid reds, greens, yellows, oranges, blues, and even purple. Blaise couldn't rightly say he'd ever seen unicorn scat before, but he figured Zepheus knew more on the topic than he did.

<Ugh, unicorns.> Emrys snorted at the droppings. <They're the worst.>

<Not worse than griffins,> Oberidon pointed out, swishing his tail.

Blaise left the stallions to bicker over the topic. Jack walked in a broad circle around the house. Blaise watched him for a moment, then called, "Can I have a minute alone?"

The outlaw flapped a hand at him, concentrating on whatever he was doing.

Blaise saw the oak Lucienne had mentioned the previous night. He started toward it, though he paused when he heard the crunch of hooves following him, a sign that the minor argument had been abandoned. He almost told Emrys that *alone* meant without him, too, but he didn't have the heart. Blaise approached the tree, slowing at the sight of disturbed dirt beneath its spreading branches. There was no gravestone, but someone had taken a knife and carved *DH* into the trunk. *Daniel Hawthorne.*

Blaise went down onto his knees, digging his fingers into a mound of dirt. "I'm sorry. So sorry I wasn't there for you." Emrys lowered his head, muzzle brushing the ground beside Blaise. "You didn't have to love me like your own, but you did. I never got to thank you for that, so I'm telling you now." *He didn't have to love me, especially with all the problems my magic caused. But he did.* "I won't ever forget that."

He rubbed a tear from one cheek. "I...I have a bakery now. Can you believe it? I hope you're proud of me." Blaise couldn't keep it in anymore. The cool dirt in his hand only emphasized how real this was. A part of him had wanted to deny his father's death. But he couldn't—not now. He choked back a sob as something occurred to him. "And I'll follow your example. You could have turned your back on me, but you never did. I won't turn mine on Mom. Or Luci or Brody. I'll do whatever I can to protect them."

His tears fell with the promise, dampening the dirt. Blaise pulled out a handkerchief, dabbing at his eyes and blowing his nose.

<You would do those things anyway,> Emrys pointed out gently.

Blaise nodded. "I would. But this is a reminder of why I do what I do." He swallowed. "Because someone else did it before me." Then he rose, folding his handkerchief and tucking it away as he rejoined Emmaline, who was pretending to not watch him and failing miserably. "What's your father doing?"

Jack crouched down, studying the pattern of footprints in the dirt. Emmaline shook her head. "I don't know. He's not exactly telling me what he's up to."

The outlaw must have heard their exchange. He lifted his head. "Trying to figure out which mages were here. There were seven of 'em." Jack rose to his full height. "That alone tells me they came expecting trouble."

"How do you figure that?" Blaise asked. *And what sort of trouble were they expecting?*

"Seven's a powerful number."

"Oh, like lucky number seven?" Emmaline's full attention was on her father, no doubt hoping to glean every bit of magical knowledge she could.

"Yep," Jack confirmed. Then he looked Blaise in the eye. "I want to go in and take a look. You coming?"

There was nothing challenging or surly in the question, which was unusual for the outlaw. Blaise didn't like it—didn't like feeling as if he were being coddled. He wanted Jack to treat him like normal—rudeness and all. If anything, it would make him feel less like damaged goods. "Yeah." He strode over to Jack, following him onto the porch. Before the Effigest opened the door, Blaise added, "You don't have to treat me like this."

Jack glanced over his shoulder. "Like what?"

"Nice."

The single word distracted the outlaw from their investigation. He wheeled, scowling. "And why shouldn't I?"

"Because it's a constant reminder of everything I've lost, and it's not like you."

A sort of recognition flashed across Jack's face, as if he understood Blaise in a way. All the same, the outlaw shook his head. "You forget, I've been where you are now. I know the hurt, how it cuts to the bone. All I had to help me back then was Zeph. I'm not being nice to cosset you. I'm doing it because I *understand*."

Blaise blew out a breath, then nodded. "So this...okay." Then, in a whisper, he added, "Thanks."

Jack grunted, pivoting again. He pushed into the home, cursing softly as he moved to open a window. "What's that smell?"

Blaise recognized the rotten-egg smell immediately. "Dragon sulfur." He edged around Jack, taking in the room. It was a small parlor that led to the kitchen and dining area. His family was tidy, but at the moment, the place was a mess. Broken glass and pottery littered the floor. A wooden chair leg was propped against the wall, the rest of the chair on its side nearby.

Light from the window flooded the room. Blaise crouched, gesturing to a broken vial. "She didn't go without a fight."

"Oh?" Jack sounded interested.

"Don't know if she succeeded, but she used Hydra Spit on one of 'em." When the outlaw raised a brow, Blaise figured he'd better clarify. "Not actual hydra spit. It's an offensive potion, probably what the dragon sulfur was in. It burns skin."

"Was gonna be impressed if she knew someone capable of milking a hydra," Jack said, amused at the prospect. "Em?"

"Yeah?" The younger Effigest had followed them inside, though she had been quiet, her lips pursed with concern as she took in the scene.

"Go with Blaise and see if you can cobble together a poppet to track 'em. Marian's the most likely, but if y'all find anything from one of the Copperheads..." Jack chuckled. "Oh, that would be quite the surprise for them."

"Well, there's blood spatter for one, but no way to know who it came from," Emmaline observed, gesturing to a dark spray on the wall Blaise hadn't noticed. He glanced away, wondering if it had been from his father. She stepped closer to him, lowering her voice. "Sorry. But blood would be really good if we knew who it was from."

"I know," he murmured. Blaise swallowed, gathering his resolve once more. "Mom's lab would be down below."

While Jack poked around on the first floor, Blaise picked up a mage-light, and he and Emmaline descended into the basement that had served as his mother's alchemy lab. They found an apron, and Emmaline used a knife to cut a one-inch strip from a string. Blaise was dismayed to see that the lab had been ransacked. The beakers, glass tubes, and ceramic bowls Marian used were shattered on the floor. Metal containers had been dented, as if someone had stomped on them. He went over to a cupboard where his mother would have stored her reagents and discovered that anything rare had been taken, too.

"Now I wonder if they were after her or the reagents," Blaise said.

"Maybe both?" Emmaline suggested. "If you're going for one prize, may as well snag another."

Blaise made a face. "I hate that your idea makes sense." He sighed. "Let's go back up."

Emmaline started up the stairs, but Blaise paused at the base as something caught his eye. A small measuring spoon, not fancy or remarkable, but one he recognized. It brought to mind the time he'd needed to measure something and hadn't been able to find a measuring spoon in the kitchen, so had raided the lab. His mother had been horrified, and Blaise had quickly learned that alchemy and cooking utensils should never cross. He turned it over in his hand, transported to happier memories for a precious moment.

"Blaise? You coming?" Emmaline called.

"Yeah." He tucked the spoon into a pocket.

When they reappeared, Jack's flinty eyes settled on Blaise, as if assessing to make sure he wasn't about to fall apart like a rickety wagon. Blaise was surprised he hadn't, either. The anguish was still there, but now he could try to *do* something about it, and that made all the difference.

Emmaline held up the strip of fabric. "Got something. I'm gonna go put together a poppet."

Jack nodded to her, and Emmaline swept out the door to retrieve materials from Oberidon's saddlebag. "Did you find anything?" Blaise asked.

"Nothing we didn't already know," Jack admitted, gesturing to the surrounding mess. "I thought about dragging a local Necromancer out to see if they could get us anything else, but I reckon it wouldn't be any more than what we have." His lips twisted. "And I'm not eager to disturb the dead."

Blaise blinked. That hadn't occurred to him. "You think my father's spirit is still around? He didn't go to Perdition?"

Jack shrugged. "Sometimes, when a soul dies a violent death, they don't go to Perdition right off. Especially if they got unfinished business." He rubbed his forehead. "But I don't much care for spooks. Rather not invite trouble."

Blaise was tempted to ask for the Necromancer, anyway. Maybe he could at least tell his father he loved him one more time if his spirit was still around. But he didn't want to ask—wasn't sure *how* to ask—for that small favor. He hoped that his moment by the grave would be enough. Instead, he asked, "What do we do now?"

"Get supplies for the road. And pray to Faedra that Em can track them."

CHAPTER SIXTEEN
The Diamond of Ganland

Jefferson

The Gulf of Stars glittered like a rich, azure carpet tipped with sparkling diamonds. After leaving Seaside, they had hugged the coast, and favorable weather meant that it only took a single day to fly to Nera. Jefferson marveled at the speed of their travel. Discounting their stay in Seaside, it only took five days to travel from Fortitude to Nera. *Astounding*. If only the Confederation hadn't forced him to scrap his airship work by turning it into a weapon. Travel could truly have been revolutionized.

The Gannish capitol perched on the coastline a few miles ahead. It was so large that they could see the outskirts from a distance, as well as the lighthouse that helped to guide merchant ships into the harbor. As they closed in on the city, Jefferson hazarded a glance at Kittie and Mindy's faces. Behind the flurry of pegasi wings, the awestruck expressions they wore delighted him as they drew ever closer.

Nera was known as the Diamond of Ganland for good reason. Every building was painted white, with flecks of hematite incor-

porated into the roofs. It gave the impression that Nera was a
sparkling gemstone, the illusion a power play to show exactly
what anyone coming in to barter would deal with: wealth, afflu-
ence, strength, and beauty.

Jefferson gave Seledora a sturdy pat to get her attention. She
flicked an ear back, and he leaned forward, straining against the
wind resistance. "Take us down!" She bobbed her head once in
acknowledgment, snorting mightily as she began a spiraling
descent that the other pegasi soon mirrored.

A few minutes later, all the pegasi were on the ground.
Mindy's eyes were still wide, and she glanced over her shoulder
toward the city. Jefferson smiled. They would be there soon
enough.

He had explained to them before they set off from Seaside how
they would need to land in advance of their arrival. It was much
too dangerous to fly directly to the Boss's estate, and no one
wanted to be shot down by the Bossguard or attacked by a
defending theurgist. Everyone agreed, going in on the ground
made the most sense.

<Shall we keep our wings out or hide them?> Seledora asked,
craning her head around to study him with a single dark eye.

"Keep them out," Jefferson said, though he felt rather bold with
the assertion. "It's no secret that we're coming."

"It sets the tone for who and what we are," Kittie agreed,
nodding at the logic. "We don't hide it."

Well, not all of us. Jefferson glanced down at the pair of rings on
his fingers. One that hid his true visage, and the other his magic.
Would a day ever come when he wasn't beholden to one secret or
another? Probably not, judging by the way his life had gone so far.
He cleared his throat. "Yes, that's another reason. They'll have no
way to mistake who we are."

To further that cause, they had dressed in their better outfits
for the day. Not their best—Jefferson had cautioned that they save
those for when they reached their destination. But they all looked

serviceable, and Jefferson fancied he looked rather debonair in his greatcoat with the flight goggles. He snapped them onto his fore-head, no longer needing them to protect his eyes from the slicing wind.

They rode toward the limits of Nera two abreast. Kittie stayed alongside Jefferson, while Flora and Mindy rode close behind.

"What's that?" Mindy asked, pointing at a long, sparkling wall that curled around the city. It joined another section that appeared to burrow under the part of Nera closest to the water.

"The seawall," Jefferson replied, glancing back at her. "I don't recall where you hail from. Have you ever experienced a hurricane?"

Mindy pressed her lips together. Many a maverick mage was reluctant to admit where they came from. She shook her head. "I'm not from the coast."

He nodded, knowing that was all he would get from her. And that was fine. He didn't need to know more than that. "Count yourself fortunate. Some hurricanes that come ashore are mild, but others..." Jefferson shook his head. "One of the most destruc-tive forces you can experience and hope to tell the tale of. A hundred years ago, such a storm rolled ashore in Nera, and the storm surge was so overwhelming, it killed thousands and scoured the city down to nothing."

Even Kittie raised an eyebrow at that. "And they bothered to rebuild here?"

Flora cackled. "Humans can be pretty stupid sometimes. No offense to present company."

"They did rebuild, but after the disaster, they knew the city was too low and would face the same fate if another powerful hurricane threatened it," Jefferson said as they ambled onward. The pricked ears of the pegasi proved they were interested in his tale as well. "This was before Ganland was part of the Confedera-tion, but they petitioned for all the Earth and Stonemages they could get from Phinora. Those pleas set the stage for Ganland to join the Confederation—but that's not the answer to your question." He shook his head to get back on track. "The Earthmages raised the city twenty feet, while the Stonemages created the seawall."

Jefferson could have told them more, but as he considered it, he suddenly didn't want to. They were mages—*he* was a mage—and he didn't want to think about the harm that had been done to the theurgists who helped. The Stonemages had been tasked with using their magic to draw quartz to Nera. It would have been too costly and slow to have it shipped by conventional methods. The effort had exhausted the theurgists, and most of them eventually succumbed to the incredible strain. The Earthmages hadn't been any better off. It was a daunting task to move enough dirt to raise a sprawling city, and six of the seven Earthmages had been found with blood leaking from their noses, dead from the effort.

No, Jefferson couldn't tell them that. Not when they were trying to establish good relations between the outlaw mages and Ganland. He clenched his jaw.

Fortunately, Mindy and Kittie were impressed by the feat and didn't press him for further details as they approached the gleaming quartz wall. A pair of guards rode out to greet them, and while they appeared calm, Jefferson saw by the set of their shoulders they were nervous. Mages on pegasi had a *reputation*.

Time to pull on his charm. He smiled brilliantly at them. "Good afternoon! Always a pleasure to see Nera's finest out here to greet weary travelers."

His greeting caught them off guard. They hadn't expected such exuberance. Jefferson was pleased to see that Kittie, too, offered a friendly smile. The guards studied their group. One man cleared his throat, urging his gelding forward. "Ah, right. You're the delegation from the Gutter?" He spoke incredulously, as if he hadn't expected to be approached by a group of well-dressed, orderly outlaw mages.

"We are," Kittie agreed before Jefferson could say as much. She sat tall in the saddle, her back ramrod straight and head high. As regal as a queen, Jefferson thought. "Boss Clayton invited us to Nera to treat."

The guard who had spoken grudgingly nodded. "We were told to watch for you." He turned in the saddle, gesturing to the gate that would admit them to the city. "The register is there. You'll tell us your names, and if they match our information, we'll admit you." Judging by the way his forehead wrinkled, he seemed to be puzzling out how they would keep a pegasus and its rider out of the city if they wanted to get in.

Once they had identified themselves—including the pegasi— and the guards were content, they were allowed through the gate.

"Do you need a guide to Silver Sands?" the guard asked, referencing the Madame Boss's estate and government offices.

Jefferson smiled and gave a shake of his head. "I'm quite familiar with Nera, though I appreciate the offer."

"That's *Jefferson Cole*, you dolt," a female guard hissed to her helpful counterpart. "He's Gannish. He's been to Nera countless times."

It was nice to be recognized. Jefferson acknowledged her with a wink and led his group into the city.

Many of the older Confederation cities boasted streets that were a confusing knot, as if a child had purposely tangled a skein of yarn. Nera, courtesy of the hurricane, wasn't among them. The streets were laid out in symmetrical blocks, with enough room for carriages to park on one side of the thoroughfare and for wagons or riders to pass by going both directions. Every road bustled with so much activity that even if the pegasi had wanted to land on one of them, it would have been an impossible task at this time of day.

"So many people. So much *everything*," Mindy commented.

"Nera isn't the oldest city in the Confederation, but it *is* the largest," Jefferson said. And the wealthiest. He knew that went unsaid as their heads swiveled about taking everything in.

They threaded through the crowds, and it didn't take long before people were stopping to stare at *them*. Word had already gone out that their delegation was coming, and at first, many of the faces that greeted them were borderline hostile. But that changed as soon as they saw the pegasi.

The equines were a feast for the eyes, their coats and feathers glossy in the warm afternoon sun. They ruffled their wings, extending them when the crowds allowed to show their impressive spans. The pegasi arched their necks, strutting with each step, glorying in the awestruck attention they received.

The Boss's personal guard allowed them entry to Silver Sands, which was nestled in the heart of Nera. It surprised Jefferson to discover Madame Boss Rachel Clayton awaiting them outside the executive stables, her Bossguard nearby.

"I received word you had arrived." Boss Clayton was in her middle years, her short brown hair touched by a few streaks of grey, but her eyes were as shrewd as anyone's. Right now, though, her eyes were wide with the glee Jefferson had seen on many a face of a horse-loving person as they had paraded through the streets. A small boy peered out from behind one of her legs while a girl stood nearby, her gaze on the pegasi, too.

"Mama said we could see the peggy-skies," the boy announced before hiding his face again.

"*Pegasi*," the girl, who was no doubt his older sister, corrected with a long-suffering eye-roll.

Madame Boss Rachel Clayton, who at that moment was also serving in her other important role as a mother, reached down and took her son's hand. "Only if you behave, though. Mama's working." There was a giddy gleam in her eyes, excited at the prospect of meeting the pegasi, too. She cleared her throat, remembering herself. "On behalf of all of Ganland, I offer my deepest greetings to the honored delegation representing the Gutter." She followed the formal words with a slight incline of her head.

"Hiiiiiiii!" The little boy waved enthusiastically.

Jefferson couldn't hold back his grin. Beside him, Kittie had a delighted smile on her lips. The young girl looked mortified by her brother's lack of decorum, but Rachel seemed to have expected it and ignored the behavior.

Jefferson knew Rachel well—he had dealt with her often as Malcolm Wells, but that hadn't stopped him from reaching out to her occasionally as Jefferson. "And we return the greeting to you. We are pleased that our arrival has been a source of wonder."

"Can we pet them now?" the boy asked.

Rachel sighed. "May I present Mary and Romie, my children. If the equines find it tolerable, could they pet them?"

In answer, Seledora and Tylos stepped forward without waiting for their riders. They both lowered their heads, and for a moment, Jefferson wondered if the usually acerbic mare would allow it. But she almost seemed like a different pegasus when faced with the children. Mary reached up and tentatively stroked her forehead while Romie giggled as Tylos sniffed at his chest.

<All a part of our diplomatic work,> Seledora explained to Jefferson privately. Though her mental voice held a contented edge that made him believe she was enjoying the caresses. So, the hard-hearted mare had a soft spot, after all.

A few minutes later, Rachel shooed her children away as a group of hesitant grooms filed in from the depths of the stables, eyeing the unusual equines with concern. Clearly, they didn't know how to comport themselves around the pegasi or understand what the expectations were.

"The executive grooms will see to the care of your pegasi," Rachel announced.

Jefferson pulled the hackamore reins over Seledora's head. He and the mare stepped closer to one of the grooms, a boy who looked to have just come into his teen years. "This is Seledora, and she is to be treated as a guest." The boy's eyes widened at the term.

"You may remove her saddle and bridle and then groom her well and bring her any food she may request."

"*Request?*" the lad gulped.

<Yes. Oats mixed with sweet feed would be a good start. Perhaps a rich dessert of some sort. A cheesecake? I am rather fond of those.> Seledora's ears pricked at the groom, who stared at her as if she had sprouted a second head.

The mare had broadcast her suggestion so that others could hear. The Bossguard perked up, suddenly on guard. Rachel was delighted, her face split by a brilliant grin. "I believe our cook was making a cheesecake for tonight. Apple crisp cheesecake, from what I recall of the menu. If that suits the mare, you can bring out as much as the pegasi need, Pip," she informed the stable boy. "I think it likely Seledora isn't the only one who would enjoy it."

The dapple grey mare arched her neck, appreciative. To Jefferson, she said, <I see why you get on well with her.>

The grooms escorted the pegasi into the stables. With their steeds no longer a distraction, Jefferson got down to business. He was going to be the Ambassador, after all. *Might as well own it.* "Madame Boss Rachel Clayton, allow me to introduce our delegation." When everyone had turned to him, he continued.

"Firebrand Kittie Dewitt." At her name, Kittie offered a genial nod, her face a serene mask.

"Hospitalier Mindy Carman." Mindy stepped forward and gave a quick bob before moving back behind Kittie.

"And my aide, Flora Strop." The half-knocker was playing her role well, keeping her features bland. Her hair was pulled back into a severe bun, which made the audacious pink less noticeable. Jefferson knew beneath that facade, she was watching everything, probably entertaining herself with a running commentary.

"It's a pleasure," Rachel said, gesturing toward the expansive residence. "Please, come in. My staff will help you get settled. I look forward to our dealings."

Jefferson nodded. *So far, so good.*

THE WELCOME DINNER THAT EVENING WAS A PLEASANT AFFAIR, WITH Mindy finding nothing amiss during any of the courses. Jefferson doubted anything underhanded would happen around the Madame Boss, but it did no harm to be cautious. The Gannish Doyens—Aaron Thatcher, Matthew Cohen, and Maude Harrington—joined them. The Board, the group of men and women who appointed the Boss and kept her in check, also attended.

In his time as Malcolm, Jefferson had worked closely with Aaron and, to an extent, Matthew. Maude had been the one selected to fill the seat left vacant in the wake of Malcolm's supposed death. Jefferson liked her feisty spirit—she was young, though not as young as he had been when he first claimed the position.

As the festivities wound down for the evening, Aaron slipped over to him. The red-haired Doyen smiled, though the lines framing his eyes were a clear tell that something was on his mind. "Mr. Cole, I understand you were close friends with Doyen Wells."

Aaron's opening foray caught Jefferson off guard. He had expected many things but not mention of his old, dead self. If he hadn't had years of experience at keeping his expressions unreadable, no doubt he would have made a mistake that would tip Aaron off. Instead, Jefferson gave a small nod. "Indeed. We were distant cousins, actually."

The Doyen's gaze flicked across the room to where Maude was engrossed in a conversation with Mindy. "Someone like Malcolm is difficult to replace. We miss him." Aaron sighed heavily, and Jefferson had to look away to regain his composure. He couldn't help the lump that formed in his throat at the sentiment.

"Yes, I attended the funeral, and I recall you spoke well of him," Jefferson murmured.

Surprise registered on Aaron's face. "My apologies. I didn't realize you had attended. Otherwise, I would have greeted you then as well."

Jefferson shook his head. "It's no matter." He glanced across the room at the members of the Board. One of them was speaking with Kittie, though the expression on the white-haired woman's face was that of someone forced to do something against her will. "Tell me, Aaron, as I've been out of the loop for a while, what is the temperature toward mages in Ganland now? Do you think it bodes well for an agreement with the Gutter?"

Aaron pursed his lips as he considered the question, his gaze also roving to the Board members. "I'll be honest. It varies. There are pockets of those who don't trust them and will think that allying with the Gutter will lead to our downfall. Others still think we should because the ultimate profit will be worthwhile." He paused, shaking his head. "And others who subscribe to Confederation ways would rather we scour the Gutter."

Jefferson nodded. He'd suspected as much, but it was good to receive confirmation. "Little has changed, then."

The Doyen crooked a finger at one of the Board members. "They're the ones you have to convince. The Board."

"Mmm," Jefferson agreed, having suspected that would be the case. "I appreciate the information. I look forward to more dealings with you in the future, Doyen Thatcher."

Aaron's smile thinned. "We'll see how things proceed, Mr. Cole. I won't lie—we're going to get some guff from the Mossbacks on the Council for even giving your delegation the time of day."

Oh, the Mossbacks. Rub their noses in it, then. Jefferson cocked his head. "Oh? I thought the Faedrans on the Council didn't grovel to that lot."

The Doyen shrugged. "It's been a challenge ever since the Breaker Inquiry." He gave a rueful shake of his head. "Don't get me wrong, we're trying. But so many mavericks are flooding out of the Confederation that it's causing problems."

Problems. Yes, problems like they can't find new mages to subjugate. Such a shame. "Problems for the Mossbacks don't equate to problems for your faction, though." Unless things had changed in the few months that Malcolm had been gone.

"No, you're right on that point, but it has made the Mossbacks grumpy." Aaron shrugged.

"I presume you're being charitable by calling them *grumpy,*" Jefferson said, which earned a chuckle.

"You're right. *Unreasonable* is the better word," the Doyen agreed, though he still laughed. Then he sighed. "Anyway, the hour is late, and I have meetings early in the day. As do you, I would imagine."

They said their goodbyes, everyone going their separate ways. Jefferson and his delegation walked to their cluster of rooms together, as they had planned. But as they reached the first door—Kittie's room—the Pyromancer coasted past it.

"Your room is—" Jefferson began, then cut himself off at the look she arrowed at him. "Never mind. I suppose we *should* have a lively discussion." He gestured grandly to the door leading to his room, which he supposed was Kittie's destination.

"You spoke to Doyen Thatcher privately. Why?" Kittie didn't mince words as she flopped down in the middle of the cream-colored, cameo-backed settee. Flora claimed the seat to one side of Kittie while Mindy took the other. It was a clear sign they had all noticed—and wondered.

"I knew he could give me honest insight into what we're getting ourselves into," Jefferson explained. "He's got connections and information the other Doyens don't, so I knew he would be a good one to ask."

"And what did you find out?" Kittie asked.

"We have to win over the Board." Jefferson sighed. "Means more wheeling and dealing. More proving our value."

"As you suspected," Kittie said.

"Yes," he agreed. Jefferson glanced at his saddlebags slumped by the door, a reminder that they still needed to unpack. And take care of other pressing matters. "Tomorrow will be a preparation day before we set to work."

"Preparation day?" Mindy repeated, puzzled.

Jefferson nodded, glancing at Flora. "Yes. Can you make sure our schedule is clear for the day? We need to get to the tailor."

Flora cocked her head. "But you have an entire wardrobe in your house outside of town."

Yes, but it's been a few months since I've been able to treat myself to a proper fitting. He waved a hand, leaving it unsaid. "I need whatever the latest fashion is, and you know it. And we need clothing for Kittie and Mindy, too."

Kittie scowled. "We *brought* clothing." She gestured to the saddlebags. Then, no doubt realizing that might not be sufficient, she added, "*Good* clothing."

Good, but not up to the standards of the Diamond of Ganland. No, Jefferson wanted his outlaws to shine just as brightly. "They're serviceable, yes. But trust me on this. We need something better. My treat."

Kittie crossed her arms, no doubt wanting to deny the offer. Conflicting emotions warred in her eyes before she finally relented. "This is part of the plan?"

He grinned. "All part of the plan."

CHAPTER SEVENTEEN
No-Account Greenhorn

Blaise

"The Untamed Territory is huge and unfriendly. We're gonna need supplies," Jack said.

Blaise stared at the outlaw with disappointment, though in his gut, he knew the pronouncement made sense. They had convened in the stables so that their pegasi could hear their plans, too. Blaise idly scratched Emrys behind an ear, thinking. When they had set out from Fortitude, none of them knew what lay ahead. Now they had a better idea, and with the outlaw's years of experience, Jack knew what they would need to have a chance of success.

"Do we have enough funds to do that?" Blaise asked. He had brought some coin, but probably not enough.

Jack gave him a crooked smile. "Who says we have to use our funds? Throw your beau's name around. Let's see how useful he is."

Blaise frowned, not wanting to take advantage of his connections. He wasn't as embarrassed as he had first been about his relationship with Jefferson—no, he had grown more comfortable with it. But he didn't like using Jefferson's name and influence that way. Would people think that was all Blaise wanted him for, a free ticket?

<He would want you to have the things you need to be successful,> Emrys reasoned, prodding Blaise with his muzzle. <Especially important things like sugar for your loyal pegasus.>

Blaise hid a smile at the stallion's suggestion. "Fine. If we do that, can we leave today?"

Jack pursed his lips, pulling a pocket watch out to consult the time. It was mid-morning, and Blaise thought it couldn't possibly take long to gather whatever they needed. But to his dismay, the outlaw shook his head. "Wouldn't be as smart as making a fresh start in the morning. And Em's still trying to get that poppet to work." Something unreadable flashed across the Effigest's face at that. Emmaline had trekked back out to the Hawthorne home with Oberidon to get another personal item. She'd had no success with the bit of apron they'd snatched the previous day.

Blaise's shoulders tensed with frustration. He wanted to be under way, hunting down the Copperheads. It was hard to tell himself that if Jack thought it was a bad idea to hare off after them immediately, then he needed to listen. "Okay. Let's go shopping, then."

Jack rubbed his hands together. "This'll be almost as good as robbing him."

Blaise narrowed his eyes. "I don't appreciate you talking about robbing Jefferson."

"All in good fun," Jack said with a shrug.

They left their pegasi to start on their tasks. Blaise followed Jack to the Mercantile. The Effigest sauntered in, and the shopkeeper seemed to know him from previous visits. They shot the breeze for a few minutes before Jack hitched a thumb at Blaise and casually dropped Jefferson's name. The woman hadn't recognized him—which had been nice—but her demeanor changed as soon as she knew she was in the Breaker's presence. Her eyes went wide, not from fear but from—respect? Awe? Something like that. Blaise wasn't sure what to make of it. But Jack was right. As soon as the shopkeeper learned who he was—and who he was connected to—she was quick to get whatever they needed. And, of course, Jack was tickled that it went on Jefferson's account.

"Don't think I'll ever get used to that," Blaise muttered as they headed to their next stop.

"What's that?" Jack asked.

"People looking at me like I'm special. Or scary. Or something in between."

Jack snorted. "If it makes you feel better, you're always going to be a no-account greenhorn to me."

It was ridiculous, but that *did* make Blaise feel better. The people who knew him—really *knew* him—understood him. They knew he didn't want to be any of the things others thought of him. There was solace in that.

Blaise rubbed his chin, moving on to another train of thought as they headed to the Dry Goods Store. "Why do you think Em is having trouble with her spell? That strip of fabric definitely belongs to Mom."

The Effigest slowed, that unreadable expression clouding his face again. "Sometimes spells don't take right the first time. Least, not for Ritualists. We're not like you, just touching things and having your magic do its job."

Blaise wrinkled his nose. That wasn't how his magic worked—not at all, now that he understood more about it. Something about Jack's deflection struck him wrong, too. "But that's not what this is, is it?"

Jack grunted. "You're getting more savvy than I like, greenhorn."

So he was on the right trail. Blaise figured there was some-thing Jack didn't want to tell him—but whatever it was would have to come to light eventually if they were to succeed. "If it's not Emmaline's spell itself, then what is it?"

The outlaw moved aside as a laden wagon rumbled by. When

it had passed, he stopped and turned to Blaise. "The mages we're going after. I told you they're bad news. I was trying to figure out who came out here but didn't have any luck. But they have magics that can cause us problems."

"Starting with Emmaline's tracking?" Blaise guessed.

"Starting with her tracking," Jack confirmed, grim. "They've got a Dampener—a damn good one, too. That might be enough to block Em, or at least make it difficult. There's also a Warder. One of those who knows what they're doing could send her off the trail without a problem."

Blaise grimaced with dismay, thinking of how expansive the Untamed Territory was. He had been counting on Emmaline's magic. "Finding them is going to be a needle in a haystack, then?"

Jack waggled the fingers on one hand, an indecisive gesture. "Yes and no. We have the advantage of flight, and they're on the ground, so it's possible that we might catch up to them if we can figure out where they are. But the important bit is I know where they're going."

Blaise arched his brows. "And where is that?"

"Thorn," Jack said. "Hank brought news about a month ago that the Copperheads had laid claim to it."

"Oh." Blaise wasn't sure what to make of that, but judging by Jack's expression, it didn't sound good. He chewed on the information for a moment, then realized why knowing where they were going wasn't the best thing. "But it would be in our favor to catch up to them before they get there, huh?"

"Yep," Jack agreed.

After stopping at two more storefronts, the outlaw declared he was satisfied. Everything he'd requested would be delivered to their hotel before dusk. With that task done, they headed to the hotel to meet up with Emmaline, whose attempts at tracking Blaise's mother were still unsuccessful.

Jack waved a hand. "Not worth wasting all your power over."

Emmaline chewed on her bottom lip, glancing at Blaise. "But I want to *help*."

"You are," Blaise assured her, knowing exactly how ineffective she felt. He was about to tell her he felt the same when Trudy, the hotel concierge, approached.

"Excuse me, Mr. Hawthorne. We have a guest who has requested to speak with you. Would you like—?"

"What's her name?" Jack cut in.

Trudy frowned, as if trying to decide if she should answer him or not. Jack smiled at her, though he didn't use his scary smile. No, this time, he used one that Blaise had only seen him use around Kittie. He lifted his eyebrows enough to give himself an open, affable expression as his lips split to show his teeth. It was an *aw shucks*, friendly look that lent him an air of approachability the outlaw didn't otherwise possess.

Emmaline noticed, and her face contorted, a *who are you and what have you done with my father?* sort of look. Jack ignored it as he tried to work his dubious charm on the concierge.

Trudy cleared her throat, then held up a finger as she pivoted and crossed the lobby to the front desk. She conferred with the clerk before returning to their cluster. "The name on the books is Jane Herald."

Not a name Blaise recognized, and neither did Jack from the way his eyes momentarily narrowed. The outlaw shrugged, letting Blaise decide.

"We'll see her," Blaise said.

Trudy smiled and beckoned them down one of the long, ornate hallways. Blaise stayed close on the concierge's heels, with Emmaline behind him. Jack brought up the tail end as if he were guarding their backs.

The concierge halted outside a room and tapped on the door. It opened little more than an inch, blocking any hope they had of seeing the occupant. Trudy conversed with the woman on the other side of the door in a soft voice, then turned back to their group.

"Miss Herald requests that she only meet with Mr. Hawthorne." Trudy spread her hands in apology.

Jack scowled, no doubt suspicious—which, to be fair, was his default. Blaise was conflicted, torn between the safety of the people he knew and whatever tidings this messenger brought. Had she come bearing news about Jefferson and the delegation?

"Up to you," Jack said.

Blaise exhaled softly. "I'll see her." But his eyes were on Jack and Emmaline, shadows of uncertainty in their depths.

Jack grinned at him, slouching with one shoulder against the wall. He pulled out a poppet—not his own, but Blaise's. He didn't particularly like Jack having it, but so far, the Effigest had behaved. "Go ahead. We're not going anywhere."

It was both a promise and a threat to whoever was on the other side of the door.

THE LATCH MADE A SOFT CLICK AS THE DOOR SHUT BEHIND BLAISE. He found himself in a suite like his own, though while his room was decorated in deep blues and warm yellows, this one was the red of a ripe apple with chocolate-colored accents. It wasn't an unpleasant combination, but it made the rooms appear darker, even in the glow of the mage-lights hanging from the walls.

A woman perched on the edge of a compact loveseat in the sitting room. Her clothing was a mix of black and charcoal, though it was well-tailored. Her long skirt shushed across the floor as she adjusted to study him. "Mr. Hawthorne, I presume." Her voice had almost no inflection.

Blaise paused. Something about that didn't sit well with him, though he decided not to hold that against her. He wasn't a brilliant orator, either. He nodded, then remembered to add, "I am."

Her eyes stayed on him, and she looked as if she either didn't know what to say next or was waiting for him to say something.

Blaise shifted his weight, his gaze darting around the sitting room. "Um, Trudy said you needed to speak to me? Should I sit?" *Stop it. Be more sure of yourself. You're not a pushover anymore.* But it was so hard when speaking to someone he didn't know.

The strange woman nodded. "Yes, please sit." She gestured to an armchair diagonal from her position.

Blaise sat. He folded his hands in his lap. "Thanks." He cleared his throat. "You know my name, but I don't know yours." It was a lie, but he hoped she wouldn't know that. Besides, it was simple manners.

"Herald will do," she replied, still watching him intently. "You are friends with Jefferson Cole."

It was a statement, not a question, but all the same, Blaise gave a small nod. Her voice was so odd—she didn't add any emphasis to the word *friends*, as others might if they wished to imply their relationship went beyond that. Just as well, since he didn't want to discuss that with a stranger. "Is this about Jeffer—Ambassador Cole?" Blaise asked.

Herald smiled at that, though no warmth touched her eyes. It was as if she were only going through the motions, mimicking something she had seen others do. "Yes, it is. How close are you to him?"

There it was, though once again, she didn't add any weight to the words. "We're business partners. Is this about the delegation?" As much as her words agitated him, he couldn't take the chance that she might not tell him something crucial.

It was as if his question had opened a floodgate. She swept into action, leaping up from the loveseat in a blur of motion as she dove toward Blaise, a pale hand outstretched. Alarmed, he yelped as she latched onto his arm, hauling him to his feet with more strength than he thought she could possibly possess. He stumbled, unbalanced by the unexpected movement. Herald dragged him upright, his boots scuffing against the floor.

"Stop! Wait! What are you doing?" Blaise tried to dig his heels in, but he still hadn't recovered his feet, and all he could do was valiantly try not to fall on his face.

She pulled him closer to the window—no, not the window. The wall? Outside, there was a pounding and a frustrated roar as Jack hammered on the door. Emmaline shouted Blaise's name.

Herald laid her palm against the wall—and then her hand sank *into* it. Blaise stared. *Did she really*—yes, the rest of her arm followed her hand into the wall as easily as a knife cutting into warm bread. And she seemed determined to drag him along with her.

No. Her magic coiled around him as her left shoulder vanished into the wall. Blaise's own power raced up at his call like a stampede of pegasi. His magic slammed into Herald's, shredding the tendrils that sought to spirit him away. The woman screamed as if the Breaker magic had directly harmed her. Maybe it had. Blaise didn't care at the moment. He just wanted to get *away*.

Herald released him, and Blaise fell onto his backside, grunting as the air whooshed out of his lungs. By the time he had the wherewithal to scuttle away, she had regained her composure, too. Herald pulled her arm back out of the wall, the limb returning with an unsettling sucking sound. She flexed her fingers, preparing to pounce.

"You will come with me," Herald said. "Your presence is required."

"Go lick salt-iron," Blaise rumbled, limbering his own fingers. Silvery wisps of magic played across his skin.

The door exploded inward, falling from the hinges with a resounding crash as Jack and Emmaline hurtled into the room. Jack's face contorted into a snarl, his sixgun out and ready though he didn't fire as he took in the scene. Emmaline's was out, too. She smoothly slid to block Herald's access to Blaise while Jack set his sights on the woman.

Blaise thought he might fire, judging by the way Jack's finger caressed the trigger. "Who are you?"

Herald had regained her stoic composure. She didn't look in the least bit concerned to stare down the business end of a furious outlaw's sixgun. She cocked her head and smiled, then took a quick step to the side, palm extended to—

"Don't let her touch the wall!" Blaise yelled, but Herald moved more quickly than his words. The Effigest cursed as the opposing mage sank into the wall and disappeared.

"Bloody souls of Perdition. What was that?" Jack growled, moving to occupy the same space Herald had been in seconds earlier. He ran a hand over the wall as if searching for a secret door, and Blaise was relieved that he wasn't sucked into it. Jack glanced back at him. "You okay?"

Blaise blew out a breath. "I think so. I was almost pulled into a wall, though." He wanted to sit, but he didn't trust any of the chairs in this room.

"Daddy, what *was* that?" Emmaline asked, her eyes on the wall.

The elder Effigest was quiet for a moment. Then he shook his head. "Don't know. A Walker unlike any I've seen before." Experimentally, he ran his hands over the wall again. "Doesn't mean they can't exist, though. Walkers are like other mages: each one a little different."

Blaise grimaced. He didn't like the idea that someone could just drag him into a wall and off to who knew where. He laughed, and he knew it had a hysterical edge from the look Emmaline gave him.

"What is it?" she asked.

Blaise ran a hand through his hair, no doubt mussing it. He didn't care. "I know Jack said the Untamed Territory would be dangerous, but I can't help but think it may be safer for me than here."

Emmaline canted her head, confused. "Why's that?"

"No walls," he explained, shaking his head.

CHAPTER EIGHTEEN

Turn Them into Flour for a Cake

Blaise

Blaise hadn't expected the Untamed Territory to be beautiful. Upon reflection, though, it made sense—Jefferson loved it, after all. There was a wild fierceness to the tall grasses that swayed in the wind, interspersed with late-autumn wildflowers in a riot of colors. The terrain was mostly flat, though Blaise saw hints of rolling hills far to the north. Trees were sparse, usually growing in clusters ringing watering holes or small springs. An endless blue sky sprawled overhead, littered with wispy clouds at the highest elevations. It was a little chilly, but Blaise's dark blue duster soaked up the sun, providing all the warmth he needed.

A smile pulled up the corners of Blaise's mouth as he peered over Emrys's shoulder. The stallion tipped an ear back in his direction. <Enjoying the scenery?>

Blaise rubbed the stallion's neck, knowing Emrys would read his pleasure. It surprised him that he felt so...okay. They had a target to pursue, and now that they were giving chase, it soothed the part of him that desperately needed to do something.

And it didn't hurt that it put distance between him and the strange Walker who had tried to whisk him away. He shuddered at the thought. They hadn't spoken of her since that night, but Jack had been so agitated by it, he had declared Blaise would bunk in the same room as him and Emmaline. Blaise hadn't questioned it—he felt better knowing they were close enough to intervene if needed.

He still didn't know what she had wanted. It was possible that she only wanted him because of what he was. As so many others had. Blaise shook the thought away, instead taking in the sights below them. The Untamed Territory was home to so many creatures, many he'd never seen before. Emrys was happy to name them as they flew over.

<Do you see the tan and white deer with the short antlers? They are antelope.> The antelope bounded away in alarm as the pegasi's shadows swept over them, leaving Blaise to observe their white tails flung upwards as they scrabbled away.

Huge, shaggy bovines with humped backs were bison. <Not related to the Knossans. Bison aren't magical, but they can be dangerous,> Emrys advised. <They look small from up here, but they would make even Clover think twice.>

Not long after, they caught sight of a grasscat, a feat difficult to achieve, according to the stallion. The predator stalked a weak bison calf, its lanky feline body low in the grass. It was challenging to make out—Blaise only saw a shadow skulking along, then realized it was a form that looked grassy, covered in wildflowers.

He had a better view of it when the beast leaped at its prey, a blur of vegetation making a terrifying yowl. The calf bleated in dismay as killing teeth clamped onto its neck, and the mother bison bugled her rage. But already, the pegasi were gliding away from the life-and-death struggle, so Blaise would never know how it ended.

He was glad for it, though. Even though the grasscat needed to

eat, he didn't want to see the calf torn apart. Emrys snorted agreement when he said as much.

"I can't believe we saw a grasscat!" Emmaline crowed her
excitement as they dismounted for their mid-day break at a
watering hole shaded by post oaks. "Those are rare to see, aren't
they, Daddy?"

Jack was loosening Zepheus's girth to give the stallion a
breather, but he turned at the question, pushing his wide-
brimmed hat up from his brow. "Yes and no. Most people don't
see 'em 'til they're coming at them." He frowned, scanning the
area. "And that one was near enough that we have to be vigilant.
They usually live in prides, so there're likely more grasscat
lionesses with that one."

The news made Blaise uneasy. "Do we need to be worried?"

"The pegasi would hear them before they got too close, right?"
Emmaline asked at the same time.

Jack glanced between them. "Yes to Blaise and no to you, Em.
They're big cats. They move silent as ghosts, and they smell like
grass."

<This is not comforting,> Emrys remarked, which was exactly
what Blaise was thinking.

"This is going to be a short break," Jack announced, pulling
jerky from his saddlebag. He tossed a chunk to Emmaline and
another to Blaise. "Only long enough to let the pegasi rest and
eat."

Emmaline loosened Oberidon's girth, then sat down cross-
legged beside the small pond. "You ever had to fight a grasscat?"

Jack had a chunk of jerky in his mouth and was busily chewing
it as he double-checked his sixgun. Once he'd seated the sixgun in
its holster again, he waggled the fingers of one hand, an indecisive
gesture. "Fight? No. Escape from, yes." He winced at whatever
harrowing memories accompanied his words.

Zepheus had been drinking from the pool, but he lifted his
head to regard them, silver droplets falling back into the still

water. <We had robbed a Confederation stagecoach. Jack was wounded because—> The stallion stopped abruptly, and Emrys and Oberidon lifted their heads. The trio of pegasi turned, suddenly on alert as they stared to the east.

Jack pulled his sixgun and poppet. Emmaline scrambled to her feet, mirroring her father. Blaise got up as quickly as he could, though he would never match either of the Dewitts.

And then they heard what the pegasi had. A distant bellow, flavored with notes of warning and fear. Jack tilted his head, lips pressed together. "That's a Knossan."

A Knossan? Like Clover? "They sound like they're in trouble," Blaise said, moving closer to Emrys.

<What are we doing?> the black stallion queried as Blaise checked his girth, then put a boot in the stirrup.

"If it's a Knossan, we should see if they need help," Blaise answered.

Jack pivoted, eyes narrowed. "Whatever's after the Knossan, better them than us."

Emrys quivered beneath Blaise, sharing the outlaw's sentiment. But the stallion wouldn't go against Blaise's wishes. Blaise closed his eyes for a moment, gathering his will. Then he shook his head, eyes flashing open. "I won't let someone suffer while I stand by and ignore it." Then softer, he added, "Let's go, Emrys."

The Effigest cursed, then moved to tighten Zepheus's girth. Blaise didn't look back to see if Jack mounted or not. Emrys was already turning, trotting out of the cover of the post oak trees to head in the direction of the bellowing Knossan.

A short distance from their impromptu camp, they found a trio of Knossans. They stood back to back, ringed by grasscats. Only the oddly shifting shadows in the grass told the tale of their impending peril. The Knossans were massive, perhaps ten feet tall at the tips of their long, sweeping horns. Blaise thought Clover was tall, but these bulls would easily dwarf her. They were garbed in clothing made from simple linens and reinforced with leather.

One of the bulls had a shotgun, and another had a bow. The third bull was unarmed, blood weeping from a ragged gash down his right arm.

Zepheus and Oberidon pulled up beside Emrys. Jack sighed. "Okay, bleeding heart, now what?"

Blaise watched the ever-shifting grasses that hinted at the felines' movements. "If we scare them, will they go away?"

Jack scowled. "How are *you* going to scare them? Turn them into flour for a cake?"

Blaise licked his lips. *By doing something they've probably never encountered before.* And it wouldn't be pretty. "Something like that."

"Wait, *what?*" Emmaline gaped.

"Emrys, can you drop me by the Knossans?" Blaise asked, ignoring Jack's worried scowl. He tried to pretend like the fact that Jack was *concerned* wasn't worrisome all on its own.

The pegasus cupped his nostrils, snorting uncertainly. <Pardon me?>

"Those cats are going in for the kill any moment. I need to be there to stop them."

"Offering yourself as an appetizer ain't the way to do it," Jack growled. "Can't believe I have to tell *you* this, but don't be reckless."

Blaise swallowed. "I'm not being reckless. If they attack me, I can stop them." He uncurled a fist, silvery wisps of magic wafting from his palm.

The outlaw narrowed his eyes. "You can manifest your magic?"

"Is that what this is?" Blaise asked. He hadn't had a name for it. Just knew it was something that happened now.

"*Yes,*" Jack said, exasperated. He pulled out a poppet, hefting it up. "Go do whatever ridiculous thing you have planned. I got your back."

"Me, too," Emmaline said grimly, sixgun in hand.

Emrys arched his neck as Blaise urged him forward. The stallion vaulted into the sky, though he gained little altitude. <Are we good for a touch and go?>

Blaise hated touch and goes. But they were something he'd practiced since he'd returned to Fortitude. He would never pull it off as effortlessly as Jack or Emmaline, but he could do it. "Yeah, no other choice."

The pegasus circled over the Knossans once. <We are here to help!> Emrys announced, though no acknowledgment came from below. The bulls were too busy keeping their formation against the predators.

As soon as Emrys's hooves touched the ground and his wings mantled, Blaise jumped from the stallion's back. In a great gust, Emrys pushed off and returned to the sky. Blaise botched the landing, his left leg buckling, and he had to throw out his hands to keep from plowing the ground with his face. Something thorny bit into his palm, but he ignored it as he struggled to his feet.

The black and white bull closest to him blew out a breath. "It is not every day one sees a human offer themselves up to the grasscats."

They're about to bite off more than they can chew. Blaise didn't take the time to speak to the Knossan. His gaze flicked over the grasses as they bent and swayed, brimming with nearly invisible cats. He rubbed his hands together, wincing at the gash in his palm. But his magic was there and ready.

Blaise knew that alongside the Knossans, he looked insignificant and weak, like the bison calf. Prey. He held up his hands, willing a thin shield of Breaker magic to take form. It shimmered before him like a heat mirage, almost imperceptible if not for the tiny motes of silver dancing in the sunlight.

There was no warning roar. Something lunged at him. He saw a flash of limber feline covered in a short hide of grass with a mane shot through with flowers. Eyes that gleamed like fireflies. Mouth gaping *wide, wide, wide* with teeth that looked more like sharpened wooden stakes than anything else. Forelegs reaching out, paws tipped with root-like claws.

More shapes were on the move. Blaise only had eyes for the one coming at him. An outstretched paw battered against his shield. For an instant, Blaise feared it would fail, popped like a bubble by the force of his attacker. The grasscat was heavy, and he felt every bit of her weight as she struck.

The lioness yowled, a horrific, agonized cry as his power took hold, unmaking her. The grass shredded, revealing a skeleton made of knotted roots and vines covered in clay-like soil that served as muscles. The wooden fangs fell harmlessly to the turf. The flowers that had been a part of the cat's mane flitted away on the breeze, as if a child had blown the fluff from a dandelion.

The other grasscats in the pride roared, the sound a mix of alarm and outrage. They became visible, heads popping up above the grasses, staring at him with those firefly-eyes. And then they charged.

Blaise lost track of the action after that. Everything was a blur. The bulls were on the move, firing at the grasscats with shotgun and bow. Jack was somehow around, moving preternaturally fast, armed with sixgun and a fat knife Blaise hadn't known he owned. Emmaline stayed at the fringe, and Blaise heard the report of her sixgun when she had a clear shot.

At the end of the dust-up, a dozen grasscats were dead—some of them shredded on Blaise's shield, others hacked by Jack's knife or shot full of arrows or bullets. One of the bulls had taken a bite on the leg, and claws had raked Jack's arm, but otherwise, they were alive, which Blaise thought was something.

He rubbed the back of his neck. "Um, sorry. I didn't know that trick was going to make them come after us like that." Jack gave him a heated look that clearly said they were going to have words about that *trick* when it was safe.

A nearly white Knossan, the one who had the gash on his massive forearm, shook his head. All three were breathing hard from the exertion and seemed on edge. "It was not your ability that spurred them, mage. They were compelled."

Compelled? Blaise blinked, wondering about that, but didn't ask because the black and white bull was staring at him. "You are the Breaker."

Blaise sighed. Great, he had a reputation even this far out. Just what he wanted.

Before he could answer, Jack spoke up. "You say they were compelled? Y'all seen any mages who might do that, by chance?"

The third bull, so dark brown he was almost black, nodded. "Indeed. Two days ago, we came across the Copperheads. They attempted to goad us into a fight." His dark eyes narrowed, no doubt angered by the memory. "But their leader said there was no time. One of the desperadoes said something about sending us to do their dirty work." His hands clenched at his sides.

"*Beastcaller,*" the white bull said, disdain in his voice. "He tried to command us as if we were animals. When he could not, he grew angry and used his power to send a swarm of wasps after us. We ran, and as we went, it was as if more and more creatures were sent to hunt us down. We fought those we could, winning our way through. But we were too tired by the time the grasscats came."

"Elementalist," Jack said, seemingly to himself. When the Knossans turned to him, he shrugged. "Beastcaller couldn't have influenced the grasscats. They're not animals, not really." His blue eyes flicked to one of the dead creatures. "They bothered to have two mages send minions to stop you. To stop us." Jack's mouth was drawn, eyes glittering with something indecipherable. "We've got a camp. Join us. We can mend our wounds together and recover."

It was odd to hear Jack downright hospitable, but Blaise figured the outlaw knew what he was doing. Together, their motley group returned to their camp.

Emmaline slipped up beside Blaise as they walked back, their pegasi on their heels. "That was amazing. What was it?"

Blaise shrugged. "Something I learned in the Golden Citadel."

Her eyes widened in understanding. "Oh. I'm sorry I asked but...you should know it was really impressive."

He nodded, knowing that it *was* impressive. No one besides Jefferson and Flora knew he had used the same trick to shatter a bullet. He had practiced it little by little, gradually weaving the shield into something larger. Blaise wasn't sure how he felt about others knowing about that ability, but he knew eventually, it was going to get out. He had to have ways to use his magic to protect himself.

<It was impressive, but I was afraid the grasscats were going to *eat* you,> Emrys said, shoving his head into Blaise's back. <Don't do that again.>

Blaise sighed. He couldn't promise that, and Emrys knew it.

When they reached their campsite, Emmaline pulled a first aid kit from Oberidon's saddlebags. The Knossans tended to their own wounds, and Emmaline helped her father take care of his. Before long, everyone was bandaged, a tentative silence growing between the humans and Knossans.

"You're awfully far from Knossas," Jack observed as he filled his canteen with fresh water.

The dark brown bull huffed. "We travel to the Black Market. It is scheduled to be nearby tomorrow, and there are certain supplies we require." His eyes glittered. "And information."

Information. One of Jack's favorite things. The outlaw cocked his head, though he feigned boredom. "Oh? What sort of information are you after?"

The Knossans exchanged looks, as if debating how much to tell them. After a moment, the white bull spoke. "Precious things have been stolen. Relics." He heaved a long, drawn-out breath. "Younglings."

Jack scowled. Blaise knew for certain the Effigest didn't like that one bit. He was close with Clover, and while Blaise didn't know her history, he could guess. "Young-uns, you say?" The outlaw rose, screwing the cap back on his canteen. "Slocum doesn't traffic."

The black and white bull nodded. "We know this. But he deals with rare items. And he is well-informed."

Jack seemed to chew on that for a few minutes. "We could use a stop at the Black Market, too. Maybe we can travel together."

"There is strength in numbers," the white bull agreed. "We would welcome this."

Blaise frowned, wondering what Jack was up to. With the Knossans, they would be landbound—which Blaise preferred to flying, but they would travel so much slower. But he would trust Jack and hope the outlaw's savvy wasn't leading them astray.

CHAPTER NINETEEN
Attitude is Everything

Jefferson

Zuzanna is a genius, but also a pain in the ass. Jefferson had been giddy at the thought of visiting his favorite tailor in Nera, until he recalled how she enjoyed tormenting him. But the quality of the items she produced was worth it. Zuzanna was more than just a tailor. She was a Fibermage, capable of weaving her power to create amazing outfits. Her designs were unlike anything else.

Most people didn't consider Zuzanna a mage. Fashion icon? Designer? Genius? All of those, and mage last. Jefferson wondered if it was because she was a tailor before anything else that set her apart. Tailors were comfortable. They were *normal*.

Not like Breakers. Or Dreamers, Jefferson considered as he held his arms out while Zuzanna moved around him, making thoughtful little noises and murmuring to herself. Flora waited nearby, somehow looking bored and vigilant at the same time. Kittie and Mindy were speaking with Zuzanna's assistant, going over fabric options since the tailor had finished with them. "I saved the fussiest for last," Zuzanna had informed them as she beckoned Jefferson over.

He glanced at the ring on his left hand, then grunted when Zuzanna poked him in the ribs. "I told you not to move!"

"I didn't," Jefferson muttered. He had barely turned his head at all. But Zuzanna was demanding when she was at work. All a part of her magic, or so she claimed. Jefferson wondered if she just enjoyed bossing the elite around. He couldn't fault her for that.

"You *did*," she insisted, ramming the tip of her index finger into his ribs. "Be still as a statue. Don't move again."

"I have to *breathe*," Jefferson reminded her.

"Oh, I have to breathe, you say? Breathe *later!*" Zuzanna snapped, which sent Flora into a laughing fit.

Jefferson sighed. Yes, she definitely enjoyed playing with the elite. And she still saw him as one, even though she knew he kept company with outlaw mages.

"No sighing!"

"Sweet Tabris, Zuzanna! I'm paying you enough, so at least allow me to *exist*."

She kept her dark-haired head down, though Jefferson suspected she was grinning. "That's an extra charge."

"Then I will pay the existence fee. Gods, I forgot how impossible you could be."

"And yet here you are, and you go to no other. Because you know you will only get the *best* from me," she bragged, stepping back as she took the last measurement. Zuzanna wasn't much taller than Flora, but like the half-knocker, she had a *presence*. Her work had stooped her back, but she was still full of vinegar. "I have everything I need. I'll have your outfits ready by end of day and can send them to you. Shall I send them to your estate?" Her voice turned sly, a sign that she very well knew where their group was staying but wanted him to say it.

"Please send them to Silver Sands."

Zuzanna whistled. "That will be an extra fee."

Jefferson rolled his eyes. "How is that any different from sending it to my estate?"

Zuzanna favored him with a beatific smile. "As I hear it, you call the Gutter home, so foreign shipping. Export fees."

Jefferson's mouth opened to argue, then he snapped it closed. He knew better. The more he said, the more she would tack onto her price because she knew that her shop was the only one he could—and would—turn to. He ran a hand through his hair. "Yes. Fine. It's worth it to be dressed respectably in a Zuzanna Original."

"Of course, it is," she agreed, then put an arm around him to shuffle him toward the door. "And now you must go so that I can begin work before my next appointment. I need time to work my magic." She waved to Kittie and Mindy. "It's been a pleasure, my darlings."

Jefferson nodded, filing out the door with the others. He was quite happy to swing into Seledora's saddle so they could return to their other obligations. And so that he could stop being poked and sniped at.

"How much is Zuzanna milking you for this time?" Flora asked, not even trying to hide the glee in her voice. She enjoyed watching the tailor antagonize him a little too much.

Jefferson sighed. "I don't want to even think about it. Enough that I intend to have this clothing shipped to Fortitude and not crammed in our packs when we're done."

"We're going to look so *good*, though," Mindy cooed. She had taken to Zuzanna right away—Jefferson suspected their magic types were akin to one another. "I can hardly wait. Did you hear what she's making for Kittie?"

The Pyromancer rolled her eyes. "It's going to be ridiculous."

Jefferson smiled. "You'll have attire befitting your station."

Kittie gave him a withering look. "I'll have attire declaring loud and clear that I'm a mage. And not just any mage." She blew out a frustrated breath.

Ah, so that was it. As soon as Zuzanna learned who she was dressing, she insisted on going all-out—as she always did. The tailor had determined she was going to have Kittie declare boldly who she was, insisting that she would design clothes reminiscent of dancing flames. The Pyromancer had argued with Zuzanna at that point, and they'd settled with a handful of different items, including a form-fitting red dress that Kittie seemed to like, though she didn't openly admit it.

"What happened to reminding them who we are?" Mindy asked.

Kittie's cheeks reddened. "It's one thing for them to know I'm a mage. It's another to flaunt the fact that I play with fire."

Jefferson understood. He would feel much the same if more knew about his magic. "You'll have an assortment to pick from. If you really dislike it, no one will make you wear it." That mollified the Pyromancer, and they continued their trek back to Silver Sands.

A few minutes later, they arrived at the gates and found that they weren't the only ones trying to gain entry. A contingent of mounted men and women in the scarlet and gold of the Salt-Iron Confederation milled around, barred by—

<Unicorn,> Seledora warned when the wind shifted to carry the scent. And then the beast turned, revealing the gleaming horn that Jefferson hadn't seen at first, either.

A Tracker, then. Jefferson touched a finger to the ring Blaise had given him, simply as reassurance. He swallowed, the only sign of unease he allowed himself. *Keep up appearances. Not the first time you've misdirected from who you really are.* Kittie and Mindy had seen the unicorn as well, and both knew what it meant. Mindy's yellow eyes were wide, while Kittie's face had paled. Their pegasi drew to a stiff-legged halt, on edge. Except for Tylos. Flora urged him forward, her lips peeled back over her teeth in a threatening smile.

"Do we run?" Mindy asked, breathless.

"That will only make it look as if we have something to hide," Kittie said, though her voice was tight. She glanced at Jefferson for confirmation.

"They have no claim to us," he agreed, though he privately wished they could skulk away and leave the Confederation forces none the wiser. But they had been spotted, and that window of opportunity was lost. That meant he had to move on to their next best option. "Come on. We *belong* here."

Seledora glanced back at him. <We do, but they may still try to detain us.> She started forward anyway.

When they drew closer, Jefferson saw the green and white garbed Gannish Bossguard holding the Salt-Iron Confederation forces at bay. Jefferson smiled when he recognized the guard captain from previous visits to Silver Sands.

"Captain Cerulean!" Jefferson called cheerfully, drawing the attention of friend and foe alike. Cerulean flicked their gaze in Jefferson's direction but didn't budge, arms crossed over their chest as they physically barred the Confederation group. "What seems to be the problem?"

The Tracker aboard the unicorn turned, sizing him up. The unicorn's nostrils flared, drinking in their unfamiliar scents. Its ears pricked forward as it made a throaty nicker, pulling in their direction as it scented the mages. The Tracker suddenly grew more interested in them, narrowing his eyes. "*Mages.*"

"Oh, they're not a problem," Jefferson said, gesturing to Kittie and Mindy. "I do believe you'll find that they're guests of Madame Boss Clayton."

Cerulean scowled. "I've been trying to convince Tracker Norris and his friends of that for the past twenty minutes."

Norris's mouth twisted into an ugly snarl. "We're here by the authority of the Salt-Iron Confederation to apprehend the *outlaw mages.*"

Jefferson leaned forward, resting his arms on the crest of Seledora's neck. "There are no outlaw mages here. Tell me, sir, do you possess a handbill for either of these ladies?" The question was a gamble. Flora had sought any information regarding the Wanted status of both Kittie and Mindy, and had found nothing. Jefferson wouldn't put it past them to fabricate a handbill, though.

Norris ground his teeth as the unicorn tugged at the reins, insistent. "Doesn't matter. They're mages and—"

"They're free." Jefferson held up a hand, ticking off reasons. "They are not Confederation citizens. They are here as delegates and have diplomatic immunity. You have no just cause to hold them as they have done nothing wrong."

Fury tinged Norris's face with scarlet. "They're *mages*." He said it with the same intensity as someone would speak of vermin. The Tracker gestured to the other soldiers. "Take them all into custody."

Seledora flung up her head at the decree, and out of the corner of his eye, Jefferson saw Flora pull out her knives, ready for a skirmish. Kittie's head was high, her eyes burning with anger. Mindy looked ready to ask her pegasus to flee.

Jefferson didn't move a muscle as six soldiers cautiously moved to circle their pegasi. Seledora's ears flicked all around as she surveyed the situation, waiting for direction. Jefferson crossed his wrists over the pommel of his saddle, giving the soldiers a disdainful look. *Attitude is everything.*

"No, I don't think so. Not today, at least." He was quite satisfied by the way the Tracker's jaw hung open at his refusal. The Confederation soldiers shifted, uncertain what to do. "Unless you're certain you wish to cause an international incident."

Norris sputtered something that might have been words if he hadn't been so furious.

Cerulean smiled, stepping forward to break through the circle. "Mr. Cole has the right of it. And I will add, Ganland is a *nation*, not a province of the Confederation. We do not answer to you. If you interfere with the wishes of Madame Boss Clayton, there will be quite an *incident*."

Norris's unicorn edged backward, eyes rolling at the tension in the air. The creature tipped its head toward the mages. Its rider, meanwhile, radiated his annoyance. "Our superiors tasked us with bringing in the outlaw mages. What am I to tell them?"

"How about *no?*" Flora suggested sweetly.

Norris made a sound that fell somewhere between a growl and a frustrated exhalation, yanking the unicorn's head around and digging his heels into the beast's sides. It jolted into a startled trot. The other Confederation soldiers fell away from their circle, turning to follow the Tracker, though they were on foot.

When the Confederation forces had turned a corner and were no longer in sight, Jefferson rubbed his forehead, turning to Captain Cerulean. "Thank you for the support."

Cerulean's gaze was steely. "I was only doing as was right. I won't have the Confederation prancing in here and running rampant like they own everything." They straightened, then turned to gesture to the other guards to open the gates. "Sometimes we have to remind them we are allies, but we call the shots in our own land." Then they chuckled. "Besides, Boss Rachel would dock our pay for a year if we allowed them to snap any of you away in the middle of negotiations." Cerulean cleared their throat. "Madame Boss Clayton, I mean."

Jefferson hid a smile, appreciative that the Gannish leader allowed herself to curry the trust of those around her with familiarity. Sometimes that was an effective way to gain unfailing loyalty. "We're expecting a delivery this afternoon. Will you have someone bring it directly to our rooms?"

Cerulean nodded. "I'll make certain the shift manning the gate later is aware."

With the Gannish guard continuing to monitor the gate, Jefferson turned to survey his cohorts. Mindy looked shaken but was recovering. Kittie looked ready to light something—or someone—on fire.

"I'm not going back to them," the Pyromancer whispered.

"No, you will not," Jefferson agreed. "Neither of you." He aimed an encouraging smile at Mindy. "The danger is past, and we're all safe." He glanced down at his magic-concealing ring. The unicorn hadn't been worried about him at all, only the Pyromancer and Hospitalier. Maybe, just maybe, it was worth the price of inhibiting his magic. He touched the band with his index finger. *Thank you, Blaise. Wherever you are.*

CHAPTER TWENTY
Supply and Demand

Blaise

"Why are we going to the Black Market?" Blaise asked Jack quietly the next morning as they broke camp. The Knossans had rested nearby, though they kept their own watch as well, wary of any wildlife that might attack in the darkness.

"Because the bulls are right—Slocum gets around. Knows things. I've gone to him often enough to barter for information." An ironic smile touched his face. "Believe it or not, there are times I think information is better'n a sixgun and magic."

Blaise pursed his lips but nodded. "If you think it'll help."

"I do," Jack said simply. He buckled up his saddlebag. "Now, finish getting Emrys saddled before the bulls leave without us."

The Knossans—they had introduced themselves as Gore, the white; Roam, the black and white spotted; and Deal, the nearly black bull—had little to gather and were ready to hit the trail before the outlaws. Moments later, they started on their way. The bulls took the lead, with Blaise and Emmaline just behind them and Jack bringing up the rear, watching for trouble.

By midmorning, they had the first sign that they were near their destination. A faded bandanna hung from the gnarled branch of a half-dead tree, the only tree standing on the horizon as far as Blaise could see. He rose in the stirrups, squinting into the distance as the Knossans implacably continued forward. He thought he saw a dark speck on the horizon, but it was impossible to know if that was their end goal.

Fortunately, it was. As they traveled, it grew larger until it took on the shape of a lone building, standing defiant in the endless emptiness that threatened to swallow it. There were no hints of wildlife anywhere around, not even a scattering of dried buffalo chips. It was as if the animals and magical creatures openly avoided the area.

"That's strange," Blaise said to Emmaline.

Behind them, Zepheus must have overheard. <The Black Market has an aura about it that mystical races dislike, and even mundane animals can sense it.>

Blaise frowned. It had been ages ago, but the family pony Smoky hadn't minded the Black Market. Though Smoky had been there many times and was generally unflappable. "Do you sense it, Emrys?"

<I do, and I don't like it. But I will go there because we must.>

Blaise rubbed his chin. "Why don't we feel it?"

Emrys glanced back. <Please do not take offense, but humans lack the sensitivity to feel it. That includes mages.>

Blaise nodded. That made sense, in a way. In the same way he couldn't track a fox, but a hound could. "None taken."

"That's the Black Market?" Emmaline asked, wrinkling her nose as they drew closer. "For all I've heard about it, I thought it'd look more impressive."

As in Blaise's past experience, the Black Market looked like an abandoned building. This one didn't resemble a saloon but had the look of perhaps a barn. Or maybe a house that had fallen into disrepair. It was difficult to tell. Whatever it was, it was near a natural spring that gave them the chance to drink fresh water and refill their canteens again.

"Lotta powerful things don't look that impressive," Jack commented, then jerked a thumb toward Blaise. "Him, for example."

Blaise ignored the dig, though he recognized it meant Jack was through coddling him. That was good. He was more concerned about the Black Market itself. He hadn't had the best experience on his last and only visit.

The Knossans slowed as they arrived, shifting their considerable weight as if they, too, were nervous around the building. Gore turned to them, dipping his horns. "We will no doubt part ways now that we've reached our destination. Thank you for accompanying us, Scourge of the Untamed Territory." His large eyes flicked to Blaise. "And Breaker of Fort Courage."

Blaise swallowed but nodded, unsure what to say. Thankfully, Jack spoke up. The Effigest touched the brim of his hat. "Best of luck finding your young-uns. Remember that the outlaws of the Gutter ain't half bad unless you're an enemy."

The trio of bulls bobbed their heads, then filed into the building. Blaise thought Jack would follow and was surprised when the outlaw stayed put and dismounted.

"What was that about?" Emmaline asked. "I need to get me a nickname."

Jack chuckled. "You'll earn one, no doubt. But that was all politics." He made a face, as if he'd tasted something rotten. "If the Gutter is a nation, it'll help if any Knossans we come across think well of us."

Blaise arched his brows. "Look at you, learning to play nice with others."

The Effigest snorted. "It's called savvy."

"It's called being diplomatic. Jefferson is going to be so proud."

Emmaline hid a smile behind her hand. Jack glared at him, but Blaise didn't mind one bit. Zepheus must have made a private comment because he nickered his own sort of laughter, butting Jack with his head.

"I'm going in," Jack announced, apparently deciding not to rally against their remarks. "You can stay out here if you want."

As Jack strode toward the door and hauled it open, Blaise swallowed, his mind suddenly back on their current focus. Emrys blew a warm breath against the back of his neck.

Blaise shook his head and plowed toward the door. "No, I'm fine." He wasn't fine, but maybe he would be. *I'm not the green as grass, scared kid I was then.* No, he had come a long way. Endured much. He squared his shoulders and pushed open the door, though he was more mindful of its fragile status than Jack had been. It would only take a nudge from his magic to shatter the hinges.

Jack was leaning against a wall, arms crossed, as he waited for the Knossans to finish their business with the Black Market's proprietor. Tom Slocum, Blaise supposed, was a mage, though he didn't know what sort. The Black Market was unlike anything else he knew—a building that shifted each day, forever cycling through predetermined locations. Maybe some sort of Walker, though Blaise had never heard of one like that.

But I never knew of a Walker who could move through walls. Blaise's eyes widened at the thought, wondering if Slocum knew anything about such a mage. And if their magic was related.

Roam finished speaking with Slocum and lumbered to the door. He paused when he got to Blaise, dipping his horns in farewell. Gore and Deal ambled after, and without another word, the bulls set out on their way.

With the Knossans gone, Jack eased over to the shabby, over-turned barrels covered in knotty boards that served as a counter. Slocum's eyes weren't on the outlaw, though. They were on Blaise.

"You're still around, I see, Breaker," Slocum said, his tone somewhere between a welcome and warning.

Blaise moved closer to Jack. "Against the odds, yes."

Slocum nodded, then turned to Jack. "What d'you want, Dewitt?" He leaned both elbows onto the wood, then hazarded a quick glance at Blaise. "No gloves?"

"Don't need 'em."

Jack smiled at Slocum, his expression both friendly and dangerous. "You know what I normally come to you for. Information."

The proprietor nodded. "And what do you have to trade?"

"Coin," Jack said, then scowled at the shake of Slocum's head. "Then what?"

Slocum tilted his head. "I reckon if you've come this far to see me, you're desperate. Coin won't cut it."

"*Slocum.*" Jack's voice was a guttural growl, a promise of violence. Any of the diplomacy that Blaise had teased him about earlier had abruptly vanished.

Around them, the building made an eerie wail. Emmaline's eyes went wide, and she jerked away from the wall she'd been standing near. Blaise felt the rickety floorboards come to life beneath him. *Come to life?* How could they? They were dead wood. Rotting wood.

"You're in my domain, *Wildfire Jack Dewitt,*" Slocum warned.

Amid the sudden flare of power, Blaise's magic roared up, ready to defend or attack. He flexed his arms, balling up his fists to keep it under wraps even as the ceiling overhead made a sinister rumble. Jack was armed, though he held off from taking aim. Emmaline stood frozen, reluctant to incite anything. Outside, the pegasi whinnied a warning.

"Whatever you ask will probably be more than we can give," Jack said, voice gravelly.

Blaise's heart threatened to gallop right out of his chest. They had come all this way, strayed from their trail. No way was he going to let this be a waste. He stared at Slocum. "What do you want?"

"*No.*" Jack didn't even hesitate. He angled to glare at Blaise, his blue eyes stormy with rising anger.

Slocum ignored Jack, relaxing. Around them, the Black Market quieted. They heard the resounding thud of hooves against a decrepit wall as one of the pegasi kicked, but the magical building was sturdier than it at first appeared. Blaise realized that while inside, the pegasi couldn't communicate with them. He was certain Emrys would have queried otherwise.

The proprietor smiled, eyes cutting to Jack. "What do you want to know?"

"The Breaker doesn't know what you demand of him," Jack said, shoving his sixgun back into its holster. He crossed his arms, the poppet tucked neatly into the crook of his elbow.

"The Breaker knows me. We've done business before." Slocum grinned, though it reminded Blaise of the leaping grasscat's maw. A baring of teeth from an apex predator. "I reckon you're here on his behalf. Not yours, Dewitt. Let him speak."

Jack stewed and said nothing. Blaise took a shuddering breath, then nodded. "You know my mother, Mr. Slocum. Marian Hawthorne." It wasn't a question, simply a statement, and Slocum nodded his agreement. "She was kidnapped, and the ones who did it killed my father. We're hunting them down to get her back." He licked his lips, wondering if he should mention the Copperheads. No, because that might be giving up valuable information. "Have you heard where she might have been taken? Do you know anything about those who stole her away?"

Slocum cocked his head, drawing an index finger over the rugged grit of the lumber he leaned against. "I might have information relevant to your questions, yes."

Jack took a step forward before Blaise spoke again. "Relevant? Not good enough, Slocum."

The proprietor chuckled. "More enlightening than you think." His chilly gaze remained on Blaise. "I'll provide the information for a price."

Blaise steeled himself. "What's the price?"

Slocum turned, moving to pull something small out of a box Blaise hadn't noticed at first. It was a clear glass vial, exactly of the sort he'd seen his mother use before for her alchemy. "Fill this with your blood."

"*No*." Jack was adamant, clamping an arm around Blaise's shoulder to steer him toward the door. "The price is too high. We don't need whatever piss-poor information he has."

My blood. Blaise felt light-headed for an instant, a terrifying vision roaring up. A wicked knife slicing the soft underside of his arm from wrist to elbow. The white-hot pain. The warmth of blood oozing. Dripping. He didn't realize he had slipped away from Jack to stand frozen in the middle of the floor.

"Blaise." The voice was urgent. A new hand was on his shoulder, squeezing with firm but insistent pressure. He blinked, and his eyes focused on Emmaline, peering down at him. Somehow, he'd gone to his knees as an old memory took hold.

"You don't know what you ask, Slocum." Jack's voice was tense, something about it protective, seeking to shield Blaise. "Take mine instead. Wouldn't be the first time."

"The bargain is not with you."

Blaise swallowed, shakily rising. *I'm okay. I'm not there. I have a choice in this.* He was glad that Emmaline remained nearby. *But what should I do?* Blaise knew that the Confederation had taken his blood for some dark purpose, one he never discovered. His mother had told him she had destroyed all the samples she could find, though.

But his blood was different. His magic—this magic he wasn't supposed to have, *shouldn't* have—made him unique. And in his case, being unique was dangerous. "Jack is right. That's something I can't give."

Slocum regarded him with an almost piteous look. "I respect that. A shame, since you're headed into a dangerous situation woefully uninformed."

Jack cursed softly. "Slocum, throw us a bone."

"Nothing in this building is given freely. You know that."

Blaise closed his eyes. If he had been in this alone, he might have turned and walked away. But he wasn't. Jack and Emmaline had thrown in their lots with him. And the pegasi. They wouldn't give up, not after coming this far. Blaise didn't want to put them in any more peril than they were already in. *And Mom. I promised Dad I would find her.*

"Half a vial. That's all I'll offer."

"Damn it, Blaise!" Jack growled. "*No.*"

"Half a vial," Slocum agreed, ignoring Jack's outburst. He held the vial out, and Blaise took it.

Blaise's fingers trembled as they closed around it. The glass was thick, but it would have been a simple thing for his magic to break. He stared at it. "How do you want me to do this?"

Slocum pulled out a bronze cube with a lever attached. "Let me see your arm."

Blaise stared at the unfamiliar device, fighting the urge to edge backward. "What is it?"

"Scarificator. Tool for bloodletting. Most physicians have them." Slocum held it up, displaying eight slits on the bottom of the cube. He pressed down the lever with his thumb, and rows of razor blades flashed out before retreating.

At least it wasn't a knife like at the Cit. Blaise licked his lips, then rolled up the sleeve on his left arm to bare his flesh. When he did so, the pink scar appeared, vivid even in the glow of the mage-lights that lit the interior. Slocum reached down, his other hand returning with a roll of bandages. He studied Blaise's scar but made no comment.

"I'll make the cut. You fill the vial with blood. Half, as we agreed," Slocum said, settling the scarificator on Blaise's tender forearm. He pressed the lever, and quick as lightning, the blades sliced into his skin. Slocum lifted the device away.

The sight of his own blood almost sent him back to the scarring memories. His teeth chattered as he struggled to keep it together. Blaise was aware of the heat of Jack's cloaked anger. Emmaline helped gather the required blood into the vial. She stoppered it, and then in a move that surprised everyone in the room, she put it in Blaise's uninjured hand, wrapping his fingers around it.

"*Your* bargaining chip," Emmaline said, her voice little more than a whisper in Blaise's ear. "*Your* choice."

My choice. With two small words, she had given him the power that the Golden Citadel had stripped away. Blaise tightened his grip, the vial warm in his hand as Emmaline bandaged the slashes on his forearm.

"That blood is mine," Slocum said, tone sharp.

Blaise shook his head. "Not yet. Only after you tell us what you know about my mother. And give me any information you have about a very specific mage." He heard Jack's surprised grunt at the addition.

Slocum narrowed his eyes. "You're demanding a lot for so little, Breaker."

Blaise glanced down at his fist. "You probably know this since you deal with information, but my beau is quite the entrepreneur. He's taught me a few things. Like supply and demand."

The proprietor hissed out a breath. "The Gannish are the absolute worst."

"Something we agree on," Jack said dryly.

Blaise ignored the barb. "What's it going to be? I'm happy to take this with me and toss it in a fire." At least he figured fire would destroy blood. Probably?

"The bargain is struck," Slocum said after a moment, though he clearly wasn't happy about it. He leaned against the improvised countertop. "If you give me the vial, I'll fulfill your requests."

Blaise uncurled his hand and offered the vial. The proprietor snatched it away as if it were a bag of diamonds. He swathed the precious vial in a nest of cotton, setting it in a lockbox. He leaned his bulk against the deteriorating wood planks again, as if it were an everyday occurrence to squirrel away the blood of a mage. Though, judging from Jack's earlier words, it probably was.

"Shame about Marian Hawthorne," Slocum began, giving his head a doleful shake. "Her loss will limit some of the sought-after potions I stock."

Blaise gritted his teeth, suddenly furious. "That alone should have been reason for you to tell me." His palms itched as his magic flared at his agitation.

Slocum gave him a cat that ate the canary smile. "Nah. I said *limited*, not cut off completely." He gave a lazy shrug. "I can charge more, so it's all the same to me. Supply and demand, you know."

"*The information*," Jack growled, as if he had forgotten that moments earlier, the building they stood in had been ready to attack them.

Blaise was with Jack in that. A dusting of magic played across his skin. He knew that if he looked down, his palms would have a silver sheen as his power manifested. Long ago, Slocum had warned him about those very hands.

Slocum's gaze flicked to Blaise's palms, aware of the unspoken threat. "Marian's wanted, and that's why she was taken."

"Wanted? As in dead or alive, like an outlaw?" Jack asked, the question piercing.

"Nah." Slocum shook his head. "Wanted in the same way you put something on a shopping list. She's lucrative. A brilliant Confederation alchemist out here? Yeah, people are gonna want her."

Blaise frowned, trying to think of why someone would want her. Then he realized he was looking at the situation too closely. He had grown up knowing what she was, though she hid under the guise of an apothecary. When he was a child, her alchemy had seemed commonplace. Unremarkable. Just a part of everyday life. But Slocum was right—Marian Hawthorne was gifted with her alchemy craft, and there were those who would want access to her. *Faedra knows, the Confederation probably wants her back.*

Slocum jerked a thumb at Blaise. "You're on shopping lists, too."

Blaise's gut twisted. "What?" His mouth went dry as more old fears rose.

"Why?" Jack demanded.

At the same time, Emmaline said, "No one's getting Blaise!"

The Black Market proprietor raised his eyebrows, as if surprised he had to explain why someone would want Blaise. "Why? Think about it. What band of outlaws *wouldn't* want a Breaker? Able to crack open any safe. Bust into any jail. Threaten to bring a building down around you." At that, he glanced at the ceiling overhead, as if he were acknowledging the fact that Blaise could do so to the Black Market if driven to it. "Lot of outlaws are mighty jealous of you and yours, Jack."

Blaise gritted his teeth. No time to take offense—he needed to stay focused. "What else do you know?"

Slocum aimed a finger at him. "*I* know *you* know the Copperheads are the ones behind it. 'Cause you're heading to Thorn.'" A smug look drifted across his lips at Jack's annoyed grunt. "But what you don't know is that the Copperheads have set themselves up a one-of-a-kind auction. Seems a certain alchemist is slated to be the main event, and the buyers are lining up."

"Who're the buyers?" Jack demanded.

Slocum shrugged. "I've told you what I know. Anything else I offer at this point would be a guess. And a guess, even from me, could be a lethal mistake."

Jack nodded. "Fair enough."

"Time's a-wasting, friends. You best be on your way," Slocum said, rising to his full height and picking up the lockbox.

"No." Blaise shook his head. "You still need to tell me about the mage."

The proprietor grimaced, clearly having hoped the information would distract Blaise to the point where he forgot. His shoulders hunched. "Ask."

"You don't have to tell me about your magic—I know we get touchy about that," Blaise began, "but I had a run-in with a Walker who could move through physical *walls*. You know anything about that?"

Slocum cocked his head, studying Blaise for a moment before nodding. "Wallwalker. Freaky offshoot of the Walkers. You're right—not gonna tell you if her power is related to mine. That's a mystery I'm not unveiling to you." He cradled the lockbox against his chest. "Goes by the name of the Herald. From the little I know, she's Gannish but not Saltie."

Blaise wondered if he should ask additional questions, but he didn't know what to ask. He glanced at Jack. The outlaw gave him an approving nod, so Blaise turned back to Slocum. "Thanks. We'll be on our way, then."

"Let's hit the trail," Jack said, motioning for Blaise and Emmaline to precede him to the door. No doubt wanting to guard their flank again.

"Nice doing business with you!" Slocum called in their wake.

CHAPTER TWENTY-ONE
Politics as Usual

Kittie

Kittie had thought coming to Ganland was the right thing to do, but she was having her doubts. Why had she ever thought this was a good idea, a way to find out how she was going to fit into this new world with her family? That this might be the way to find out who *she* was now?

In the past, whenever Kittie unraveled, she went for the one thing she knew would dull the pain and confusion. And now Mindy, that blasted well-meaning Hospitalier, was trying to keep her from it.

"Let me by," Kittie hissed, her voice low and full of warning. "All I need is one little drink."

"No," Mindy said, adamant as she shook her head, curly black hair snaking around her oval face. "That's not what you *need*."

Kittie had been on her way to hunt down one of the staffers with an order for them to bring her brandy. Wine. Whatever they had. Maybe everything they had. Kittie's flask had run dry, and unlike in the few towns they had stopped at on the way to Nera, she hadn't had a chance to leave Silver Sands to secretly refill it.

"How do you know what I need?" Kittie snapped. A part of her regretted the tone, knowing Mindy meant well. But a larger part of her needed a drink to get through their mission, and she wasn't about to let this buzzing gnat of a mage get in her way.

Mindy stood firm. "Because I'm a *Hospitalier*." Her yellow eyes —a rare color in anyone, even mages, Kittie knew—gleamed with determination. She took a step closer, dropping her voice to a whisper Kittie strained to hear. "I don't *just* know what food or drink will be best for you, or if it's spoiled or poisoned. My magic gives me an inkling of how the things you put in your body might harm you in the long term—"

"You're not the first to tell me to quit drinking," Kittie growled, crossing her arms. She didn't enjoy having this spat in public, so she stepped back into her room. Mindy followed. "But I'm fine. It's not a problem. I can handle it."

Mindy frowned. "You're lying to yourself, and you know it."

Kittie bristled. She hadn't said *you're lying to me*. No, because Mindy was right, damn it. She huffed out a breath, deflating. "I've been trying to stop. Or to cut down. I did, for a little while." Jack had insisted, which had been eye-opening considering he enjoyed a fair amount of alcohol, too. But he didn't *need* it, crave it, the way she did. *Jack*. She thought of him, and Kittie didn't know if she could see this thing that she'd agreed to through. It was so much harder than she'd thought.

The curvy Hospitalier smiled up at her, golden eyes bright. "That's good. That tells me right there you recognize you need to change." Mindy smoothed an errant lock of hair behind one ear. "You've got people back in Fortitude who're worried about you."

Kittie frowned. "Did Jack put you up to this?"

"No."

Kittie scowled, wondering who might have interfered if not Jack. Though maybe it wasn't interference—not really. She wanted to quit. Needed to quit, if she could. Kittie thought back to her contentious talk with Nadine. She hadn't asked for help, but the Healer had stuck her nose in, anyway. Probably because she was in the business of fixing people. Nadine had been certain that if she tried, she could succeed. *But you have to want this, Kittie. You can't half-ass it. Throw in an entire donkey train if you must.*

"I've tried," Kittie said after a moment. "I've done the things that were suggested. Get more sleep. Drink plenty of water. Focus on the good things in life." She made a scoffing sound. "All things people should do, anyway. None of it helps. I can't do this."

"Do you want to?" Mindy challenged.

Kittie opened her mouth to snap that of course she did, but it was a lie. She remembered her conversation with Jack, his disappointment that she didn't want this badly enough. Kittie shut her eyes, conflicted. How could she want something so much and not at all? "Yes and no. Maybe if I find something that works."

"*I* can help you, but you have to want it," Mindy said softly.

Kittie massaged her forehead. She really, really could use a drink, but unless she ran roughshod, that didn't seem to be in her future. "How?"

"Do you want to quit?" Mindy asked again, clearly unwilling to commit if Kittie didn't.

The Pyromancer sighed, scrubbing at her face with one hand. "Yes, damn it. I don't want to be this way. But how will what you do be any different?"

"Because I know what you need," Mindy said simply, leaning against the wall. "It's what I do."

"Okay, Hospitalier. What do I *need?*"

Mindy's face lit with a true grin. "I was hoping you'd ask." Her lips twisted, and her brow scrunched, thoughtful. "Caladrius root tea. I can ask if they have any here, and if not, there should be some in town. I saw Caladrius root growing in Ganland on the way here."

"*Tea*, ugh," Kittie groaned. "What did I do to deserve this? Will it help?"

Mindy laughed. "It won't be only tea, at least not to start. I'll mix it with whiskey."

Kittie shot Mindy an incredulous look, certain she'd misheard. "Wait. How's that going to help? I mean, I like the idea, so I don't want to complain, but..."

The Hospitalier smiled. "It's going to be a slow but steady process to wean you from alcohol and onto something not as likely to kill you. Tea is a good replacement—or at least, better than other alternatives."

Kittie pursed her lips. "I've never been much of a tea drinker."

"You'll like it, I promise. The hot water will make the Caladrius root taste sweet. And the whiskey...well, you're familiar with that." She rubbed her hands together in anticipation. "And Caladrius root will do wonders to give you a clear mind for the meeting with Madame Boss Clayton and the Board later."

Kittie sighed. "I hope you're right."

KITTIE RELAXED AGAINST THE CUSHIONED CHAIR. SHE HAD TO ADMIT Mindy was right—the Hospitalier had brought her a cup of Caladrius root tea (with the promised addition of whiskey), and it had done wonders for her constitution. She had more clarity and was less agitated, able to focus on the matters at hand.

Kittie glanced across the table at Jefferson. He was in his element. She knew, thanks to Jack, that the entrepreneur really was the best choice to come along with them. He had lived another life as a Doyen and had rejected that identity. The details behind that were unclear to her, but Jack seemed to trust him (even if he liked to pretend otherwise), and that made Kittie feel as if she, too, could trust him.

Jefferson leaned forward in his seat, the gleam in his eyes reminding her of someone preparing for a fight. *You can take the politician out of politics, but you can't take the politics out of the politi-*

cian. No matter what had forced him to shed his Doyen position, he was eager for this current opportunity.

Madame Boss Clayton sat at the end of the table. Jefferson and Kittie sat to the Boss's right while the five members of Ganland's Board sat to her left. From what Kittie understood, each Board member hailed from a different region in Ganland, appointed by their local leaders. The Board, in turn, appointed the Boss.

And that last bit? It wasn't good news for them, since it meant they could also unseat the Madame Boss, if they saw fit and had a majority in agreement. It seemed some of the Board members were dead set against anything to do with the Gutter, as Jefferson had found out from Doyen Thatcher.

"You're going to provoke the Confederation if you do this," a silver-haired woman protested, shaking her finger at the Madame Boss. She was Sylvia Westerfield. Kittie had spoken with her at dinner and had found the woman incredibly patronizing.

A man with a squat face that reminded Kittie of a hog nodded agreement—Bartholomew Tate. "I've heard talk of Phinora putting a hefty tariff on our goods. We—"

"You pass that on to the Phinoran buyers, then," Rachel interjected before Bartholomew finished his thought. "Don't act as if we haven't done that before when one nation or another sought to strong-arm us."

"But then they'll buy from someone else," Bartholomew grumped. "We'll be too costly."

Jefferson was nearly salivating at the discussion. This, Kittie saw, was a topic he enjoyed. "Then pivot. Sell them goods they can't get from anyone else. Or go to another market." He leaned over the table, more animated than Kittie had seen him the entire trip. "More and more families are moving to the Gutter each day. People who will need goods."

Rachel nodded and was about to speak when Sylvia jabbed a bony finger into the table. "But that's part of the problem right there. Do you not see?" Her finger bent at an angle that made

Kittie cringe, but the woman paid it no heed. "The people going to the Gutter are *mages*."

Kittie didn't like the way the old woman spoke. She said it as if it were an epithet. *And here Ganland is the country most favorable toward mages.* "Excuse me? What is the issue with *mages?*" Kittie kept her tone calm, though she wanted to show her outrage at the veiled insult. Her *child*—the people she cared about—would not be slighted.

Sylvia's eyes drifted to her. "The issue is that the Confederation *needs* mages, sweetie." The woman spoke with such condescension, Kittie almost imagined she was getting a swat, like a sticky-fingered child accused of stealing from the candy jar. "Even as we speak, the Confederation is devising ways to keep the mavericks from leaving."

What? Alarm shot through Kittie, and judging by the way Jefferson sat up straighter, he was surprised by this, too.

"Mages—mavericks—are *people*. Not wild horses to be brought in and tamed." Jefferson squared his shoulders as he spoke his heated words. He was no longer entertained by the conversation. "The Confederation has no right to detain them."

A handsome young man who reminded Kittie of a swan shook his head at that. Marcus Funk appeared to be similar in age to Jefferson. "But that's just it. The law of the land still states that mages are not equal to normal humans. Regardless of the dog and pony show that happened with the Breaker."

At mention of Blaise, Jefferson went tight-lipped, his green eyes smoldering coals. Rachel scowled at the trio of Board members, though her eyes darted briefly to the pair who had made no objections yet. She leaned forward as she spoke. "Ganland has always prided itself on being the most hospitable nation in the Salt-Iron Confederation for mages."

Kittie somehow reined in the laugh that threatened to tear from her mouth at that. This wasn't *hospitable*.

"We won't be party to keeping any mages who wish from traveling freely to the Gutter or elsewhere," Rachel declared.

"Even if the Salt-Iron Council issues a decree?" Bartholomew asked. "They're meeting on this very topic when they reconvene."

Kittie hated all this back and forth and posturing. The veiled threats. The derision and condescension. Time to do something about that. "We will, of course, understand if Ganland isn't forward-thinking enough to ally with the Gutter. It takes courage and savvy to do something like that, and, well..." Kittie allowed her words to trail off as she glanced around the table. Was she taking an enormous risk by insulting the lot of them? Probably. But she was *over* being treated as if she weren't equal because she was a mage. Confederation law didn't make that true.

Sylvia's eyes bulged, and Bartholomew's piggy mouth dropped open. Marcus's graceful neck snapped around as he stared at her. Jefferson was smiling, the look on his face that of a cat about to pounce. He seemed to approve of her tactic.

"You make an excellent point, Firebrand Dewitt." When Jefferson spoke, he made her title the honorific it was meant to be. Something to put her on the same level as the Board members. Kittie rather enjoyed it. "That is exactly the sort of gamble I took when I invested in Rainbow Flat, and...well, we've seen how profitable *that* was."

He made no mention that even now, he was investing in Fortitude, all because his beau called it home. Kittie liked that, since she would do the same if she had the resources. But she only had her voice, her mind, and her fierce love. That had to be enough, and she had to use them to help. "And Rainbow Flat will be a part of the new nation. Asylum, too. That would be a boon for trade, would it not?" Kittie didn't know shit about trade, but these people seemed to like it. It felt like the right thing to say.

Jefferson grinned, steepling his fingers before him. Rachel watched him expectantly, as if hoping he would do her job for her. Madame Boss Clayton had an economy of speech and seemed to enjoy seeing others nudge themselves closer to the things she wanted. Perhaps, Kittie reflected, she knew enough of Jefferson to trust him here.

"Not only that." Jefferson's voice was soft, almost seductive. The Board members around the table unconsciously leaned closer to hear what he was about to say. The would-be Ambassador took his time, making certain he had their full attention. "Think of how long the average cargo ship takes to travel from Nera to Thorn. I'm not speaking of a sleek passenger steamer—no, I speak of the lumbering cargo ships. How long?"

"Months," Marcus supplied, though the way his brows slashed down proved he was uncertain where Jefferson was going with this.

"What if," Jefferson began, walking his index and middle fingers across the table as if they were a person, "we could establish an overland trade route?"

"We have those, and the outlaws—" Bartholomew started, then cut himself off as understanding dawned on him. "*Oh.*"

Jefferson smiled, tapping his fingers against the table again. He said nothing. Anything more was unnecessary.

It was brilliant. Kittie had known about the idea, but the way he delivered it was better than anything she could have done. She was no longer the orator she had been in her youth, and she lacked Jefferson's acuity. He'd done his job, and now it was her turn. She pasted on a smile to match Jefferson's. "The Gutter outlaws would have no reason to attack an ally's convoy. And in fact..." She lifted a hand, snapping her fingers. A tongue of flame bloomed to life in her palm, and the gathering of Board members gasped. Rachel's Bossguard went on alert, though they remained in their positions when the Madame Boss gave them a shake of her head.

"Our mage *allies* could help protect the trade route from the dangers of the Untamed Territory," Rachel said. She gestured to Kittie and the fireball dancing in her palm. "As you can see, they have unique skills that a *normal* human lacks."

For a *normal* human, Kittie was beginning to really, really like Rachel Clayton. The Board members were staring, their faces a mix of fear and wonder.

"Is this a threat?" Sylvia asked.

Should it be? Jack would have asked that without hesitation—and a damn good thing she was here and not her husband. *I have tact.* Kittie closed her hand, extinguishing the flame so effectively that not even a wisp of smoke escaped. "No, it's a demonstration. The mages of the Gutter are not lightweights. Do not make the mistake of underestimating us." Okay, maybe that was a little bit of a threat. Unintentional, though.

Rachel smiled. "Thank you for the input, Firebrand Dewitt. Board members, thank you for joining us. As it seems we're only going round in circles, I see fit to table our discussion for the time being so that you might think on it."

The quintet of Board members exchanged glances. It was clear they didn't want to be dismissed, but they were following some protocol Kittie wasn't aware of. They filed out, leaving Boss Clayton alone with the delegation. Once the door closed behind the last Board member, Rachel sank back in her chair.

"That was exhausting. But you made a good show of it," she told them with an approving nod.

"Exhausting for you? We did all the heavy lifting," Jefferson replied with a chuckle, though he seemed in a better mood than when the Board had been ready to disparage Blaise. He turned to Kittie, his face animated again. "We hadn't even planned most of that, but you did an excellent job. You're a natural."

I'm definitely not a natural. She gave a weak smile. "I did what I could."

Jefferson's gaze slid back to Rachel. "Do you think we have a chance?"

The Madame Boss grinned. "When you mention safe transcontinental trade routes, there's always a chance."

CHAPTER TWENTY-TWO
More Than a Breaker

Jack

With the information provided by Tom Slocum, Jack, Blaise, and Emmaline plowed onward. Based on Jack's recollection, the Black Market had been just north of the rough-and-tumble town named Starvation. Their best bet was to cross the Untamed River to the town of Uncertain, and from there, make their final trek to Thorn.

Either the Copperheads had decided not to waste their magic on stymieing their pursuit, or they no longer had a need. Jack didn't like it one bit after their conversation with the Black Market proprietor. "They knew exactly what they were getting when they took your mother. And they had to know you wouldn't twiddle your thumbs," he remarked as they gathered their things after stopping for lunch.

Blaise frowned. "How would they know that?"

Jack snorted to himself, wondering just how *dense* the Breaker truly was.

Emmaline gave Blaise a disbelieving look. "You don't know yourself very well sometimes, do you? Word got out that you only took down Fort Courage to save your friends who were there. To save *me*."

"Oh." Blaise blinked as he took in her words. He rubbed the back of his neck, as if he hadn't equated that with heroics. And to be fair, Jack understood his confusion. Jack wasn't much of a hero, either, but he'd tear down the walls of Perdition to keep the people he cared about safe.

The problem was, folks like the Confederation or the Copperheads would use that drive against someone like Blaise. Or Jack. The more he chewed over the idea, the more certain he was that the Copperheads knew who was on their heels. The grasscats had been a test. Anyone else would have given up. Or died. Now their enemies could bide their time, planning an ambush.

That was something to think about later, though. "We gotta get moving," Jack announced, shooting a look over his shoulder. To the northwest, a wall of thunderheads had built up, the deep blue-grey clouds laced with intermittent lightning. Already, the wind was picking up.

<We can't fly in that,> Zepheus announced, nostrils flared as he drank in the wind.

"Is the wind too dangerous?" Blaise asked.

<Not only the wind, but the lightning,> the palomino answered, pawing at the ground impatiently. <Jack is right, and we must make up as much distance as we can. Perhaps find shelter.>

"Time to stop our jawing and get," Jack agreed. He shoved a foot into the stirrup and swung into the saddle. As soon as his bottom hit the leather, Zepheus surged forward.

"Coming!" Emmaline called, following suit with Oberidon. The spotted pegasus leaped after Zepheus.

<Emrys will not be as fast,> Zepheus observed, one ear pricked back to keep tabs on the other pegasi.

Yeah, Jack knew it. The black stallion wasn't built for speed, even if his rider was more competent now than in the past. "Let them keep pace, but we have to find shelter if we can."

Jack and Zepheus had flown through storms before, but only under duress. As an Effigest, he'd figured out a way around the threat of lightning for himself using a lightning rod spell, but it was harder to duplicate the effort for a creature the size of a pegasus. Maybe something to dabble with in the future, but not now with so many to protect. Never mind that the gusty crosswinds would prove perilous to their passage, too.

Jack glanced back over his shoulder. Oberidon was keeping pace, the spotted stallion snorting with every stride. Emrys was lagging, as expected, but doing his best. He refocused his gaze on the horizon, searching for any sign of shelter. Nothing was visible, aside from a few trees that would only serve as a danger with the lightning.

Then he saw something: a dip in the terrain to the west. Jack tapped Zepheus's neck. "That way!" The palomino angled his head to see where he was pointing, then adjusted his course.

The arroyo Jack had spotted wasn't much. Zepheus slowed as they approached, the outlaw peering down at its depths. In the weather that was coming, the wash would be as much a hazard as a haven. Oberidon jogged up, Emmaline scrambling down from the saddle to see what her father was looking at. Emrys arrived a moment later, lathering between his forelegs from the effort.

"We'll be lower than the rest of the land down there, less likely to be struck by lightning," Jack said, pointing to the dry bed of the arroyo.

Emmaline bit her lip. "But that was formed by flash floods." Her gaze flicked to the growing storm. "Kinda like that."

"Yeah, we're damned if we do and damned if we don't," Jack agreed. "We don't have a lot of time to figure something else out."

Blaise slipped down from the saddle, walking over. He was quiet for a moment, though Jack judged by the look on his face that he was thinking of something.

"If something's brewing in that skull of yours, this is the time to speak," Jack said.

The Breaker looked uncomfortable. "If the flash flood is the bigger concern, I could probably stop it. Or at least slow it."

Jack raised his brows. "*How?*"

Blaise pointed to the sides of the arroyo. "The soil here is dry and hard-packed. I can use my magic to break it into big chunks. Maybe big enough to form a dam to slow the water."

"That's actually not a half-bad idea," Jack mused. Sometimes Blaise was full of surprises, like with that fancy shield of his. "But the flooding is only part of the concern. We won't care about drowning or being washed away if we're struck dead by lightning. But I'm hoping being low in the arroyo will at least offer a little protection."

"I have an idea," Emmaline piped up, though she sounded hesitant. As if she worried that whatever she was about to suggest would be dismissed. Which, Jack realized, he had done before. He gestured for her to go ahead. "Remember when you were teaching me Rising Dread?"

Jack lifted his brows, curious why she was thinking of that spell at a time like this. "Yeah?"

She gained more confidence at his question. "You made a perimeter with it, and the working affects everyone inside." Jack nodded, wondering where she was going with this. "And I was thinking about the wards around Bitter End when I found Mom..." Emmaline paused, brow furrowed with thought.

Jack cocked his head. "A Warder does those." He made it a statement, not a contradiction.

Zepheus snorted nearby, glancing at the darkening sky. <I estimate we have twenty minutes before the leading edge overtakes us.>

Yeah, yeah. Jack gestured to let the stallion know he'd heard.

"Maybe we place a similar perimeter around us. I know you have the effigies in your bag." Emmaline started again, gaining momentum with each word, her eyes bright. "But we alter the spell. Could we make it *protect* what's inside?"

Jack snapped his fingers, thinking of his own lightning rod spell. "Maybe not protect, but divert." Yeah, the more he thought about it, the more he liked it. His previous iteration required affixing the spell to each individual poppet. This would cover a generalized area. He turned and stabbed a finger at Blaise. "Get to work on that dam. We'll set up about a quarter-mile away to give you some wiggle room."

He half-expected the Breaker to look flustered or afraid, but he seemed composed. As if having a purpose, a way to help, was all he needed. Blaise nodded, stepping away from the pegasi and crouching down, laying his palms against the ground.

"C'mon, we'll let him do his thing," Jack told Emmaline, climbing back into the saddle. Easier to fly down to the dry bed than to slide down the steep sides.

They dismounted again when they reached the bottom. Jack moved around to Zepheus's side, pulling an effigy from his saddlebag. He hefted it in his hand, going through the mental calculations. As with cooking, a good Ritualist could make substitutions and tweaks to a spell on the fly to produce something effective and new. The skill in doing so was what set a talented Ritualist apart from others. It had been a gift that made Jack lucrative to the Salties back in the day.

"How do you think we build this?" he asked his daughter.

Emmaline's eyes widened for an instant. Then she nodded with determination. "Um, well, I was thinking about what you told me for the Rising Dread. Set a perimeter of effigies, linking them together. Enhance them with something to protect us or divert the lightning."

"But what?" Jack prodded.

She swallowed as she thought about it. Jack hoped she came to a conclusion quickly. An outlaw mage had to think on the fly to survive.

"Hematite," Emmaline said after a moment. Then her face fell. "But I don't have any."

"I do," Jack replied with a grin, pleased by her answer. He gave a meaningful pat to the pouch attached to his belt, then dug a hand inside until he found the familiar lump of hematite.

Emmaline frowned at the single piece. "Will that be enough?"

"Gonna have to be," Jack said with a shrug. He'd done more with less. "I'm more concerned about the power drain that this working is gonna be on us."

"Oh?" she asked, hazarding a glance at the foreboding clouds. They both jumped as they heard a tremendous rumble.

For an instant, Jack thought lightning had struck nearby, which would force their hand. But he turned and saw a rising cloud of dust further up the arroyo. Blaise stood at the top of the ridge, Emrys beside him, peering down at the makeshift avalanche. Large chunks of soil had broken free to land in a jumble, partially clogging the wash. Jack feared for a moment that Blaise might think it was enough, but the young man climbed onto his pegasus, and together, they flew to the other side.

Content that Blaise had a handle on things, Jack returned to their spellwork. "Yeah, if we can get the hematite to hold, the rest of it is going to be on us to keep the casting up. That's going to depend on the amount of storm we have to hold off."

Emmaline blew out a breath. "We don't have any choice, do we?"

Jack shook his head. "Nope. And we need to get these effigies placed. That squall ain't gonna wait for us to make plans."

The younger Effigest idly rubbed at her cheek, smearing dirt across it. "We should place the effigies at the cardinal directions. The power drain will be relative to the size of the perimeter, right?" At Jack's nod, she grew bolder with her ideas. "And keep it as small as we can. Maybe ten paces apart, with the pegasi in the middle."

"Sounds solid," Jack affirmed, pride surging. Emmaline was

going to be a top-shelf mage at this rate. A pattering of fat rain-drops began to fall, heralding the coming storm. There was another dull rumble as Blaise dropped more chunks of earth into the arroyo. They were short on time, so Jack took the lead. "You go ahead and place the effigies at north and east. I'll get south and west." He tossed the pair to her, and she moved with determination, counting out the paces.

As Jack and Emmaline worked, Blaise and Emrys joined them. In his peripheral vision, Jack saw the Breaker free their yellow rain slickers from their gear, preparing for the storm.

"Mine are in place. Should I activate them now?" Emmaline called, hesitation in her voice.

"Do it," Jack agreed, doing the same to his. He felt the jolt of his magic racing between his paired effigies. "Then you need to come activate mine, and I'll do the same to yours."

"Can we do that?" Emmaline asked, surprised. "They're already active."

"Layers twine together," Jack said tersely. He didn't have time to explain, not now. He hadn't gotten to the point of teaching her this bit of spellwork, but there was no better teacher than experience.

The air rippled around them as lightning flashed a handful of miles away, followed by a tremendous clap of thunder. The pegasi clustered together in the middle of the effigies, snorting. <Hurry it up,> Zepheus urged.

"Working on it," Jack muttered. "Spell ain't gonna do shit if we get it wrong." He looked at Emmaline. "Key the hematite to the effigies, then go bury it a good distance outside of our barrier."

She nodded, expression grim as she bent down to attune the small stone. If the Effigest had been anyone else, Jack wouldn't have trusted them with the task. Done incorrectly, they were probably going to die. Emmaline finished, then jogged a distance away, hurriedly reaching down to sink the hematite into the dirt before joining them again.

"Now, what do we do?" Emmaline asked, slipping up beside him.

Pray to Faedra that this works. "Pour everything we have into it and hope we can hold off the fury of a storm."

As if summoned by his words, the wind picked up, sudden rainfall battering them. Jack shrugged into his slicker, crouching down beneath Zepheus's neck. The pegasus spread a wing to shelter him from some of the rain but had to tuck it back in when hail began to fall.

"Ouch," Jack heard Blaise grumble as a hailstone the size of a golden eagle coin struck his head, no doubt smarting even with his hat. "I guess whatever you're doing doesn't help with hail?"

"'Course not," Jack snapped. "We're protecting against lightning. What else do you need? Want me to crochet you a fancy doily while I'm at it?" Yeah, maybe it was unfair to take his frustrations out on the Breaker, but he was already feeling the effects of the spell as it chewed through his reserves. Extreme magic drain always made him grumpy.

"I'd like to not get a head injury from a piece of ice the size of my fist," Blaise said, irritation in his voice as a huge chunk of hail struck the ground beside him.

Maybe he had a point—that could take any of them out, or seriously injure the pegasi. Jack hadn't accounted for hail, and that only further annoyed him. "Can *you* do something about it?" Jack grumbled, thinking maybe Blaise would make another one of his fancy shields that broke anything that touched it.

"Maybe." He heard Blaise shift positions. They were cramped within the confines of the spell. "Can I piggyback onto whatever y'all are doing?"

"Sure, why not?" Emmaline said.

"What? No!" Jack growled, but it was too late. He felt the shift as Breaker magic joined the twined forces of Effigest power.

Jack thought for certain that was going to be it for them—that Blaise's destructive magic would chew through their fragile spell, sundering it and leaving them vulnerable to the lightning. But to his great surprise, he recognized the Breaker magic was braiding itself into their working. His breath caught. He wanted to demand to know what Blaise was doing and how he'd learned to do that. And if it would work.

But Jack didn't have such luxuries. They were in the teeth of the storm now, lightning illuminating the dark ribbons of rain around them. Whatever Blaise had done helped with their hail problem—rain got through to them, but in between the nearly deafening peals of thunder, he heard a strange crunching sound that he could only assume was the hail disintegrating. Rain plastered their slickers against them, and Jack hoped that the earthen dam Blaise had created would hold.

Beneath Oberidon's arched neck, Emmaline groaned. "I don't know how much longer I can keep this up."

Yeah, he wondered the same for himself. Their spell was working—lightning danced around them but always diverted to the place where she had buried the hematite. Their exhaustion was in direct relation to the amount of lightning they deflected with the working. Jack opened his mouth to make a response when something new flowed into their spell.

Power. Magic in its purest form, not yet flavored with a type like Breaker or Effigest.

"Take it!" Blaise called.

The Breaker was a continuous surprise. How was he able to share his reserves with them? Ritualists and Effigests could bolster others, but Jack had never heard of any other sort of mage doing so. *I've got questions for you if we survive this.*

Jack felt Emmaline's part of the working grow stronger, no longer threatening to buckle from the strain. In fact, Jack himself felt empowered by the flow of magic. Unstoppable, like a freight train with no brakes barreling down an incline. As if their strange combination of magics were capable of anything. It was a heady feeling, almost seductive. Jack reveled in the sensation.

He lost track of how long they held off the storm. By the time the gusts calmed, and clear blue sky opened overhead, the feeling of immense power had waned. He felt like a husk. Puddles formed around their boots. Rivulets flowed past them, streams of water breeching the dam but not sundering it. The dam held, but for how long? Jack panted for breath, shaking off the paralyzing exhaustion.

"Up. Up to the ridge," he ground out, getting into the saddle. The wet leather squeaked beneath him. Emmaline shook her head, gathering her strength to mount. But it was clear she was too tired, and Oberidon knelt to help her aboard.

Moments later, they were all on the ridge. Jack had a better look at Blaise's dam. Dark water churned behind its confines, pressure building. It wouldn't hold forever, but it had done its job. And Blaise...

Jack whirled to face the Breaker. "What was *that*?"

Blaise leaned hard against Emrys's rain-slicked neck, catching his breath. "Maybe start with, 'Gee, thanks, Blaise, that was really helpful. Now can you tell us what you did because we're curious?'"

Jack snorted. "That's not how I'd say *any* of that."

Blaise sighed. "I know." He struggled upright, rubbing the side of his face. "Can we make camp here? I'm tired."

Jack pursed his lips but nodded. They were all too wrung out to go further. Emmaline was much too quiet, her face pale. She needed rest. Jack dismounted, though he aimed a forefinger at Blaise when the Breaker did likewise. "You're dodging the question."

Blaise took off his hat, shaking out his soggy hair. Curls matted against his forehead. "Look, I only did it because...because I didn't want us to die, okay?"

There was a hint of fear in the young man's blue eyes. "What are you so afraid of?" Jack asked. It was odd, since the formerly skittish Breaker had grown bolder recently. Emmaline shook off her fatigue, moving closer to listen with arms crossed. Oberidon stayed close beside her, helping her remain upright.

Blaise glanced away. "I don't want people to know that...that I can do these things with my magic. It's already bad enough that I'm unique." He licked his lips. "I imagine it would only be worse if they know all of what I can do."

Jack scowled, not understanding. "You ever think that if people know what you can do that they may think twice before crossing you?" But no, of course, the soft-hearted baker wouldn't have such a thought.

Blaise ducked his head. "I have, actually. But I don't want to *be* like that."

"You can be powerful and still kind, you know," Emmaline commented, coming up alongside Blaise. "You don't have to be only one or the other."

Yeah, Emmaline hit the target. That was the problem. Blaise equated flaunting power—his magic—with force. With bullies. Sometimes, it seemed like he'd overcome that, and then others... well, this was a prime example.

Blaise closed his eyes for a moment. "I feel like I can't be both, though. Like when I find the outlaws who took my mother. Who..." His eyes flashed open, and his voice wavered as he said, "Who killed my father. I *can't* be kind then. I *have* to be hard. Powerful. Vengeful."

"Justice and vengeance aren't the same thing at all," Jack pointed out. "And you don't have to change who you are. Yeah, you may need to be hard as steel when we go up against the Copperheads. But then you'll be toe to toe with bloodthirsty desperadoes, not a bunch of mewling kittens. Don't think you have to show them an ounce of kindness, 'cause they would *never* show you the same."

Blaise sighed, rubbing his hands together. "Okay, I guess you're right." He licked his lips. "I'll tell you what I did during the storm."

"Yeah, you better," Jack grumbled, failing to hide his curiosity.

"The first part, where I added my magic to your spell? That was something I had time to think about when I was..." He swallowed. "When I was in the Cit. When I took down the *Retribution*, there were a bunch of protective spells, all woven together. I don't know who cast them—if it was a single Warder or maybe a group. The part that stuck with me was they were different, but they worked together."

"So you thought you could do the same thing," Jack marveled. It had been an audacious idea, one that could have failed spectacularly. Only it hadn't. That took natural aptitude, something he hadn't thought Blaise possessed for magic. *I was wrong.*

"Yeah," Blaise agreed softly. "As for the other...well, I knew I could lend power." Discomfort crossed his face again. "I learned that when Jefferson and Flora saved me. If I hadn't given some to Jefferson, I would have had too much."

Jack nodded. He recalled that—the potion had overwhelmed Blaise's personal reserve, threatening to shatter him and everything around him if he hadn't bled some off. So he'd siphoned some away to the peacock, and it had worked. Whatever that was about, Blaise had done it effortlessly. Without hesitation, as if it just came naturally.

If they ever caught up to Marian Hawthorne, Jack had questions for her, too. Had she made Blaise into *more* than just a Breaker?

CHAPTER TWENTY-THREE

Plans Are for Outlaws Who've Slept

Blaise

"That wasn't them, was it?" Blaise asked as they lay on their soggy bedrolls, staring up at the clear sky overhead. The sun had set, and the stars were brilliant, though the moon hadn't yet risen.

"The Copperheads?" Jack asked. He kept his voice soft. Emmaline was asleep, worn out from her magical exertion. She had crawled into her bedroll not long after they'd shared a scanty meal of jerky and dried fruit.

"Yeah. Did they summon that storm?"

"Nah," the outlaw answered. "They have a Weathermage, but a storm that size? That's only nature, and it happens this time of year in the Untamed Territory. We're lucky there weren't any tornadoes."

"The hail was bad enough," Blaise agreed, reaching up to rub a tender spot on his crown.

Jack grunted as he stretched. "Yeah. That spell you did, though? That was damned gritty of you. Didn't know you had it in you."

"Are you complimenting me?" Blaise asked, edging up to lean on one elbow so he could see the outlaw's profile better.

"Maybe."

Blaise grinned, and he felt more confident than he had when he'd made the choice to go all-in during the height of the storm. "Thanks." Then his thoughts turned to their purpose. "What are we going to do now?"

"Sleep," Jack said. "The pegasi said they have the watch, so that's what we're supposed to be doing. Really should shut your piehole."

There's the Jack I know. "I mean tomorrow."

"Same plan. Head to Uncertain, resupply, and get any new gossip we can before continuing to Thorn."

"Going to Thorn will be dangerous, won't it?" Blaise asked.

Jack sighed, as if he didn't want to have this discussion now. He probably didn't. But Blaise was too wound up to sleep. "Like whacking a beehive with a stick while covered in honey? Something like that."

"Do you have a plan?"

"Plans are for outlaws who've slept after draining themselves during a damned squall."

Blaise sighed, deciding to let the testy Effigest sleep. He hadn't fully exerted his magic, despite all he'd done. He closed his eyes, dreading what awaited him in slumber. With Jefferson no longer shepherding his sleep, the nightmares had returned.

A dark shape loomed over him. Emrys. <I am not Jefferson, but I am here if you need me.>

Blaise breathed out a soft breath, reaching up to stroke the pegasus's lowered head. Emrys's presence made him smile. He much preferred a stallion in the night to a nightmare.

UNCERTAIN WAS A FAR CRY FROM EITHER FORTITUDE OR RAINBOW Flat. It seemed to be in a location that would make it prosperous —the Untamed River rumbled in a blue ribbon just southwest of the town. Blaise was surprised that he didn't see docks or boats, as had been common in Rainbow Flat. As their pegasi landed on the edge of town, unchallenged by any sort of sentries, Blaise asked Jack about it.

Amusement glinted in the outlaw's eyes. He jerked a thumb toward the river. "This deep in the Untamed Territory, the local wildlife ain't gonna let a man put a boat in the river uncontested."

That caught Emmaline's attention, too. "But Rainbow Flat is in the Untamed Territory, and they have shipping."

Jack waved a hand. "Any critters in the Tombstone River are more placid than what's here." He held up a hand, ticking off fingers. "You got kelpies, globsters, river serpents, bunyips. People learned real quick that the water 'round here is dangerous."

"I don't know what any of those are, but I'm going to take your word for it," Blaise said.

Emmaline shaded her eyes. "Not even a bridge."

Jack shook his head as Zepheus trotted toward the town. "Nope. Globsters like to attach to 'em and break 'em down. There're a couple of spots where you can ford the river if there's not been heavy rain. Water's too shallow for most of those critters." He grinned. "Made ripe pickings for an outlaw."

No one paid them any heed as they rode into town. Uncertain was almost a ghost town. The buildings seemed to be on their last legs, the paint faded. Some of them had clearly never seen a coat of paint. Honest-to-goodness tumbleweeds rolled down the dusty street. Their pegasi halted outside a small building where Blaise could barely make out the words *Post Office* painted over the door. The elements had scoured away much of the lettering, so it looked like *ost Of ce*. The emblem of an equally faded rampant griffin clutching a letter in its talons, the symbol of mail delivery, was the best clue among the dubious signage.

"Hank travels all this way?" Blaise asked as they dismounted.

"He can go as far east as Thorn, though I imagine that route will get more scarce," Jack said, running a hand along Zepheus's glossy neck. "Only does it once a week or so."

Jack shoved open the door to the post office. Blaise and Emmaline followed him in. They watched as the Effigest made inquiries at the counter, only to discover there was nothing awaiting him. *What's he looking for? A letter from Kittie, maybe?*

Thinking of Kittie led him to thinking of Jefferson. Gods, he missed him. If someone had told him a year ago that he would pine after the egotistical Jefferson Cole, he would have laughed. Yet here he was.

Blaise ran a hand through his hair. They might—no, *would*—be going into a dangerous situation. *What if I don't make it back?* He swallowed the lump that formed in his throat. Blaise knew he shouldn't borrow trouble. But Jefferson didn't know any of what had befallen him. He could send a letter but...Blaise shook his head, dismissing the idea. This was too big, *too much* for a letter, and his predicament would only alarm Jefferson and distract him from his task.

They left the post office, though Blaise was still chewing through different thoughts. "Walkers just get to go willy-nilly into Confederation lands?"

"Walkers are hard to stop if they want to go some place," Jack answered. "Long as they don't get a bullet in 'em or salt-iron on their wrists, they can get away. So mostly the Confederation turns a blind eye to 'em." He shrugged. "And besides, many a Walker provides the same service for the Confederation. Far be it from them to shoot themselves in the foot for something of benefit."

Like the Wallwalker? Blaise didn't want to mention the Herald aloud, fearing that to do so might invite her presence.

They accompanied the pegasi to the town's livery stable. It was downright sad compared to any other stable Blaise had seen, but at least it would be a roof over their equines' heads for the night.

There were no grooms other than the gruff stable owner who took more of their coin for the stalls, so they each untacked their pegasi, groomed them, and made sure they had fresh water, clean straw, and a bucket of sweet feed.

That task done, Jack led the way to Uncertain's only diner. The food was palatable, but Blaise was of the opinion that dried buffalo chips might have better flavor. Still, it was food in his empty belly, and he was in no position to complain.

Uncertain's single redeeming feature was the bathhouse. Jack paid for a room—singular, they would have to bunk together—and then they made their way to the baths. Jack and Emmaline made efficient use of their time, but Blaise was in no rush. His sore muscles demanded a good soak after the grueling days of travel.

By the time Blaise climbed out of the tub, the water was cold, and he wished he could have his clothing washed. But there wasn't time for that, so he pulled on his clothes and boots and walked the short distance to Uncertain's sorry excuse for a hotel.

Jack and Emmaline were already in the shared room, though their damp hair was proof they'd only recently come in from the bathhouse, too. Father and daughter were sitting on the bed, and it was obvious they had been discussing something.

Jack pointed to the rickety chair in the corner. "Have a seat. We're making plans."

"About time," Blaise said and dragged the chair over. He hoped it would support his weight. A tendril of his magic told him how brittle the wood was. In fact, that made him decide against it. He pushed it back in the corner and sat cross-legged on the floor. Jack's eyebrows shot up. "It's about to break," Blaise explained.

"You can sense that?" Jack asked.

"Yeah."

The Effigest digested that, probably filing it away as more Breaker trivia for later. Then Jack went back to the matter at hand. "While I soaked, I had time to think. We know that not only was your mother wanted, Blaise, but so are *you*."

Blaise sighed, rubbing his chin. Briefly, he wondered if he could shave before they left Uncertain. He didn't like when his beard went untended for too long. "Yeah, I'm aware." Nothing new about that, unfortunately.

"I'm thinking that you and Emmaline don't go into Thorn," Jack began, then held up a hand when Blaise opened his mouth to interject. "Not *immediately*. Let me go in, do some snooping around, see what I can learn. There's an abandoned homestead ten miles outside of town. Should be safe enough for you both to hunker down there."

Emmaline's lips pressed together in an unhappy line. She didn't want to be left behind, either. "Won't it be dangerous for you alone?"

The outlaw hesitated before answering. "Alone, I can go in and keep my head down. Try not to attract attention while I get the lay of the land and dig for information. And besides, one of the engineers for our wind-pump is in Thorn. If nothing else, I can use calling on Creagen as a front." He shifted on the bed. "As long as I don't give 'em reason to pay attention to me, I should be fine."

Somehow, Blaise doubted that was possible. Jack was often quick to take offense, and he didn't back down easily. "Are you saying you'll behave yourself?"

Jack hissed out an offended breath. "I know what I'm about, Breaker. I've been doing things like this since you were in diapers."

Blaise nodded. It wasn't as if he had a better plan. At best, his only idea was to blunder into the town and somehow find his mother and free her. Not much of a plan in the grand scheme of things.

The outlaw yawned. "Anyway, time to hit the hay. Gonna be an early start tomorrow." He rose from the bed, crossing to pick up his bedroll. He unfurled it across the floor and settled down on it.

"Blaise, you want the bed?" Emmaline asked. She patted the mattress, which was about as thin as a pancake and nowhere near as soft.

He shook his head. "All yours. My bedroll dried finally, so the floor will work." He picked up his bedroll and situated it beside the wall. Although the room only had one bed, the hosteler had provided them with additional pillows. That was better than nothing. The pillow smelled funny, like it had never seen a bit of soap or water during the entirety of its existence, but Blaise was so tired he was asleep before he knew it.

A BOOT POKED BLAISE IN THE RIBS. "GET UP, SUNSHINE."

Jack. Blaise groaned, sitting up. There wasn't even the slightest hint of natural light filtering through the window yet. Blaise didn't mind waking up before the sun when he had a morning of baking to look forward to, but the exertions of the last week had caught up to him, and it was nice to sleep somewhere with an honest-to-goodness roof over his head. Factor in the nightmares that had interrupted his sleep, and he wasn't as rested as he'd like to be. "Five more minutes."

"Nope. In five minutes, you're gonna ask for five more. Not gonna happen." The Effigest was adamant. The room filled with the glow of a mage-light. Nearby rustling proved Emmaline had just finished dressing and was pulling on her boots. "Besides, we're gonna go see something before we grab breakfast and get in the sky."

Jack's words had Blaise curious. He reluctantly struggled upright, rubbing at his eyes. Blaise had slept in his clothes, so all he needed to do was pull on his boots and gather his bedroll. After the bath, his hair would probably benefit from a brush and some styling, but those were niceties for another time. He could almost hear Jefferson's exasperated sigh. *My hair probably looks like a bird's nest.* Blaise did steal a few minutes for a much-needed shave, though.

Once they'd gathered the few belongings they'd brought into the hotel, they headed to the livery. In the grey light of early morning, they fed their pegasi. While the stallions ate, Jack motioned for Blaise and Emmaline to follow him.

Rose gold blushed on the distant horizon as Jack led their procession out of town. Uncertain wasn't large, so they didn't have far to go. The morning was quiet, the silence only broken by the nearby rushing of the river and buzzing insects. In the distance, an animal bellowed, a sound unlike anything Blaise had heard before. Splashing accompanied the strange bellow.

Jack stopped on a ridge that overlooked the river. The sun peeked over the eastern horizon, illuminating the water with a pinkish-gold tinge. Emmaline made a small sound of appreciation as they saw what Jack must have wanted them to see.

Creatures were in the river, cavorting in the mist that wafted from the water. Blaise squinted. "Are those horses?"

"Look closer," Jack suggested.

Blaise studied them, observing the fluid way they rose from the water. There were a half-dozen, a small band. A pair of them tussled like juveniles at play, their soaked manes and tails splaying behind them, sending droplets flying. No, their hair wasn't wet. The animals *themselves* seemed to be made of water.

"Kelpies?" Emmaline asked, her voice soft. Jack made a noise of agreement.

"They're pretty," Blaise murmured. *I wish Jefferson were here to see them. He would like this.* "You said they were dangerous. They don't look dangerous."

"Is Emrys dangerous?" Jack asked.

"No," Blaise said automatically, then caught the error in his quick answer. "Oh. I mean, he's not dangerous to *me*. Or anyone he likes." He frowned. "But he *can* be dangerous." Blaise had seen first-hand what Emrys could do when he was motivated.

Jack jerked his chin at the kelpies. "Same for them, but they're wild. They want nothin' to do with humans. And they're carnivorous. Get too close to 'em, and there's gonna be trouble."

"Did you wake us up early just to remind us how dangerous the wildlife is?" Blaise asked.

"Nah," Jack said with a shake of his head. His eyes flicked to Emmaline. "They're pretty. I thought y'all might like to see them, and this is the best time of day to do it."

"I *love* seeing them!" Emmaline whispered. "Even if they *are* murderhorses!"

The golden light revealed the delighted twist of Jack's lips. *He's being a father.* Blaise liked that—he liked seeing Emmaline happy, liked seeing Jack attempt to do something nice. Even if he was rude with his early morning wake-up calls.

"Are there bunyips around, too?" Emmaline asked. "I've never seen one."

Jack's gaze slid to Blaise, as if he were looking for permission. Blaise smiled. "I have no idea what a bunyip is, but I'm game to see one. From a safe distance."

CHAPTER TWENTY-FOUR
The Plan is Don't Get Yourselves Killed

Blaise

They landed at the abandoned homestead late that afternoon. Sad to say, it was in better shape than Uncertain. The barn was dusty and worn, the ground dotted with holes left by various burrowing critters, but it was serviceable. There was a house, too, but Jack warned them to stick to the barn.

"Why's that?" Emmaline asked, curious.

"It's haunted," Jack said simply, as if that explained everything.

Instead, it only filled Blaise's head with more questions. "Excuse me, what?"

"Haunted," the outlaw repeated patiently, as if he were explaining the concept to a small child. "You know, ghosts, spirits, that sort of thing."

Emmaline didn't seem at all daunted by the prospect. "Oh! Do you think we'll see them?"

Blaise sighed. *Of course, Jack is leaving us at a haunted house.* But now, he understood why the homestead was abandoned. "Why didn't the souls go to Perdition like they're supposed to?"

Jack gave them both an amused glance. He nodded to Emmaline first. "You might see 'em later, and you definitely *would* if you dare set foot in the house. So *don't*." His head swiveled to Blaise. "The poor sods got murdered by the Copperheads, so as you can imagine, they're touchy about that." He rolled his shoulders. "And on that happy note, I better head to Thorn while there's still daylight."

"Let me point out you're leaving us at a *haunted house*," Blaise grumbled.

"The barn is perfectly safe," Jack replied, Zepheus turning in a circle in preparation for departure. "Bed down with the pegasi. Two days. You best give me two days before you get it in your head to come haring off after me."

"Two days," Blaise agreed, eyeing the house. "You're leaving us for two days. At a haunted house. What do we do if you don't come back in two days?"

Jack gave him a wry look. "I figure you two will rush into town with magic a-blazin' despite anything I tell you."

"You're not wrong," Emmaline agreed.

"In that case, the plan is don't get yourselves killed," the outlaw suggested.

"That's not a plan. That's a long-term goal." Blaise shook his head. Not having a plan made him nervous, but there were too many unknowns. No way to plan for every potential scenario.

Jack made no reply. He leaned forward as Zepheus swept into a trot and then a lope before leaping skyward. The stallion's wings flapped furiously as he gained altitude, and before long, the pair were a tiny, receding dot.

Blaise rubbed his forehead, turning back to Emmaline and the waiting pegasi. <We should eat soon,> Emrys suggested.

"Yeah, we should," Blaise agreed, rubbing the whorl of hair on the stallion's broad forehead. Even when staying close to Forti-tude, Emrys was always hungry. Though that wasn't his fault—his equine nature required it. And now they were spending five to six hours a day in flight, the pegasi were using more energy than they normally would. They definitely deserved a chance to graze and rest. It made Blaise feel a little bad for Zepheus, having to bear Jack into Thorn, and he mentioned it to Emmaline.

She shook her head as she pulled the saddle from Oberidon's spotted back. "You don't need to worry about Zeph. Daddy will find a stable first thing and make sure he's settled before he does anything else."

They balanced their saddles atop one of the stall partitions inside the barn. Blaise found a dusty bucket and headed out to the well, situated a stone's throw from the barn. That the homestead had access to water made it lucrative, and hard to believe no one else had tried to claim it. Though maybe people had—and had been run off by the ghosts.

He brought the water back for the stallions and found Emmaline pulling out rations of dried jerky and fruit. Blaise was so tired of dried jerky and fruit, and would have given anything for the ability to bake something halfway decent. He eyed the house again, wondering if it was worth braving restless spirits for the chance to bake. *Maybe.*

Oberidon wandered a short distance and lowered himself to the ground, writhing around in the dirt. Too late, Emmaline caught the pegasus's movement in the corner of her eye. "Oby! What in Perdition are you *doing?*"

<Dust bath,> the stallion replied for them to both hear, sounding only a little contrite. <I was itchy. Emrys, come on, it feels fantastic!>

Emrys flicked an ear at the temptation, though his brown eyes were on Blaise. "Oh, go ahead," Blaise told him. "We'll brush you both after we eat."

"I hate when they do that," Emmaline grumbled.

"I don't mind it," Blaise said. In fact, he enjoyed watching the antics of a dust-bathing pegasus. Emrys walked near Oberidon, then pawed at the dirt, raking up clouds of dust. When he had loosened a broad swath, he lowered himself down to his knees, wiggling his body and flapping his wings. He shook himself, ruffling his feathers with the brisk movement. Dust wafted up and away from the pair of pegasi.

"I should let you groom the both of them," Emmaline said, handing a stick of jerky to him.

"I can if you want," he agreed as he took the proffered meat. Anything to stay distracted and keep his mind off his worries. He was so focused on the pegasi and their dust bath that it took him a few minutes to notice Emmaline watching him intently. Blaise raised his brows, wondering if she was staring because he looked like a wild thing. "What?"

Emmaline glanced down at her hands, an unusual move for the young woman who was as spirited as her father. "Can I ask you something?"

He nodded. "Yeah, you know you can."

She took a sip from her canteen and capped it, as if she were stalling. Or like she was figuring out how to ask her question. "I've been thinking long and hard about this. Wondering if Fort Courage broke me, or…" Emmaline wet her lips, then shook her head as if unable to continue her sentence.

Broke her? Blaise leaned forward, his full attention on her. "What do you mean?" He hated to ask. Blaise understood too well the sort of memories that might haunt Emmaline. But his experience was likely different from whatever she had endured, and he couldn't help her without more information.

Emmaline scrubbed at her forehead. "They had a Healer there. Not the good kind. Not like Nadine." She bit off a chunk of jerky and chewed on it as if it had committed a grievous wrong. Blaise didn't mind the break in conversation. He was content to let her take her time to say whatever was on her mind.

"I didn't understand what they'd done to me until I got back to Itude. Until Nadine checked me out and talked to me." Emmaline rubbed her upper arm in the place a geasa tattoo would have been if they'd given her one. Blaise knew that wasn't it, though. She'd never been tattooed as he had. "They do it to women mavericks. Make sure we can't have babies, I mean."

Blaise's mouth went dry at her words, and he hastily uncapped his own canteen and took a swig. If he was following correctly—and as much as he disliked it, he was certain he was—the Confederation had forcefully sterilized her. He reined in the swell of rage that bloomed at the thought of the Salties harming Emmaline. Now wasn't the time for anger—he needed to listen. "I'm so sorry."

"Not your fault," Emmaline said with a wave of her hand, misunderstanding that he meant it as sympathy and not apology. "I never thought about it much before. But after that, I've noticed more and more..." She made a frustrated sound. "Other people my age are pairing up. And..." Emmaline picked up a new piece of jerky and stared at it.

"And they're having cake together?" Blaise suggested, deadpan.

Emmaline snorted a laugh, lifting her gaze to give him an amused look. "Is that what you and Jefferson call it?"

"That's between us," Blaise replied, though he was happy he'd jarred her out of her spiral. "What about it?"

She bit into the jerky, chewing and then gulping it down before speaking again. "I don't find that interesting. And sometimes the new townies ask why I'm not sweet on anyone." Her shoulders rose, as if the very thought irritated her. "They make it seem like that's all I should be thinking about."

Now he understood exactly why she was asking him. "Nothing wrong with being the way you are."

She crossed her arms. "But it doesn't make sense. I like the idea of romance. I think you and Jefferson are adorable. I like the idea of *other* people having that. Shouldn't I want that for me?"

Blaise shrugged. "The cake wasn't only a joke. Some people like cake and would eat it all the time, while others never want it. Some think to have cake when it's offered, or maybe crave it on occasion." He had her full attention, so he continued, "And some people only want to have cake with someone they care about."

Emmaline didn't even try to hide her amused smile. "How'd you come to learn so much about *cake?*"

"I've been paying more attention to people. Trying to figure things out." Emmaline was one of the few people he'd ever admit this to. Jefferson suspected, he was sure. Blaise wanted to understand more of the social cues he'd missed during his formative years, if only to help him navigate his relationship with Jefferson.

"Hmm." She studied him. "I'm never going to look at cake the same way again, thanks to you."

Blaise laughed. "I mean it, though. Your feelings and thoughts don't make you strange." He met her eyes. "Fort Courage didn't break you." It had changed her, just as his time in the Golden Citadel had changed him, but Blaise knew the things Emmaline had described were *normal.*

Emmaline relaxed at his assessment. "I knew you'd understand me." She pursed her lips. "You can't tell Daddy about Fort Courage, though."

Blaise scratched his forehead. It felt wrong that Jack didn't know what they had done to his child. But he knew why she requested it. Jack was fiercely protective of the ones he cared about. If Jack knew, Blaise had no doubt there would be more bloodshed as the Effigest threw himself into the teeth of the Confederation. His fury would know no bounds, and his reckless anger would be the end of him. No, Jack could never know.

"I won't tell him," Blaise agreed. Then he felt compelled to do something he rarely offered to anyone but Jefferson. He wiped the remnants of jerky grease away, then moved over and hugged her. She sank against him, her head nestled against his shoulder.

"Thanks," she mumbled against his shirt. "I wish we could have done laundry. Your shirt stinks."

"We were having a moment. You just ruined it," Blaise said,

though he wished the same. He liked the music of her laughter against him. "You don't smell like rosewater and lilies, either."

She drew back, the hint of a smile on her lips. Then she grew serious again. "Thanks for listening."

"That's what friends do. What *family* does." He watched her for a moment, assessing. Blaise wondered how she could look so strong after all she'd been through. "And don't worry about not being like other people. You're better than most."

Emmaline cocked her head. "Be sure to tell yourself that, too." He gave her a self-deprecating smile. Yeah, she knew his woe-is-me tendencies.

Emrys arose from the wallow, dust sheeting off of him as he settled his wings at his side. Emmaline wrapped the remainder of the jerky and shoved it in a pocket. "Time to go groom a certain troublesome stallion."

"I can groom Oby if you want," Blaise offered.

"Nope. I got him," she said, following him into the barn so they could retrieve the brushes from their saddlebags. "Oby, get your tail over here!"

The stallions trotted up, Emrys a dusty grey in the growing twilight. They settled down to work, brushing the dirt and grime from their coats. Emrys and Oberidon stood side-by-side, each grooming the other's wings with questing lips to make their feathers lie flat. Blaise wished he could have focused his attention solely on the bucolic scene, but he stole glances at the foreboding house every so often.

When they finished, the sun was down, and they were ringed by the warm glow of a mage-light. Emmaline chucked her brush back into her saddlebag. "Why do you keep looking at the house? You're not thinking of going in, are you?"

Blaise glanced at the house again. It didn't look any different from any other home in the darkness. It was in better repair than the Black Market building had been, though not by much. "Jack said the Copperheads killed the people who lived here. Made me wonder if the ghosts could tell us anything useful."

Emmaline quirked a brow. "You thinking about going to have a sit-down and chat with them?"

Blaise shook his head. "I figure nothing good would come of going into a haunted house."

She relaxed. "Good. I'm much more content to sleep in the not-haunted barn. Even if Oberidon does snore like a roaring dragon."

<I do *not* snore,> her pegasus said, stomping a hoof.

<You *do* snore,> Emrys said, earning a nip from the spotted stallion. <And calling it a roaring dragon is charitable.>

<Well, *you* are flatulent!> Oberidon rejoined, and the stallions devolved into trading barbs, while nipping and mock-striking at each other.

Blaise and Emmaline watched them tussle into the furthest reaches of the mage-light. The last few days had been stressful, and the stallions needed to let out some of their tensions. They squealed and spun, but after a few minutes of rambunctiousness, they calmed and trotted back over.

"All better?" Emmaline asked, sugary sweet.

<For now,> Oberidon agreed.

Blaise chuckled, shaking his head. Then they settled in for the long night.

CHAPTER TWENTY-FIVE

Oh, Biscuits

Jack

Thorn was a different town from the last time Jack had gotten this far east. The coastal city had always been a beacon for travelers—it was easily accessible to Eskela, Theilia, and Knossas by ship, which made it a strategic location for the Copperheads to take. Ravanchen wizards traveled overland through a mountain pass. The odd Confederation merchant made their presence known, too.

On his last visit, Thorn had had a laid-back air. The buildings were well-maintained, courtesy of the money changing hands constantly. To the untrained eye, the city looked the same. The buildings were as lovely as before. But the air was charged with tension, as if the citizens who called it home were constantly looking over their shoulders in fear.

Which they probably were with the Copperheads as their new *protection*.

True to his word, Jack behaved himself and kept a low profile. As much as he liked a good fight, he focused on his goal. The frustrating part was that he learned nothing at all regarding the whereabouts of Marian Hawthorne. The trouble was that he couldn't outright ask after her, lest his inquiries cause alarm. Wouldn't do to have the Copperheads come calling on him.

That meant he listened in on every conversation he could, though none of them bore any fruit. Jack didn't really care which bordello boasted the finest entertainment or which saloon served alcohol that was little more than watered-down whiskey. Such topics formed the bulk of the discussions he overheard, unsurprising with the number of visitors.

He discovered that many were in town specifically for the auction Slocum had mentioned. Anticipation rang in every voice that spoke of it, impatient for the day the Copperheads would allow the eager bidders to get an eyeful of the merchandise.

To his surprise, he found that the Knossans they'd come across had made it as far as Thorn, too. Jack was boggled they had reached Thorn so quickly. He spied them sitting across the saloon from him, and he wondered if one of them was also a shaman who might have enhanced their speed. The possibility made it curious they hadn't used magic to fight against the grasscats—unless they couldn't. *Druid, then.* He'd heard the Knossan druids were sworn to not utter a spell against a living thing.

He slipped across the saloon, pausing by their table to tip his hat to them. "Howdy, friends. Got room for another?"

The trio snorted in surprise at his appearance. Roam bobbed his head. "Please, make yourself welcome."

Jack snagged a nearby chair and hauled it over. "The next round's on me." Figured it didn't hurt to be charitable to encourage wagging tongues. "Fancy seeing you lot here."

"We made good time," Deal agreed blithely. Jack suspected the Knossan was smirking, though it was hard to tell.

"Any luck finding your young-uns?"

Gore blew out a soft breath, shaking his horns. "Not yet."

"We suspect we may have more luck soon, when the auction

merchandise is unveiled," Roam added, his voice low and dripping with disgust.

Jack whistled, scratching his forehead. The server delivered a round of beer, and he waited until she left before he spoke. "You think they're selling *people?*" Jack figured it never hurt to confirm information from Slocum.

"That is what our inquiries have uncovered," Deal murmured. "There is nothing too *exotic* for this auction—that is what the Copperheads say. It stands to reason they mean the mystic races."

And alchemists. Jack nodded, though he was glad he'd taken the chance to chat with the Knossans. This was the most he'd heard yet. "If your young-uns are there, you gonna bid on them?"

Three sets of angry eyes fell on him. "We should not have to buy back our kin," Gore said.

"No," Jack agreed, "and I know you Knossans are fierce but look around." He tipped his head to the other saloon inhabitants. "Lotta these folks gonna take offense to you trotting off without paying." *Not even gonna mention what the Copperheads would do.*

The tips of Roam's horns scraped the table as he dipped his head. "We have no choice. There is no way we could afford the prices this auction will demand." His resonant voice was suffused with heartbreak, and Jack suspected that one of the missing Knossan children was his own flesh and blood.

Damn it. Jack tried to have a hard heart, but he hated trafficking. Especially hated it when it happened to children. And to auction them as if they were a dairy cow? He bared his teeth. "I'll help you get your young-uns back."

The Knossans regarded him with surprise, their ears flicking forward as if they'd misheard him. "You will? How?" Gore asked.

He shrugged. "We'll have to figure out the particulars, but the way I see it, ain't fair to the young-uns for you to not have a shot at freeing 'em."

Deal huffed. "We are not to be taken lightly."

"No, you're not," Jack agreed. "But you're about as sneaky as bison covered in bells. You go charging in, this ain't gonna work." He splayed a hand against his chest. "I'm an Effigest. We can figure something out."

Gore exchanged glances with the other bulls. "We would be foolish to refuse your help. But what do you ask in return?"

Jack pursed his lips. "I suspect there's merchandise in the auction that's of interest to me and mine. If that's the case, all I ask is for your help to recover it. Like for like."

"That is reasonable," Roam said.

A few moments later, the agreement was struck, and Jack moseyed out of the saloon. Twilight was falling across the town, so he checked in on Zepheus and found the stallion relaxing in his stall. Though the pegasus hadn't been idle—he, too, had been listening in on any gossip from those around the stables but had heard nothing new.

Jack found a room for the night. He appreciated a roof over his head and a mattress that was softer than the ground beneath his bedroll, but it made him fret over Emmaline. And Blaise. But he had been right to handle their approach to Thorn with caution. He knew it, but that didn't mean he *liked* it.

Emmaline's tough. She'll be fine. Blaise, though…well, that was the real worry. He wasn't cut out for this, even though he had handled everything well so far. That kid was meant to be in a bakery, not traipsing across the Untamed Territory on a manhunt. Jack shook his head, banishing the thought. Nothing he could do about that.

Blaise

BLAISE SAT UP WITH A GASP, HIS HEART THUNDERING IN HIS CHEST. He swallowed, rubbing his forehead as he heard Emrys stir to wakefulness nearby.

<I'm here.> The stallion was an inky form against the void of darkness. Blaise breathed out a soft breath as Emrys moved closer, lipping at his rider's shoulder. <I'm sorry I can't keep the nightmares away.>

"It's okay," Blaise whispered, not wanting to wake Emmaline. He ran a hand along the pegasus's leg, tracing the canon bone down to the feathered pasterns. The equine form was familiar. Comforting. It was enough to anchor him in a better frame of mind.

Sleep was impossible after his nightmares. Emrys drowsed next to him until the distant horizon lightened with the coming day. But as dawn came, a heavy fog rolled in from the east.

Emmaline scrubbed at her eyes as she roused from her bedroll. She yawned and stretched, frowning. "Must be a sea fog."

Blaise glanced at her. "You think so?" He couldn't put his finger on it, but something about the fog unsettled him. Although, it wasn't unusual in the autumn. He'd seen it often enough during his youth in Desina.

"Thorn's on the coast, and we're close enough for it to roll in, I imagine," Emmaline said with a shrug. "May as well eat. Can't do a thing about the weather."

They'd added oatmeal to their supplies when they stopped in Uncertain. Emmaline had foraged and found fresh berries, so they added them to make their meal more appealing. Blaise and Emmaline were sitting down to eat when both stallions came to attention, ears pricked.

Emmaline stopped eating with her spoon halfway to her mouth. "Oby?"

The spotted stallion snorted uncertainly, shaking his mane. <Hoofbeats. We hear hoofbeats.>

<A *lot* of hoofbeats,> Emrys agreed, shifting uneasily.

Oh, biscuits. Blaise's mouth went dry. Jack had said the Copperheads had a weather mage, but not one capable of creating the storm that had assaulted them. That didn't mean they couldn't do something like create this fog.

"We can't ride in the fog, can we?" Blaise asked, his sinking feeling growing. He swallowed, not even bothering to ask if the pegasi could fly in it. It was thick, making it difficult to see the house from the barn, even though the distance wasn't great.

<Not without risk of taking a misstep,> Emrys said.

Emmaline clambered to her feet. "We need to get deeper into the barn. *Now.*"

Blaise picked up his saddlebag, hauling it back into the dark interior. The pegasi crowded into the furthest depths of the barn, their riders crouching beside them. Emmaline extinguished the mage-light, and they huddled in the surreal darkness together.

In the distance, hooves pounded a foreboding rhythm. The blanket of fog dampened equine squeals and snorts, along with the voices of men and women.

<Unicorns,> Emrys said. <I smell unicorns.>

Blaise's heart raced. The Copperheads had found them. They heard equines milling outside. Laughter. The solid slap of boots hitting the ground from a dismount.

"Breaker! We know you're in there. C'mon out," a gruff voice called.

Unicorns. It had to be the blasted magic-scenting unicorns that had tracked them down. Blaise traded a look with Emmaline.

Emmaline licked her lips, reaching for the sixgun at her side. She pulled it from the holster, metal whispering as she checked her ammunition. "Do we fight?"

Blaise closed his eyes, stomach sinking as he remembered what Jack said about the Copperheads. Emmaline was good. Fierce. But she was only one brave girl, and he—well, he was a Breaker, but he didn't know how to fight. Not when he was surrounded like this. Not when to fight might mean his friends would pay the price. They were woefully outnumbered. He would never forgive himself if Emmaline or one of their pegasi died on his account.

"No," he said, shaking his head as he opened his eyes.

"What do you mean?" she hissed. "They want you!"

They did. And in turn, the Copperheads had something he wanted, too. Maybe, just maybe, he could turn that in his favor, given the time and room to maneuver. Time to leverage the situation.

"Exactly," he agreed softly.

<I don't think you understand what that means,> Emrys said, urgent. He leaned his great head against Blaise's back. <They will take you from me. And they will take *us*.>

That was the part Blaise didn't like. But, in his mind, a peaceful surrender was preferable to being taken by violence and possibly hurt. Or worse. He turned, planting a kiss in the middle of the stallion's forehead. "I know it sounds like a terrible plan. But trust me in this."

<I *do* trust you,> Emrys said, though he was sorrowful. <Now I wish I had run off with you into the fog! I would risk a broken leg to keep you safe.>

But I wouldn't risk you breaking a leg to keep me safe. Blaise shook his head, then glanced at Emmaline. "Are you okay with this?" He knew only too well that she might have horrible memories rearing up of the last time she'd been taken by force.

She tightened her grip on the sixgun. "No. I hate this." Emmaline tried to hide it, but Blaise saw the tremor of her hands.

He took a step closer to her, looking her in the eye—something he did with very few people. "I know. But we can't run, and we can't fight—"

"We *can* fight," she whispered, sounding very much like her father.

Blaise shook his head. He understood her fear. "We can, but *not now*."

Emmaline made a frustrated sound. "You think they'll give us another chance?"

"I don't know," Blaise whispered. He had to be honest and not sugar-coat the situation. "But we're at a disadvantage here. And I have an idea."

She narrowed her eyes at him. "What—?"

A voice from outside interrupted her. "Breaker! Time's up! Come out now, or we come in by force."

"Later," Blaise promised. "Trust me."

Emmaline sighed and shoved her sixgun back in its holster. Blaise mustered his courage, raising his voice as he called, "We're coming out! Don't shoot."

CHAPTER TWENTY-SIX
Slap in the Face

Jefferson

Jefferson smiled behind the rim of his glass of cider, watching as Kittie flowed through the throng of curious Gannish elite like a hummingbird going from flower to flower. No, not a bird—like a spark prepared to gut a forest. The elite were quite aware of who and what she was, but since she was well-dressed and approachable, she had become a charming curiosity. She seemed to comport herself well, so he contented himself to watch from a distance.

Mindy and Flora were in attendance, too, though they kept lower profiles. Mindy had dressed simply, insistent she didn't want to stand out. She wore a demure black outfit that allowed her to blend in with the staff. Flora was being typical Flora—invisible, but no doubt somewhere nearby.

They had been invited to an early Bounty's Eve gala, hosted by one of the Board members. Bounty's Eve wasn't for another week, though Jefferson and Madame Boss Clayton were optimistic they might sign the declaration that day. It would be symbolic to do so on an important holiday. With that plan in mind, refusing the invitation to the gala had never been an option.

He realized, though, as he watched the elite flow around the great room like schools of fish, that galas no longer excited him as they once had. Or maybe the problem was that he missed Blaise. All the elite with attachments attended with their partners or had brought a guest, which made him feel the odd man out. And it made him a target.

To be fair, in the past, he wouldn't have minded the flirtations of a lovely lady at all. But now? He found it irksome. *Especially* considering the woman who had set her sights on him.

Cinna Smithstone smiled up at him. She was a petite beauty, with wavy tresses such a deep red they were nearly burgundy. She had been the woman Malcolm Wells had been engaged to—not an engagement of love, but one of power. After they had broken it because of Malcolm's wayward inclinations, she had moved on to marry an elderly lecher who had since made the long walk to Perdition.

And now, for Tabris knew what reason, she had attached herself to Jefferson.

It was my fault. She had sat next to him at dinner, and he had held a polite conversation with her. Cinna had taken it as a doorway to monopolizing his time, and no amount of begging off would dissuade her.

"When you're not in meetings, you should absolutely come and walk the Hanging Gardens with me," she nearly purred, threading her arm through his in a gesture he remembered too well from years ago.

Jefferson carefully extracted his arm, simultaneously sliding a few inches away to allow some breathing room. "That is most kind of you, Ms. Smithstone, but my schedule is, as you may no doubt imagine, jam-packed."

She pouted at him. "That's no fun at all!" Then her pout shifted into the alluring smile that used to make his breath hitch. "But you're free *tonight*. No meetings after this, hmm?"

Cinna closed the gap between them again, tracing her fingers down his lapel, nudging the button that kept his greatcoat closed. Jefferson knew exactly what she was doing. Any gamble to win her target. What did Cinna want from someone representing the Gutter? Was it because he, too, was a curiosity? Or did she covet his wealth, hoping to add it to her own? "You're kind to offer, but I'm no longer available for such sport. My heart belongs to another."

She canted her head, baring the pale curve of her neck. "But she's not here, is she?"

"*He* is not," Jefferson corrected, once again wishing that Blaise were there.

Her face contorted with indignation, her mask slipping for an instant. Then it fell back into place as she ran the nail of her index finger around the ridges of his button. "He doesn't have to *know*." She glanced up at him through her long lashes. "It could be our little secret."

Our secret, and one everyone in this room would be privy to. Not that she tempted him. She was a reminder of the life he'd left behind, and he wanted nothing more than to get away from her. But even if she weren't...even if she *were* someone he might find alluring... He shook his head. "I must refuse, Ms. Smithstone. While my beau wouldn't know, *I* would."

An ugly gleam flashed in her eyes at being spurned. Before he could even react, her open hand flew up, slapping him across the face. She spun on her heel and marched off, huffing.

"Oof, that didn't look pleasant," a voice said at his shoulder.

Jefferson rubbed his cheek, wondering if her fingers had left a mark. It wasn't the first time someone had slapped him—but in the past it had been after he'd made propositions of his own. He glanced at Kittie, who had ghosted up behind him. "I assure you it wasn't."

The Pyromancer was watching Cinna, not him, which he found interesting. "Good thing I didn't have to scorch her."

"You what?" Jefferson blinked, thinking he'd misheard.

An amused smile played on Kittie's lips. "Jack told me you're a playboy. He said I should keep an eye out for Blaise's interests."

"I am *not* a playboy," Jefferson grumbled, then sighed when Kittie raised her brows at him. "Okay, maybe a little. But I wouldn't dare go with her. Or anyone else, for that matter." *That life is dead and buried, too. And I'm fine with that as long as I have Blaise.*

"Glad to hear it. So, why was she so adamant, then?"

"You heard? Wait, you *knew* I wasn't propositioning her?" Jefferson uttered a frustrated sigh at Kittie's innocent look. "I don't know why she was so interested. There are many reasons. I *am* quite the catch, you know."

"So I'm told," Kittie agreed. She was about to say something else, but her mouth clamped shut at the sound of heels approaching.

"Firebrand Dewitt! Ambassador Cole!" A young woman with black hair approached them with her arms spread wide. He recognized her from his past. Her name was Tara Woodrow, and her family had been in league with his father. "You simply must join us for the traditional Bounty's Eve toast."

"A bit premature, isn't it?" Jefferson asked. Toasts were often made on Bounty's Eve to encourage a prosperous future, and there were some who reasoned it was bad luck to do so before the proper date.

She flung an arm around his shoulders as if they were old friends. "Oh, Mr. Cole, please don't tell me you're a superstitious sourpuss! In my mind, the more toasts, the better."

"I'm more inclined to ask for Tabris's fortune at the proper time, personally," Jefferson replied, smoothing his lapels and wishing he could shrug out of her grip. But there was no way around this without looking like poor guests. "We won't turn away your hospitality, however."

Kittie gave him a questioning look, and he answered with a slight shake of his head as Tara beamed at them. She scooped her other arm around the Pyromancer. "Wonderful! Come along, then."

Tara herded them to a circle of elite across the great room. To Jefferson's surprise, he noted that they had snubbed the Board members from this gathering. They clustered on their own, flashing suspicious glances at Jefferson and Kittie as they joined Tara and her cronies. Cinna numbered among their group, though she crossed her arms and turned away when she saw him.

Jefferson was troubled by the fact that he recognized many of the group. All people who'd had dealings with Stafford Wells in the past. *My father is dead and gone, along with everything he represents.* Jefferson fervently hoped that had been the nail in the coffin for trafficking, though he doubted it. It made him a little suspicious of the supposed well-wishers, though logically, he knew they may very well support the Gutter if they thought it might fill their coffers.

"Ah, there he is. The good Ambassador." Jefferson recognized the speaker: Phillip Dillon, a man who had close dealings with his father. The very same man who had bought Jefferson's sister as a wife. He bit his tongue to stave off the comments he longed to make.

Phillip picked up one of the shot glasses arranged on the antique table before them. The alcohol in the glasses was a rich amber. As Jefferson drew near, he caught a glint in the bottom of each shot glass. A freshly minted golden eagle, a traditional addition to a proper Bounty's Eve drink.

"Hello, Phillip," Jefferson greeted the other man, feigning a smile he didn't feel.

Phillip grinned at him, then offered a respectful nod to Kittie. "Welcome to Firebrand Dewitt as well! We're honored by your presence, truly." He laid his free hand over his heart, then gestured to the shot glasses. "We wanted to have a toast with you, optimistic that it will help us prosper in all our endeavors."

A deep frown lined Kittie's face. Jefferson didn't understand what the problem was until Mindy slid into their group, sidling alongside the Pyromancer. Mindy whispered something, and Kittie lifted her chin. "I appreciate the invitation, though I won't be able to partake." There was regret in her eyes. And a longing.

Tara scowled, exchanging a look with Phillip. Something about that glance rubbed Jefferson the wrong way, though he couldn't rightly say why. Tara's face shifted back to a friendly smile. "That's no problem. We have other toasting options. Cider?" She removed one of the shot glasses.

Kittie nodded. "That will be fine."

"One for me as well, please," Mindy piped up.

Annoyance flickered on Tara's face, but she feigned the look of a properly polite lady. "Of course."

Jefferson didn't miss the intensity with which Mindy was studying the shot glasses. Tara returned with the two non-alcoholic drinks, offering them to Kittie and Mindy. The Hospitalier murmured her thanks, though her yellow gaze never left the small glasses.

The rest of the elite picked up shot glasses from the table, and Jefferson did likewise. Phillip cleared his throat, lifting his own high. "Now that we're all here, please lift your glasses and…"

Mindy wobbled where she stood, and for an instant, Jefferson feared something was wrong with her. The Hospitalier caught herself on Kittie, locking an arm around the other mage. There was a sharp tinkling as their shot glasses collided, and Mindy made a small yelp of dismay. Everyone stopped what they were doing to stare at the pair as Mindy righted herself.

"Oh, clumsy me. Still getting used to these heels," the Hospitalier said, her shoulders shrugging with embarrassment.

"Did any of the drinks spill?" Tara blurted the question. "On your clothing, I mean. It would be a shame to ruin them." She focused on Kittie, assessing the amount of liquid in the glass.

Kittie recovered, holding her glass in one hand and running her other over the front of her dress, the flame-licked number she'd gotten from Zuzanna. "Luckily, no. Dry as a bone."

Tara nodded, mollified. Mindy continued to look properly embarrassed, though Jefferson had the sneaking suspicion she hadn't been clumsy at all. Her stumble had been deliberate. He frowned down at his own shot glass with concern.

Phillip chuckled. "Now that the excitement is out of the way, let's make this toast properly, shall we?" He lifted his glass again. "To bright futures and fruitful connections!"

"To bright futures!" the others chorused, glass clattering against glass as they chimed together. They drank.

Jefferson followed suit, noticing that Kittie and Mindy did likewise with their ciders. The golden eagles rattled musically, falling against their lips. Dillon had served them a smoky Canenite rum. He wondered if the smoky flavor had been a nod to Kittie or just a coincidence.

_____

"WHAT HAPPENED BACK THERE?" KITTIE HISSED, A TRACE OF ALARM in her voice as they piled into Jefferson's suite at Silver Sands. Her eyes were on Mindy, demanding an answer.

"Wait for Flora," Mindy said, sounding tired. The ride back had been awkward, full of pensive silence, as none of them dared speak without the assurance of privacy.

"I'm already here," the half-knocker declared as she blew in from the door that led to the bedroom. Of course, she had made it back before them—Kittie and Mindy didn't know about her affinity for salt-iron, but Jefferson had made certain that a tiny swaddled nugget was nestled in the drawer beside his bed to serve as a beacon for her.

Kittie gave a sharp nod, turning back to Mindy. "Explain. You switched our drinks. Why?" Apprehension crept into her tone, and Jefferson realized she wasn't angry at Mindy—she was worried about the young Hospitalier.

"I was watching when the shots were prepared. No one pays much attention to me because I'm not important like either of you." She gestured to Jefferson and Kittie. "And that's fine because it lets me do what I'm here for."

"They put something in our drinks?" Kittie asked.

Mindy's golden gaze flitted between Kittie and Jefferson. "Only yours. I didn't see what they spiked it with, so I don't know what their intent was. But my magic..." She frowned, as if she were struggling with how to describe it. Jefferson could commiserate. "It sat up and took notice. Until I convinced Kittie to order a different drink, I wasn't sure who they were targeting."

Kittie's eyes widened in understanding. "And here I thought you were trying to keep me dry."

Mindy shrugged. "Well, that was part of it. But I thought it odd when that woman took your drink back and dumped it, then replaced it with the cider and added something from a vial to it."

"A vial?" Jefferson asked. "Like an alchemical potion?"

"Or poison," Flora suggested helpfully.

"I don't know which," Mindy admitted. "I only knew Kittie shouldn't drink it."

Kittie crossed her arms. "But *you* did. After you switched glasses with me." Her forehead creased as her eyebrows lifted.

Mindy waved a hand, dismissive. "I'll be fine. Whatever was in your glass won't hurt me." They stared at her. Jefferson cocked his head, the motion silently requesting an explanation. Mindy shifted uneasily. "Okay, I try to keep this quiet. My magic makes me resistant to anything harmful put in food or drink."

Flora whistled. "That's handy."

"It is," Mindy agreed softly. "I'm not comfortable with people outside Fortitude knowing about my magic, especially that. For a Hospitalier, it's a powerful ability."

I know that feeling. Jefferson offered her a smile. "Your secret is safe with us. So, you won't have any ill effects from whatever they tried to dose Kittie with?"

The Hospitalier winced. "I'm *resistant*, not immune. It depends what was in there. If it was a poison meant to kill, I'll be violently sick and try to puke out my guts."

"I'll hold your hair," Flora offered valiantly, earning a wan smile from Mindy.

"I don't think they would try to kill Kittie," Jefferson said, though he was thinking aloud. "That would be too obvious. All the signs would point back to the gala, unless it was some sort of slow-acting poison. Would something like that work, Flora?"

The half-knocker pursed her lips. "I don't do a lot with poisons." At the looks her words earned her from Kittie and Mindy, she backtracked. "I mean to say I have definitely, positively never killed anyone with poison. So, I can't help you with that sort of information."

Jefferson nodded. "Well, I suppose we'll just have to wait and see what happens."

"How do you feel?" Kittie asked, assessing the Hospitalier.

Mindy rubbed her temples. "I have a headache coming on, but that's not anything unusual."

Jefferson's gaze slid to Flora, but the diminutive woman was already on it. "C'mon. Let's get to your room and get you settled. I'll keep an eye on you."

"If she feels poorly through the night, Rachel should have a Healer on call," Jefferson suggested.

Mindy's eyes widened at that. "No. No Healers. Please. Nadine knows but…" She shook her head, fearful. "I'll be okay. A Healer can't do anything, anyhow."

Jefferson nodded, though the brave face she put on bothered him. Intellectually, he knew the reason she had accompanied them—it was to do exactly what she had done. But that didn't mean he *liked* it. "Is there anything we can do to help?"

She allowed Flora to help her to the door. "Don't eat or drink anything until breakfast for a start. I don't want to worry about you."

Kittie sighed. "We won't. It's our turn to worry about *you*."

Flora eased the Hospitalier out into the hallway. The Pyromancer turned to Jefferson, her expression like that of a hunting cat. Focused and wary. "Do you have any idea why those in that group would attempt to drug me?"

Jefferson licked his lips. "Without knowing what the drink they intended for you would do, it's hard to say. But I don't think they would kill you." He paced, hands laced behind his back. "Make you ill so you can't attend the next few days of meetings?" Jefferson paused, making a frustrated noise. "Beyond that, my imagination isn't vivid enough to know what they might do."

Kittie rubbed her hands together, a move that reminded Jefferson of Blaise and made his heart pang. Then the Pyromancer spoke, refocusing his attention. "So, we don't know what they're planning or if they're an enemy—though I'm going with enemy if they were spiking my drink."

"I think that's a safe assumption," Jefferson agreed, thinking back to his sister, Phillip Dillon, and his business enterprises. "But until we know more, there's not much we can do."

"So we wait, and we watch," Kittie said. She yawned. "Though first, we sleep."

Jefferson couldn't help it; he yawned, too. Yes, sleep sounded like a good idea. *If only I could Dream.*

CHAPTER TWENTY-SEVEN

Dream or Die

Jefferson

efferson rolled over, pulling the sheets around him as something tugged at the corners of his sleeping mind. Whatever it was roused him, and he groaned softly as he rubbed away the grit in the corner of one eye. It had to be the middle of the night, but something had woken him—

Shouts. Running feet thudding down the hallway.

He scrambled into a sitting position, flicking the nearby mage-light on. Its silvery-blue glow illuminated the room, and he unsteadily wobbled to retrieve a pair of pants and pull them on. Jefferson was rising to button them when Flora appeared beside him with the soft pop of displaced air that always announced the use of her magic.

"Get out of here," the half-knocker urged, as serious as he'd ever seen her. "There's a fire."

"Fire?" Jefferson repeated, his fuzzy mind still catching up with the idea that he was awake and needed to take action. Then her words hooked their talons into the primordial part of his brain, and his eyes widened. He let out a soft curse as he snatched up his greatcoat. "Right, I'm going. How's Mindy?"

Flora shook her head. "Not great. Whatever she drank did a number on her stomach."

"Help her to safety," Jefferson said. "Should I get Kittie?" Did a Pyromancer need help to escape a fire? He would think not, but he didn't want to make assumptions.

"I saw her pelting down the hallway toward it," Flora said, her expression grim. "We gotta get out of here fast. The fire's tearing through this place."

Jefferson nodded. "Go help Mindy. We'll meet at the stables if it's safe—"

"They're burning, too," Flora said tersely.

No! The pegasi. Jefferson swallowed, waving Flora away as he pulled his shoes from beneath the bed. By the time he had them on, the half-knocker was gone. He caught the telltale scent of acrid smoke wafting through the cracks in his door. Their rooms were on the third floor, making it a sheer drop to the ground below. Jefferson glanced at the bed. Make a rope with sheets? He'd read of that being done in adventure books, but it wasn't a tactic he wanted to bet his life on.

"Stairs it is," he murmured, hoping that at least one of the two stairwells that served the building was passable. He formed a plan in his mind. Step one, get out of the building. Step two, get as close as he could to the stables to ensure the pegasi were safe. Step three...well, he hoped everyone was safe by the time he reached step three.

Jefferson reached the door and had his hand on the doorknob when it flew open. The hardwood rammed against his face, striking him squarely in the nose, and he staggered backward with a surprised howl of pain. He heard voices, but it was difficult to focus on them through the aching corona that was his face. Jefferson backpedaled until he fell against the bed, sitting down on it, stunned.

"Is this Jefferson Cole?" he heard someone ask. Male.

"Yes."

Cinna. It was Cinna's voice. Why was she here, in the middle of a fire? He heard the tap of feet on the floor, hushing when she reached the rug beside the bed. Jefferson cradled his bleeding nose with one hand, his vision blurring as he stared up at her.

"Don't fight us," Cinna advised him.

Jefferson blinked, struggling to clear his vision, trying to figure out why she might say that. Had she come to help evacuate people from the danger? Two dark shapes flanked her. He blinked three more times, his vision finally clearing enough to see. Cinna fidgeted, and he realized she held something in her hands. A square of fabric. Cinna popped open a small vial and soaked one side of the cloth with the contents.

A vial. Suddenly, his brain caught up with everything. Mindy had mentioned a vial. Someone had tried to drug Kittie's drink.

They failed to take out Kittie, and now they're after me?

Jefferson surged to his feet, fear taking hold. If he could slip past them, make it to the door, maybe he could lose himself in the crowd escaping the fire...

"Don't let him get away! Keep him still!" Cinna snapped. "We don't have much time."

The men loomed over him. Reaching hands grasped for him, clamping around his upper arms. Panic took hold as he bucked in their grip, the men's curses echoing his attempts. Frightening memories of a similar incident flashed through his mind. *Can't let them hold me. Have to get free!*

But there was no way. They were stronger than he was, and his face was a distracting beacon of pain that made it difficult to react. *Think. What advantage do you have?* None. His only advantage was a gutsy half-knocker who was evacuating the ill Hospitalier. Seledora was no doubt escaping the inferno, too. He had nothing.

Nothing except his secret magic, stifled by the precious ring on his finger.

There was no other choice. As the men held him down and Cinna struggled to shove the cloth into his face, Jefferson desperately clasped his hands together, working the ring off his finger. Blaise had asked him not to remove it, but neither of them had expected anything like *this* to happen.

The ring came free, slipping from his fingers to fall on the floor with a metallic clank. Jefferson's heart sank, but he promised himself he would find it later. Once he was safe. He couldn't focus on that right now. As the ring fell away, his magic breathed to life. Jefferson hadn't realized until that moment how much his magic had become a part of who he was. But now it was back and at his command. He was glad for it. *This is who I am now. A mage. The Dreamer.*

He grunted as one man held him down with such force it was difficult to breathe. Or maybe the smoke was drifting into his room—everything was confusing. Jefferson called on his magic, and it roared like a pack of hunting dogs eager to be on the trail. It was damned hard to focus when he was fighting for his life, but he had to. There was no other option. Dream or die.

Jefferson sent a tendril of magic arrowing up at the man who held him down, curling it around him, layering it around his assailant like a parent tucking a child under cozy blankets on a chill winter's night. He felt the man struggle against the drowsiness. Jefferson poured more magic into the effort.

Cinna rammed the cloth into Jefferson's face while he was distracted. She sealed the fabric around his nose, and he tried to sputter as he inhaled the sickly-sweet scent. Jefferson didn't let go of the man with his magic, doing all he could to keep him asleep while trying to twist away from Cinna.

But he had already inhaled too much of whatever was in the cloth. *Why is everything so hazy? Is it the smoke? Is—?*

CHAPTER TWENTY-EIGHT

I Am the Fire

Kittie

K ittie's magic had stirred her from sleep. She was sensitive to fire, but normally its presence didn't bother her. If a hearth held fire in the winter or a stove was in use for cooking, she was aware, but it served as background noise to her senses.

This was different. This was raw, blood-curdling *danger*, like wolves on the hunt. Like a griffin stooping on prey, talons outstretched. *Wrong, wrong, wrong.*

She moved to her window, throwing back the curtains. The world outside danced with gold, firelight reflecting on the nearby hematite-encrusted rooftops. Kittie licked her lips, summoning her magic. She lifted a hand, pushing it out, an invisible spy flitting through the air to bring back news.

She normally used this facet of her power to find easily combustible objects. Kittie could call up flame from thin air, but it was always easier with a source. Her thread of questing magic would also tell her of any neighboring fire, like the town gossip returning with news.

It took only seconds. Her magic retracted, and she chewed on her lip as she took a precious minute to sort through the information. She couldn't describe it to anyone else, but her magic brought back data. How far she was from the fire. The intensity. Natural or man-made. How it was spreading. Kittie assessed it all, her heart sinking.

Someone had set the fire on purpose. It was an inferno, and it was going to *kill*.

Kittie tugged on a robe, tying it around her waist as she pulled on a pair of boots. She had to help. The fire was ravaging the wing Madame Boss Rachel Clayton and her family called home.

The hallway outside her door had turned into a mad rush of people bolting, searching for escape. Someone yelled something indistinct. Men and women crushed together, seeking an exit. Kittie hoped Jefferson, Flora, and Mindy were in their number. Their wing was in danger from the blaze but not as much imminent danger as the Clayton residence.

Kittie gritted her teeth, pushing against the flow of frightened people. They threatened to sweep her away with them like a frenzied tide, but she won her way through their tear-streaked, coughing clusters. Someone grabbed her elbow and yelled for her to follow, but she ignored their plea. No time to explain that she was a Pyromancer and the fire and smoke wouldn't harm her. She didn't *enjoy* breathing smoke, but it wouldn't choke her lungs as it did anyone else.

She thundered down the stairwell closest to the residence. In the distance, she heard a crash as a structure fell beneath the fury of flames. Tongues of fire scorched a garden as she raced through.

In the haze of smoke, she saw movement as figures fell out of a broken window on the lowest floor of the residence, stumbling to catch themselves. Kittie rushed to them.

A middle-aged man and two children rolled onto their backs, coughing. Grime smeared their faces, and dark blood soaked the man's arm. Kittie slid to her knees beside them, recognizing the children from her first day in Nera—the Clayton children, Mary and Romie.

"I'm here to help. Is anyone else still inside, Mr. Clayton?"

The man's eyelids fluttered, and he struggled into a sitting position. Then he moaned and sagged onto his back again. He looked as if he'd suffered burns during their escape, but Kittie couldn't help with that. "Yes."

"Mama's in there," Mary rasped. Despite the soot on her face, the girl was still the spitting image of her mother. Determination and fear gleamed in her eyes. "She promised to get my kitty!"

Romie, the little boy who had shyly hid behind his mother's legs the day Kittie had met him, burst into tears. "Mama! Mama!"

Kittie swallowed, glancing over her shoulder at the fire. She steeled herself, turning back to the frightened family. A searing gust of wind blew hair into her face, and she smoothed it behind her ear. "It's okay. It's going to be okay. You want to hear some-thing funny? *My* name is Kittie. How about I go check on your mama and the furry kitty?"

Mr. Clayton dragged himself onto one elbow. "The Pyro-mancer." There was a quiver in his voice, as if he feared she was the source of this.

It wasn't the first time Kittie had heard that. She licked her lips. "It's not my doing. But I'm going to help however I can."

"Can you extinguish it?" he asked plaintively.

Kittie didn't have the time to explain that stopping this fire would be the equivalent of jumping onto a wild horse bareback and expecting it to respond to her commands. "I'll do what I can. Get your children somewhere safe."

She rose, stalking toward the burning home as ash rained down. Mr. Clayton called after her, but the symphony of popping flames and crack of failing timbers drowned out his words.

"No, no, no. Not again," Kittie whispered, shaking her head as she drew closer to the home. The crackling dance of flames brought back a rush of memories. She'd lost her own parents to fire. *My fire. No. This isn't that. It's not the same.*

Anyone else would die charging into such a building unless magic of some sort protected them. Black smoke billowed out the doors and windows, trailing up the sides of the structure like thick, inky vines. Kittie crouched low as she prowled inside, her eyes tearing from the smoke.

"Rachel!" she called, though she knew it was futile. If the Madame Boss still lived, she wouldn't hear Kittie over the roaring flames.

She checked every room on the first floor, begging Faedra to reveal the woman lying low beneath the smoke. But she was nowhere to be seen. Kittie was spending all her magic on holding the growing fire at bay, allowing her a path through the destruction. It was the only thing she could do, since she couldn't bring the inferno under her command and quell it.

Stairs. Kittie found them looming in the dense haze of smoke. If Rachel was upstairs, in all likelihood, she was already dead. No one would fault her for turning back now—except they would, she realized. She rubbed ash away from her eyes.

Those children deserved to have their mother back if there was any chance at all.

I am the fire. The flames cannot touch me. Nothing will stop me. Kittie summoned all her courage, all her past regrets, as fuel for her inner fire. *No regrets now.* She had to get up the stairs, but the fire was chewing through them. The Pyromancer gritted her teeth, lifting her hands in a placating gesture. The flames on the stairs paused in their greedy expansion, reluctant to obey.

It was going to have to be enough. Kittie's feet flew up the stairs, the wood groaning and fracturing beneath her weight. When she reached the top landing, she peered into the burning nightmare before her. Impossible to see anything but smoke. She fumbled forward, hoping she would blunder into a door.

And she did. The first was closed, flames licking at the framing around the door. They hadn't breached it yet. Kittie pressed her magic hard against the fire, fighting to hold it back. The blaze strained against her, wanting to consume.

"Later," she promised the fire. *I just need a few minutes. Please.* She opened the door and slammed it behind her, though a belch of smoke followed her in.

A small bed claimed one corner of the room, toys sitting on a table, and books lining the low shelves. A child's room. Kittie was about to turn and continue her search when she spied a dark lump in the corner. It moved feebly, then coughed.

No, she.

Rachel lifted her head, her face dark with soot, eyes streaming tears. She opened her mouth to speak, but another fit of coughing cut it short.

"I've got you!" Kittie called, frantic as she crossed to the woman. Gods, only the fact that the door was closed had spared the Madame Boss's life. There wasn't time to think or explain, only to act. She reached down and pulled the woman to her feet, where she swayed before thrusting a furry mass at Kittie.

The cat.

It was a tiny kitten, and in the face of disaster, it was almost inconsequential. But it was a life, and that meant it mattered. Kittie took it in her hands, the little creature limp though she felt a sluggish heartbeat. Maybe not too late. She tucked the kitten into the large pocket of her robe, hoping it would be safe there.

Now for Rachel. The Madame Boss wobbled on her feet, almost going down. There was no way she was walking out of here. Kittie moved to face Rachel, grabbing her right hand and draping her arm over her own shoulder. It took more maneuvering, but seconds later, she had the Gannish leader slung over her shoulders, Kittie's right arm securing the woman's knees and one of her arms to keep Rachel in place.

Go, go, go. Time was against them. Kittie threw open the door with her free hand, the fire screaming at her impertinence. She shoved her dwindling magic against it, fighting to keep it from advancing on them as she made her way to the precarious stairs.

Later, Kittie still didn't know how she got Rachel out of the home. She only knew one moment they were inside, and then the next, she was lumbering out the door, smoke billowing behind them. Someone yelled. Hands reached out, pulling Rachel from her back.

"Healer. She needs a Healer," Kittie whispered, exhaustion washing over her as a reminder that there was a price for the amount of magic she'd used. Something wiggled feebly at her side. The kitten. "Beast Healer, too." She pulled the furball from her pouch, holding it out as an offering.

Someone took the kitten from her. Kittie staggered forward, away from the inferno, going down to her knees. A blurry form asked her something, but words no longer made sense. Kittie scrubbed at her forehead, her vision going fuzzy, before collapsing face-first into the grass.

EVERYTHING WAS TOO BRIGHT. THE HARSH SMELL OF AN ANTISEPTIC potion assaulted her nostrils. Kittie winced, cracking her eyes into narrow slits.

"She's awake!" Mindy's voice, heavy with relief. Shadows moved closer, blocking out the rude light that assaulted Kittie's face.

She felt the nearness of people leaning over her. The warmth of a Healer brushing fingers beneath her wrist, checking her pulse. "Firebrand Dewitt, my name is Healer Imogene Ames, but you may call me Genie. You're at the Providence Infirmary. You collapsed after magical exertion."

Yeah, I figured. Kittie gave a tiny nod. Her throat hurt, as if the fire had raced down it and tried to burn her lungs to ash. In any other person, it would have. She had a headache and felt shaky, probably from lack of food. A little brandy would hit the spot, but with Mindy nearby, that didn't seem to be in her future. A nurse came in and helped prop her up in bed.

Genie gave her a thorough going-over. The Healer frowned when she finished her check. "You over-extended. You're going to feel the drain for a while, perhaps up to a week."

"Is Rach—Madame Boss Clayton well?" Kittie asked, the words coming out like gravel. She gingerly touched a hand to her throat.

"I'll get you something for that in a moment," Mindy whispered.

Genie offered Kittie a reassuring smile. "Madame Boss Clayton will recover. She had a few burns, but she's doing better than you are." Her words hinted at the fact that the leader had received a dose of healing magic to soothe the burns. It would be her due, after all.

Kittie sagged against the pillows with relief. A few minutes later, Genie and the nurse left the room to tend to other patients. No doubt their beds were full after the catastrophic fire. Mindy eased toward the door, but Kittie raised a hand to stop her.

"What did I miss?"

Mindy swallowed. "You're still weak. I'll tell you soon. I *will*. But let me get you some food and drink. You really need it." Her eyes glistened with helpless tears.

This is all she can do. Kittie nodded. "Okay, I'll wait."

The Hospitalier slipped out the door. Kittie sighed, deciding to enjoy the quiet and the softness of the sheets. She must have been unconscious, as someone had removed her night clothing and robe, cleaned her up, and then dressed her in a cotton shift. She closed her eyes, grateful for the news that Rachel had survived. *Those children still have a mother.* She knew the pain of a shattered family too well and didn't wish it on anyone.

Mindy returned, an orderly trailing her with a tray bearing what smelled like a rich and salty chicken soup. Kittie's mouth watered as the scent wafted to her, and she was more than happy to adjust, allowing them room to place a bed tray over her midsection. A bowl of fresh strawberries sprinkled with sugar and a tea of some sort accompanied the soup. Kittie didn't care too much about the details. Her stomach demanded food, and she set about answering the request.

Once she slurped the last of the soup from the bowl and moved on to the strawberries, she glanced at Mindy. "What's happened?"

The young woman sighed, pulling a chair closer to the bed as she sank into it. "It's...I don't know how else to describe it. A *nightmare.*" Mindy's voice cracked with the word. She sniffled and rubbed at her nose. "Flora got me out, and then by the time I felt well enough to walk, we found you...well, they had brought you here, but there was so much trouble."

"Trouble?" Kittie asked, popping a slice of strawberry into her mouth. It was the sweetest thing she had ever tasted, the flavor parading across her taste buds. "Over what?"

"*You,*" Mindy whispered. "Some of the Board members. They were here, demanding your arrest. Accusing you of setting that fire!" Fury rose in the Hospitalier's voice, her eyes sparking in outrage. "They said since you were a Pyromancer, and the fire was so intense, it must have been you."

Kittie chewed on the amazing strawberry and said nothing as the juices soothed her throat. This turn of events did not surprise her.

Mindy pulled out a handkerchief and dabbed at her nose, which had started to run. "But by that time, the Clayton family was here, too. One of the children heard—the girl, brave little thing! She pulled away from her father and marched over, hands on her hips, and hollered that you had run into the fire to save her mama and nothing more. By that time, Mr. Clayton came over and said that was so, and he was ready to do anything in his power to keep you here to get the care you needed."

Kittie licked a bead of strawberry juice from her lips, heartened by that. "So, they're the reason I'm not in salt-iron shackles right now."

Mindy nodded. "Yes."

"And Jefferson and Flora?"

Mindy stared down at her hands. "I sent a messenger to tell Flora you were awake when I went for the food. I expect she'll be here soon."

She didn't mention Jefferson. Kittie felt the bottom drop out of her stomach at the realization. She didn't feel like eating anymore, but her body demanded it, anyway. Kittie toyed with the rest of the strawberries, eating them slowly to bide her time.

True to Mindy's word, Flora barged into the room a short time later. She didn't bother to knock, as was her habit. The small woman's pink hair was disheveled, and her glasses hung crooked on her face, but she didn't seem to notice. An air of desperation and stark grief clung to her like a second skin.

"Flora?" Kittie asked gently, moving the tray aside and trying to sit up.

The half-knocker swallowed a lump in her throat. "I wasn't there when he needed me." Her head bowed, and her thin shoulders racked with silent sobs. The normally bold, happy-go-lucky, fierce spitfire was broken.

"Tell me," Kittie urged, her voice soft. She knew it would hurt, but her mind was already catching up to speed, thinking. *What would the Firebrand do?* She would gather all the information at any cost. Then use it to decide the next move.

Flora sucked in a ragged breath, then lifted her head. A fat teardrop journeyed down one of her grey cheeks. "He's dead. They...they found him in his room. Must have been trapped, I guess. There...there wasn't much left." She scrubbed the back of her hand against her face, wiping away the tear. Flora uncurled a hand, revealing a ring. "This was near his body."

Kittie's heart sank. No, this couldn't be. Jefferson was a puzzle, but she had come to like his keen mind and boundless determination. What would they do without him?

They would see this through. *This is a tragedy—but we can't let this spell the end for the Gutter. We can't.* She thought Jefferson would want them to continue the fight if he could not.

"I'm so sorry, Flora. I know he meant the world to you." Kittie didn't understand the half-knocker's tie with Jefferson, but whatever it was ran deep. Jefferson's loss cut them all to the core, but Flora the most. "Did the pegasi survive? I saw the stables were engulfed."

Mindy nodded. "Yes. Our pegasi evacuated all the normal horses, in fact. Not a single equine died."

That was a small bit of good news, at least. Kittie would take anything at this point.

"What do we do now?" Mindy asked softly. "Do we...do we go home when you're up to traveling?"

Kittie shook her head. "No. We finish what we came here to do. We do it for Jefferson. And for ourselves." She vowed to see this through if it was the last thing she did. "Mindy?"

The Hospitalier snapped to attention at the sharp query. "Yes?"

"I'm going to need Caladrius root tea. A *lot* of Caladrius root tea."

CHAPTER TWENTY-NINE

Dreams and Nightmares

Jefferson

"Well, it's been a while since I've been here," Jefferson mused as he turned in a slow circle, examining the dreamscape uncoiling around him. It felt *good* to be back—natural. Though, the manner of his return was alarming.

His mind was a little fuzzy, and he wasn't sure if his memories were accurate or if something hazed them. There had been fire. Flora helping Mindy out. A door slamming into his face. A struggle. An old lover from his past. His brain refused to connect any of the dots.

Jefferson frowned, trying to figure out how he had gotten back here. He had *promised* Blaise he would keep the ring on. The only reason he'd be able to reach the dreamscape was if he had taken it off to use his magic. "But *why* would I do that?" As much as he'd missed his magic, his vow to Blaise had been *important.*

He shook his head, frustrated. *Might as well take advantage of my time here.* Jefferson squared his shoulders, calling up his magic. Mists of the dreamscape swirled around him, thickening until they obscured his vision. Then they melted away, revealing the stone hallway that led to the dream prison.

His steps rang out against the floor, echoing back at him. Jefferson strained his ears for any sign of his prisoner, but there was nothing. He quickened his steps, shifting from a jog to a flat run as worry took root. Full of dismay, he drew to a stiff-legged halt in front of the cell that had once held the psyche of Gregor Gaitwood.

It was empty, the door open as neatly as if someone had unlocked it and released the vile Doyen for good behavior. "No, no, *no*," Jefferson murmured, stepping closer to the threshold.

He considered checking the interior but decided against it. He remembered too well the ending scene in the theater production *Song in the Crypt*, where the erstwhile hero had been tricked and bricked into a mausoleum. All the same, Jefferson's heart thundered at the revelation that Gregor Gaitwood was no longer suffering for all the pain he had inflicted.

Gaitwood was free, and he didn't deserve it.

Jefferson balled his fists at his sides, shaking his head. What could he do? Perhaps he could find Gregor and drag him back kicking and screaming, but then what? While that would be satisfying, Jefferson had the uncomfortable feeling that there were more pressing things he needed to worry about.

Was it something to do with Blaise? It almost went without saying that he had his share of concerns for the Breaker. But no, that didn't feel right. Blaise wasn't related to whatever had made him end up in the dreamscape again.

Think. There was the fire. Wait. Am I dead? Is this Perdition? Jefferson didn't like that thought. Though, he would expect Perdition to have a lot more souls. And it stood to reason it wouldn't be something he could shape with his magic. That logic soothed him, and he turned, striding back the way he had come.

"Let's see. Mindy was...yes, Mindy was ill after drinking the shot meant for Kittie." Jefferson decided that mulling it over aloud might help. It wouldn't hurt. "We went back to our rooms. Flora stayed with Mindy." He nodded to himself, hands clasped behind his back as he puzzled through his memories. "I went to bed, but noises woke me. People yelling about the fire."

Jefferson slowed, frowning. "Flora popped in to warn me. I told her...I told her to get Mindy out." He recalled putting on shoes and hurrying to the door—and the hardwood ramming into his face. Jefferson swallowed as his lost memories fell into place. Cinna had been there with two men. She had shoved something into his face as the men held him down.

Oh. He'd removed the ring, hoping to haul one of attackers to the dreamscape and out of the action. But Jefferson remembered nothing beyond that, except for a too-sweet smell.

"They drugged *me*." He frowned. But why? Jefferson sighed, wondering what his next move should be. He had his magic again, so perhaps he should take advantage of that?

Maybe I could reach Flora? He discarded the idea immediately. Jefferson didn't think much time had passed, and even if it had, it was likely daytime, and he wouldn't find her slumbering. Then a dread thought clutched him. Was he still in his room? Was he going to burn to death while he tried to come up with a plan in the dreamscape?

"That won't do at all," Jefferson murmured. No, it was time to wake up and meet whatever lay ahead in the real world.

SILK SHEETS WHISPERED AGAINST HIS SKIN AS JEFFERSON STIRRED TO wakefulness. He kept his eyes closed, ears straining for voices or anything that would clue him in to impending danger. But he would know the cool, smooth feeling of silk anywhere. The pillow his head rested upon was the softest he'd had since his own bed at his estate outside Nera. The amount of comfort was puzzling, though welcome.

His eyes snapped open. He reclined in a dark room, though light filtered in around thick drapes covering the sole window. Jefferson slowly sat up, taking stock of himself. He was a little sore, but that was to be expected. Lifting a hand, he trailed his fingers along the bridge of his nose. It was tender, but no puffiness or traces of sharp pain followed his exploration. No crusts of blood, either. *A Healer must have tended to me.*

Jefferson was bare-chested, though his mystery attendants had left his drawers and pants on. He swung his legs over the side of the bed, then reached over to flick the mage-light on the nearby bedside table, illuminating the room in its glow. A glance around showed a fresh set of clothing laid out on an armchair in the corner. A dresser with a mirror claimed one of the walls, though he was dismayed to discover it held no grooming items. He strode over to the mirror to check his nose.

His mouth went dry when he saw the face in the mirror. No. No, *no, no.* Roguish, dark-haired Malcolm Wells stared back at him, complete with the fading geasa tattoo on his bicep. Jefferson closed his eyes, certain he was mistaken. But when he opened them again, nothing had changed. Swallowing, he glanced down at his hand. His beloved cabochon ring was missing.

"No, this can't be." Jefferson shook his head, moving to take stock of his personal items. He found his pocket watch in the drawer of the bedside table. But of his ring, there was no sign. There had to be a reasonable explanation. He would get it back. Everything would be fine. "One thing at a time, Jefferson," he murmured to himself. "You've been in plenty of scrapes before. This is no different."

After taking a calming breath, he assessed the rest of the room. Beside the door, a small, rectangular wooden panel had a winking sapphire gem embedded in the middle. He raised his brows at that. A call button, either powered by one of the new electrical currents or enchanted with magic.

Where in Perdition am I? Everything about this was puzzling.

Jefferson moved to the laid-out clothing. *Well, I may as well be presentable.* He shucked off his pants, setting them aside as he pulled on the replacements. The new clothing was a little large, but not too bad. The provided shoes were the right size, and they were new and unbroken. He knew the logo stamped into the leather. Caesuras. Top-of-the-line shoes, at that.

As he moved, Jefferson's bladder reminded him it needed attending to. His stomach added to the protests. Jefferson pressed the call button. He didn't hear any sort of ring or other response from it, but that meant nothing. It likely sent the ring to somewhere deep in the home, maybe the kitchens or elsewhere the staff might be. Jefferson tried the door but found it locked. Not surprising.

A few moments later, the lock on the door clicked, and a young man in the garb of a well-appointed footman pulled it open. "Good afternoon. My name is Abernathy. May I be of service?"

He had half-expected thugs or a mustache-twirling villain straight out of a theater production on the other side of the door, so the appearance of a benign footman caught him off guard. Jefferson recovered quickly, however. "Yes. I need the quincy and perhaps food, if it's no trouble."

Abernathy inclined his head, then turned. "Your every need will be met." He beckoned for Jefferson to follow.

It wasn't long before his bladder felt relief, and his stomach was pleasantly full. Abernathy had brought a tray to the room, so Jefferson didn't get a chance to wander and figure out where he was. When he asked the footman, Abernathy simply responded, "With the Quiet Ones." Jefferson had never heard the term before, but he decided not to press for more answers. The footman bade him wait and rest in the room.

The Healer returned, though the middle-aged woman said even less than Abernathy. She didn't even give her name. She merely ran her hands over him as if he were a prized racehorse she was assessing for soundness, made a *harrumph* of approval, and left.

A short time later, a knock sounded on the door before it swung open. "The Quiet Ones will see you now," Abernathy said, making a grand gesture for Jefferson to follow.

He didn't know who or what the Quiet Ones were, but this didn't bode well.

CHAPTER THIRTY

Unicorns Are Assholes

Blaise

The Copperheads were a level of bad-tempered Blaise hadn't expected, even with Jack's warning. He'd always considered Jack mean—or maybe ornery was the better term. But the Copperheads? They were something else.

The enemy outlaws had surrounded them, the fog lending them an additional layer of malice. The desperadoes had been ready to claim their prisoners. They relieved Emmaline of her sixgun, reagent bag, and poppets. For the pegasi, they had prepared halters with O-shaped rings made of salt-iron. Blaise clenched his jaw as Emrys squealed at the touch of metal.

A frowning woman, who the others called Maureen, glared at Blaise as she strolled over. "Where's your weapon?"

Blaise swallowed, lifting his chin. "*I* am the weapon." He flexed his fingers meaningfully.

She gave him a dubious look, as if she didn't think he could possibly be serious. Blaise had to admit it was refreshing to see someone who wasn't frightened or awestruck in his presence. "You look awful soft."

He tensed, stung by her words. It rankled that her assessment bothered him, but it did. Blaise had wanted none of the difficulties life had thrown at him, but he had earned his scars. In his time back in Fortitude, his body had filled out again from the ravages inflicted on him by his time in the Golden Citadel. He wasn't naturally slender, not like Jefferson—he skewed toward a sturdiness reminiscent of Emrys. He narrowed his eyes. "Don't mistake softness for weakness."

He still didn't impress her. Maureen glanced at the leather gloves in his pocket, ignoring his words. "Put those on, Breaker."

To his annoyance, after he slipped his gloves on, another outlaw strode over with a pair of burlap bags, which they tied over his hands. Blaise decided not to point out that the layers of supposed protection would do nothing against his magic. Not even the salt-iron cuffs they had clamped to his wrists. Those surprised him more than anything, though he realized they had brought along an outlaw without a lick of magic to handle the wicked metal.

As before, the salt-iron did little more than irritate his skin and make it impossible to mount. The Copperheads wanted him to ride one of their unicorns, but the temperamental beast refused to kneel to allow him to get aboard. Snorting in frustration, Emrys knelt as a plea to allow Blaise on his back. The Copperheads grudgingly allowed it, though they kept the stallion in the middle of their knot. Oberidon and Emmaline followed along behind, the young Effigest's face a mask of anger.

The Copperheads bantered amongst themselves on the ride back to town. Blaise took the opportunity to learn what he could. It sounded like Maureen had led this expedition, though she wasn't the Ringleader. She had authority, though, and was some sort of Healer.

The unicorns they rode were as rough as their riders. Their scar-crossed coats gleamed with all the colors of the rainbow. Some of them had brands, which made Blaise curious, but he didn't ask. They were all ill-tempered, and the equines enjoyed attempting to skewer the grounded pegasi with their deadly horns. The Copperheads didn't even attempt to dissuade their mounts, and Emrys and Oberidon were soon bleeding from puncture wounds.

Blaise closed his eyes, fighting back angry tears. He had known his plan was a risk to the safety of the pegasi, but he hadn't expected this outright cruelty. His magic itched beneath the layers of bondage. Blaise knew he could break free, but then what? There was nothing he could do to help the pegasi. He couldn't take on a dozen armed outlaws and their belligerent unicorns.

Relief washed over him when the town of Thorn came into view. The unicorns stopped pestering the stallions, more intent on getting back to their stable.

No one paid them any attention as the Copperheads escorted them into town. They threaded through the busy streets, eventually ending up near the docks. The tang of saltwater was heavy in the air, and gulls and other shorebirds cried out as they wheeled overhead. The outlaws didn't stop until they'd reached a building he thought might be a warehouse. It was a three-story affair, constructed from heavy-framed timber with rusted iron cladding. One of the Copperheads dismounted and rolled the massive door open.

Blaise glanced over at Emmaline, but she gave a small shake of her head. She didn't have any better idea of their whereabouts than he did. Their escort urged them inside.

The interior was lit by a mix of lanterns and mage-lights. Sturdy posts of timber supported the high ceiling. Blaise thought the building might be full of ship cargo, but it wasn't. At least if it was, it wasn't anything like he'd expected. Rows of steel cages and stalls took up one half of the vast building. Stacks of crates lined up into long aisles claimed another section. The remaining area looked to be under construction, as if someone were building seats and some sort of staging area.

Oh. Slocum had mentioned the Copperheads were having an auction. *And this is it.*

"Get off, Breaker," one of the Copperheads commanded, taking Emrys's halter and yanking hard on the lead rope. The stallion pinned his ears, eyes rolling as he jerked his head back.

Blaise hissed out a breath. It was clumsy work, but he dismounted without falling onto his face. Maybe his rising anger had given him the grace he normally lacked. "Hurting my pegasus really frosts my cookies."

The outlaw guffawed at the expression, slapping his knee. His eyes glinted with a meanness Blaise had seen in bullies before. "I'll frost your coo—"

Blaise closed the distance between them, lifting his salt-iron-bound hands. He thought about calling up his power to chew through his bonds—and he could. Oh, he could. But that would give away too much, and he wasn't prepared to do that yet.

Instead, he brought the salt-iron shackles up to the man's throat, holding the chain taut against the tender flesh. The man yelped, struggling to twist away, but Blaise followed him, relentless. The outlaw was a mage, as Blaise had thought, and he squealed like a pig as the metal seared his skin. Just as quickly, Blaise yanked it away, though the Copperhead now had a bright red lash across his skin, as if he'd been scalded.

"I'm gonna—"

"You ain't gonna do shit, Calvert," Maureen snapped, sauntering over to them. The wounded man cowered beneath her ire. "The Breaker is not to be damaged."

"But he—"

"I heard what he said, saw what he did, and it's damned clear he knows exactly how to frost *your* cookies." She put her hands on her hips. "If you keep this up, what I do to you will make that salt-iron burn feel like pox from a bordello girl." With Calvert slinking away, she turned to the others. "Sanguine and Cottonmouth, you take the pegasi. Eunice, with me to get the Breaker and young Effigest settled."

A pair of men broke off, each moving to stand by the pegasi. Blaise tensed as one of them took Emrys's lead rope. "If you hurt a hair on either of those stallions, I'll bring the roof of this place down."

"They're not yours anymore," the man said with a shrug.

Blaise gritted his teeth. Nearby, Emmaline stewed, fury lining every crevice of her face. He wanted to argue, but it would do no good. In fact, it might harm the whole reason he had given up so easily.

Emrys rolled a dark eye in his direction, nostrils fluttering. Blaise wanted nothing more than to go to him, so they could reassure each other that it would be okay. *You're my pegasus, and I'm your rider. Nothing can take that from us.* Blaise clenched his fists within his bonds, giving Emrys the smallest of nods. The stallion's hooves echoed hollowly on the stone floor as he was led away.

"Let's move," Maureen said, giving Blaise's shoulder a shove as they started up an aisle.

Maureen and Eunice hustled Blaise and Emmaline into a shared cell at the furthest end of the row. Every other cage had occupants, and he was surprised—and horrified—by the variety. Knossans, Theilians, goblins, knockers, harpies, and more represented the two-legged mystic races. Basilisks, chupacabras, jackalopes, wolves, grasscats, and creatures he didn't recognize occupied others. Blaise glimpsed the occupants of the stalls, too. Bison, antelope, kelpies, bunyips, griffins, unicorns, kirins...the variety was mind-boggling.

The Copperhead women left them in a salt-iron-reinforced cell, along with a bucket in one corner for bodily needs. Blaise and Emmaline waited until they were certain they were alone before they took the chance to speak.

"For the record, I hate this idea," Emmaline hissed, a pained expression on her face.

Blaise winced with sympathy, knowing the salt-iron was leeching magic from her. Maureen had removed his shackles and the sack, so Blaise shucked off his gloves and stuck them in his pocket, flexing his fingers. "I know. I'm sorry, I just didn't know any other way that wouldn't end up with us dead or wounded." It wouldn't take much for this to end the same way, though.

She sighed, rubbing her forehead. "Sorry. Bad memories make me snappish."

"No apology needed." Blaise paced the perimeter of their cell, studying the bars.

"What are you doing?"

He smiled and, in answer, laid a hand against a slat. It wasn't pure salt-iron. He figured that would have cost a fortune, but he felt that they had somehow incorporated it into the steel. Hardly enough to so much as annoy him, though the same couldn't be said for someone like Emmaline. Her eyes widened in surprise.

"We're not as trapped as you think," he whispered.

Emmaline relaxed, sitting down in the middle of the cage, as far from the bars as possible. "What are we gonna do?"

Blaise abandoned his place by the bars and moved to sit beside her. "Still deciding that part. But the way I figure, Jack's going to find out what happened to us."

"The odds of him doing something stupid are pretty high. That move of yours would have impressed him back there, by the way," Emmaline commented, drawing an index finger along her neck.

Blaise grimaced. He wasn't particularly proud of his actions, but it had been the only thing he could think of to get his point across without using magic. Blaise didn't want to hurt other people, but he wouldn't abide bullies, either. That didn't make what he did *right*, though.

Emmaline must have noticed his distress. She bumped a knee against his. "You did what you had to."

Blaise nodded. That was as good a segue as any into what he had to tell her next. "Jack won't let us rot here. You know that."

When she nodded, he continued, "And come what may, if you get out, I need to stay in."

She crossed her arms, giving him a stubborn look that was a ghost of her father's. "I am *not* leaving you here with these... these...well, calling them *outlaws* is an insult to outlaws."

He wiggled his fingers, a reminder. "You're not leaving me here. I'm choosing to stay. This is my best shot at finding my mother." Blaise nodded to the expanse of cages all around them.

Emmaline frowned. "You think they have her here somewhere?"

"I don't know, but I intend to find out."

CHAPTER THIRTY-ONE

Malcolm Who-Is-Not-Dead

Jefferson

The footman showed him to a lavish parlor. As he entered, the murmur of light conversation greeted him. Men and women filled the room, some seated and others standing. Staff hovered around the edges, seeing to every whim of the well-dressed elite. His arrival must have served as a signal. As soon as he strode inside, the help slipped out of the room.

Jefferson had little love of being thrown into a situation where he didn't know what was afoot, and he felt vulnerable without his ring. Without his *identity*. Any sign of weakness could very well be like the scent of blood in the air near a murder of chupacabras, and he did his best to hide how flustered he was by the entire scenario. Jefferson doubted he succeeded.

His gaze flicked over the occupants, surprise jolting through him when he saw Cinna in their midst, arms folded across her chest. Jefferson swallowed, realizing he knew everyone in the room. Some came from families his father had dealt with in the past. Others he had come across in his time as a Doyen or in his entrepreneurial guise. A few of them had been in attendance at the gala the previous evening and had taken part in the toast. Familiarity didn't mean he was safe, no matter how well he had been treated to this point.

"Good afternoon," he greeted them, deciding to seize whatever minor advantage he could. "I appreciate the invitation to join you." Jefferson offered a polite nod to the group.

Their eyes fell on him, and he felt a bit like a butterfly pinned down for an exhibit. Phillip Dillon cut through the group like a shark through the surf. A broad smile played on his lips, teeth flashing. *My sister's husband?* "We're pleased you could join us, Jefferson." He paused dramatically, tilting his head. "Or is it Malcolm?"

"Yes, which is it? I feel as if I've seen a ghost," a taunting voice added. *Gaitwood.* Gregor slipped in through a door on the far side of the room, joining the knot of elite.

You did this. Jefferson sucked in an outraged breath. For once in his life, he was utterly speechless. He felt naked, as if they had stripped away every part of his being. And there was nothing he could do about it. Small wonder Cinna had slapped him last night if they had already clued her in to his secret.

"Oh dear, he's overwhelmed." Saccharine-sweet, Tara Woodrow ambled over, offering a wineglass. "Perhaps this will help with the jitters."

Her words snapped him out of it. Jefferson took a step back, glaring at her. "You spiked Kittie's drink."

Tara shrugged. "But this one's fine. Promise." When he shook his head, she took a sip herself. "Your loss."

"Jefferson Cole. Malcolm Wells." This from Phillip, who moved closer, interest etched on his face. "I'm intrigued. I must admit, I doubted Gregor's story, but now that I see it's true..." He pursed his lips as if he grudgingly admired Jefferson's masquerade. "So, *who* are you?"

Remember who you really are. The Dreamer. An entrepreneur. "I am Jefferson Cole."

"He's lying," Gregor said. "You see the proof in his face. Malcolm didn't die in the fire at the Wells Estate."

Yes, he did. Jefferson knew they would never accept it, though. Not with the face of a younger Stafford Wells in their midst. Gregor knew it, *knew* he didn't want to be that person. It took every bit of willpower Jefferson possessed to not let Gregor see how much this was undoing him.

Tara made a frustrated noise. "Are we just going to stand around and hurl accusations? There are perfectly good refreshments going to waste. Ones that are definitely *not* laced with hallucinogens."

"You have a way of making that sound foreboding," Everett Duncan, a magnate from Phinora, observed.

"It's true," Tara insisted. She flounced over to a chaise and claimed a seat, then leaned over to pick up a plate and fill it with her choice of finger sandwiches and pastries.

"Yes, have a seat, Malcolm-who-is-not-dead," Phillip said, sounding almost amiable. "Is there a need for introductions?"

"I believe I'm familiar with everyone here." Jefferson let the weight of his bitter words sink in. They thought they knew him as Malcolm? Well, he had the advantage of knowing *them*, too. He picked out a single chair in the circle, following up the move by filling a plate. Gregor wanted to make him a fish out of water, did he? Jefferson had years of practice having his feet in two worlds. *I can do this.*

He noticed Gregor claim a seat as far away from him as he could. Jefferson smiled in his direction. "Doyen Gaitwood, I couldn't help but notice the bags under your eyes. Not sleeping well?"

Gregor's mouth tightened. "I'm sleeping like a baby now."

"Because babies are notorious for sleeping well," Jefferson said dryly. The rest of the elite had taken their seats and selected refreshments as well. Jefferson took a bite of his sardine sandwich, gulping it down before deciding to make the next move. "I will admit, I'm unclear why I'm here." *And where here is. And why you want Malcolm Wells.* Did it have something to do with Alice? Had Phillip discovered his wife had fled and sought to use him to recover her somehow?

The other elite exchanged looks. After a moment, Phillip spoke up. "You're here, Malcolm, because we've decided you would be a worthy addition to our group."

Jefferson bit into his tart to hide the fact that this new information spurred more questions than it provided answers. *Their group? What group?* He recalled his sister's reference to *corruption.* Was this what she meant? After he swallowed the bite of tart, he asked, "Ah, is this a social group? Like a country club?"

Amused titters met his question. Megan Brew, a woman with straight black hair and eyes like a pair of emeralds, laughed as she lifted her glass to him in a toast, as if he had made a jest. "Oh no, Mr. Wells. We're so *much* more than either of those, I assure you."

"We are the Quiet Ones, the true power behind the Salt-Iron Confederation," Phillip added, his eyes glittering. "Seven powerful men and women who drive every aspect of the Confederation." He cocked his head, thoughtful. "Well, six currently. We've had a gap left by the untimely death of Stafford Wells."

"Yes, very sad," Jefferson said. "Anyway—"

"You're his replacement." Tara cut him off with a grin.

Wait, wait. What? Jefferson's brain ground to a halt as he suddenly caught up to their meaning. Stafford Wells had been part of this shadowy group of political puppeteers? How could that be? Stafford had never mentioned the Quiet Ones, even when he had groomed Malcolm as his successor. But maybe this group didn't work like that. Suddenly, things made a lot more sense. Such as how adamant his father had been that Malcolm would capitulate and undo all the legislations he had worked so hard on. It hadn't been only for the sake of his trafficking rings. It must have been for this group, too.

Jefferson cleared his throat, then took a sip from the glass offered to him. Water, which was welcome, as he didn't know if he could tolerate anything else at the moment. "I'm flattered that I made the top of what I'm sure is an esteemed list of nominees. Though, I'm not sure I would be a good fit."

The pressure in the room seemed to build like a thunderstorm. "An appointment to the Quiet Ones isn't something you can decline," Everett, the magnate from Phinora, said with a shake of his head. "In most cases—such as yours—it's an *inherited* position."

"You either join us, or you're never heard from again," Tara piped in pleasantly, as if mentioning that the weather outside was rainy.

Somehow, Jefferson maintained his composure in the face of such a bald threat. "I'm certain adding me to your roster would have my father rolling in his grave. Or did you forget he disowned me?"

"We have long memories. *Very* long." Cinna leaned forward, her eyes narrowing. "*None* of us have forgotten that, I assure you."

But you're not holding a grudge about it, I see. Jefferson met her gaze, unflinching. "The fact of the matter is, Malcolm Wells is dead. Most of you were at the funeral. You can see how it would be problematic if he..." Jefferson took a breath, correcting himself. "If *I* appeared again."

Phillip nodded. "You're not the only one in this room with secrets, Malcolm. But sometimes, when those secrets come to light, they can be quite helpful."

A chill zinged through Jefferson. They were going to undo all of his hard work; resurrect Malcolm Wells. The one thing he absolutely didn't want. "No." When their icy stares settled on him, he decided he needed to qualify his refusal. "How would that be explained away? It would force too many questions." Questions that he was reluctant to answer.

"Perhaps you had a mental breakdown and wished for time away. And you were quite dramatic about it," Gregor suggested acerbically.

Jefferson gritted his teeth. The expressions all around him showed this was an argument they wouldn't let him win. He tried to think of some way around it, some loophole, but the fear of being forced back into a role he didn't want overwhelmed him. A life he didn't want to lead—a life he had rejected. "What benefit do you even get from Malcolm Wells returning to life?"

"Your seat might have been filled, but your name still has political pull," Tara pointed out, twirling a finger in the air. "We love having politicians in our pocket, as you can see."

Jefferson glared across the room at Gregor. "We don't work well together."

"No one is saying you have to. We know you're Faedran and Gregor is a Mossback. We like playing both sides," Tara clarified.

"And as for why?" Phillip said. "You throw your support behind the Gutter. It's needed to outweigh the Gannish Board."

Jefferson narrowed his eyes. They could have asked Gregor to do that—but no, they couldn't. Gregor would never support such a move, and it would be out of character for him to do so. "What, you don't have Aaron Thatcher in your pocket?"

"Alas, no," Tara said. "He's the sort we don't want privy to our existence."

"So you chose me."

"So we chose you," she agreed with a smirk.

"Because your father was a Quiet One, and his father before him," Phillip explained. "And once we learned you were still alive, it made the most sense."

None of this makes sense. Jefferson shook his head. "The problem with your plan is that Jefferson Cole was in the midst of dealings with Madame Boss Clayton. It would make more sense for me to continue in that guise." *Please agree. Please.*

Gregor made a *tsk*ing sound. "Oh, you haven't heard? A shame about that. Jefferson Cole died in the fire at Silver Sands. Ironic how history repeats itself, is it not?" He held up something small and shiny between his thumb and index finger. A red jewel winked. Jefferson's pulse raced as he realized it was his cabochon ring.

"You give that back!" Jefferson was up and out of his seat before he even realized it. Then he was on Gregor, grappling with the shorter Doyen. Gaitwood had already slipped the ring onto his finger. Jefferson was grateful the ring was keyed to his blood and would work for no other. Shouts rose from the Quiet Ones around them as Jefferson grabbed Gregor by the shoulders. He didn't strike him, though.

No, he called up his magic, sending it pouring into Gregor as the other man yelped, realizing what lay in store. Jefferson chased him into the dreamscape, furious. He didn't care that the Quiet Ones were probably seeing Gregor go limp in his seat and Jefferson stare at the ceiling as if he were daydreaming. *He. Didn't. Care.*

The dreamscape was formless as Jefferson roared into it, but already his subconscious twisted it based on his emotions. Black storm clouds surrounded him, intermittent lightning striating the darkness. Gregor stumbled backward as Jefferson appeared, grabbing the Doyen by the lapels of his coat.

"What have you *done?*" Jefferson growled. Around them, the shadows took shape, eerie howls coming from them. A great serpentine silhouette lurked at the periphery of Jefferson's vision.

"What I promised I would do," Gregor choked out. "You should have known you would pay the price for your treachery."

"I'm not the treacherous one!"

Gregor laughed, despite his dire situation. "You lie to everyone, including yourself. You think it's not treacherous to deceive everyone by living two lives? And now...oh, Malcolm. Now you conceal your magic. How's that working for you?"

Jefferson huffed a breath, the stark realization like a slap to his face. Blast it all, but Gregor was right—about the last part, at least. Here he was amid the enemy, using his magic. That was a dangerous, sloppy mistake.

"This isn't over between us, Gregor." Jefferson let go of him. "I will free you from the dreamscape, and when I do, you'll return my ring to me."

"I don't think I will," Gregor said, straightening his jacket. "And if you force me to—*or* if you haul me into this gods-forsaken place one more time—I'll tell them about your sorcery. And won't they find *that* intriguing?"

Jefferson fisted his hands, but he didn't have a response. Angrily, he banished Gregor from the dreamscape, then followed him out. He found Tara nearby with a pitcher of water in her hands, clearly about to douse the both of them.

"Oh, whatever palsy has taken them is over. That's too bad." She set the pitcher down with disappointment.

"Have a seat, Mr. Wells," Phillip said with a long-suffering sigh.

Jefferson glared down at Gregor, then stepped away, stalking back to his chair. He ignored the curious looks from the Quiet Ones, as they no doubt wondered what their strange encounter had been about. Neither man enlightened them.

"It should be abundantly clear that you're Malcolm Wells at present." Phillip gestured in his direction. "You'll conduct yourself as such. Like it or not, you serve as a Quiet One now."

Jefferson crossed his arms. "And if I don't? If I act against your wishes?"

"Accidents happen," Cinna hissed. Jefferson suddenly wondered if the death of her first husband had been as natural as had been publicized.

Another thought occurred to him. "The fire. That was you?"

Tara shook her head. "That was the Board's doing. They hope to discredit your delegation."

Jefferson's brow knit. The Board would do something so heinous, an act that would threaten the lives of so many, including the Madame Boss? Were they mad? Then he considered the company he was currently in. The elite would plumb any depths to give themselves an advantage.

"Come now, Malcolm." Phillip gave him an encouraging look. "It's quite clear you want the Gutter recognized as a nation. That's why you came to Nera, after all. This is what we want, too. Why is this so difficult? It doesn't need to be."

Because I don't trust you. "Why do you want that?" That was what he really wanted to know. It bothered him—everyone in this room had dabbled in trafficking or working to keep mages oppressed and vulnerable. Why would they suddenly support a nation of free mages, especially outlaws?

Phillip shook his head, regretful. "We play a long game, Malcolm. And honestly, none of us are ready to show our hand to someone just joining the game. It could jeopardize years of work."

Jefferson knew he was in an impossible situation. Gregor had his ring, and the Quiet Ones had him exactly where they wanted him. And blast it all, they were right—he would support the Gutter no matter what. No matter the face he wore. Maybe it would be best to concede for now. Buy time to figure something out.

He bowed his head. "I see. I suppose it's in my best interest to work with you, then."

"If you want to live to see another day, it is," Tara agreed, far too chipper.

"Welcome to the Quiet Ones, Malcolm," Phillip said, lifting his glass. Around the room, everyone joined the impromptu toast. The gestures reminded Jefferson of the toast the previous evening. *Fruitful connections, indeed.*

CINNA SHOWED HIM BACK TO HIS ROOM AFTER THE SOCIAL gathering ended. She was frosty as she walked beside him, her eyes cutting to him every few strides. "You should have come with me when I propositioned you last night. Your mage wouldn't have been poisoned, then. But we needed the distraction, you see."

Her audacity was boggling. "I'm sorry, I was under the impression you wanted a tryst, not to upend my entire life."

"That isn't your life."

Jefferson ground his teeth, breaking his stride to glance at her. The loss of his identity hurt, and for it to be disregarded as if it were nothing was even worse. "What were you planning to do? Seduce me before drugging me and hauling me off to your Quiet One friends?"

She gave him a sour look. "Don't act as if you wouldn't have liked it. I haven't forgotten all the things you enjoy." Cinna continued onward, her heels echoing down the stone corridor. "We could have been a powerful couple, you know."

Her words surprised him, though they shouldn't have. Back in the day, he had assumed she was simply a gold-digger with a family eager to attach themselves to someone with a good name. "Was your former husband the Quiet One or one of your parents?"

"My mother," Cinna answered with a smirk. "She retired a few years ago. To enjoy her happy golden years."

"How wonderful for her," Jefferson muttered, not meaning it at all.

"Why did you do it, Malcolm?"

He chafed at her use of the name. "Do what?"

She stopped, turning to look at him. Curiosity burned in her eyes. "Give up everything. Become someone else." She gestured broadly around them. "You could have *anything* as a Wells."

Not anything. He swallowed. "You know why. I could no longer tolerate the things my family was doing. I wanted to oppose it." Jefferson shook his head in frustration.

"All things you did as Doyen Malcolm Wells," she reminded him tartly.

He started walking down the corridor, and she hurried to catch up. Cinna would never understand that the simple act of looking at his face in the mirror made him ill. Reminded him of the man who cared more for money and power than his own children. She was right, of course, that he had opposed his father as Malcolm. But the reasons *why* were too personal to explain to someone like Cinna.

"You're not so different from us, you know!" Cinna called.

His shoulders tensed. "I am *very* different from you."

"You're not," she insisted. "Look at you, Malcolm. Doing every unscrupulous thing you can to gain an edge. That's what this Jefferson Cole act was, wasn't it? An elaborate lie, a farce." When he made no reply, Cinna plowed on. "And we're like you. We have pet mages, too."

Pet mages? He whirled at that. "Blaise is not a pet."

She smirked, clearly amused that she'd gotten to him. "We saw your tattoo. The Breaker is the lover you mentioned, hmm? I heard rumors, but I didn't believe that you were really—"

"Don't talk about Blaise," Jefferson snapped, trembling with fury.

Cinna waved a hand. "There's no shame in taking a mage as a lover. Tara even *married* her pet—though, to be fair, he's an alchemist." She shrugged, as if it made no difference. "The fact is that you have a mage at your beck and call. A powerful one. And now so do we."

"I wouldn't ask Blaise to use his magic on my behalf." But it was a lie. He had. And Blaise had paid the price. Jefferson's stomach turned as he recalled the ruins of the airship at Fort Courage. Gregor was *right.* Cinna was *right.* He was a liar. He had used Blaise. *But I promised Blaise...I promised myself...to never do that again.*

She sighed. "Malcolm, don't be so stubborn about this. You can't shirk your responsibilities anymore. We hold all the cards. Don't you see how tenuous your position is?"

The problem was, he *did* see. There was no way out that didn't destroy everything he'd worked for. With a frustrated huff, he stopped in front of the door to his room. "You've seen me to my room. Now leave me in peace, Cinna."

She quirked a brow. "The offer I made you yesterday still stands." Cinna lifted a hand, brushing her fingertips against his chin. "You only need to say the word."

He squeezed his eyes shut at her touch, shivering. Though it wasn't from lust—it was from the shadow of his old life smothering him. "I may not have a choice in many things at the moment, but I have a choice in that. My heart belongs to someone else, and I won't betray him. That's where I draw the line."

Cinna bristled, stepping back. "Your loss." She stormed down the hallway as Jefferson withdrew into his room.

CHAPTER THIRTY-TWO
Legends Aren't Made by Bluster

Jack

Jack grabbed a simple breakfast in the inn's common room before heading out. Zepheus reported that he was fine, and a groom had already visited, delivering a bucket of oats sprinkled with sugar. Satisfied that his pegasus was in good shape, Jack headed to Creagen's Engineering Works to lend some credibility to his visit.

"Well, well, well, if it ain't Wildfire Jack."

Jack narrowed his eyes. *I know that voice.* He paused mid-stride, pivoting and gracing the speaker with a broad smile. "Well, if it ain't Seymour Arce, the outlaw with the most unfortunate name in history." He leaned on the soft C in the last name, drawing it into an *S* sound.

"Arce rhymes with *dark*," Seymour growled.

Jack shrugged. "Honest mistake." They both knew it wasn't. The Copperhead Ringleader had gotten a lot of grief over his name, which was probably what had made him hard enough to claw his way to the top of their gang. Maybe it wasn't smart to beard him, but there were some things Jack couldn't resist. Besides, it would have been uncharacteristic if he hadn't given the outlaw some guff.

"What brings a Gutter Rat out here?" Seymour drawled, clearly wanting to give as good as he got.

"Aw, gotta import your insults from the Salties?" Jack asked. He shrugged a single shoulder, as if he didn't care enough to commit both to the effort. "Oh, you know. Wind-pump's acting up. Thought I'd chat with Creagen." He nodded to the building a dozen paces away.

Seymour's slitted eyes studied him. "That so? Thought you might have gotten wind of the auction." The Copperhead Ringleader advanced a step closer. "We just got something in that may *personally* interest you."

Jack tried not to let his surprise register, but he was too slow to catch it, judging by the smirk that slunk across Seymour's face. His mind whirled, piecing through all the possibilities of what the other man meant. He didn't like any of the conclusions he came to.

"Don't make an enemy out of me, *Arse*," Jack growled. "'Cause it ain't gonna be pretty."

The Copperhead chuckled, reaching out to clap Jack on the shoulder. "Wildfire Jack, I know you think you got stones as big as the Griffin's Crest Mountains, but you forget your place."

Jack's hand brushed against the collar of Seymour's shirt as he ducked out of the other man's grip. "What'd you take?"

Seymour smiled. "The question isn't what, but *who*?"

That confirmed Jack's suspicions. "I'm not gonna rise to your bait like a yearling pegasus to a sugar trap." The Copperhead leader was a bully, and he was no doubt hoping Jack would make a rash decision and take a swing at him. Seymour was a Strength mage. It wouldn't be a fair fight unless Jack pulled a sixgun. As much as he'd love to wipe that arrogant look from Arce's face, he was savvy enough to know this wasn't the time. "Now, get out of my way. I got places to go."

Seymour checked his shoulder against Jack's. "Didn't know you were a coward, Dewitt."

Jack sidestepped away from the Copperhead. "Legends aren't made by bluster. Don't cross me." He trudged past Seymour, heading to the Engineering Works.

"That's right, Dewitt. You should be scared!" Seymour called after him.

Nah, you *should be scared.* Jack flashed a feral smile over his shoulder, smug about his acquisition of the loose hairs he'd liberated from the Copperhead Ringleader.

JACK MADE GOOD ON HIS FALSE PRETENSE, SHOOTING THE BREEZE with Charlie Creagen before heading back to the stables. Every moment of his visit to the Engineering Works had been agonizing —he wanted nothing more than to race out to see if his fears were founded. But Jack was determined not to blow his cover. He'd come damned close with Seymour as it was.

Zepheus's head was over his stall door, ears pricked as he waited for his rider. The pegasus kept a low profile so he didn't gain the interest of the unicorns ridden by the Copperheads. None were stabled in the livery where Zepheus was, but he wasn't taking chances.

Jack let himself into the stall, crowding close to the stallion. "You got any word?"

The palomino's nostrils roved over Jack's shirt, reading the scents. <No, but you're upset. What is it?>

The Effigest glanced up the stable aisle. No humans were in sight, and mundane equines occupied the rest of the stable— horses and mules. And a donkey, judging by the sudden braying. "We need to fly out to the homestead. Now."

Zepheus peered at him. <What? Why?>

"Ran into Seymour." Jack was already on the move, grabbing the saddle blanket and spreading it across the stallion's back.

<And? What happened?>

"He dropped hints he has Em and Blaise." Jack swallowed, shoving away the fear and anger that threatened to take root. "I need to check before I do something I might regret."

Zepheus nickered with worry as Jack slung the saddle onto his back, deftly tightening the cinches. <You can't take on all the Copperheads.>

"Nah. I just gotta take on *one* of 'em." And in such a manner that would make any of the others think twice. If they had Emmaline and Blaise, Jack had an idea for retaliation. It was dangerous. It was reckless. In short, it was the sort of thing Jack excelled at. "I figure we can make a quick flight, check into things, and then..." He trailed off. Jack didn't need to say more. Zepheus understood.

Moments later, they were underway. Zepheus's wings pumped the air, the stallion pushing himself to his top speed with no urging. The homestead was in view before long, and as the stallion descended, Jack nearly choked when he saw the imprints of cloven hooves that had churned up the dirt all around the house and barn.

"Emmaline!" he shouted, jumping out of the saddle and hoping against hope that she'd hidden. "Blaise!" Zepheus joined him, whinnying and sending out mental queries for any within his range who might hear.

<I don't sense them,> Zepheus said after a few minutes. He rested his chin on Jack's shoulder, an attempt at comfort. <And all the scents they left behind are stale.>

Jack shook his head in frustration, his eyes stinging. He had been foolish to think they were out of the Copperheads' reach here. Seymour Arce and his gang thought they had bested him, but he wasn't done. He would not let this go unanswered.

<What will you do?>

"Get 'im where it hurts." Jack turned and scratched beneath the stallion's forelock. "Let's get back to town. I got some spelling to do."

CHAPTER THIRTY-THREE
Weaponized Crochet

Jack

Two hours later, Jack strolled up the street to his hotel as if nothing was amiss, a paper sack concealing new supplies clutched under his arm. When he reached his room, he took stock of his few possessions, making sure no one had tampered with them while he'd been out. But everything was undisturbed. He pulled a skein of yarn and two crochet hooks from the sack, and an almost-complete project from the bottom of one of his saddlebags.

Only Kittie and Emmaline knew that he'd taken up crochet after the trauma of his experience with Gaitwood in Phinora. He wasn't ashamed of it, but he also didn't want to have to explain himself. That would only end with him stabbing a crochet hook through some Nosy Nelly's eye. The simple act calmed him as he was consumed by creativity. Didn't hurt that he'd figured out how to craft some damned handy poppets.

This project was a good example. With the proper cleansing, it was a simple matter to reuse poppets. Jack was pleased with the design of this doll. It had a pouch in its belly, making it easy to keep binding materials or reagents in place. He didn't want to risk anything disrupting the spells he had planned for Seymour Arce.

Jack removed the hairs from his pocket, stuffing them into the poppet's pouch. Aside from nabbing people Jack cared about, Seymour's biggest mistake had been letting an Effigest within arm's reach of himself. Once the hairs were secure, he stowed the crochet hooks and yarn in his saddlebag. He hadn't planned on bringing the supplies for his new hobby along, but now that he'd spent coin, he wasn't about to leave them behind. Jack tucked the doll into the reagent pouch at his side. He'd have to do additional shopping to complete this specific working.

He stopped by the Mercantile first. Sometimes, especially in the Untamed Territory, a good Mercantile stocked reagents. That wasn't the case here, though. The shopkeeper directed him to a new store that had opened since Jack's last visit, and before long, he stepped into Botanica Magica.

A dryad ran the place, and she eyed him warily as soon as he entered. A trash griffin perched on her shoulder—sort of like someone had the brilliant idea to cross a raccoon with a goshawk, and the result had come out ornery.

"You're not one of our outlaws," the dryad observed, arms crossed. The daisies rooted in her hair swayed as she tilted her head.

"Nah, but guessing my coin is still good here." Jack jingled his coin purse for emphasis.

The dryad might not trust him, but money spoke, and before long, he was the proud owner of flashfire pepper, bittercress, serpent's bite, and a tin of bunyip fat. He took his prizes back to his room to complete the assembly and start the spell.

The working he had in mind wasn't pleasant, but Jack wasn't here to go easy on anyone. In a town full of outlaw mages who would have no problems with sending him to Perdition, he couldn't pull any punches. He held the poppet in the palm of his hand, tightening his grip as he called on his power to activate it. A soft glow washed over the poppet as the sympathetic magic took hold, binding Seymour Arce to the tiny doll.

This was either going to be the power play he needed to gain the upper hand, or it might be his biggest mistake. *Only one way to find out.*

Before heading to his room for the night, Jack paid a visit to Zepheus. The stallion had no new information, though he was curious about Jack's spell. The outlaw had brought the poppet with him, and in the growing darkness, he crouched down to tuck the tiny figure far beneath the manger in Zepheus's stall.

<I smell pepper,> the pegasus observed. <You didn't...?>

"I did," Jack hissed, waving a hand at the palomino. He raked some straw beneath the manger, hoping it would help cut the scent of pepper. A human nose wouldn't detect it, but he worried a unicorn might since Zepheus could. Though, the odds of a unicorn understanding what the pepper meant were low. "I ain't here to be nice."

<This working is quite a bit further south than *nice*. It's downright cruel.>

Jack shook his head. As far as he was concerned, Seymour Arce was already playing dirty and deserved the consequences that were coming for him. With a vengeful smile, he whispered the last words that would activate all the spellwork on the poppet.

With that task done, he retreated to his room. Jack slept with his sixgun and poppet on the bedside table—he wouldn't put it past Seymour to send someone to kill him in the middle of the night. But the night passed without disruption, leaving him to wonder if his working hadn't taken. Did Seymour have protections of some sort in place?

After he breakfasted, he stopped by the stables to check in with Zepheus again. As he was about to leave, the stallion's ears pricked forward. <There's some gods-awful caterwauling coming this way, and someone is screeching your name.>

"Well, that's good news. I was starting to worry I fizzled and didn't know it." Jack stretched, rolling his shoulders to loosen the muscles. A moment later, he heard the same sound: a high-pitched squeal headed their way.

<You're not worried they're going to shoot you on sight or turn you into a toad?>

"The worst Seymour could do is shoot me or rearrange my face with his fist." Though, to be sure, that wouldn't be pleasant. Any blow the Strength mage landed would make one from Jack feel like a love tap by comparison. "But that hex ain't gonna poof if I'm dead." He only hoped that the Copperhead Ringleader understood that very important detail.

<I'm coming with you,> Zepheus said, nosing his stall door open to follow his rider out into the bright morning sunshine.

Jack knew it would be a futile effort to dissuade the stallion. Besides, they were partners. Zepheus had saved his hide many times before. It was good to have him at his back. He simply nodded his agreement, swaggering out into the dusty street in front of the stable.

Seymour stood at the head of a group of Copperheads. Mostly, the rest of the desperadoes did a fair job of looking properly menacing. They either had revolvers or rifles in their hands, or sprites of magic glimmering on their fingertips. Seymour, though…well, Jack had a difficult time not guffawing at the man.

Seymour's face was red, his eyes bulging as he shrilled Jack's name like a piglet calling for a sow. Each step was delicate, as if he were walking across a patch of cacti. Jack's favorite part was the way Seymour frantically clutched his groin.

"What…did…you…*do?*" Seymour finally wheezed the words out amid his extreme discomfort. The rest of his gang fanned out around them, hemming in Jack and Zepheus.

Jack cocked his head. "Looks like you've rolled in the hay with one too many ladies or gents, Seymour. Might wanna think about seeing a Healer."

Seymour made a frustrated rasp. "*Magic.*"

Maureen the Dread Surgeon, Seymour's second, stepped forward. "He saw *me*. And I know a hex when I see it."

Jack had been counting on that. He knew the Copperheads boasted one of the most fearsome Healers in Iphyria. Nadine was scary in her own way but overall had good intentions for her patients. Maureen wasn't the nursemaiding sort, aside from when it came to the Copperheads who rode at her side. Though, maybe not even then. It wasn't healthy to get too close to her. Maureen had earned her moniker after using her magic to amputate key appendages from anyone who got on her bad side.

Jack smiled, allowing some of his own sadism to ooze into the expression. "Then you'll also know I'm the only one who can break it." That was a half-truth. If another Effigest found his poppet, they could cancel the spell. At his words, the enemy outlaws stepped closer, the circle constricting like a noose. Jack crooked a finger at them. "That poppet ain't on me, friends."

Seymour glared at him through watering eyes. Maureen eyed the outlaw leader, and in that long look, Jack knew she was wondering if the time was ripe to take over leadership of the Copperheads. Something to watch. "What do you *want*, Wildfire?" Seymour growled through gritted teeth.

Jack smiled. "Show me the merchandise you think I'll be interested in. Then maybe I'll do something about that pickled pepper pecker of yours."

SHADY WAREHOUSES DOWN BY DOCKS WERE A FINE PLACE FOR AN ambush. Izhadell had boasted a warehouse district, and Jack had seen his fair share of ambushes there. Even conducted some of them himself in his time as a theurgist. Tension laced the back of his neck with every step as the Copperheads showed him and Zepheus to the building that was to serve as their auction hall.

The malevolence surrounding them made him downright itchy. *Pretty sure I ain't gonna be welcome in Thorn again.*

He followed Seymour into the depths of the warehouse, surprised by the pungent bouquet of scents that assaulted his nose. The sounds, too. Muted growls, the call of birds, lowing, hisses, and quiet voices. Crying. Moans. It was like stepping into a menagerie. Jack narrowed his eyes.

Beside him, Zepheus flicked his ears, taking in all the sounds. <So *many*.> Awe and horror were ripe in his mental voice. Jack felt the same way.

"The pegasi first," Jack suggested, eyeing Seymour lest the man make some sort of double-cross. Jack figured if he got the pegasi, it would be a lot easier to make an escape.

"You don't call the shots here," Seymour said, though he didn't sound very convincing, what with the nasal whimper that punctuated his speech as he continued to experience discomfort in a man's most precious region.

Jack smiled. "Yeah?"

Seymour trudged down a row of stalls, stopping midway along. A snort of surprise echoed in the depths, and a moment later, Oberidon's head thrust over the partition. A rope with glittering beads tangled around his neck, stifling his magic. Jack frowned at the round, weeping wounds dotting Oberidon's flanks. *Unicorns. I hate unicorns.*

Emrys was one stall over. The stallion's head was low, eyes dimmed with depression. Jack's lips pressed together in displeasure. The black stud was taking his and Blaise's capture hard. *Don't you worry, you contrary pie-licker. We're gonna spring you both.*

Jack pivoted on his boot heels. "These two stallions are sentries from out of Fortitude. You release 'em to me, and I'll drop the spell that's making your pecker feel like you dipped it in a hill of fire ants."

Seymour's face contorted at his crass words, while a handful of his compatriots guffawed—including Maureen, who still looked ready to stage an overthrow at any moment. Jack needed her to wait a little longer.

"Agreed. Do it *now*," Seymour snarled.

Jack shook his head. "No can do—or did you forget I don't have the poppet on me? But you have my word that once they're free and I get back to the poppet, it'll happen."

Seymour blew out a frustrated breath. "Then go ahead. Leave and do it!"

"Nope." Jack leaned against the stall, rubbing Oberidon between the eyes to soothe the pegasus. Spotted ears pricked forward, following the conversation. Emrys had lifted his head, too, finally realizing that help had arrived. "I reckon you got something else of interest to me. *Personal* interest."

Tight-lipped, Seymour spun and gestured for him to follow. Jack shook his head. "Nope. Release the pegasi first."

Seymour tightened his fists, and for a moment, Jack feared he'd pushed the man too far. But then the ongoing hex reminded the Ringleader that he needed Jack in one piece. "Get those bang-tails out *now*."

Seymour's outlaws hustled to obey his order, and moments later, Emrys and Oberidon clopped beside Zepheus, free of the infernal salt-iron.

<We're getting Blaise?> Emrys asked, his ears pitched forward and renewed hope in his eyes.

Jack tightened his mouth and gave a small nod. He and the trio of pegasi followed the Ringleader down a new row of cells, and at the end—well, he had to fight back the urge to run to the bars to check on his daughter for himself. Instead, he ambled up as if he had all the time in the world, though his gaze flicked over her, assessing her for injuries. *Faedra help you lot if you harmed my daughter.*

Emmaline appeared unharmed. Blaise was beside her, his steady gaze on Jack as if he were trying to make the outlaw understand something. Jack couldn't figure out what, though.

The Breaker glanced at Emrys when the stallion pawed at the ground.

Jack glared over his shoulder at Seymour. "You have my daughter and my—" He paused. *Damn it, Blaise.* "Friend. Let them go."

He saw Blaise's eyebrows lift in surprise at the admission of friendship. Then the young man gave the tiniest shake of his head. Jack narrowed his eyes.

"No," Seymour said, drawing Jack's attention. "You can have the girl, but not the Breaker. You've had him long enough."

Jack saw Blaise's shoulders rise in agitation, then fall back down. The young man was annoyed at the situation and clearly didn't want to be thought of as a possession, but he didn't want Jack to spring him?

Jack clenched his fists until the nails bit into his palms. Even if Blaise wanted to stay here—*why?*—the outlaw needed to make it look like he wouldn't let go of the Breaker easily. "No, he's *mine.*" Behind him, Emrys snorted in outrage. Jack hoped the blasted stud wasn't about to bite him for playing along with whatever Blaise was up to.

Seymour smiled. "I'll cut you a deal, Wildfire." Then he paused, taking a moment to scratch frantically at his groin. "You dispel the hexes on me, and you get the pegasi and the girl. *And* you get to leave town alive." Around him, the Copperheads all took a step forward, as if they had choreographed it. "Quite charitable of me, to be sure."

Jack glowered around at the group, though overall, that was a fair deal. "The *alive* part better include my daughter and the pegasi."

Seymour waved a hand. "It does. We'll be right generous and even let you stay for the auction. We're happy to take golden eagles from Fortitude."

I bet you are. Jack glanced at Blaise. *Hope you know what you're doing, Breaker.* "Deal."

CHAPTER THIRTY-FOUR
It's What I Do

Blaise

I can do this. Blaise closed his eyes, grounding himself. He had underestimated how much Emmaline's presence had encouraged him, but he focused on his relief that she was with her father. And the pegasi were free, too. Blaise wished he'd had some way to explain what he was doing to Emrys. He trusted Emmaline would tell him, but there was a possibility the stallion would be too upset to listen. *This is going to take a lot of apology cakes.*

Blaise spent the late afternoon watching and learning. He noticed that the men and women who patrolled the area where he and the other mystical races were kept weren't gifted with magic. Normal humans—they looked tough, but he wondered if they were simply hirelings and not true outlaws. Security capable of wandering around the salt-iron without feeling the drain and ache.

He also noticed they were lazy. Judging by the routes of the more stringent guards, he figured they were supposed to walk up and down each aisle to check on their charges. But many of them were lax, simply peering down the aisle before moving on, heading off to other entertainments.

The closest prisoners to his cell were a full-blooded knocker and a young Theilian. The white-furred Theilian curled up in a ball in the middle of the cage, trembling. The knocker spent her time pacing, frowning with concentration.

When Blaise was certain no guards were going to sneak up on him, he edged closer to his neighbors. "Howdy."

The Theilian growled and made no other response. The knocker gave him a mistrustful look. "What?"

Blaise glanced at the windows lining the upper third of the cavernous warehouse. Despite the dirt riming the huge panes of glass, he judged by their dimness that night had fallen. Fatigue dogged him, but he couldn't sleep. Not yet. "Do either of you know anything about an alchemist?"

The knocker's frown deepened. "Ew. No, why?"

"Because I'm looking for one," Blaise said. "And once I find her, I can escape."

The knocker snorted a laugh. "You hear that, Furball? This joker here thinks he's going to escape the Copperheads!" She slapped a hand against her knee. "You lost your chance when you didn't go with your friends."

The Theilian lifted her head, uncurling and creeping closer, dark nose quivering. "You're the Breaker." The lupine's voice was soft, reverent. "The howls of your lifesong have made it as far as the mountains of Theilia."

Blaise blinked. "What?"

The Theilian cocked her head. "Your scent was added to the lifesong by the outcast Kur Agur."

That sounded all kinds of strange. Kur Agur, the only Theilian to call Fortitude home, had howled about him? Blaise had a lot of questions and no time to ask them.

"The Breaker?" The knocker edged over. "Okay, I've heard of you. At the very least, this may be entertaining." She rubbed her hands together, and Blaise wondered if she was related to Flora or if most knockers were this eager for dangerous entertainment. "Furball, your sniffer got anything useful?"

"Lirra, *not* Furball," the Theilian corrected with a grumble. She sucked in a deep breath, lips curled and nostrils twitching with the action. "There are too many scents."

"Wait." Blaise dug into his pocket. The measuring spoon. Would it be enough? It had seemed like such a small, inconsequential keepsake at the time. "This belongs to her. Would it help?"

Lirra's eyes lit up. "Yes. Though I will do you little good in a cage."

Blaise grinned. "What if you weren't in the cage?"

"You can do that?" the knocker hissed, incredulous.

In answer, Blaise moved to the rear of his cell. It was darker at the back, and he doubted anyone would easily notice his handiwork if he were careful. He closed his hands around the bottom of a slat, his magic chewing through it. Blaise duplicated the effort at the top, then gently shifted the slat out of the way, concealing it in a shadow. He squeezed through, easing out the hand span of inches between the cage and the wall. It wasn't comfortable, but he managed.

"Guess you *can* do that," the knocker said, eager. "Can you free us?"

Blaise pursed his lips. "In time. First, I have to find the alchemist." He paused outside Lirra's cage. "I'll let you out on the condition that you have to go back in when we finish."

The Theilian growled. "I don't wish to."

Blaise understood. Oh, how he understood. He sighed. "Do you trust me?"

"No," the knocker said.

Lirra whined, her ears flattening. "I don't *want* to, but I know what the lifesong says." She hunched her fuzzy shoulders. "You won't let us be sold?"

"No," Blaise said softly, shaking his head. "I won't." He only hoped he wasn't making a promise he couldn't keep.

Lirra scratched a clawed hand at her throat. "I will work with you and return here when we finish."

With her promise, Blaise set about releasing her. The knocker watched, her jealousy obvious. Blaise hoped she wasn't the petty sort who might call for a guard. Lirra stepped cautiously through the gap he created, then took the spoon into her hands, sniffing deeply.

She gave him a toothy grin. "I have the scent. Are you able to stalk quietly? We don't wish the guards to catch us."

"I'll try," Blaise said.

"Come." And then she was off, her feet whisper-soft on the stone floor.

Blaise hurried after her. Other mystic creatures stirred at their passing, but none called out. Lirra kept to the shadows as best she could, and Blaise mimicked her, though he would never have her grace. As they made their way through the warehouse, he was awestruck by the size of the place—and the sheer amount of *merchandise* the Copperheads had collected.

At the end of an aisle, Lirra paused, stretching as tall as she could with her nose in the air. Her eyes gleamed in the dim light, and she turned again, leading him onward. "We are close."

Blaise hoped she was right. They were no longer in the area that housed the mystic races and creatures, but were surrounded by crate after crate of items. Some of them appeared to hold books—rare ones, Blaise guessed. And...his eyebrows raised. Grimoires? One of them appeared to be bound in leather that looked a bit too much like human skin for his comfort, and he hurried to keep up with the Theilian. Another crate held glittering dragon scales, while yet another had Knossan horns. His stomach turned at the sight.

"Ahead," Lirra murmured, extending a claw down the aisle. She cocked an ear. "The guards have been here recently, so you may have a window of time. I will return to my cell." Her eyes bored into his. "And *you* will return?"

Blaise swallowed, nodding. "I will."

With his agreement, she ghosted away. Blaise turned, quietly slipping down the aisle of crates. He thought Lirra had been mistaken until he saw the cell nearly hidden by stacks of stolen goods. It was like the one he had been in, though it was furnished with a cot. Someone was asleep on it. Blaise crept closer, eyes straining in the low light. Dark curls drooped over one side of the cot. *Mom.* His heart raced, and his magic swelled, ready to be unleashed. *No, we have to be careful. Need a plan.* But first, he had to be sure she was okay.

"Mom." Blaise kept his voice low, and for a moment, he thought he was going to have to speak louder to wake her. But then her head jerked upright, and she stared at him as if he were a phantom.

Marian slowly sat up, the rough blanket falling away from her. "Blaise?" The word echoed off the crates surrounding them, and she winced, dropping her voice. "Gods, Blaise. What are you doing here? You...you came for me?" Her eyes glistened, tears building in the corners.

"Of course, I came for you." Blaise felt tears well in his eyes, too. But there wasn't time for tearful reunions, not yet. They were both still in danger. "You're my Mom."

"Even after...everything?" Marian swallowed, as if she couldn't bear to give voice to the alchemical experimentation she had put him through.

"You'll always be my Mom, even if you did things you regret," Blaise whispered. But did she regret them? The question was on his lips, but he didn't speak it.

She answered anyway. "Not a single day has passed when I didn't wish I could change the things done to you." Marian rose from the cot, stepping over to the bars nearest him. "I wish I could change *everything*." Grief etched the curve of her lips. "Everything I've done has hurt the people I care about the most."

Suddenly, Blaise saw that no matter how angry he was with his mother, she was even more so with herself. Marian Hawthorne wasn't blind to the long-term consequences of her choices. He swallowed, unsure of what to say.

His mother shut her eyes. "Your father is dead because of me. Maybe Luci and Brody, too."

"No," Blaise whispered, shaking his head. "No, they made it." He reached out and placed one of his hands on hers. "They're safe. I got them." Blaise hoped they were still safe, but he trusted Nadine.

Marian's eyes flashed open, hope in their depths. "Oh, Blaise." She shifted her hand, her fingers moving against his. She gave him a light squeeze. "You shouldn't be here."

Relief at finding his mother filled him, replacing the anger he'd felt toward the Copperheads. He didn't need vengeance. He only needed to get her away from here. "I'm going to get you out."

She frowned. "They want you, too. You're not safe here."

"I know. They already got me."

Marian blinked, startled. "What? Wait...you freed yourself?"

Blaise couldn't help his smile. He was ridiculously pleased he was finding uses for his magic. "I'm a Breaker. I broke out. It's what I do."

His mother took a shaky breath, thinking. Then she nodded. "Okay. What's the plan? Are we escaping now?"

Uh-oh. Here we go with people assuming I have a plan. He rubbed the back of his head. "I could break you out, but it's not that simple. It'll take some time. I wanted to be sure I could find you first."

Marian studied him. "Well, you found me." A wavering smile flitted on her lips, and she reached out, cupping his cheek with one hand. "Thank you. You're capable of such amazing things, my Dandelion."

He paused. *Dandelion*. When he had been small, she'd called him that as a pet name—but he hadn't heard it in years. "What do you mean by that?"

She took a deep breath before answering. "Tough. Resilient. Filled with goodness in a way that's not easily destroyed."

Her words and faith warmed him. For a moment, he felt like a small child, safe with his mother. He relaxed against her hand for a dozen heartbeats before pulling away. "I'll be back, Mom."

"Get some rest, Blaise. You look exhausted."

He chuckled, shaking his head. *Still my Mom.*

CHAPTER THIRTY-FIVE
At Least We're Disasters Together

Jefferson

It was ill-advised, but Jefferson had drunk himself into a stupor. It seemed his best way of coping with his current situation. And it was the only thing that helped to send his worried mind to sleep.

At least he had the dreamscape again, though it was little solace. His magic sang as it filled the surrounding void, rolling out like retreating thunderheads as Fortitude took shape. The familiar town made him feel a little better about things, though he knew it was a temporary balm. Then he paused. *Should I?* Jefferson glanced at the cheerful yellow bakery, Blaise's name boldly scrawled over the awning. *Will he be angry with me? Maybe not since the Quiet Ones haven't figured out my magic.*

Besides, Jefferson missed Blaise terribly, and under the circumstances, he would be the easiest person to locate. Finding Blaise, *being* with Blaise, had become second nature.

He reconsidered, though. As much as he missed Blaise, his beau was too far away to help him. Kittie or Flora, though... Yes, he decided to err on the side of being a responsible mage. While he wasn't as familiar with Kittie, he stood a good chance of being able to locate Flora.

Jefferson sent out a tendril of his dream magic, then stopped when he felt it butt up against a barrier of some sort. *Strange.* He tried again, but once more, his magic came up short. Or rather, it was like a seedling trying to break through stone. Not impossible, but quite difficult.

What's stopping me? Jefferson pulled his magic back, assessing the situation. *Oh.* The Quiet Ones must have the estate warded. That made sense—it would block enemies from scrying their location, too. That didn't bode well for him, though.

Except... He frowned, turning in a circle in the empty dream-streets. It was difficult to describe, but the warding that surrounded him wasn't all-encompassing. There was a tiny crack, allowing something from the outside in. It reminded him of a poorly hung carriage door he'd come across once that had allowed a breath of winter's chill inside.

Jefferson pursed his lips. No, this wasn't a something. It was a *someone.*

Blaise. He nearly laughed with joy. His tenuous connection to the Breaker was a tiny chink in the ward, but it was there, and it was enough. Jefferson hoped Blaise was asleep.

He sent his magic arrowing towards that tiny gap, relieved when he felt it pass through. It was like threading a needle, and Jefferson suspected this would only work with Blaise. *Why? Because I love him? Or because his blood made me what I am? A combination of both? Or is it something darker, like a remnant of our geasa? No, that's long gone.* He didn't know the cause, but he was glad for whatever it was.

Now, he only had to hope Blaise was sleeping. He felt the other man's distant presence, and Jefferson was tempted to crash through to him. But he knew better than to do that to Blaise. No, instead, he approached the dream door that separated them and imagined giving it a polite knock.

Jefferson felt Blaise's response. There were no words, only surprise followed by assent. And then Blaise was there, in the dreamscape, with him. The Breaker closed the distance, throwing his arms around Jefferson and tugging him close.

"Is it really you, or do I just miss you this much?" Blaise mumbled into his shoulder.

Jefferson relaxed, enjoying the feel of Blaise against him. "Can't it be both?"

The Breaker stayed in the embrace but pulled back to look him in the eye. "Have you made it back to Fortitude?"

Wouldn't he know if I'd made it back there? Jefferson blinked at the question. "I...no. I'm still in Ganland." He winced at the admission as Blaise frowned. "It's a long story." Jefferson raised his brows at his beau. "And I take it your question means *you're* not in Fortitude?" He hoped it meant Blaise had gone to Rainbow Flat to reconcile with his mother, as he'd said he would.

It was Blaise's turn to look rueful. "No, and that's also a long, unhappy story." The Breaker sighed, resting his chin atop Jefferson's shoulder. Heartbreak radiated through the younger man.

"Do you want to go to the bakery?" Jefferson asked softly. "We can talk."

Blaise nodded, and together they crossed to the building. The younger mage seemed to shed some of his nerves as soon as he entered, though they both knew it was the dreamscape and not real. But for the moment, it was real enough. Blaise set to work, doing the thing Jefferson could always count on him to do when he was worried: bake.

Jefferson moved companionably beside Blaise. It had taken some doing, but he had learned his way around the Breaker's baking workflow. He banished his greatcoat and then rolled up his sleeves so they wouldn't get in the way.

"Shall I go first, or you?" Jefferson asked.

Blaise swallowed, closing his eyes for a moment. "You."

Whatever had spurred Blaise to leave Fortitude was painful. It almost made Jefferson wish Blaise would share first, but he would wait. As they worked, he explained the chain of events that had led to the kidnapping attempt, the revelation of his identity, and losing his rings.

"Oh, Jefferson," Blaise whispered when he'd completed his tale. The Breaker set aside the ingredients he had pulled out, wiping his fingertips on a towel. Then he closed the distance between them, wrapping his arms around Jefferson. While the dreamscape wasn't real, the reassurance and love in Blaise's embrace *was*. "I know how much you didn't want that ever again."

"The worst part is they killed *me*." Jefferson hissed out a breath. "I mean Jefferson. I can't be who I want to be anymore." *I should have known I couldn't escape the clutches of my family name. All I had was a respite, nothing more.*

"That's not true," Blaise pointed out, reaching up to touch his face. The face he always wore in the dreamscape. *Jefferson.*

"I mean out in the world."

Blaise met his eyes, and for a moment, the Breaker's gaze was like an anchor. "I know. That's what I mean, too. They may have brought you down, but Jefferson Cole is too smart to be done away with so easily."

Blaise's faith made him feel a little better, but Jefferson knew that was an easy thing for his beau to say, not knowing the full gravity of the situation. "But if I can't…if I never get my cabochon ring back…" He would be forever cursed with a Wells family face, no matter the name he used.

"I know it took me a while to come to this decision, but I love you no matter what you look like," Blaise said, leaning in to deliver a soft kiss. "And we'll get your ring back. Somehow." When Jefferson smiled, Blaise continued, "Are Kittie, Mindy, and Flora okay?"

Jefferson shook his head. "I don't know. I certainly hope so. The warding here is too tight, and you're the only one I could reach." Jefferson sincerely hoped the Board had made no new attempts on his friends. It chafed that he wasn't around to do anything to help them. He sighed. "And you? What's happened?"

Blaise went back to the pie lattice he had been constructing, a sure sign he needed a distraction to help him through. As he worked, he recounted the days after the delegation had left. The shocking letter delivered by Hank, and Blaise's frantic journey to Rainbow Flat. Finding his siblings unharmed but afraid, and his father dead. His mother stolen away in the night.

Jefferson sucked in a surprised breath as Blaise continued with his tale. He hadn't thought that anything could possibly be worse than his own situation. But this? It was horrific. *I should have stayed with him.*

"You're not hurt, are you?" Jefferson asked when Blaise finished. He knew of the Copperheads from his travels in the Untamed Territory. They weren't known for being polite. Even Flora would be reluctant to tangle with them, which said something.

Blaise shook his head. "I'm not hurt, though I can't say the same for Emrys and Oby." Anger flashed in his eyes. "But Jack got them out. And Em."

"But not you?" Jefferson asked, curious. Though, he suspected Blaise was someone everyone wanted—and not for the same reasons as Jefferson. Others would want to use him for his power.

"No," Blaise said. "I stayed in the auction warehouse. I found my Mom."

That seemed to be the first bit of good news in the entire awful situation. "And did you free her?"

"Not yet."

"Hmm." Jefferson rubbed his smooth cheek. "So, you're stuck in an auction house run by the meanest desperadoes in the Untamed Territory. I'm stuck in the estate of a shadowy cabal. Fortunes of Tabris, we're a mess, aren't we?"

"We're kind of a disaster," Blaise agreed, sounding much calmer about everything than Jefferson would have expected.

"At least we're disasters together," Jefferson murmured, winning a smile from Blaise. He picked up a towel and dabbed a spot of flour off Blaise's beard. "I don't know how you manage to cover yourself with flour in the dreamscape."

"Would you have me any other way?"

"No. You're perfect as you are," Jefferson admitted, savoring the sweetness of that truth. Then he straightened, returning his attention to their problems. "Do you have a plan?"

Blaise pursed his lips. "Why does everyone assume I have a plan? My plan ended with 'find Mom.' So no." He glanced at Jefferson. "Why? Do *you* have a plan?"

"Finding *you* was my plan," Jefferson said, and Blaise's smile nearly illuminated the bakery. "They unwittingly blocked my ability to get my magic past whatever wards they have set up—aside from my link with you."

Blaise froze, looking at him sharply. "The geasa is *gone.*"

"I don't mean the geasa." Jefferson bumped his shoulder against Blaise's in apology. "Maybe it's because my magic spawned from you. Or a connection of a more romantic nature."

Blaise's brows slammed down over his eyes at that. "What?"

Jefferson sighed. "Because I *love* you. Honestly, I thought I'd made that clear on multiple occasions."

Blaise's expression softened. "You have. I was just…" He shook his head, rubbing the back of his neck as he did when he was feeling especially awkward. "You think so?"

"I think love is a sort of magic all its own," Jefferson murmured, meaning every word.

The Breaker paused in his work, all traces of agitation from the moment before gone. He looked as if he were gathering his thoughts, as if Jefferson's simple truth had struck a target. But when he spoke, he did a very Blaise thing: he changed the subject. "Do you think we could find Jack in the dreamscape, like we did before?"

Jefferson shifted closer to Blaise, wrapping an arm around

his back. Blaise glanced at him, an apologetic cast in his eyes. Sometimes, Jefferson had learned, his beau was at a loss for how to respond. He was getting better, little by little. *I know you love me. You're just figuring out that bit of magic, along with everything else.*

Jefferson pursed his lips, releasing Blaise from the embrace. The Breaker stayed comfortably close, though he went back to work on his pie. "I don't know. You're the only one I could reach..." He let the words trail off, puzzling through things. "Oh. Do you suppose you're acting as a bridge?" That made sense in a strange way.

"Won't know unless we try," Blaise reasoned, slipping the pie into the oven. "And this time, I know Jack is close to where I am. Physically, anyway. Not sure what that translates to in here." He waved a hand to indicate their current surroundings.

"Would he be sleeping now, do you think?" Jefferson asked.

Blaise shrugged. "Maybe. I think you're stalling."

"Maybe I'm trying to savor every moment I have alone with you."

"Try it, Dreamer," Blaise said, though there was amusement in his tone. It was music to Jefferson's ears.

Gods, I've missed this. Missed him. Jefferson took a deep breath and blew it out slowly, focusing his magic on finding Jack. He came up against the same resistance at first, but then he felt something strange—as if Blaise were guiding his magic. *There.* He found the shape of the Effigest's slumbering mind. Jack was well and truly asleep, though his dreams were troubled, full of worry and anger. Small wonder after what they had been through. It was a simple matter to coil his power around Jack and shepherd him into the dreamscape.

The outlaw materialized in the bakery, frowning at the pair. He glanced around. "This the real thing, or am I so busy fretting I'm dreaming about your damned dreamscape?"

Jefferson huffed. "Of course, it's the real dreamscape. Have some appreciation for the difficulty it took to bring you here." He gestured at Blaise.

Jack cocked his head, turning to the Breaker. "That the real you?" When Blaise nodded, the outlaw's shoulders relaxed, though annoyance carved his face. "This business of staying in the warehouse is a piss-poor idea. I was going to get you out!" In a rare occurrence, Jefferson found himself agreeing with the outlaw.

Blaise grimaced. "It was the best idea I had to find my Mom. And I *did* find her."

Jack snorted. "You got a plan I need to know about?"

The Breaker sighed. "Why does everyone assume I have a plan?"

"'Cause if you've got the balls to sneak out of a Copperhead cage and hunt down your mother, seems like you should have figured out more than that," the Effigest said.

Blaise frowned. Jefferson watched the exchange, realizing what Jack was doing—he was goading the younger man into talking through a plan. The outlaw liked to teach in his own cantankerous way. Jefferson had personal experience with his methods.

"Could you or Em cast Obfuscation on my mother, and we sneak her out that way?" Blaise asked after a moment.

Jack considered it. "I'd need something of her essence."

The Breaker became more animated. "I have one of her old alchemical measuring spoons. We can do this. We can get my Mom out." His relief was almost palpable. Then he glanced away, guilt flashing across his face.

"What is it?" Jefferson asked.

A muscle in Blaise's jaw tightened. "There's so many...so many people stuck here. Other mystic races. I met a Theilian and a knocker." As soon as he spoke, Jefferson understood. Blaise wouldn't leave them behind.

A smirk spread across Jack's face. "Good. I got no tolerance for outlaws who steal *people*." Sometimes, Jefferson decided, the brazen outlaw was downright likable. This was something that he, too, could support. Then Jack's gaze settled on Jefferson. "How's my wife doing?"

Jefferson swallowed. "Ah, she was well the last I saw—"

"What do you mean by *the last I saw?*" The outlaw glowered.

"Another long story." Jefferson sighed, then launched into an extremely abridged version, heavily stressing that Kittie had been doing well until the fire.

Jack waved a hand at that. "Fire ain't gonna hurt my wife. I'm more concerned about the Salties who might blame it on *her.*"

Jefferson blinked. He hadn't even thought of that, though he'd been distracted. He cleared his throat. "I should see her again soon, though. I hope. My captors want to put me back in the action as Malcolm Wells."

"She knows who you are," Jack said bluntly.

Jefferson had suspected as much. He'd doubted Jack would keep that from his wife for her own safety. And she had done well to keep that information to herself. "Just as well in this situation."

"You got a plan to get out of the thorn patch you're in?" the outlaw asked.

Well, now he knew exactly how Blaise felt. "It's a work in progress." Jefferson hoped it was, at any rate.

"You'll figure somethin' out," Jack drawled, in a surprise to both Jefferson and Blaise. "You got more lives than a cat."

"I think you just complimented me. I truly *am* dreaming," Jefferson muttered, earning a laugh from Blaise.

The outlaw ignored him, turning to Blaise. "We can't let the Copperheads see this auction through. This is what I'm thinking…"

Jefferson didn't like the idea of Blaise taking on the Copperheads, but the showdown seemed inevitable. As he listened to their plan formulate, he decided that if Blaise must take on the most feared desperadoes in the land, he had no better ally than the Scourge of the Untamed Territory.

CHAPTER THIRTY-SIX
The Only Idea

Jack

Jack eyed the poppet sitting between him and Emmaline. It was Seymour's crocheted poppet, though he'd deactivated the spells as promised. He didn't want the Copperhead leader to have any reason to come after him prematurely. Of course, Seymour didn't know he still had a poppet keyed to him. He'd demanded Jack hand over his poppet, and it had only taken a simple bit of sleight of hand to give Seymour a blank. No way would he ever know the difference.

"You sure about this?" Jack asked, glancing at Emmaline.

His daughter shrugged. "No, but I think it'll work. Hope so, anyway." She picked up the poppet in one hand and a small seashell in the other. Jack had nullified the poppet with mugwort, rendering it a fresh slate for her to work on aside from the hairs still keyed to Seymour. He watched as she carefully tucked a tiny conch shell into her ear.

Jack was antsy to ask if it had worked. She ran her fingers over the poppet, making small, silent adjustments to the spell. Pride soared in him. She was truly becoming a natural at her magic, and it was possible that one day she might even be better than him.

After a moment, she grinned. "I can hear 'em!"

"That's my girl," Jack rumbled, leaning over to kiss her forehead. "I'm gonna go do my part now."

She gave him a thumbs up to show she'd heard, though she was now intent on magically eavesdropping on the Copperhead Ringleader. Jack smirked. *Yeah, this might actually work.*

He slipped out of their shared room, stopping by the stables to update the stallions. Emrys was still upset about the whole mess, pacing a furrow into the straw at his feet. As soon as he saw Jack, he demanded they rescue Blaise immediately.

"Workin' on it," Jack told the impatient stud. Zepheus and Oberidon were more receptive to his news, and they were ready and waiting to do their part. With the equines fully informed, he headed to his next meeting.

The dark alley behind the warehouse stank of rotting fish and shit. The trio of Knossans snorted continuously, as if they were trying to clear the vile odors from their nostrils. Jack almost pitied them, but the alley made the perfect rendezvous point for exactly that reason. Others would avoid it unless they had a compelling reason to go there.

"Let us be done with this place quickly," Gore rumbled, his alabaster tail flicking behind him with clear irritation.

"Yeah, I hear you," Jack agreed. He kept his little trick of an odor-blocking spell on his poppet to himself. As soon as he'd found the alley, he'd whipped it up. "I've got three keys here. Not enough for all of us, but the more of us opening cages, the better."

The Knossans nodded, their horns sweeping with the motion. "That is fine. We will leave Roam unhindered, so that once our younglings are located, he may see them to safety," Deal said.

Jack figured that wasn't the worst plan. The Knossans had been barred from viewing the *merchandise*—clearly, the Copperheads had figured out they were up to something. Jack didn't think it likely they'd be kept from the auction itself, though. The desperadoes were happy to take a coin from anyone, as Seymour had said.

The outlaw handed keys to Deal and Gore, then pointed to Roam. "When it's time, you're with me. I can try to keep you hidden, at least for a short while."

The spotted bull's ears twitched with concern. "Magic?"

"Well, I reckon putting a blanket over your head ain't gonna work," Jack said with a shrug, earning an amused snort from Gore. "I know I got a bit of a reputation as a top-shelf pisspot, but in this, I'm your ally." He glanced at the foreboding, mold-covered brick of the warehouse beside them. "I know the Scourge of the Untamed Territory don't seem the most trustworthy."

"You have proven to be more trustworthy than the Copper-heads," Roam said.

"That don't take much," Jack muttered.

It wasn't long before he had a rudimentary poppet with hair from the Knossan. He meant every word he'd told them—he respected the bulls, and he intended to dispose of the hair when all was said and done. Jack finished making arrangements with the trio, then headed back to the hotel.

As soon as he opened the door, Emmaline leaped up, rushing over to him. "Daddy, we've got problems."

He raised his brows. "What kind?"

She chewed on her bottom lip, pointing to the small conch shell she had removed from her ear and left on the bedside table, beside a notebook she'd used to jot down notes as she listened. Emmaline crossed to it and picked up the notebook, thrusting it at him.

Jack scowled as he pieced together her shorthand. "You telling me Marian Hawthorne was never going to be a part of the auction?"

She nodded, moving beside him to point at another line. "Yeah, exactly. They just used her as a draw. An attraction." Emmaline's face grew serious. "And now they have *Blaise* as the star feature."

Yeah, well, neither us nor the Breaker are gonna allow that. Jack nodded. "What's this here?" He ran his fingertips over a handful of words he couldn't quite make out.

Emmaline smoothed a lock of blonde hair behind one ear. "A group from Ravance has offered double the buy-out price for Blaise's Mom, so the Copperheads are going to accept."

"Yeah, that tracks," Jack said. "When is the deal going down over the alchemist? Did you hear that much?"

"The Ravanchen wizards are delivering their payment at the end of the auction."

Jack digested her information, pacing as he mused on how to handle it. It was a delicate situation all around, in a town full of so many dangerous individuals that it was almost ridiculous. He could cast Rising Dread to sow confusion and violence, using the opportunity of chaos to free Marian, but that would make it hazardous for the alchemist. And possibly for Blaise, Emmaline, and the pegasi, too. No, they needed to figure out something else.

"I don't suppose we can sneak in there beforehand and free Marian and Blaise?" Emmaline suggested hopefully.

Jack shook his head. "Nah, with the auction tonight, that would be like sticking our hand into a wasp's nest." *Hmm.* He'd hoped to extract Blaise and Marian in the chaos he planned to create during the auction.

Emmaline gave him a dubious look. "Won't we be cutting it close otherwise?"

He grinned. "Probably."

She swallowed. "Is that a good idea?"

"It's the *only* idea."

Blaise

No guards stopped by to deliver an evening meal. Blaise suspected it was because the buyers were already filtering in, claiming their seats around the ring. He heard the clatter of many feet along with rumbling, indistinguishable voices.

"Not much longer now," the knocker commented, her tone gloomy.

"The auction has to happen," Blaise said. "But that doesn't mean the deals are going to go through."

"I hope that is true. We're quite outnumbered," Lirra commented, whining as she spoke.

Blaise shook his head. "We're not outnumbered."

They were quiet after that, listening to the happenings around them. Small groups of guards—or maybe auction workers, Blaise wasn't sure—filtered down the aisles. Some of them removed the more placid creatures. Others carried boxes from the goods area.

In time, they came for Blaise's neighbors. Neither Lirra nor the knocker spoke as the Copperheads hustled them away, though they both shot looks over their shoulders, as if they felt betrayed by his broken promise.

Once they were gone, Blaise heard a soft scuff. He whirled, agitation flaring. Then he relaxed at the lithe, blonde-braided form of Emmaline slipping up beside the cell. Her expression was grim, but she flashed a brief smile at him. "Howdy, Blaise. You miss me?"

"You know it," he murmured. "How's the plan coming?"

"Eh, so far, so good. No one saw through my Obfuscation. Handy spell, that." Emmaline shifted her weight. "We have a bit of a problem, though."

Blaise raised his brows. "What?"

"You're the last on the auction block."

Of course, I am. Blaise rubbed the bridge of his nose. Their original plan relied on his sale being earlier in the auction, giving him time to play his role. "Why'd they do that? I thought my mother was going to be last."

"Yeah, um, sounds like the Copperheads are selling her to someone for an excessive buyout." Emmaline made a face.

"That's not good." Blaise shifted his weight unhappily.

Emmaline gave him an encouraging smile. "Don't worry. We're sticking with the plan. It's a good one."

Bold words, considering how often their plans went sideways. But he *had* to believe this would work. It had to. "This changes the timing." He wasn't supposed to be at the *end*. If anything, he and Jack had thought the Copperheads might put him on the block first. "What if it doesn't work?" Blaise swallowed. When plans had gone awry in the past, he had been the one to suffer. He felt light-headed, and he squeezed his eyes closed to ward off the rising panic.

"*Blaise*," Emmaline's voice was urgent, slicing through the old memories that swelled like a tide. "This was *your choice*. You own this. And you're not alone."

His eyes flashed open. She was right. In the past, those things had been done *to* him. He had been a victim. But this? Blaise had been the one to decide on this course of action. *I'm not helpless. Not anymore.* Blaise hissed out a breath. "Thanks."

"Sometimes, we all need a reminder," Emmaline whispered. "I gotta go before I'm seen. We're gonna do this." Then she opened her fist, revealing a poppet. She whispered something and faded from Blaise's immediate view, though he knew in his gut she was still there. But no one else would. Emmaline slipped away.

CHAPTER THIRTY-SEVEN
Buyer Beware

Blaise

Lirra and the knocker returned a short time later. Lirra trembled, her eyes wild as the cell door slammed behind her. The knocker muttered curses under her breath. Blaise had no time to speak to them, however, because the guards had come for him.

He didn't recognize them, but they handled the salt-iron manacles with such ease that Blaise suspected if they were outlaws, they didn't boast magic. He allowed them to clamp the shackles to his wrists, then once more placed his hands inside burlap sacks.

"C'mon, you," one man grumbled. "The sooner we get this done with, the sooner I get back to my dice game."

If we do our job right, you'll never get back to that game. Blaise made no response, though. He allowed the men to lead him down the aisle, doing his best to keep calm. His magic awaited his command. *Not now. Too soon.*

The guards brought him up behind the area set aside for the auction, leading him to a large wooden stage—though unlike any stage Blaise had seen before. It was enclosed by a mesh of barbed wire with what he suspected were salt-iron beads strewn throughout. The Copperheads left nothing to chance.

Blaise stepped onto the stage, the door creaking closed behind him. He looked out at the throng of attendees. A makeshift spotlight cobbled together from a lantern and mirrors focused on him, nearly blinding him with its glare. Blaise shielded his eyes with his bound hands, squinting to see the crowd. It was a full house, and every single face in the audience was either unfriendly or covetous. So many races were in attendance, not just humans. Knossans, elves, Theilians, knockers—others Blaise didn't recognize, too. They jostled one another, the crowd's agitation palpable.

"Here he is, ladies, gentlemen, and creatures of all variety! You asked for him, you got him! The Breaker of Fort Courage, a man with such rare magic, you'll never see it again in your lifetime." The auctioneer, a man Blaise didn't recognize, leaned over a podium, enthusiasm in his every movement. "Who will start the bidding at five hundred golden eagles?"

Five hundred golden eagles? Blaise boggled at the number, even as someone in the audience raised a card to place the first bid. No time to wonder how high the bids for him might go, however. He tapped his magic, and it came flooding to his fingers, unhampered by the salt-iron. Blaise let it chew through the sack first, the fabric falling away in jagged strips.

The crowd was loud, and if anyone noticed what he was doing, they wouldn't be heard over the masses. With his hands free of the bags, Blaise wrapped his fingers around the shackles on his opposite hand, pouring more magic into the effort.

The people in the front row saw *that*. A couple of them even rose, waving their cards to get the attention of the Copperheads. Blaise paid them no mind. He hoped Jack, Emmaline, and the Knossans were doing their part. If not, Blaise wouldn't get very far. Here, on the auction block, the enemy outnumbered him.

The bindings fell away from his wrists, landing on the timbers at his feet with a sharp metallic clatter. That made even the auctioneer stop to take notice, and he stared at Blaise, bewildered. Then he found his voice again. "Copperheads! Get this man back in shackles."

The Copperheads and their hirelings advanced on the auction block even as Blaise traced his fingers over the barbed wire, creating a gap. It parted with a twang. The approaching men and women only paused when the first screams rang out from the back of the auction gallery.

A blue and black-feathered anzu soared overhead, its lion's head agape with a guttural roar, talons raking the tops of heads with abandon. Shots rang out as someone tried to take the creature down with bullets, but it was moving too quickly. And it wasn't alone.

Bison bellowed, charging into the crowd with heads lowered, sending attendees scrambling to get out of the way. A pair of harpies shrieked, picking up a crate and smashing it against window after window, creating an escape for the winged creatures. A canine-bodied aralez howled, a rallying cry to the other flyers before bolting through an opening.

More terrestrial creatures and mystic races appeared. Blaise saw the bright flash of Lirra's fur as she wove through the crowd. She wasn't fighting, though—simply trying to find a way to freedom, the knocker close on her heels. Jackalopes hopped around in confusion. Freed bears and wolves streaked through the crowd, growling and clearing the way with calculated bites and unforgiving swipes.

A bunyip appeared, water sluicing from the sleek fur on its warm brown back as it crashed into the hapless buyers. It opened its massive mouth, grabbing a Copperhead and snapping the man's arm in two. A kelpie joined it, whistling a whinny. It fixated on a Copperhead, and the man climbed onto its back. The water horse splashed away with its unwitting prey.

No one paid attention to Blaise. They were too focused on

surviving the onslaught of the angry menagerie. At last, he had a large enough gap to squeeze through—though his safety outside of the enclosure was uncertain.

A mighty roar cut through the bedlam. The largest grasscat Blaise had ever seen leaped atop a stack of crates, looking down on the chaos. Sharp claws kneaded the crate before it jumped to the ground to stand before Blaise, leafy tail lashing.

Uh-oh. I hope it's not mad for what I did to the other grasscats. Blaise swallowed. He didn't want to use his magic on the elemental, but he would if it came down to it.

Firefly eyes peered at him, the grasscat so large that it was on a level with Blaise and didn't need to look up to meet his gaze. The beast yawned, displaying serrated, rooty fangs. Then it laid down, giving Blaise a bored look.

"I don't understand," Blaise told the feline. "And there's somewhere I need to be."

The grasscat blinked those gleaming eyes at him, slow and steady. Then he gave a regal nod, as if in understanding. The grasscat made a deep sound, almost a purr.

"I'll be on my way, then," Blaise said, easing around the creature and feeling extremely awkward about the entire conversation.

Suddenly, impossibly, the grasscat sank into the floor. Patches of grass and moss writhed toward Blaise like a shark fin cutting water. Then the grasscat flowed out of the stone beneath him, wood and vegetation reclaiming form. Blaise yelped, pulling on his magic.

The grasscat rose from the floor, Blaise squarely on the elemental's back behind a mane of dandelions and trumpet vine. The grasscat didn't speak, not in the way of a person or even a pegasus. Instead, he sent a series of images and emotions to Blaise. A grasscat leaping at Blaise, then falling to pieces, blown away like chaff on the wind while a malevolent human form watched. A profound sense of sadness tempered with understanding. The scene changed to a peaceful stream, butterflies flitting over it on a sunny day. The grasscat lounging by the water, Blaise at his side, companionable.

Peace. The grasscat sent a message of peaceful intentions. The creature was intelligent enough to know friend from foe. And he didn't blame Blaise for defending himself and others against the compelled felines. Somehow that made Blaise feel even more guilty for having dispatched the others. But now wasn't the time for regrets. It was time for action.

"Can you take me to the alchemist?" Blaise hoped his mother was unharmed in the ruckus.

The grasscat glanced back at him, making a rumble of assent. Then he made an impressive leap, pushing off with powerful hind legs to summit the crates again. The grasscat purposefully stalked along the top, allowing Blaise a better vantage of the warehouse.

Shouts and screams filled the air as men and women stampeded, trying to avoid their attackers as they sought escape. The Copperheads were in disarray, shouting orders to the crowd and one another that no one listened to. Some people were already down, unmoving from injuries they'd sustained. Blaise felt pressure in the air, magic swelling as mages called on it to fight, and mystic races answered with power of their own.

Everyone was too busy fighting or struggling to survive to pay any mind to the grasscat with the mage aboard. Blaise recognized the area they were over, pointing ahead. "That way. I think she's that way!"

The grasscat continued onward. To Blaise's dismay, they discovered that the aisle where Marian was kept bustled with activity. People were trying to claim the alchemist for themselves in the chaos.

Jack was there, too. He must have dropped his Obfuscation spell. There were so many people, he realized the spell would never work as they'd planned. The outlaw attempted to slink around the knots of people trying to slip past each other to get to

Marian. The Effigest had resorted to bodily shoving people out of his way.

"Get me down there," Blaise told the grasscat. "Please."

Reluctance shivered through the great cat, but he sprang down. Blaise dropped to the floor, and as soon as he was off, the grasscat whirled away, no doubt eager to make an escape. A dandelion puff floated in his wake. Blaise caught his breath at the sight. *Mom called me a dandelion.*

He swallowed, turning back to the throng. Someone had removed Marian from the cell, gagged and blindfolded, rendering her unable to put up much of a fight—though she was certainly trying, judging by the way she was stomping on insteps. Blaise recognized the men and women directly around his mother as Copperheads. They were no doubt trying to wrest their prize to a safer location.

But others who had gathered were having none of that. "We told you, she's *ours!*"

"Not yours until you make payment," the man who Blaise thought was the Copperhead Ringleader shouted over the cacophony. "We—*stop that man!* Stop Wildfire! He's going to take her!"

Jack had almost gotten to Marian. As one, the surrounding auction attendees turned, all staring at the outlaw. Jack was moving *fast*, but not fast enough. One of the nearby men spun, a book tucked under his arm as he raised a hand and made a grandiose gesture. Jack slowed to a crawl, and Blaise fancied he could almost hear the outlaw's outraged growl. The enemy mage made a gesture that looked suspiciously as if he were lifting a middle finger, and Jack jerked backward, thumping against a wall.

No. The Effigest struggled against the onslaught of magic holding him in place, but he was like a mouse pinned by a cat. The Copperhead Ringleader laughed at Jack's predicament. "I'm gonna enjoy this, Wildfire. You shoulda kept your nose out of our business." Then he cocked his arm back, his knuckles glowing red with power.

Blaise knew what would follow. There was no way he could reach Jack or his assailant in time. But he was close to the mage with the book. Blaise charged at the man.

The mage saw him coming, though. With the book tucked securely in place, he lifted his other hand, and Blaise felt him send the same spell out in his direction. It caught him by surprise as it shoved him back a step. The meaty crunch of a fist smashing into Jack's face split the air. Blaise gritted his teeth and called up his magic, slamming it against the tendrils that sought to drive him back. His power severed the sorcerous threads as easily as if he'd snipped a ribbon. But he didn't stop there. His magic followed the truncated wisps, bridging across to those that held Jack, severing them.

"What?" the mage gasped in surprise as his spell broke.

Jack slumped to the ground, blood pouring from his nose like a grotesque fountain. One of his eyes was screwed shut, but that didn't stop him from lashing out at his attacker now that he was free of the spell. But the outlaw he was fighting was far stronger than he. Another blow from him would do Jack in.

<We're coming!> Emrys's cry filled his mind.

"*Breaker!* That's the Breaker!" someone said excitedly, pointing at Blaise. It was the Copperhead who clutched Marian Hawthorne by the arm.

"Small wonder," the mage with the book huffed, limbering his fingers. "Now I know why my spell failed." He glanced at others who stood nearby. "Get him. He was going to be ours, anyway."

"He ain't yours to claim! He's *ours*," the Ringleader growled, sidestepping an attack from Jack to move into a better position, eyeing Blaise.

The bookish mage shook his head, gesturing for his companions to step closer. "Then you'll have to stop us."

If Blaise thought things were bad before, they suddenly got

worse. Magic, bullets, and blades were flying. He crouched, barely able to crawl to Jack, who had pulled himself up onto one elbow, clutching a bandanna tight against his nose.

"You okay?" Blaise asked, though his eyes were on his mother. Her captors were shielding her from the battle, at least. She was too precious to lose.

"Been bether," Jack lisped, spitting blood as he spoke. "Pegathuth coming."

Blaise nodded. "I heard Emrys." All they needed was for the pegasi to arrive—and to extract Marian, somehow. And for no one to get shot, stabbed, punched, or otherwise magically injured. *Easy. Haha, no.*

Jack palmed a poppet, working a spell with a trembling hand. After a moment, the blood stopped running from his nose, so Blaise guessed it was some sort of spell to staunch the wound. "You dithract them."

"What?"

The outlaw glowered, which was a hundred times more menacing when his face was a bloodied and bruised mess. "Dithract!" He waved a hand as if that would help explain what he meant.

"Oh, *distract*."

"That'th thwhat I thaid," Jack griped, clambering to his feet.

Heart thundering in his chest, Blaise stayed low to the ground and wondered what in the world he could do to distract everyone —especially those who held his mother.

<Almost there!>

Blaise swallowed, laying a palm flat against the ground and uncoiling his magic into it. The hard-packed dirt split into great furrows, cracks splintering out from Blaise like a massive spider-web. People yelled as cages, cells, and stacked crates wobbled and collapsed. Blaise narrowed his eyes, sending a crack toward the Copperheads who had his mother. With a shout, they leaped aside, Marian falling away from them.

Bloody, messy, and glorious, Jack snagged her, tugging her sideways as Zepheus and Oberidon came to the ground, snorting as they struggled to find footing. Emrys landed at the end of the aisle, where he had more room to maneuver. Jack removed Marian's blindfold and helped her climb onto Oberidon's back. As soon as the spotted stallion was airborne, he vaulted onto Zepheus and followed.

<Our turn,> Emrys announced as he charged up the aisle, bulling people out of his way.

Blaise withdrew his hand, pulling back his magic. The ground quieted, though the massive cracks remained. He rose, not realizing the trouble he was in until too late.

A dark-clad hand whipped around him, shoving a square of fabric into his face. Whatever it was, it smelled sickly sweet. Blaise grunted in surprise, trying to twist away but unable to do much of anything.

"I learned from last time," the Herald said, triumphant, as she dropped the cloth and latched onto Blaise's arm.

Blaise wanted to fight back, but he couldn't. It was difficult to even stand, must less try to get away or use his magic. Dark spots swam before his eyes.

He heard an enraged whinny, then the Herald screeched as a large, dark shape plowed into her. Blaise was nearly jerked off his feet by the impact. Too late, he realized it was Emrys, slamming against the Herald to free his rider.

The Herald sank into the wall with a groan, taking Blaise and Emrys with her. Everything went weirdly dark, followed by the sensation of falling sideways.

CHAPTER THIRTY-EIGHT

Crazier Than an Outhouse Fly

Jack

<Emrys and Blaise are gone!> Zepheus's frantic mental cry made little sense to Jack at first. His head still rang from the mighty punch Seymour had dealt, and it was difficult to breathe through his nose. Thank Faedra he'd had enough sense to throw up a weak Stonewall spell, or that blow might have caved his face in. Jack frowned, trying to deduce Zepheus's meaning. *Dead or...?* The palomino was already adjusting his course, retracing his path back to where Emrys would have landed.

<Gone,> Zepheus repeated, adamant. <Magicked away!> His tail lashed in his wake.

Magicked away. Anger flooded through the outlaw's veins as he absorbed the information. Who would have taken the pair? And how? Zepheus touched down in the middle of the ruined ground, mindful of the massive furrows Blaise had wrought.

The Salties and Ravanchens were still squabbling with magic and weapons, though few remained on either side. Seymour was face-down in the dirt, blood leaking out from beneath him. Jack reined in the urge to shoot the prone outlaw out of principle; it would be a waste of bullets. And he wasn't one to waste bullets.

<They're growing tired,> Zepheus advised, backing up to stay out of the line of dangerous magics. Jack narrowed his eyes, noting the glossy burn-marks on the nearby wall from arcane magic.

Good. Fancy-pants Ravanchen wizards probably ain't used to a proper magical brawl. And they had shitty aim. Jack glanced around for anything he could use to give him an edge. There was nothing readily available, though the stalls where the pegasi had been held were nearby. He slipped over to them, pleased to discover salt-iron halters and lead ropes. He picked them up, mindful of the salt-iron beads. Jack gritted his teeth against the leeching of his magic.

He returned to the impromptu battlefield. The combatants were breathing hard, sweat glistening on their faces, hair matted against their scalps. They had ignored him until that point because Jack hadn't been fighting them. That was about to change.

The outlaw pulled out his poppet, clutching it tight in his right hand. He dropped the Staunch Wounds spell he'd activated earlier, glad that it had been enough to ease his pain and make it easier to speak. To pull this next trick off, he was going to need as many layers of Speed on his poppet as he could manage. It was going to be a walloping drain on his magic, not counting the slow siphon of the salt-iron.

Jack ignored the blood trickling from his nose as jitteriness washed over him. It was suddenly impossible to stand still. He wanted to *gogogo*. Jack rushed forward, moving so fast his boots barely seemed to touch the ground.

Jack had never layered so many Speed spells on his poppet, and afterward, he vowed to never do so again, without good reason. The sudden, intense burst of speed was like the stoop of a falcon, so quick that his stomach felt like he'd left it behind.

Everything around him slowed, as if time itself froze as he flowed forward like living lightning.

He raced to the quartet of attackers who still stood, snatching bits of hair or a dab of freely flowing blood from the pair of Copperheads and attaching them to spare, unattuned poppets he'd kept ready in his pocket. For the Ravanchens, he wrapped the salt-iron halters and ropes around them. *They're going to be pissed.*

That task done, Jack retreated to Zepheus, activating the two new poppets. Then he dropped his own Speed spell and hurriedly threw Paralysis up over the pair.

His spell almost didn't take. Jack felt the magic waver, nearly too brittle to bring the Copperheads to heel. Gods, but that Speed spell had sapped him fast. Jack had a decision to make. If he split his reserves between the pair, they were likely to break the Paralysis quickly. But if he focused it on just one, he stood a better chance.

"Guess I gotta do this the old-fashioned way." Jack drew out his sixgun as he refocused all of his magic on the female Copperhead. He sighted his revolver on the newly freed man, shooting him in the leg to make escape or fighting back difficult.

"Faedra's tits, man!" the wounded outlaw swore, whimpering as he rolled onto his side.

The two wizards from Ravance howled in agony at their salt-iron bondage. They had fallen to the floor, tripped by the ropes, and they writhed as the beads literally burned their flesh. Mages hated salt-iron because it blistered their skin and hurt like the blazes, besides sapping their magic. Wizards were an entirely different thing. The metal was even worse on them. Jack knew he wasn't making friends with anyone here today.

"Which of you assholes are the ones who took the Breaker?" Jack snarled, gaze flicking between the two groups.

The wizards were too busy whining. The paralyzed Copperhead couldn't speak, though her eyes were wide with terror. Good. Jack liked that she was afraid. They should all be afraid.

"Ravance or someone else?" Jack demanded again, swiveling between his captives. "Someone better talk, and soon. I got enough bullets for the lot of you."

"S-stolen from us," one wizard cried after a moment. "Take this off. Take it off!"

Stolen. Blaise was never yours to start with. Jack fought the urge to plant one of the promised bullets in the wizard's skull. But outright murdering wizards from Ravance might cause problems down the road, and he figured it was best to avoid that. The Copperheads, though? They were fair game.

"I want answers, then maybe I'll do something 'bout that." Jack turned to the Copperheads. He loosened the Paralysis spell enough to allow the woman to speak. That was a relief for him as well, using up a little less of his precious magic. "Start talking."

"A Walker took him," the woman rasped.

A Walker. That made sense. But gods, the Walker had taken a *pegasus* too? That would be a huge drain, unless it had been an accident. "Who here has a damned Walker on their side? How did this Walker travel?"

The outlaw shook her head. "Don't know who she belongs to. But she came out of the wall, then back into it. The Breaker and a pegasus went with her."

Jack stared, then cursed softly. The Herald, the same Walker who had tried to get Blaise before and failed. This time, she'd been luckier. And Emrys was with them? *Damn.* At least Blaise wasn't alone with an enemy.

"Any of you lot see that?" Jack demanded of the wizards. One of them whimpered but nodded.

"I've seen her around," the paralyzed Copperhead said. "She was here for the auction, but she'd made inquiries about the Breaker before. Sounded like she got sent to fetch him, no matter what."

"And take him where?" Jack asked.

"Ganland. They—"

Jack hadn't paid attention to the wounded Copperhead, and that had been a mistake. The man had pulled a knife, and he lunged at the paralyzed woman, slitting her throat in a quick motion. Blood fountained, spraying the man and blinding him. Jack growled with renewed rage, sighting his sixgun on the Copperhead and firing. He dropped atop the female desperado, the right side of his face a ruined mess.

The bloodshed made the wizards sob even harder. Jack had learned what he could from the Copperheads. He spun on the wizards. "If I let you up, you gonna play nice?"

They nodded, tears streaming down their faces.

Jack reached down and untangled the halters and ropes, carefully freeing the men. The salt-iron sapped the last dregs of his magic, and he fervently hoped he had no need for it soon. He was done. And damn, but his face hurt, and the blood was becoming more distracting as he tasted it on his tongue. He tossed the ropes aside, his sixgun still out. Not *wanting* to shoot the Ravanchens didn't mean he wouldn't if it came down to it.

The wizards jerked upright. The two men had lost their grimoires in the fall, and Jack took the time to kick them away, far from the pair. Wizards could cast without their spellbooks, but the grimoires strengthened their abilities and made them capable of greater magics than were otherwise possible.

"My father gave me that grimoire!" the dark-haired wizard protested. The telltale signs of salt-iron damage peppered his left cheek. Jack hoped that meant the man would have too little magic left to call the book into his hand.

"Don't care," Jack drawled. "Y'all know anything about these folks in Ganland?"

"N-no," the same wizard gasped. "I promise, we don't. We were only here to purchase the alchemist and the Breaker."

Jack narrowed his eyes. Again, why would Ravance want Marian Hawthorne? As far as he knew, wizards didn't care a lick for alchemy. They figured they were superior to anything an alchemist could whip up. He didn't have time to follow that line of questioning, though. "Get out of my sight. Leave town. If I see you again, I have a bullet with your name on it." Jack glowered at them.

The wizards staggered to their feet, limping over to retrieve their grimoires. Then they turned tail and fled, only glancing over their shoulders to make sure Jack wouldn't shoot them in the back.

Once he was certain they weren't coming back, Jack shut his eyes for a moment. He felt Zepheus move closer, warm equine breath blowing against his face. Jack turned, resting his forehead against the stallion's cheek. "Em and Marian outside with Oby?"

<Yes. Oby keeps demanding to know what's happened.>

Jack's shoulders slumped. He wasn't looking forward to telling Emmaline or Marian Hawthorne that Blaise wasn't coming back with them. Scuffing a heel against the ground, he laid a hand on Zepheus's neck. "Let's regroup with 'em."

"Wildfire!" a voice bellowed. Jack stiffened, expecting to come face-to-face with another of the Copperheads. But when he turned, he saw the white Knossan, Gore, picking his way through the ruined ground. Blood spatter speckled his coat, though Jack saw no visible wounds.

"Gore," Jack acknowledged with a nod of his head.

"I wish to thank you. Our younglings are safe." He snorted, glancing over his shoulder at the surrounding wreckage. "Without your aid, we would have lost them."

Jack relaxed. That was the first bit of good news he'd had, and it was welcome. "Glad to hear it. We weren't as lucky."

"You did not recover the one you sought?"

"We did, but the Breaker got stolen away in the middle of it all."

Gore lowered his horns, his dark eyes somber. "I wish I could assist, but our concern is with our younglings now."

"Nah." Jack waved a hand. "You've the right of it. Get your

young-uns to safety." He turned, preparing to mount, though he paused when a thought came to him. "When you go back to Knossas, remember who helped y'all."

The bull surprised him, stooping into a bow so low that the tips of his horns grated against the ruined floor. "We do not forget these things. May Veruc the Great Bull grant you strength." Gore straightened to his impressive full height, turning to plod away.

Jack sighed, swinging into the saddle.

The entire short ride out of the disheveled warehouse, he racked his mind for ways to catch up to the Walker who had stolen Blaise away. What did they want with him? Revenge for Fort Courage? To use him? Or was it a strike against the Gutter? All of those thoughts set Jack's nerves on edge. They were all potential reasons.

Emmaline raced up when they emerged from the warehouse. Marian was nearby, mounted on Oberidon. Good. If the alchemist needed a quick escape, the spotted stallion was their best bet. Emmaline's eyes widened at the mess of his face. Then her gaze searched behind him. "What happened to you? And where's Blaise?"

Jack wiped at the blood trail leaking from his nose. "We'll talk about that some place else." He was painfully aware of the number of people still lurking around the area—and not all would be friendly toward them. He needed to get Marian somewhere secure so that all of this would have been worth *something*, damn it.

Marian stared at him, a lump in her throat. Her knuckles, clutching the pommel of Oberidon's saddle, were white as fresh snow. "They killed him?" Her voice was soft but with a warning rumble reminiscent of a dragoness protecting a clutch of eggs.

"No," Jack answered sharply. *I don't think so, at least.* "C'mon."

They returned the pegasi to the stables. As they walked out, crossing to the inn for a little privacy, Jack froze when he saw a familiar figure looming nearby. Maureen the Dread Surgeon.

She smiled like a crocodile, sauntering over to them, flanked by a handful of Copperheads. They sported a variety of wounds, many of them limping with the effort.

"Wildfire Jack, seems I owe you my thanks," the Dread Surgeon said, cocking her head at him. Jack narrowed his eyes—well, his one good eye. The other was too swollen to cooperate. His fingers twitched, ready to pull his sixgun if needed. "You got rid of Seymour for me, and I didn't so much as have to lift a finger. My hands are clean as a drake's fangs."

He pursed his lips, trying to figure out if she truly was thanking him or if another shoe was about to drop. "I reckon that's not the full truth, but Seymour deserved what he got." Jack shrugged, deciding not to explain that he'd only indirectly been responsible for Seymour's demise. Let them think he was the one who ended the Copperhead leader. More renown for the Scourge of the Untamed Territory never hurt. "Now, if you don't mind, I got things to do."

Jack started forward, though he was still ready to draw if the Copperheads threatened them or made a move to seize Marian.

Maureen held up a hand. "Whatever you may think, I *am* beholden to you for offing Seymour. Let me heal your face, at least."

Jack wondered what Seymour had done to make her so happy the outlaw was dead. And why hadn't she used her own fearsome magic against him to unseat him before? He remembered the shock of Seymour's magic-enhanced fist meeting his face—yeah, that alone might be reason to fear the man. His throbbing face reminded him that he needed to decide. Could he trust the Dread Surgeon? Nadine was one thing. Maureen was something else.

His indecision must have been obvious. She took a step forward. "Wildfire Jack Dewitt, I don't *want* to be beholden to you. But right now, I am—and I'm going to be pissed if I don't get to pay this off with a simple healing."

"I take a life, and you repay me by closing wounds? Seems imbalanced," Jack remarked.

"Think of it as a life for a life," Maureen said, her grin downright threatening.

She's crazier than an outhouse fly. Jack's thumb nudged his holster, debating. But as unhinged as she was, she seemed somehow...sincere? He sighed. "Fine."

She moved over to him almost too eagerly, and Jack had to fight back the desire to strike out as she laid her hands on his face. He'd suffered healing from terrible Healers before, and he figured she might be similar. Jack felt the warmth of her magic flow into him, probing his broken nose, the bruises and battered flesh of his face, and his swollen eye. He prepared himself for the jagged glass feeling he feared might accompany her working but it never came. Instead, her magic was more like being covered by a warm blanket: comfortable and soothing.

So at odds with the woman wielding the power.

When she stepped back, Maureen watched him expectantly. "Well?"

"I'm good, thanks," Jack said gruffly. He decided not to remark on her abilities. She was called the Dread Surgeon for a reason, but her healing was skillful. Nurturing. He suspected she curated the rough reputation to protect herself. "Your debt is paid—as long as y'all keep your grubby hands off the alchemist. She's under my protection."

Maureen nodded. "You have until dusk tomorrow, Wildfire Jack. Any of you and yours who linger at that point are fair game."

"Good enough," he rumbled, pointedly aware that this meant he would no longer be welcome in Thorn. Not unexpected, all things considered. Jack watched as Maureen and her gang sauntered away before turning and gesturing for Emmaline and Marian to head into the inn.

"I was ready to kill her if she did anything to you," Emmaline whispered as they climbed the stairs.

Jack smiled. "Glad you've got my back." He pushed open the door to their room and ushered them inside.

As soon as the door closed, Marian whirled on him. "Start talking. Where is my son? What's happened to him?" Emmaline stood beside her, hands on her hips, the same questions afire in her eyes.

With a resigned sigh, Jack recounted what had happened and the scant information he had learned. "So, Blaise is half a continent away or more." Suddenly, he felt exhausted, as if the sum of his exertion for the day had finally come crashing down on him. But he couldn't stop, not now.

"We have to go get him!" Emmaline didn't even hesitate. She looked ready to bolt out the door right at that moment.

Jack sat on the bed, wishing he could lie down and lose himself to the oblivion of sleep. "We will, but it's going to take time. We have to find another pegasus to hire for Marian. And even then, Zeph and Oby need a break. They're as dog tired as we are." He closed his eyes. "Or we could find a ship, but..." That would allow all of them a chance to rest and recover, but a voyage by sea, even aboard a fancy steamer, would take too long. It was far from a direct route.

"If you think you know where he is, one of you could take us there. You're mages, after all," Marian said.

Jack cracked an eye open, scowling. "We're Effigests. Neither of us can manage a spell like that." And even if that *was* in an Effigest's bag of tricks, a working that size would take the collaboration of a coven.

"You're *mages*, and you *can*," Marian insisted.

He wanted to argue that she knew nothing of mages or what they could or couldn't do, but that wasn't right. She *did* know mages. She had *made* a mage. Jack glanced at Emmaline, who shrugged. She was as uninformed as he was on this idea, at least. "Explain."

"What separates a mage from a wizard?" Marian asked.

Jack pressed his lips together, annoyed that she would stall with a question. "Mages specialize in magic that comes naturally to them and takes minimal training—sometimes none." When she nodded, he continued, "Wizards don't have any specialties, can only cast a couple of spells without reading from a grimoire. But their pool of magic is deeper than a mage's."

The alchemist snapped her fingers. "There were grimoires in the warehouse."

Jack cocked his head. "You think we can cast a travel spell if we find a grimoire with one?" He didn't like the sound of that—it seemed awfully risky.

"Yes."

Hope gleamed in Emmaline's eyes at the simple word. "We should try, Daddy."

Jack shook his head. "I'm wrung out—no way would I have the reserves needed to cast a wizard-class spell. Even if you bolstered me."

Marian sat at the foot of the bed. "Do you remember the potion that Doyen Gaitwood used on Blaise?"

Immediately, Jack turned, eyes narrowed. "That was *you?*" The potion had almost been the Breaker's end, threatening to tear him apart and take everyone nearby with him. Would this woman's evil never end? Gods, had it been a mistake for Blaise to come after her?

"I didn't have a *choice*," Marian said hotly, arms crossed. "They had my family. And I didn't know they were going to use it on *Blaise.*" Her voice broke when she said his name, frustrated tears glistening in her eyes. She raked a hand through her curly hair. "Gods, do you think I *want* to hurt him?"

"Didn't stop you the first time," Jack growled, ignoring the way Emmaline's eyebrows slammed up in surprise. He forgot there were some things she wasn't privy to.

"That's not an argument for here, but I'll be damned if you think I haven't regretted every moment of suffering that I've caused him." She trembled. "No matter what anyone may think, I'm his *mother*. I *love* him." Marian's face crumpled, helpless tears streaming down her cheeks.

Jack almost felt sorry for making her cry, but not fully. Blaise didn't deserve a lick of what had happened to him. He was just another soul thrown into the hungry maw of the Confederation, as Jack had been. "Fine. Tell us about your *potion*, then."

Emmaline offered Marian a handkerchief, and it was a moment before the alchemist composed herself enough to speak. She swallowed. "It's the Elixir of Overwhelming Magic. They gave Blaise a modified version because they..." Marian shook her head. "They didn't care if it killed him in the end. It floods the mage who takes it with a deep river of magic, replenishing anything used as quickly as it's spent."

"What's the cost?" Jack asked. There was always a cost, some detrimental side effect.

"When the effects wear off, the mage is exhausted and helpless."

Ha. Already there. Jack frowned. "And you think it'd be enough to power a wizard spell?"

Marian rubbed her forehead. "That was part of the ultimate goal."

Jack bit back a comment at that. Sounded like the Confederation was hoping for their own wizard-class mages. *Small wonder Ravance was so interested in Marian. They wouldn't want magical competition from the Confederation.* "There's a reagent shop in town."

The alchemist shook her head. "This isn't your run-of-the-mill potion. It's specialized. It requires rare reagents." She gave a grim smile. "Reagents that I'm fairly certain are in that warehouse."

Jack rose from the bed. "Sounds like we better get back to the warehouse, then."

CHAPTER THIRTY-NINE
Globetrotter

Blaise

Blaise didn't know how long he fell sideways into the darkness. He knew he was screaming. Someone else was screaming, too—the Walker who had grabbed him. And there were snorts and throaty sounds from Emrys, the clatter of hooves failing to find purchase on...wherever they were. *Emrys.* Blaise couldn't let the stallion come to harm.

He wanted to slam his power against the Herald's, shattering her hold on them. Blaise tried to call on his magic, but it was sluggish. Slippery, like trying to catch a minnow from a stream. Out of his grasp for the moment.

"Let go of me, or I'll make sure you get turned into glue!" the Walker howled as they traversed the void of miles.

Suddenly, they stopped. Blaise was breathless, as if he had run the distance they'd covered himself. He fell down onto the ground —*grass*—panting and rolling onto his side. He felt dizzy, his muscles non-responsive from the sweet-smelling fabric.

Wherever they were, the sun was still up. Emrys was a dark, thrashing shape, snorting and shrilling his anger. Blaise groggily fought to sit up, to go to the stallion, but a hand grabbed his arm—

"No!" Blaise wailed. He was about to be dragged back into the Walker's world, and he had no way to fight back. Then the Walker went flying, releasing his arm.

A shadowy form loomed over him. Blaise was vaguely aware of Emrys trying to talk to him, but his mind was too clouded. He felt as if he'd been spinning in circles. His stomach lurched with nausea, and he fought dry heaves for longer than he liked. Eventually, he rolled onto his back, staring at the sky.

They were outside. They must have traveled westward—the sun was still up, though it was low. Emrys stood over him, a protective bulwark against the unknown. Blaise groaned.

<Can you hear me now?>

"Yeah," Blaise grunted, slowly easing into a seated position. The movement agitated his nausea again, and he had to take a deep breath before he trusted himself to speak. "Sorry."

<Are you okay?> Emrys asked, head lowered as he sucked in Blaise's scent. <You smell ill.>

Blaise nodded, then regretted that, too. "I think if I stand or move, I'll throw up. Or if I do...anything." He wanted to curl into a ball and sleep, but he was afraid if he did that, he would never wake up again.

The stallion made a concerned rumble. <Then stay still. I'll watch over you until you can move.>

That made Blaise feel a little better. He was somewhere far away from Jack, Emmaline, and...oh gods, his mother. He swallowed, tears stinging his eyes. *No, don't dwell on that. I'm not with my friends, but I have Emrys. I'm not alone.* All the same, he couldn't shrug off the utterly helpless feeling.

"What happened to the Walker?" He had seen no sign of her.

<I kicked her into the wall of the barn, and she vanished.>

Well, at least he hopefully wouldn't have to worry about the Herald coming after him any time soon. Not unless she wanted another attack from the pegasus. "Do you know where we are?" Blaise whispered, squeezing his eyes shut. He felt less queasy when his eyes weren't open.

<Not yet. A farm, maybe? Lots of grass. Rolling hills. I smell cows and pine trees in the distance.>

Cows and pine trees. "Desina, maybe?" Blaise couldn't help but feel hopeful at the prospect. Just thinking of Desina made him homesick. Made him think of his mother...

A velvety nose brushed his face, and a rough tongue swiped his cheek, catching a salty tear. <I don't know. But stop with those thoughts, whatever they are. We are together. We are safe for the moment. I will let no one hurt you or take you away from me.> Blaise imagined the stallion had his ears laid back flat against his head at that fierce declaration.

"Thank you," Blaise murmured. Gods, he didn't know what the Walker had planned to do with him. *Don't think, don't think.* He focused on breathing and taking in everything his senses told him. The evening wind tousled his hair, carrying the earthy fragrances of the countryside to him. Grasshoppers sang, and sandpipers trilled. It was peaceful, and in other circumstances, he would have enjoyed his surroundings.

Night had fallen by the time Blaise trusted himself to stand. Clutching Emrys, he shakily got to his feet, momentarily proud that he no longer wanted to puke. But then he realized they were alone in the dark, with no idea where they were or if there was a safe place to spend the night. Or get food, when his stomach felt like keeping something down.

<I am saddled, and your canteen is still attached. There may be food in the saddlebags, too,> Emrys reminded him. <If you get on my back, we can start traveling and perhaps orient ourselves.>

That wasn't a terrible idea. Blaise didn't have any better ones. He took a swig of water, checking the saddlebags. Emrys was right—there were a few scanty rations, mostly dried fruit and jerky. But it would do, when food appealed to him. *Things are looking up.*

Emrys hid his wings, and a few minutes later, had found a road. Even with the moon out, it was dark. Blaise couldn't see a thing, but the pegasus assured him he could see well enough.

They didn't find a town, but Emrys located a clearing off the beaten path that would serve for the night. Blaise wished his bedroll had been packed along with the rest of his gear, but he was exhausted, and honestly, he had slept in worse conditions.

Jefferson didn't visit his dreams that night. Blaise was so tired that not even nightmares invaded his sleep. He had hoped for the Dreamer, though. While he knew they could do little for one another with the distance between them, there was much to be said for finding comfort in the one you loved.

In the morning, Blaise's stomach felt better. He kept down a handful of dried fruit before setting off with Emrys again.

<I wish I dared to fly. That would be the easiest way to figure out where we are,> Emrys said as he trotted along.

"Not worth the risk," Blaise agreed. Then he raised his brows when Emrys slowed, nostrils flared. "What is it?"

<Salt and surf.> He flicked an ear. <We're near the coast.>

But the coast of where? Though a coast was a good sign—they were more likely to run into fishing villages or ports. As they continued on, they came across wooden signs listing the names of a few small towns, though Blaise didn't recognize any of them.

"Could be Desina. Maybe Mella? Even Ganland." His breath caught. What if they were in Ganland? But the odds of that were slim.

<If we are in Desina, it would be a simple thing to fly to the Gutter,> Emrys reasoned. <I don't think we're in Mella. I would smell the mountains, and we would see them to the north.>

True enough. They plowed onward, and all the while, Blaise worried about what they would do. He didn't have any coin, so it wasn't as if he could pay for food once his meager supplies ran out. Or lodgings. He was so busy mulling through his limited options, he didn't notice the sound of hooves approaching them.

A pair of riders came into view—local wardens, judging by their clothing. Green and white: the colors of Ganland.

Blaise swallowed, nodding to the wardens as they loped past. The riders vanished down the road, no doubt on pressing business that had nothing to do with Breakers who had been spirited far away. "We're in Ganland." He wasn't sure if that was fortuitous or not. If they ran across a Salt-Iron Confederation contingent, they'd be in trouble. But Ganland also meant people he knew. Flora, Kittie, and Mindy. And somewhere, *Jefferson.*

<I saw. Should we follow the wardens and ask for help?>

Blaise shook his head. "No." He wasn't sure who he could trust. "I'd rather find our people. Let's get to a town and ask for directions to Nera."

Emrys arched his neck. <Sounds like a plan.>

EMRYS'S NAVIGATION INSTINCTS WERE THEIR SAVING GRACE. BLAISE never came across anyone he felt confident asking for directions to Nera, but it wasn't long before the stallion recognized their surroundings from their previous ill-fated trip to Ganland.

<This is the road we traveled from Seaside to Nera,> Emrys insisted with certainty, though Blaise didn't feel so sure. He didn't recognize the scenery at all, but that was no surprise. The last time he had taken this road, his murky future had distracted him.

But Emrys was right. By mid-afternoon, Blaise's breath hitched at the welcome sight of Jefferson's ostentatious estate situated outside the city. The gate from the road to the house was open, and Emrys trotted up unhindered. Though, the pegasus drew to a stiff-legged halt when he heard a throaty whinny.

Emrys's nostrils flared, his head held at attention. Then he surged forward. <Seledora is here!>

Seledora? Did that mean Jefferson was here, too? Blaise's heart galloped along with Emrys's hooves as the stallion bolted toward the stables. The grey mare appeared in a paddock, though it took her little effort to flit over the fence and greet them. A groom walked out of the stable, scratching his forehead in puzzlement.

"Wasn't expecting any visitors—oh, it's you." The groom's eyes went wide when he recognized Blaise from his last visit, though it had been several months. He straightened. "You have my condolences, Mr. Hawthorne."

Condolences? Blaise frowned at the confusing words as he slid out of the saddle. "Um, thanks. Can you see to Emrys? Give him a good rubdown and some oats—though make sure he doesn't eat them too quickly."

"Of course," the groom agreed, giving a deferential nod.

Emrys was busy catching up with Seledora. The mare was still frosty toward the black stallion, but she was curious, wondering how—and why—they had come to Ganland. She flicked a black-tipped ear at Blaise, then turned to him once Emrys followed the groom into the stable to be pampered.

Seledora's eyes gleamed like amber in the afternoon light. <What is this Emrys tells me of a Walker dragging you across half a continent?>

Blaise sighed. "That's a story I'd rather not recount multiple times. Is Jefferson here?"

The mare lowered her head, and Blaise got the sense that she was mourning. But why? <He is...not. But Flora, Kittie, and Mindy are.> She paused again, ears pricked toward the house. <I've told them you are here, and Mindy is directing one of the staff to bring refreshments to the parlor. Ask them to open a window for me.>

"Okay," Blaise agreed, too worn to do anything else. He turned and strode to the house, but he didn't get far before Flora appeared at his side.

The half-knocker looked as rough as Blaise feared he did. Her pink hair, which was normally well-kempt, was scraggly, with flyaways framing her face. Her eyes were red, as if she'd had little sleep or had cried a lot...or both. Flora's mouth opened, and Blaise half expected some catty remark, but she closed it again, shaking her head.

"Flora, what's wrong?" Blaise asked, bothered by...well, everything. It was so un-Flora-like.

She swallowed a lump in her throat, stopping to look up at him. "I know we should wait until we're inside, but...oh gods, Blaise. I'm so sorry." Flora surprised him by wrapping her long, slender arms around him in a hug. She released him quickly, sniffling. "Sorry. Forgot you don't like that." Flora wiped away a tear.

"It's okay," Blaise murmured. He was still shy of touch from most people, but he felt safe around Flora. "I've never seen you like this. What's going on?"

Flora sighed heavily. "There's no good way to tell you. Jefferson's dead."

Her words chilled him to the core. Blaise staggered backward as if he'd been physically struck. "What? How?"

"There was a fire."

Oh. Blaise immediately relaxed. His foggy brain had forgotten that not everyone knew what he knew. "Jefferson's not dead."

The half-knocker reached out and patted his hand, and Seledora bumped him with her nose, as if offering her own form of support. "I know you don't want to think that, Blaise. But there's no way he could have survived. We found a body. I thought you'd heard, and that was why you came."

Blaise shook his head. "That's not why I came. And he's *alive*."

Flora gave him a pained look. "I wish he were, too. But if he were, we would have found him by now. Some Healer would have brought him forward."

Gah, Blaise hated trying to explain things to people. Especially when he was as exhausted as he was. "Let's go inside and talk."

That would give him a little breathing room to puzzle out an explanation.

Flora nodded, leading the way into the elegant home. Everything about it was Jefferson, from the fine artwork adorning the walls to the plush rugs lining the hallways. They filed into a parlor where Kittie and Mindy awaited, the promised refreshments laid out on a table. Kittie watched him closely when he walked in, questions bright in her eyes.

"Hi, Blaise," Mindy greeted him, though her usual warmth was missing. The trip had been hard on her, too, it seemed. She frowned at the food, then glanced at him. "The ham and mustard sandwich. That's what you need."

"Howdy. And thanks," he replied, sinking down onto the softest couch in the room. Oh, what he wouldn't give to peel off his boots, stuff his face with food, and then sleep. But that had to wait. He appeased his stomach by loading a small plate with food —complete with Mindy's sandwich recommendation—before turning back to the matter at hand. "Seledora was hoping someone would open the window for her." At his request, Flora pulled one open, and the mare thrust her head inside.

"You're a long way from Fortitude," Kittie said, her tone neutral yet somehow still bristling with questions.

"And that's a long story for later," Blaise replied. First things first. "Like I was telling Flora, Jefferson's *not* dead."

"How do you know?" Kittie asked sharply. Almost defensive, as if she were protecting herself.

<The dreamscape?> Seledora asked, nostrils flared as she made the private query. <He dreamed to you?> Then, before he could even think to reply, she snapped her teeth. <Wait, say nothing.>

Blaise winced. He had forgotten that of those present, only Flora and Seledora knew about Jefferson's magic. It wasn't his place to divulge that secret, even among friends. Too late, he realized it would have been wiser to make his explanations outside to

Flora and Seledora. His brain raced for a plausible explanation and failed entirely.

"I just do," he said, though he knew he sounded like a petulant child, unwilling to acknowledge the truth of the matter. "It's *Jefferson*. He's cunning."

"Even the most intelligent people die," Mindy said, staring down at her plate of food as if she'd lost her appetite.

Blaise glanced at Kittie, and an idea came to mind. "Everyone thought *you* were dead for years. But Jack never gave up hope."

The Pyromancer's eyes narrowed, and her mouth curled as if his words made her thoughtful. "You're not wrong about that. For your sake, I'll hope that you're right." She leaned forward. "Now, will you tell us what you're doing here, hundreds of miles from where you're *supposed* to be? And why do I suspect my husband is tangled up in it?"

As much as he hated being the center of attention, Blaise recounted the entire mess to them. Kittie didn't seem surprised that both Jack and Emmaline had accompanied Blaise, but the pride that glittered in her eyes was unmistakable when Blaise spoke of their deeds.

When he finished, Kittie crossed her arms. "So, what will Jack and Emmaline do now that they've rescued your mother?"

Blaise shook his head. "I don't know." By now, they had to know he'd been stolen away. How would they react? Would Jack come unglued? Or after the chaos they'd sowed at the auction, were they fleeing from Thorn for their lives? He couldn't even imagine what they would do now. He hoped they'd go back to Fortitude, where they would be safe.

But this was Wildfire Jack Dewitt, and when had he ever done something that would guarantee his safety? Still, perhaps he would—if only for Emmaline. And maybe Marian.

"You've been through a lot," Flora announced at the tail end of his accounting. "Blaise, you look like you need a good soak in the tub and then rest in a decent bed."

"I do," he agreed, and he rose from his seat with a groan. His muscles were happy to remind him of everything he'd been through the last few days. A soak in a warm tub sounded downright amazing. He bid Kittie and Mindy goodnight and followed the half-knocker to the suite of rooms reserved for Jefferson.

Flora wasn't lying about the bath. She called for a staff member to prepare one, and the man hurried off to see to the request. But when the door closed behind the staffer and they heard the distant sounds of preparations, she held up a hand. Flora marched over to a window and hauled it open, revealing Seledora. Mare and half-knocker eyed him. "Start talking. How do you know he's alive?" Hope clung to Flora's words like the last golden leaf on an autumnal tree branch.

"The dreamscape," Blaise whispered. "He pulled me into it..." He paused, trying to figure out what day it was. "Not last night. The night before, I think? Anyway, not more than three nights ago. When was the fire?"

"Four days ago," Flora replied, pensive. She traded looks with Seledora. "How certain are you it was him? And that you weren't just dreaming *about* him?"

"Absolutely certain," Blaise answered without hesitation. "He told me he lost the ring I gave him, and I was mad at him for that, but also sort of glad because I missed him. And *no*, before you ask again, I didn't just dream that. I know it was real because we brought *Jack* into the dreamscape, too. That was how we planned the auction escape."

Seledora laid back her ears. <If that's true, then why hasn't he shown up? Is he hurt? What happened?>

"He said a group called the Quiet Ones have him," Blaise said. No recognition flared in Flora's eyes at the word, and with chagrin, he realized they truly were a shadowy organization. "They attacked him during the fire, and he took his ring off so he'd stand a chance against them."

"Then why hasn't *he* tried to tell me any of this? He's pulled me into the dreamscape before," Flora pointed out, as if she were reluctant to believe him.

"He can't," Blaise said. "Wherever he is, it's warded. And somehow he can only get to me because..." He shrugged. "I guess because my magic broke a crack in the ward?"

She stared at him. "All of that sounds absolutely unhinged, and that makes me think you're probably right."

"Er, thanks." Blaise rubbed the back of his head. "One more thing, though. The Quiet Ones are forcing him to be Malcolm again, declaring Jefferson dead in the fire. They took his cabochon ring away."

Anger flashed across Flora's eyes. "*Schist.*" She shook her head, plainly understanding how painful that would be to Jefferson. Seledora made a fierce rumbling sound, shaking her head. "But you say the Quiet Ones will send him back to Nera? To continue to campaign for the Gutter?"

Blaise nodded. "That's what he said."

Flora chewed on her lower lip, thinking. "Okay. I'll figure out something to tell Kittie and Mindy."

A knock sounded on the door, and the steward returned, eyeing their odd group. "Mr. Hawthorne, your bath is ready. Do you need help undressing?"

Flora bit back a laugh, which made Blaise suspect she was feeling a little better about things. Meanwhile, he kept the horrified look off his face that would normally crawl across it at such a question. "Um, no, thank you, I'll be fine."

"As you wish." The steward slipped out.

The half-knocker released a long sigh. "I'll let you get cleaned up. You look like you really *were* dragged across half the continent. Then get some rest." She paused at the door. "You think you'll see Jefferson tonight?"

I hope so. But there was no way he could guarantee it. "I don't know. He wasn't in my dreams last night." He paused. Was it last night? He'd lost track of time.

<Jefferson is a man of many surprises. We won't count him out,> Seledora said, withdrawing her head from the room.

Flora ran a hand through her mussed hair. "Yeah. Get yourself cleaned up now. You stink." On that note, she left him to his privacy.

Blaise sighed, then shucked off his boots, leaving them by the door. He had learned from his previous visit that Jefferson's steward would no doubt slip in, remove his worn clothing, and replace it with something fresh. Any other time he would have thought that intrusive, but he welcomed it now. Blaise was glad that he was nose blind to himself, figuring that Flora was probably right about the smell. He piled his clothing in a stack beside the boots, then headed to the bath.

The warm water and suds were so delightful he nearly fell asleep as he relaxed and washed away grime. If only the troubles that dogged them would be as easy to wash away as the dust of travel.

CHAPTER FORTY
Portal Fantasy

Jack

They weren't the only ones with plans to loot the ruined warehouse. Other outlaws and thieves had fallen on the damaged structure like carrion birds to a rotting carcass, and Maureen's Copperheads had their hands full trying to dissuade the interlopers.

"That's gonna be a problem," Jack grumbled as he, Emmaline, and Marian huddled outside the building. If he had the magic for it, he could use Obfuscation again on himself, and Emmaline could do likewise. But he was too depleted to cast it on himself, much less Marian, and he didn't want to suggest Emmaline cast on the alchemist.

"No, it's not," Emmaline said, stepping forward. Jack's brows shot up, and he caught her arm. She stiffened, looking over her shoulder at him. Defiance and self-assurance gleamed in her eyes. "Daddy, let me do this. I can be a distraction."

Inwardly, he growled. He was the one who wanted to take risks, to be the distraction. But Emmaline was coming into her own, trying to show that she was capable. And damn it, she was.

Jack would only cause more harm by denying her this chance. Besides, he had done a thousand more feats of derring-do by the time he was her age. "Don't do anything I'd do."

"Nah, I'll be smart about it," she quipped, flashing him a grin as he released her arm.

Be careful. I love you. He watched her stride off, the words unspoken but on his lips. But she knew, he hoped.

"That's a good girl you've got there," Marian remarked.

"The best," Jack agreed, voice gruff. He cleared his throat, shifting his weight from foot to foot as he waited. Emmaline would need time, but he was impatient. He wanted to get this going.

After several minutes, he heard shouts and the steady thump of boots on the ground. Jack took that as their signal, and he and the alchemist slipped inside the warehouse. The interior was dim, many of the mage-lights broken during the havoc they'd created. As they walked down the long aisle of overturned cages, dark remnants of blood spatter were visible.

"There," Marian whispered, pointing at the toppled crates in the far corner of the warehouse, near the location where the Copperheads had kept her.

Some of them had come open, the contents spilled across the floor. Gems glittered amid dried herbs, cracked vials of powder, and harvested bits of once-living creatures. Jack recognized the flexible, feather-like scales from dragons, gleaming like sun-fired copper. The spiraling horn of a unicorn. The tanned skin of a chupacabra, the runic patterns dull on the musty hide. He curled his lip as Marian crouched down, picking through the items.

"Awful, all of it," Jack muttered.

The alchemist glanced up at him. "Plenty of blood on your hands, or so you've told me." He fought the urge to sneer at her comment. "You should look for a grimoire."

The grimoires. Jack didn't like being told what to do, but the sad fact was he'd been distracted from his purpose, and Marian was right. But that didn't mean he had to acknowledge her rightness. He made a face and spun, heading over to a promising area that held a jumbled collection of scrolls.

Something caught his eye on the way over. Jack diverted from his course, eyeing the small upside-down crate. He shoved a mess of scrolls out of his path, crouching to right the crate. Jack recognized the rising sun insignia painted neatly on the box, and he wondered if he dared believe it was legitimate.

He pried the top open, whistling when he saw its contents. *Rare.* A single fire pot nestled in a protective cover of phoenix feathers, a strip of dragonhide wrapped around the feathers to keep them together.

"Can't believe they got their grimy hands on one of these." Jack wondered if the Copperheads even knew what they had. It was likely they didn't. He carefully closed the top of the crate again, then picked it up. Though his primary mission was to find a grimoire, he saw nothing wrong with liberating a little something extra. He rose, returning to his original search.

It was downright strange that the Copperheads had snagged grimoires for their auction. From what Jack knew, wizards didn't let go of their spellbooks easily. The Ravanchens gifted grimoires to young wizards when they showed an aptitude for magic, and they kept the book with them for the rest of their lives. *Grave robbers, maybe.* When a wizard died, their tome went to the grave with them.

Jack found a toppled crate of grimoires, the books a disheveled mess. He pursed his lips. The magic wafting from the tomes was palpable, akin to holding a hand over a flame and feeling a halo of warmth. The outlaw crouched down, studying the pile of books. He reached out, snagging the nearest one to pull it closer, nose wrinkling at the musty bouquet rising from it.

He frowned at the tome, expecting it to be warded against use by anyone other than the owner. But he was able to open it without issue, and he thumbed through the contents, searching for something helpful. *Damn cocky wizards, leaving their grimoires where any old cuss can read 'em.* Jack wasn't going to look a gift pegasus in the mouth, though.

Footsteps announced Marian's arrival, a heavy bag slung over her shoulder. "Any luck?"

Jack kept his eyes on the page, unwilling to admit he'd been distracted on his way to the spellbooks. "Not yet, but there's more to go through."

The alchemist shrugged the bag from her shoulder, resting it on the floor. "I could have a look, too." She reached for one of the nearest books.

Inwardly, Jack cringed at an alchemist handling anything magic-related. It was just plain *wrong*. But he wasn't about to turn down an offer to go through the mess of grimoires. Besides, it wasn't as if she were unfamiliar with mages—she'd raised one. "Have at it."

"I'll look, too."

Jack nearly jumped out of his skin, sixgun at the ready, when he realized Emmaline had snuck up on him courtesy of her Obfuscation spell. She wore a broad grin, no doubt enjoying the opportunity to toy with him. Emmaline had the invigorated look of someone who had stirred up trouble and had a grand time doing it.

"Son of a bat-eared harpy, don't *do* that." Jack glowered at her, then gestured to a stack of grimoires. "Get to readin'. I take it you had luck?"

She nodded, not contrite at all, as she picked up a tome. "Yeah, we have maybe twenty minutes."

Twenty minutes. It would have to do. They set to work, flipping through the grimoires on the hunt for the right spell. One of the books was devoted entirely to turning people into different animals, while another seemed to be some sort of magical cookbook. The cookbook made him think of Blaise, which only served to further his irritation as book after book proved useless.

"This one, maybe?" Emmaline asked a few minutes later, her fingers tracing the handwritten words.

Jack set his book aside and scooted closer, leaning over her shoulder. His excitement grew as he scanned the words. "Portal. Yeah, that's exactly what we need."

"Good, because I don't think this one was even a grimoire," Marian said, shoving her current read aside. "Unless there's something magical about treating toenail fungus."

"This is solid," Jack murmured, nodding with satisfaction. He still wasn't convinced they *could* cast the spell, but it was certainly worth a shot. The only problem was the amount of power drain that would come with it. The note at the very bottom of the page gave him reason to suspect that this portal would bankrupt even a wizard.

Marian tossed a canvas sack over to them. "Stow it in that."

Jack nodded. He held the sack open while Emmaline carefully tucked it inside. Then he glanced at the stack of other grimoires, debating if they should try to run off with more. No telling what might happen if they fell into the wrong hands.

"We should go," Marian said, turning at the sound of boots treading their way.

"Yeah, let's get out of here," Jack agreed, though he scooped up an armful of additional grimoires as they hurried out of the warehouse.

JACK STEEPLED HIS FINGERS, STARING AT THE GRIMOIRE SITTING ON the bedside table. It was almost dusk, and they needed to get out of Thorn before Maureen made good on her promise.

He straightened to alertness when the door creaked open, but it was only Emmaline and Marian. They had gone outside to allow the alchemist to make the final touches on her potion—she feared that the fumes from her creation might make them ill if she continued to work in the small room.

"All done?" Jack rumbled, eyeing the flask in Marian's hand.

"Yes," she answered, though she traded a glance with Emmaline.

They'd been scheming away from him, no doubt. He frowned. "Out with it."

"Daddy, I think I should be the one to cast the portal spell," Emmaline said, her words coming out in a flurry. "And I know you don't want me to, but it makes sense. We're traveling more than half a continent away. Marian says the magical draw is gonna be huge, and whoever casts it is probably going to be unconscious when we arrive." She held up a hand when Jack opened his mouth to interject. "It can't be you. *First,* you're still wanted in the Confederation, and you'll be impossible to defend if you're sense-less. *Second*, you've been to Ganland—and my single rescue trip there doesn't account for much." She sucked in a breath. "And if Blaise is in trouble, you stand the best shot of helping him."

Jack pursed his lips, shaking his head. "You don't give yourself enough credit, daughter of mine." The smile that bloomed on her face warmed his heart. And damn, he didn't want to allow this, but it made sense. His reservoir of magic had refilled a bit, but he wasn't at full power yet. Emmaline was fresher than he was, and with the potion, she would be a veritable locomotive. "You got this."

Her eyes lit up, and she turned to take the flask from Marian. "I won't let you down, Daddy."

"I know you won't." Gods, but he was so proud of her. And scared. But mostly proud. Jack swung his gaze to take in the room. Most everything was loaded in the saddlebags. He watched as Marian stuffed the grimoire back in its carry sack. "Let's get down to the pegasi."

Together, they went to the stables. Zepheus and Oberidon were already tacked up, raring to go. The stallions pranced out of their stalls, heads high. The palomino snorted at the sun dipping on the western horizon. <Running out of time.>

"Yeah, we're getting to it," Jack muttered, patting Zepheus's glossy neck.

Emmaline studied the spellbook, worrying at her lower lip. "This says I need turquoise to anchor it."

Jack nodded. He had studied the spell to know what Emmaline was up against. Judging by the way the spell was written, the wizard liked to use an actual door with a turquoise-inset frame. But the caster had apparently made it work without the same set-up as well. The grimoire's owner had jotted notes in the margin, detailing that without a doorway, the turquoise had to be placed north and south. Jack dug in his carry pouch and pulled out a pair of the blue-green stones, passing them to Emmaline.

"Didn't know you carried these," she remarked, then crouched down to place them in position, about six feet apart. Emmaline's goal was to create a portal large enough for the pegasi to pass through, so they would leave no one behind.

"I—" Jack began, then a braying laugh cut him off.

"Wildfire Jack! I thought you would have left town by now," Maureen called, standing in front of the livery. She was flanked by a half-dozen other Copperheads, all spoiling for a fight.

Emmaline's eyes widened. "Marian, give me the flask." She held out a hand, and without a word, Marian thumped the flask into her palm, its contents sloshing.

Jack turned away from his daughter and the alchemist, though he desperately wanted to make sure all went according to plan. But he had to trust Emmaline in this. The pegasi moved to flank him, presenting a unified front. Jack made a show of lazily pulling out his pocket watch. "Huh. Judging by my watch, we still have a few minutes." He hazarded a quick glance behind him. The lowest edge of the sun touched the distant horizon.

Maureen put her hands on her hips. "Cutting it close, aren't you?" She smiled. "It'll be fun to play with you and your pony."

Zepheus snorted at the insult, mantling his wings.

C'mon, Em. "We had a bargain, Maureen."

Behind the pegasi, Emmaline made a gasping retch. *Must have drank the flask.* Jack fought the urge to spin and make sure she was okay. He narrowed his eyes, keeping his attention on the Copperheads.

Maureen tilted her head, taking a step forward. She smiled, but it wasn't a pleasant expression. "Time's running out for you."

"'Scuse me, Maureen, but looks like that girl has a *grimoire*," a gap-toothed Copperhead pointed out.

Shit. Jack grimaced, exchanging looks with Zepheus and Oberidon. "Stampede, boys."

The pegasi surged forward, charging at the formation of Copperheads. Fearsome they may be, but in the face of a pair of 1,200 pound animals plowing toward them, the men and women broke ranks with a yelp. Self-preservation was like that sometimes. Zepheus and Oberidon stirred up a dust cloud with their hooves and wings, obscuring the Copperheads' vision.

"We gotta go!" Jack growled, whirling to check on the status of the working.

Emmaline's back was straight as a fence post as she stood between the turquoise stones. Her hair was swept back, as if blown by a gale—and most alarmingly, her eyes glowed like the moon through clouds on a starless night. Jack had seen the shimmer of magic on the hands of some mages but never had he seen it in their eyes. No, that was a *wizard* thing. Gooseflesh crawled across his arms as he stared at his daughter.

The *bang* of a revolver caught his attention, and Jack turned back to their assailants. He pulled out his sixgun as the pegasi surged back to join him. Jack caught sight of a grey shape in the cloud and fired, satisfied when he heard a yelp and saw a man stagger to the ground.

Suddenly, the air behind him howled and rippled with the force of the spell being wrought. A shockwave burst forth from

Emmaline, forcing Jack to stagger backward and the stallions to stumble. Jack's ears rang, but he righted himself and found Emmaline. Her eyes had stopped glowing, the color cooling back to her normal green as a slit of radiant light opened in the air before her. There was a great tearing sound, as if someone were ripping a piece of fabric. The opening yawned wider, revealing a verdant, well-manicured garden.

"She did it," Jack whispered.

"Let's go!" Marian shouted, pointing at the portal.

<We'll guard your back,> Zepheus announced, half-rearing, wings flared out dramatically.

Jack didn't even argue. He put an arm around Emmaline, wincing as she sagged against him from exhaustion. Her eyelids fluttered.

"Just a little longer, darlin'," Jack murmured to her, watching as Marian slipped through. When the alchemist seemed to be on the other side and no worse for wear, Jack followed. Crossing through the portal was unlike any sensation he'd felt before. For the heartbeat it took to step through, it was as if someone had jabbed thousands of needles into his flesh. He hissed against the unexpected pain, though it vanished just as quickly. Jack glanced down at his daughter. Emmaline shifted against him but made no other sign of discomfort as he guided her onto a gravel path.

Even through the portal, he heard the sounds of the Copperheads. Zepheus and Oberidon stormed through. "Close it, Em. We're good." Hopefully, none of the Copperheads planned on following them through. Jack grinned at the idea. Well, if they did, they'd be fish out of water.

Emmaline's head lolled, but not before she closed the portal. It made a soft pop and faded from existence. Then she sagged against him, unconscious, just as Marian had predicted.

CHAPTER FORTY-ONE
Don't Press Your Luck

Blaise

The water in the tub trembled. Blaise had been relaxing, motionless with his eyes closed as the warm water eased his tension. His head whipped up at the sudden, strange sensation that rolled through the air. Something like the change in pressure from an incoming storm, only not that. His magic came alive, on edge.

Blaise stumbled out of the tub, dripping as he grabbed the fluffy towel awaiting him. He barely mopped up any of the water trailing down his body before he wrapped the towel around his midsection, barreling into the bedroom proper. As he'd suspected, the steward had replaced his worn clothing with a new set. He tugged on pants, shoved his feet in boots, and shrugged the shirt on, attempting to button it as he raced out of the room.

Ahead, he heard pounding feet and exclamations of surprise. He broke into a run, barreling out of the house, across the expanse of the wrap-around porch, and then down a short flight of stairs. He heard whinnies and cursing.

Blaise followed the sounds into the garden and stopped in surprise, his magic dissipating at the tableau.

Jack stood there, propping up Emmaline, who drooped against him as if she couldn't walk. Kittie was already rushing over to her with a sharp exclamation of worry. Zepheus and Oberidon were there, too, though they stepped aside, crushing a bed of marigolds as they made room for the humans.

My mother. Marian Hawthorne was there. Her eyes found him, and she gasped with surprise, then jogged over to him, wrapping her arms around him.

"Blaise, Blaise," she crooned, holding him as if he were a small child and not a grown man. "You're safe. You're here? But how are you *here?*"

"I have the same question for you," he replied, utterly baffled. Flora appeared nearby, eyes wide as she took everything in.

"It's complicated," Marian said, not releasing him from the embrace.

"Usually is with this group," Blaise agreed, though he couldn't help the sense of relief that his mother was here and safe. Far from the Copperheads, at any rate.

Kittie ushered Emmaline into the house with Flora's help. With his daughter in someone else's care, Jack turned to Blaise, his eyes glinting dangerously. "Didn't expect to find you here. What happened?"

His mother released him at last, and Blaise took a step back. He glanced down and realized that every button on his shirt was off by one, but he decided not to care. "It was the same Walker who tried to get me in Rainbow Flat. The Herald. She latched onto me, but Emrys bit her and didn't let go." He ran a hand through his soggy hair, raking it back until he hit a snarl.

<And I'll do it again if she dares to show her face around Blaise,> Emrys declared, pawing at the ground. He and Seledora had come to see what the fuss was about.

"Yeah, I figured it was that blasted Walker, but how did you get *here?*" Jack asked.

"We ended up somewhere in Ganland, and Emrys kicked her away. Didn't see her again after that." Blaise gestured around to their current location. "Emrys figured out we were close to Nera. To Jefferson's estate."

"Is the peacock here?" Jack asked gruffly, no doubt recalling their last conversation with him.

"No."

The outlaw nodded. "Was afraid of that. Well." He turned in a circle before facing Blaise again. "Glad you're safe."

Blaise raised an eyebrow. "Were you worried about me? As in, you cared if something happened to me?"

Jack made a face. "Don't press your luck, Breaker." He waved a dismissive hand. "I'm gonna go check on Em and catch up with my wife. I trust you can have one of your beau's grooms see to the pegasi." Without waiting for an answer, Jack stalked to the house.

"He *was* worried about you," Marian murmured.

Blaise smiled. "I know."

CHAPTER FORTY-TWO

Everyone Loves a Mystery

Jefferson

"Y ou'll make your triumphant return to Nera tomorrow," Phillip informed Jefferson at breakfast the next morning.

He stopped eating, raising an eyebrow at that. The very idea made him lose his appetite. He didn't want to go, didn't want to be Malcolm Wells. "Must I?"

"Yes," Phillip said, making a sour face. "We would have preferred more time to indoctrinate you to our ways, but it can't be helped. The Board is attempting to unseat Madame Boss Clayton."

Jefferson didn't even try to hide the show of surprise on his face. "What? Why?"

Phillip sighed. "They've been attempting this since the fire. They're declaring her unfit to govern and recalling her, citing *hysterics*."

Jefferson narrowed his eyes, offended on Rachel's behalf. "Rachel Clayton has never been hysterical a day in her life."

Phillip nodded, and it felt odd to have anything at all in

common with the Quiet One. "If they succeed, the Board will seat one of their own in her position and scuttle any hopes of recognizing the Gutter." His lips puckered as if the idea left an unpleasant taste in his mouth. "Your job will be to return to Nera and help ensure Madame Boss Clayton wrests back control."

Jefferson frowned. "And how am I supposed to do that?"

Phillip shrugged. "That's up to you. You have a good head on your shoulders. And more than that, people trust you."

"Who's going to trust a man coming back from the dead?" Jefferson asked, once more hoping against hope that Phillip might see the sense of his argument.

"Everyone. They're going to eat up the sob story you and Cinna will feed them—"

"Cinna?" Jefferson set down his spoon, the metal rapping sharply against the surface of the table. "I don't need a nanny, especially her." The very thought of his ex-fiancée accompanying him turned his stomach.

Phillip waved a hand, dismissive. "She's part of your cover story, Malcolm. After your breakdown at the traumatic loss of your parents, you faked your own death and sought an old flame to heal your shattered heart. And then, when it became apparent that Ganland needed your leadership once more, you rose to the challenge." He had the nerve to back up his words with a smile. "It's hopelessly romantic. People will eat it up."

The disgusting thing about the narrative was the fact that it *was* romantic. Exactly the sort of thing that made a compelling story and would earn him favor once more. "I don't want Cinna. Pick anyone else."

"She's the only one among us that makes sense, Malcolm. Regardless of your opinions, she is going with you." The Quiet One laced his fingers together. "You go in there, help Madame Boss Clayton keep her authority, and then push the Gutter's recognition through."

Something about that rubbed Jefferson the wrong way. "And after that?"

"That's none of your concern."

Jefferson straightened in his seat. "If I'm to be a Quiet One, then it absolutely *is* my concern."

Phillip raised a brow, gesturing with an index finger. "I like your spirit, but I don't trust you. Not yet. You're ours to use as we see fit until you've proven your value."

Jefferson's hackles raised. He stared Phillip down, drawing on every bit of haughtiness he possessed. "And what will happen if I don't prove my value?"

"The same fate as anything without worth." The calculated glint in Phillip's eyes made Jefferson's stomach churn. "But don't worry. I'm certain you'll live up to our expectations." Then Phillip smiled in a manner that telegraphed he had one more nugget of information to dole out. "Oh, and Malcolm? Once Ganland recognizes the Gutter, you'll need to hold a celebration."

Jefferson frowned. "I don't have a home in Nera." Not as Malcolm, anyway.

Phillip gave a bored shrug. "Use the Cole estate. I have it on good authority that's where you stay when you're conducting business in Nera. Everyone knows you were so *close*." He chuckled. "And now we know why."

Jefferson clenched his fists beneath the table, annoyed at being commanded. But holding such a celebration in his own home made things more promising. He might, just might, wrest back control of this horrible situation. "The Cole estate it is, then."

TO JEFFERSON'S FRUSTRATION, THE WINDOWS OF THE CARRIAGE conveying him to Nera were covered in heavy drapery, making it impossible to gain his bearings. If he so much as twitched in the direction of a window, Cinna adjusted her grip on the pretty little pistol she had produced from the folds of her dress.

She sat across from him in the carriage. Cinna had tried to sit beside him, but he had made a point to move when she did so. The Quiet Ones might have forced her along with him, but that didn't mean he had to tolerate her. Though Cinna seemed to have other plans, judging by the mostly one-sided conversation she kept up.

"You know, Malcolm, it wouldn't be such a terrible thing if we wed," she said. "We don't have to do it for love, only our combined might. You can keep your mage to warm the bed if you like." Cinna smiled. "Though I wouldn't mind warming it as well."

"I will *not* marry you," Jefferson insisted, crossing his arms. "You're out of your mind."

She leaned forward, a swell of cleavage peeking out of her bodice. "You will if the Quiet Ones demand it." Though, he didn't miss the brief stricken expression on her face, as if his declaration had actually stung.

Jefferson huffed out an exasperated breath. First, the Quiet Ones had stripped him of his preferred identity, and now this was a possibility? He hated it. Had to come up with some way for that to *never* happen.

Cinna shifted, the fabric of her long skirts rustling as she recrossed her legs. She glanced down at the pistol, then back at him. "For this venture, you *will* treat me as if we are engaged again."

Jefferson stared at her, wanting to argue but realizing that to do so would only put him in more jeopardy. Cinna was watching every move he made and would report back to her cohorts. He *had* to play their game to have any chance to escape. "Very well."

Mollified by his agreement, Cinna peeked out the curtained window. She made a satisfied sound and drew it open, revealing the pristine beauty of Nera. "Your public awaits."

"What do you mean?" Jefferson leaned over to get a glimpse of his own, though he was disappointed they were in Nera. He had no clues that would lead to where he had been held. He blinked when he saw curious citizens lining the road to Silver Sands. "All these people want to see me? Why?"

"Everyone loves a mystery." Cinna smirked. "It doesn't get more mysterious than a beloved politician they thought to be dead returning to the scene."

He hated how right she was. Jefferson stared down at his bare fingers. He fervently wished for his ring. Both of them, actually. He wanted to *look* like Jefferson, and he wanted to be safe from any potentially snooping unicorns and Trackers. But he had neither and would have to carry on without.

The carriage rolled up to the Silver Sands entry gate. Captain Cerulean strode over and spoke to the driver before coming around to the side. The guard pulled the door open, peering inside.

"They claimed you were Malcolm Wells, and I had to see for myself," Cerulean said, their eyes wide. The guard captain was familiar with the former Doyen and didn't even attempt to hide their surprise. "Is it truly you?"

Jefferson had no choice but to incline his head. What else was he to do, claim that he'd been kidnapped as Jefferson Cole and returned as someone thought to be deceased? "It is."

Cinna reached out and placed a hand on his knee, as if in comfort. "He's had a long and challenging road." She smiled warmly at the guard.

Cerulean raised their brows, curious but unwilling to ask. "Go on through." They shut the door and motioned for the driver to continue once the gates were open.

As the carriage rolled in, Jefferson got a better view of the damage wrought by the fire. The residential wing was a burned-out husk of tumbledown brick and charred timber, the guest wing bearing similar damage. The only building that seemed to have suffered minor damage was the executive wing. Their carriage halted outside.

A footman approached, opening the door to see them out. As soon as she could, Cinna snagged Jefferson's hand in hers, claiming him. She smiled demurely as the Bossguard approached to guide them through a throng of gawking Gannish politicians and staffers.

Their escort left them in a small parlor, along with a selection of brunch items. Jefferson wasn't hungry. He was still trying to puzzle through how he was going to play this. Cinna sat nearby, loading a plate as if nothing were wrong.

The door opened without a warning knock. Flora hustled inside, staring before rushing over, throwing her arms around him. She hugged him fiercely, as if she would never let go. Cinna stopped eating, eyebrows lowering with disapproval at the spectacle.

"Don't you ever make me think you're dead again," Flora whispered in his ear.

Jefferson chuckled. "It wasn't my intent. But I'm glad to see you, too." It improved his outlook to have Flora back on his side.

"Malcolm, why is your creature here?" Cinna asked, setting the plate aside as she locked eyes with Flora, no doubt attempting to overpower the half-knocker with her air of superiority.

Jefferson squeezed Flora's wrist, a silent plea for her not to verbally or physically attack. "Cinna Smithstone, allow me to introduce you to Flora Strop, Jefferson Cole's aide."

"And *problem solver*," Flora added, baring her teeth in an aggressive smile.

Cinna scowled, connecting the dots. Clearly, she disliked what she found. "I know what she is. You may greet Malcolm and then be on your way. We're here on business."

"As is Flora," Jefferson snapped, unable to hold his temper at her dismissal of his oldest and dearest friend.

"If I were you, I'd take an extended trip to the powder room," the half-knocker advised the Quiet One. Cinna stared, unsettled at the demand from someone she towered over. Flora pulled out her butterfly knife, the one she liked to toss around for show. That helped Cinna decide, and she retreated from the room.

Jefferson relaxed as soon as she left. "What have I missed?"

Flora grimaced, looking up at him. "I could write an entire book about what you've missed. But first, *how are you not dead?* There was a body in your room!"

"Ah, that was probably one of the men Cinna brought along to kidnap me." He hadn't gotten a good look at the man, but the fire might have only left enough behind for his friends to believe that any corpse in the room had been Jefferson.

Flora gave him a long look, no doubt reading the subtext that he had used his magic. She knew him too well—Jefferson wasn't a scrapper, wouldn't have been able to fight back against those odds. "Gotcha. Well, to answer your question, the Board is trying to unseat Rachel and discredit our delegation. Blaise somehow got to Ganland, and Jack and Emmaline appeared not long after—"

"Wait. Blaise is *here?*" Jefferson asked, hope rising again. He was almost certain he'd misheard her. Guilt pulled at him—he'd been too depressed about his own situation to seek Blaise out in the dreamscape. Jefferson knew Blaise had his own difficulties, and he had no desire to add to them.

"At your estate. Jack, too. That's a long, weird story," Flora confirmed with a nod. "Blaise is the one who told us you were still alive. And that you had to be..." She waved a hand to encompass his body. "This."

Blaise is here. That knowledge soothed him more than anything else. If things went well for the day, he could retire to his estate and see Blaise. He slouched against his seatback. "I heard about the Board's machinations. But I also have it on good authority *they're* the ones who set the fire."

Flora looked up at him. "Do you have any proof?"

He shook his head, voice still low. "None aside from the word of someone who will see me dead if I don't do as I'm told."

Flora scowled. "Not while I'm around."

Oh, he had missed her spirit and fierce protectiveness. He thought about trying to dissuade her, but he knew it wouldn't do much good. "I want to meet with Rachel as soon as I can."

Flora sighed. "That's going to be difficult. The Board's had her locked away 'for her own good,' they say." She made a face, gritting her teeth. "Ever since she refused to implicate Kittie as the source of the fire, they've been dogging her heels."

Kittie? Jefferson paused, then recalled Jack had suggested this might happen. Of course, the Board would be the ones responsible for the fire—and attempt to pin it on an outlaw mage. That would have guaranteed Ganland cutting ties with the Gutter. Instead, it seemed Rachel had doubled down on her determination to acknowledge the Gutter. Jefferson grimaced. He had a vested interest in the Gutter's nationhood, but it annoyed him he would be doing exactly what the Quiet Ones desired if he stayed the course.

Maybe they're not so bad, a distant, niggling part of his brain rationalized. *There's always going to be some group vying to be at the top, to be dominant. Why not be among that group?* After all, wasn't that exactly the game he had played as a Doyen? But that had been different. He had been the one calling the shots, crafting the policy. The Quiet Ones...well, he wasn't sure what their end game was. Maybe he would have gone along with them to see where things led. But now he had too many people he cared about who might suffer if things went awry. No, he would figure something out.

"Do you think I can see the Board, then?" Jefferson hazarded after a moment.

Flora gave him a toothy grin. "As a matter of fact, you can." Without even asking, she tugged out his pocket watch and checked the time. "Yep. In a half-hour, the Gutter is on their docket again. As soon as the rumor mill brought word that you were coming, I took some liberties with their schedule." She snapped the watch closed. "I penciled Malcolm Wells into their meeting with Kittie."

"You are a true wonder, Flora," Jefferson chuckled, shaking his head. He took back his watch and replaced it in his pocket, smoothing his lapels. "Oh. Do you have my ring? The one Blaise gave me."

Her face softened. "Yeah." Flora dug it out of her pocket and offered it to him. "For a while, I thought that was really all I had left of you. What is it with you and leaving jewelry behind?"

"Not a trend I hope to continue," Jefferson said wryly. He held the ring in his palm, debating if he should slip it on or not. His magic might be the only ace he had, and it was worth protecting. Wrinkling his nose, he slid the ring on, shivering at the sensation of his power abruptly cutting off. Flora watched him, curious, but didn't comment on his choice. "Where's Kittie? We should get ready to go shark fishing."

CHAPTER FORTY-THREE
Hostile Takeover

Jefferson

"So it seems the tales of your demise were exaggerated, Mr. Wells," Board member Sylvia Westerfield commented as they took their seats at the long table. The rest of the Board stared at Jefferson with beady eyes. Despite their *heart-felt* greetings and feigned relief at his appearance, he wasn't welcome. Neither was Kittie, who sat beside him, sipping a cup of tea as if her life depended upon it.

"Yes, well, everyone needs time away from the limelight," Jefferson said with a shrug. "I had some issues to work through."

"Most people would just step down or retire," Board member Marcus Funk muttered.

"I'm not most people," Jefferson shot back, thinking that was the most profound truth he'd ever spoken. "But I didn't travel all the way to Nera to justify how I spent my secluded time. Let's move on to the matters at hand."

"As you can understand, Pyromancer Dewitt and Mr. Wells—"

"Doyen." Jefferson had no qualms about interrupting Bartholomew Tate. "Even when we no longer hold the position, we keep the honorific." As much as he disliked the role he had to play, he wasn't going to allow any slights from this group.

"*Doyen* Wells," Tate corrected through gritted teeth. "We must table the request by the Gutter to be recognized as a country. Ganland is a leaderless nation at the moment, a ship without a rudder—"

"You've put the ship in dry dock, and it hasn't even sprung a leak," Kittie interjected, narrowing her eyes.

Jefferson braced his elbows on the table, steepling his hands together. "You must admit, it is offensive to refer to our Madame Boss Clayton in nautical terms. Makes it easier to dismiss her, I suppose." He smiled at the tense glances the rest of the Board traded.

"Now see here, Doyen Wells, we have nothing but respect for Madame Boss Clayton," Tate retorted, crossing his arms. "Her health has been delicate since the fire. Surely you, of all people, understand that."

"What I understand is that this Board has tried all the lowly tricks in their power to undermine the Gutter delegation from the day they crossed the border into Confederation lands." Jefferson chose his words carefully, remembering his role. Malcolm Wells had not been at the attack, but he *could* pretend to have heard tales of it.

At his accusation, even Kittie's head snapped up. This wasn't something he'd discussed with her. No, the pieces had only now fallen into place. He was more certain than ever that the Board was responsible for the attack near Fort Courage. "The Board isn't working for *Ganland*, is it? You're working on the Confederation's behalf."

All around the table, Board members sputtered in indignation at the allegation. "That is malarkey, Doyen Wells! Ganland is a part of the Confederation." Funk slammed a palm against the table.

"As long as we stay in lock-step and bow to the Confedera-

tion's whims, we are," Jefferson agreed. Yes, that was something he
had been painfully aware of as a Doyen. "You think you stand to
lose too much if mages have a chance at freedom in their own
land. So, you hired thugs to take out Jefferson Cole the first night
he and his delegation were in Mella." Memories of the attack
stirred him to anger, and he shook a trembling index finger. "And
when it became clear Madame Boss Clayton was willing to break
with the Confederation—potentially jeopardizing Ganland's
standing—you couldn't bear it, could you?"

"What are you on about? This is ridiculous!" Westerfield
protested, shrill with outrage.

Jefferson grinned savagely. He wasn't done, not yet. "You're the
ones behind the fire. You sought to discredit Pyromancer Dewitt,
to cast doubt on the delegation." He debated his next words.
Should I? At the moment, he was doomed to his identity as
Malcolm Wells, so what did he have to lose? Jefferson slammed a
palm against the table. "You killed Jefferson Cole."

Tate's face reddened. "Doyen Wells, you are out of line. We
understand the Pyromancer may not have caused the fire. It may
have just been an accident. A terrible accident."

Kittie rose from her seat, placing her hands flat against the
table and leaning over them. "It wasn't an *accident* that someone
stacked oil-soaked bales of hay against Silver Sands. Nor an accident that someone set them ablaze."

"It sounds as if you know exactly what started the fire, Pyromancer. Are you confessing?" Funk asked.

"Knowing the *source* of the fire doesn't mean I *set* it," Kittie shot
back.

Tate gestured to the nearby guards, who came to attention as if
this had been planned. Jefferson suspected it had been. "Arrest
Pyromancer Dewitt. Cite that she has confessed before the Board
to setting the fire."

Kittie recoiled, eyes widening with horror. "What? No!"

"She did no such thing!" Jefferson growled. The guards in the room closed ranks around them. Jefferson narrowed his eyes. "So, this is how it's going to be? Staging a coup?"

"Not a coup. We're acting within our rights as the Board," Tate said tightly. "Guards, arrest Doyen Wells on the charge of conspiring with an outlaw mage."

Well, this escalated quickly. Jefferson stood, shoving his chair away to block the nearest guard. "Stand down, man. This is madness. You really think the lot of you will get away with this?"

"I *do* think so because we *are*," Tate said with a grim smile.

Jefferson sighed. "Very well. This is all on you, then." He squared his shoulders as if he were about to make a speech before a crowd. "The Gutter is allied to Ganland, and thus Madame Boss Clayton, the rightful leader. As such, we'll rise in her defense." As soon as the words left his mouth, he realized he had spoken as if he were Jefferson. No one seemed to catch his mistake, though. Everyone focused on the rising tension instead.

"Good luck with that. You're outnumbered," Funk sneered.

"Outnumbered, perhaps. But not outmatched." Kittie glanced at Jefferson as she spoke. They hadn't made any plans to handle a hostile takeover. He trusted her instincts, though. They couldn't allow the Board to arrest them. Not only would it sink their plans for the Gutter, but they would likely end up in the Confederation's clutches.

The Firebrand snapped her fingers, a circle of flame blooming to life around them, cutting off the guards. Jefferson didn't particularly *like* being enclosed in fire, but he trusted Kittie could handle it. The Board took her display of power as a new threat.

"She's going to burn us all! Just as she tried to do to the Madame Boss!" Tate yelled, doubling down on his accusations against Kittie. "Shoot her! Don't take her alive!"

"I don't think so," Kittie murmured, lifting a hand as the guards aimed revolvers at her. Jefferson didn't see exactly what she did, but she gestured, and an instant later the guards dropped their weapons, yelping as if they were hot coals. A single revolver misfired as it struck the ground, the bullet punching through the ceiling.

But the guards had Jefferson and Kittie hemmed in, and it wouldn't take long for the Board to bring in reinforcements if needed. Kittie glanced over at him. "What now?"

Good question. His mind whirled through the possibilities, but none of them seemed likely. Except for one, in which he made a display of his own magic. Gods, were all his secrets to be forced into the light now? He didn't see any other way around it.

"Now it's my turn," Jefferson said softly. He worked the ring off and slipped it into his greatcoat pocket for safekeeping. His power breathed to life. *Sorry, Blaise. I tried.*

He called on his magic, and the dreamscape boiled up in his subconsciousness, ready. Jefferson focused on Tate, curling a tendril of magic around the man, luring him into slumber. His body hit the ground hard, and a guard cried out, moving to pull his limp form away from the ring of fire. "They killed Board Member Tate!"

"Oh, for Tabris's sake, he's sleeping like a baby," Jefferson muttered. Then, one after the other, he dragged the rest of the Board into the dreamscape.

Never had he forced so many to slumber against their will. Sweat beaded his forehead at the exertion. He was going to pay the price for this later, but at least that might mean he *had* a later in which he wasn't behind bars. When he finished, all five Board members lay dozing on the floor or slumped across the table, some of them snoring. The guards stood over them, uncertain.

Kittie kept up her wall of fire, though her forehead wrinkled when she looked at Jefferson. "Was that you?"

He wanted to deny it, but there was no use. She was a mage and would no doubt see through his lies. And he couldn't afford to alienate any allies. "Yes."

"You and I are going to have a talk later." She set her mouth in a thin, determined line. "Once we figure our way out of this mess."

He winced. "That's fair." Jefferson turned to the guards. "Put your weapons down!"

"You're not in command of us," a guard snarled petulantly.

The door swung open. "No, but I am." Madame Boss Clayton strode in, frowning at the sleeping lumps of Board members, then at Kittie's fire shield. Flora and Mindy were a few paces behind her. Jefferson had wondered what the half-knocker was up to. Springing the Madame Boss with the help of a Hospitalier, it seemed. "Stand down."

"But—"

"I said *stand down*," Rachel repeated, firm. "As you can see, the Board is incapacitated. And as such, *I* am the only authority." Puzzlement was clear on her face as she tried to figure out why her treacherous Board members had taken a nap in the middle of a meeting. Her eyes flicked to Jefferson—to *Malcolm*, as that was who she saw. "Put the weapons away, or I'll relieve you of duty. Permanently."

With a grumble, the guards did as she commanded and moved back to their defensive positions. Kittie dismissed her fire, the smoke curling away and dissipating into nothing. Jefferson glanced down. The floor and furniture didn't bear so much as a single scorch mark. She was *good*.

"So, what did I miss?" Rachel asked. "Aside from the miraculous return of former Doyen Malcolm Wells." Her eyes were sharp, as if she were trying to peel back the layers of lies and half-truths.

"That's a topic for another time," Jefferson said stiffly, hoping it was a conversation that would never happen. But he knew better. He gestured at the Board. "They were planning a coup, from the sound of it. Discrediting us, overthrowing you. You know, the usual."

Rachel raised her brows. "What happened to them, anyway?"

"I suppose I bored them," Jefferson said with a shrug that didn't fool anyone.

"Explanations later," Rachel murmured, and Kittie smirked in agreement. Then she turned to the guards. "Arrest the members of the Board on charges of treason."

"And arson," Kittie added without hesitation. She picked up her cup of tea, peering into the golden liquid before taking another sip.

Rachel nodded. "Arson." Her face darkened with anger as she understood the true meaning behind the charge. "Attempted murder."

Kittie shook her head. "Not only attempted."

The Madame Boss tensed at that, bowing her head with such grief that a wave of guilt washed over Jefferson. "I stand corrected. Charge them with the death of Ambassador Jefferson Cole."

Jefferson turned away so no one would see the flicker of remorse in his eyes. He wanted to yell at them, to declare that Jefferson Cole stood before them. He puffed out a frustrated breath.

The guards were reluctant to do her bidding, and Rachel seemed painfully aware of this. She strode into the hallway and had one of her staffers run off on an errand, and moments later, her Bossguard arrived on the scene. They hauled the sleeping Board members into custody as Jefferson strained to keep them in the dreamscape. He knew they were confused about where they were and how they'd gotten there, but he didn't much care. A part of him wished he could spare enough focus to give them reason to regret their actions.

Once the Board had been cleared from the room, Rachel released a haggard sigh. She turned, giving Jefferson and Kittie a grateful smile. "I appreciate what you did. You took a significant risk for me. For Ganland."

Kittie inclined her head. "Doyen Wells proclaimed that the mages of the Gutter are your allies—Ganland's allies—and that much is true. The least we could do was stand firm."

"And then some, it seems," Rachel murmured, eyeing Jefferson. "It's time for an explanation, isn't it?"

Jefferson sighed. "I suppose it is."

"TEA. I'D DRINK A WHOLE KETTLE RIGHT NOW," KITTIE MUTTERED, massaging her forehead with her thumb and index finger.

"I've got you covered," Mindy said, pushing a fresh cup in front of the Firebrand. Steam rose from it, and the rich, sweet scent drifted across the table to Jefferson. Kittie sighed and took another swig, as if the tea were a balm for her soul. Jefferson didn't know what was going on with her, but he suspected it was. If only tea would help his situation.

They sat around a table in a small assembly room that Rachel had commandeered—a room that gave them the privacy they sorely needed. Jefferson didn't enjoy it one bit, despite the snacks delivered to them by a perky staffer.

"Where do you want to begin, Doyen Wells?" Rachel prompted.

He swallowed, reluctant to unearth his secrets. Not that he wanted to mislead anyone—there were some secrets that simply needed to remain buried. But now, he had no choice if he wanted to stay in their good graces. And he would need every advantage against the Quiet Ones. His stomach twisted as he ignored Flora's persistent attempts to catch his eye.

Jefferson looked up, meeting the Gannish leader's eyes. She wouldn't like what he was about to say, but he saw no way around it. "Let's begin with the fact that you also know me as Jefferson Cole."

Rachel's mouth dropped open, then snapped shut as she absorbed the news. Her cheeks flushed with anger. "I'm sorry, *what*? Jefferson Cole, as in the man whose death we just accused my former Board members of?"

Mindy's lips tightened, as if she, too, felt betrayed by this new information. The Firebrand kept her mouth shut, wisely concealing the fact that she was very aware Jefferson Cole was alive and well when she'd made the suggestion.

"Yes, *that* Jefferson Cole," he agreed, wishing he were anywhere but here. Well, maybe not anywhere. He certainly didn't want to end up back at the Quiet Ones' estate.

"How is that even possible?" Mindy asked, the hurt clear in her tone.

Jefferson didn't meet her eyes. He liked Mindy, and he truly had not wanted to hurt anyone with this. "It was a lot of work, I assure you." He rubbed the bridge of his nose, thinking. "I don't want to get into the details, but trust me when I tell you I am also Jefferson Cole."

"What game have you been playing with us?" Rachel asked. "Malcolm Wells is supposed to be dead, too. Yet here you sit, telling us that somehow, you are *two* people." Her voice rose with each word, her frustration getting the better of her. "I should have you arrested for this."

Jefferson sighed. "Please don't. There was no game. Everything I have done, I have done to *help*." Inwardly, he winced, knowing he hadn't always been so virtuous. "I know this doesn't look good, but I had my reasons for this masquerade."

"Ones that you won't share with us?" Rachel needled.

Jefferson thought back to his family's wicked ways and how he'd tried to separate himself from them. He didn't want to recount any of that at the moment. It was punishment enough that Malcolm Wells stared back at him in every mirror he passed. "Perhaps in the future, but not today, with so many other things afoot."

"Just as well because *I* have questions about what you did to the Board members," Kittie said, fire in her eyes.

"Yes, do tell us about that," Rachel agreed.

Jefferson rubbed his forehead, debating how much truth he

could tell them. He felt Flora's gaze on him but still refused to meet her eyes. "I'm a mage."

Kittie cocked her head. "I've never heard of a mage who puts people to sleep."

"I'm unique, and we need to leave it at that," Jefferson said. He might have to bare every aspect of himself to them, destroy his lifelong web of lies, but he refused to betray the secret of Blaise's blood.

"And when, exactly, were you planning to share this information with us, Malcolm?" Rachel prodded, her eyes flinty as she stared Jefferson down.

He'd withstood her withering gaze before. And he'd be damned if he would cringe under it now, though her use of his old name stung. "To be quite honest, I was never planning to share it with any of you." This admission earned him nothing but deepening scowls, and Jefferson flapped a hand. "Not because I'm trying to deceive you—I'm *not*. But..." He shook his head, struggling to figure out a way to explain his situation without connecting his magic to Blaise. "I was *not* previously a mage. And you must understand that magic showing up at this stage in life is problematic."

"On so many levels," Rachel agreed. She shifted to match Kittie's cross-armed stance. "You were gunning to be the Ambassador as *Jefferson Cole*. How can I trust you with such a position after keeping this from me? I'll need to consider someone else."

No. His eyes widened at that. Blast it, but he wanted that position! It was perfect in every way for him, for his goals. To be with Blaise and still do something meaningful. But the Quiet Ones would use him...*wait, the Quiet Ones*. He was safe behind the Madame Boss's walls, with her Bossguard, wasn't he? With his outlaw mage allies around him.

"You can trust me because I'm about to tell you something I shouldn't." Flora jerked upright at his words, her eyes wide as she no doubt wondered what he was about to say. "The night of the fire, I tried to escape like everyone else. I was attacked and kidnapped, held against my will."

"What?" Rachel's voice went gravelly with stark disbelief, and Kittie's brow furrowed. Mindy blinked in surprise. "Who would do such a thing? At Silver Sands, of all places?"

I hope they believe me about the next part. "There's a powerful group of elite called the Quiet Ones. They seek to set things in motion, to fall in place to their design." Jefferson licked his lips. "They said that I had to join their group as Malcolm Wells and ensure that Ganland recognize the Gutter as a nation."

"So, they like mages?" Mindy asked, uncertain.

"Mages are useful to them, and they see value down the road in having the Gutter tightly allied to Ganland." Jefferson rubbed his chin. "I don't know what their long game is. They didn't seem overly concerned about the Confederation taking umbrage to any of this."

"Why is this the first time I'm hearing of this group?" Rachel asked.

"Because they operate behind the scenes," Jefferson said. "They're shadows, lining things up just so. I may be in dire straits for telling you this much."

"And you're joining these Quiet Ones?" Rachel frowned.

"I have little choice," Jefferson said, his shoulders tense. "I have to do what they tell me, or…" He shook his head, averse to telling them how truly grave his situation was. "They sent Cinna Smith-stone along with me to make sure I stick to their plan."

"I wondered why she was with you," Rachel murmured. "I knew that engagement was broken years ago."

"Cinna and the rest of the Quiet Ones don't know about my magic. It has to stay that way," Jefferson said urgently.

Rachel frowned, clearly reluctant for the secrets to continue. "If they're as connected as you say, they're going to find out."

"I would rather they find out from me," Jefferson replied. "On my terms."

"Well, you and Kittie stood up for me and for Ganland, so I'm grateful for that. I'll keep the secret of your magic, though note that I'm *not* happy about that," Rachel said. She stared at him for a dozen heartbeats, then straightened as she moved to a new topic. "I believe tomorrow I can arrange a time to sign the declaration recognizing the Gutter as a nation...and Ganland's newest ally. It will be noteworthy to do so on Bounty's Eve."

Kittie made a soft gasp. Jefferson's shoulders sagged with relief. "Just tell us when, and we'll be there."

CHAPTER FORTY-FOUR

Flair for the Dramatic

Jefferson

"It was still stupid, even if you think you had no choice," Flora pointed out, dogging Jefferson's steps as they crossed from the Silver Sands executive wing to the portion of the stables that had been untouched by the fire. The half-knocker had made arrangements to delay Cinna, and Flora was clearly determined to use every moment to her advantage.

He stared straight ahead as they walked. "It was the only thing I could do that might give me some power back. And offer protection."

She scowled. Jefferson knew he had just insulted her—Flora considered herself his protection. And she was, but there were some things even she couldn't guard against.

"The more people who know, the harder your secrets are to keep." Her voice was soft, the words meant only for his ears.

Oh, how he knew. "No sense dwelling on what's done."

"I'm only dwelling on how *stupid* it was."

"Oh look, there's Seledora," Jefferson said, deciding a change of subject was best. He was glad to see his pegasus attorney—it meant he wouldn't have to ride a mundane horse back to his estate.

<Why did I hear Flora say you did something stupid?> the dapple grey mare asked, ears pricked forward.

Jefferson sighed. *And here I thought perhaps you missed me.* "No reason."

Seledora must have broadcast to the half-knocker as well. Flora harrumphed at his response, though she glanced over her shoulder. Cinna Smithstone strode toward them, not yet near enough to overhear. "Dreamer here flaunted something he should have kept to himself."

<She's right. That's stupid.>

"It's quite unfair that you outnumber me," Jefferson complained as he swung into the saddle.

"Malcolm, you wouldn't leave without me, would you?" Cinna asked as she finally caught up. A Silver Sands groom led a glossy bay gelding out for her. She frowned at the animal. "Wait. Where is the carriage?"

Jefferson stroked Seledora's sleek neck. His attorney fluffed her wings, settling them against her sides. "No carriages. I prefer the saddle." Carriages were for *Malcolm*. Riding Seledora was a spark of defiance. A subtle nod to who he wanted to be. "I'm certain Madame Boss Clayton's staff would find accommodations for you if you don't wish to join us."

Cinna crossed her arms, glancing at the pegasi. "I'll take one of those, then."

"One does not simply *demand* to ride a pegasus," Jefferson said, happy that in this, at least, he had the upper hand. "However, since you don't have the advantage of flight, we'll keep to the ground." He nodded to the bay gelding. For a fleeting instant, Jefferson entertained the idea of flying off into the sunset, leaving this mess behind him. If only it were so simple.

Cinna narrowed her eyes and, assisted by the groom, got into the saddle. She joined Kittie, Mindy, and Flora who were already waiting on their pegasi.

"Ready?" Kittie asked, glancing at Jefferson.

"We may proceed," Cinna said with a nod.

"So very ready," Jefferson agreed, meaning every word. *I'll get to see Blaise soon. And I'll be in my own home.* Though Blaise was definitely the best part. His only worry was what Blaise would think of Cinna's presence.

Dusk was falling as the open gates of the estate came into view. Mage-lights illuminated the windows, lending the home a cheerful glow. Jefferson had missed this sight.

Seledora trotted to the stables, allowing Jefferson to dismount. The rest of the delegation, plus Cinna, did the same.

As soon as she was on the ground, she sidled up next to him. "Shall we go inside?" She reached over to snare his hand.

Jefferson jerked away from her. "You presume too much."

She closed the gap between them again. "No, *you* do. You forget yourself, Malcolm."

I most certainly do not. But she was right. In public, even here on his own estate, he had to pretend. The realization tied his stomach in knots. Cinna linked her arm through his, aiming a victorious smile at him. Reveling in her power over him.

He turned back toward the house. The front doors were already open, with some of the staff filing out to the wrap-around porch. Jack, Marian, and Blaise were there, too, watching their arrival.

Blaise glanced from Jefferson to Cinna. Recognition flashed in his eyes, along with something else. *Disappointment.* Before Jefferson could climb the steps to greet him, to offer any sort of explanation at all, Blaise stepped back inside.

Blast it all. He knew exactly what Blaise was thinking. He was Malcolm Wells again, and Blaise knew he'd been engaged to Cinna. *I should have asked Seledora to pass word to Emrys of this farce.*

When Jefferson reached the top of the stairs, he glanced at the staffers. He frowned—he looked like Malcolm Wells, which meant he technically couldn't command them to do anything. But he could ask politely. "Good evening. Could you prepare one of the guest bedrooms for Ms. Smithstone?"

Cinna tittered, as if it was a jest. "That's unnecessary. I'll be staying with Malcolm."

The muscles in Jefferson's jaw ached from how tightly he clenched his teeth. "I wouldn't wish to sully your reputation during our engagement." He gave her a polite smile and a gallant half-bow. They both knew he had a prolific history as a rake, but she could hardly make that argument when he mentioned an *engagement*. "I'm certain the staff will find satisfactory accommodations for you."

The Quiet One opened her mouth, no doubt hoping to find a loophole. But Jefferson was already untangling his arm from hers, uncomfortably aware of Jack's furious gaze. He hoped he could get to Blaise before the outlaw murdered him.

Jefferson left Cinna staring after him as he hurried to the suite where he suspected Blaise would be. He tapped on the door, but there was no response. Gently, he turned the knob and pushed it open.

The mage-lights were dim. Blaise sat on the bed, his face in his hands. He looked up when he heard the door close.

"Blaise," Jefferson said softly. "Please talk to me."

The Breaker quivered. "I don't *understand*. You..." He shook his head as if he couldn't bear to complete whatever thought had crossed his mind.

Jefferson moved to the bed and sat a few feet away from Blaise. This wasn't the reunion he'd hoped for. "Let me help you understand."

Blaise lifted his head, meeting his gaze. "I know who she is. What she was to you."

"*Was*," Jefferson agreed.

Confusion sparked in the Breaker's eyes. "I thought..." He

paused, then rubbed the back of his head. "Oh. I jumped to some conclusions I suppose I shouldn't have." Blaise relaxed, though now he looked embarrassed.

At least this crisis was averted. Jefferson scooted a little closer to the Breaker, though he still gave his beau room to shift away if he needed. "I will *always* choose you over her. No matter what it looks like. No matter what she forces me to do." He took a ragged breath. "That is a promise."

Blaise lifted his head, meeting his gaze. "What do you mean what she *forces* you to do? Why is she here?"

Jefferson grimaced. "She's one of the Quiet Ones. And since we have a history, they sent her along to make sure I behave." He was suddenly tired of this. Tired of the Quiet Ones and the Board. Tired of everything. "You're the only one I love. I hope you can believe that, even when I wear this face."

Blaise closed the distance between them. "I do. I was just..." He shook his head. "I recognized her and thought..."

That I would abandon you for her? Jefferson shook his head. "Never. I missed you. Gods, you don't know how much I missed you."

Blaise huffed. "You could have *done* something about that. You haven't bothered to see me in the dreamscape the past two nights."

Jefferson rubbed his forehead, mentally kicking himself because Blaise was *right*. "I was in a bad spot, and I didn't want to bring you down with all you were going through." He had a thousand questions for Blaise. How had he gotten here? What had happened in Thorn? It didn't matter, though. He was *here*. That was what mattered.

Blaise was quiet, staring down at his hands. "You helped me through one of my hardest times. Don't you think I'd want to do the same for you?"

"I know you would, but..." Jefferson trailed off, deciding how to phrase his next sentence. "You've been hurt so many times. I feared adding to it."

Blaise bumped Jefferson's shoulder with his own. "We're stronger together, you know."

Jefferson sighed. Blast it all. He *should* have sought Blaise out in the dreamscape. "Forgive me for being stupid?"

A ghost of a smile touched the Breaker's lips. "I forgive you." Blaise looked as if he were about to add something. Instead, he leaned in, claiming Jefferson with a heated kiss. The Dreamer melted into the familiarity, into the love the gesture offered. Blaise was warm and comfortable, a bulwark against the horror that was his current life. For those precious seconds, Jefferson could pretend like nothing was wrong.

When at last they parted, Blaise murmured, "That was nice, but now you should probably tell me more about what's going on."

Jefferson rubbed the side of his face. "Madame Boss Clayton knows who I really am...and about my magic." At Blaise's blank look, he realized the Breaker had no clue who he was referring to. "The leader of Ganland. Oh, and Mindy knows, too."

He'd thought Blaise might be more alarmed by the news, but the younger man merely shrugged. "I trust Mindy. And I assume you had a very good reason to tell them."

"I didn't know what else to do." Jefferson recounted the meeting with the Board. Hard to believe it had only been hours ago. It felt like ages. He pulled the magic-concealing ring out, turning it over in his hand. "You didn't want anyone to find out about it."

Blaise curled his hand over Jefferson's. "No, I wanted you to be safe. There's a difference." He sighed. "And none of that turned out as I'd hoped."

"Neither of us could anticipate the nest of vipers I walked into." Then Jefferson winced, recalling that Blaise had dealt with snakes of his own. The Copperheads weren't to be taken lightly. "Ah, sorry. Wrong turn of phrase."

The Breaker brushed the words away with a shake of his head. "Maybe it's time your era of secrets came to an end."

What? Jefferson's first instinct was to say no. His secrets had been too large a part of his life, a layer of protection he had relied on for years. "I don't want to be Malcolm Wells."

"You don't have to be," Blaise said, as if his simple words made it true. Maybe they did.

I'm Jefferson to him, no matter what. He swallowed the lump in his throat—he hadn't anticipated how much that would mean in this moment. Blaise understood. But the Breaker was only one man, and to everyone else, Jefferson would forever be Malcolm Wells. "Everyone else thinks Jefferson is dead."

"So was Malcolm Wells. You had a funeral and everything. You do have a certain flair for the dramatic."

Was Blaise teasing him at a moment like this? Jefferson blinked, taking stock of the twist of Blaise's lips and the glint in his eyes. *He is.* "What do you mean? About my secrets, that is."

"Be Jefferson. Be a mage. Just be unapologetically *you*." There was a fire in Blaise's voice, stoked with determination and love. The Breaker was thoughtful, looking down at his palms as if they held an answer. Maybe they did, for all Jefferson knew. "You said Gregor has your ring. Do you think he'll attend the signing tomorrow?"

Gregor. Jefferson bit his tongue to stave off his anger at the enemy Doyen's name. "No, I don't think the Quiet Ones would want that. Gregor opposes the mages, and it would be strange for him to attend."

"Do you think he's still in Ganland?"

"He was at their estate when I left this morning. I suspect they may keep him there in case he's needed. There's no Salt-Iron Council sessions for another month, so his time is his own."

A determined look settled on Blaise's face. "We need to find out where this estate is."

Jefferson's shoulders slumped. "It's warded, and the carriage windows were covered, so I couldn't see a thing."

Blaise cocked his head. "That's not the only solution, you know."

Jefferson frowned, puzzled. He couldn't think of any other way. "What do you mean?"

"If your ex-fiancée is so eager to be here, we may as well make her useful."

Jefferson still wasn't following Blaise's train of thought—mainly because he wanted nothing to do with Cinna. "What?"

Blaise sighed, leaning over to give him an exasperated kiss before pulling back to explain. "Bring her into the dreamscape and interrogate her. The dreamscape is real to you...and to me. But she wouldn't know that. And didn't you tell me you used it to change the memories of the guards who had..." Blaise drifted off, suddenly unable to finish his question.

Jefferson knew exactly what he meant, though. "I did. I mean, at least I think I did, based on the reports Flora dug up about the incident afterward." Now that Blaise mentioned it, he was warming to the idea. "That's brilliant. I'd much rather do that than the alternative."

"What's the alternative?"

Gods, he didn't *really* want to tell Blaise, but he'd asked. "Seduce her. Though, to be fair, I would have to put little effort into it so it wouldn't be much of a seduction." When the Breaker's brows shot up at that, Jefferson gently took his hand. "And I'd rather *not*."

"I'd rather you not, too," Blaise agreed, fingers tightening around Jefferson's. There was a veneer of possessiveness over his tone that Jefferson liked.

Jefferson glanced down at their twined fingers, savoring the contact. "What will we do with the information I get from Cinna?"

Blaise leaned over and kissed his cheek. "Leave that to me."

Jefferson disdained the idea of hosting Cinna in the dreamscape, but Blaise was right—it really *was* a good idea. And if he did it just right, she would never know what she had divulged to him. It was a stroke of genius.

He curled up beside Blaise in the partial darkness, a single mage-light casting its pale glow over them. Jefferson stole a glance at the Breaker's profile. To the observer, he seemed to be asleep, but Jefferson's magic told him he wasn't. All the same, Jefferson relished seeing Blaise relaxed, as if the world hadn't come crashing down on them.

"You're delaying," Blaise muttered, cracking one eye open. "You really don't like her, do you?"

"No," Jefferson admitted.

Blaise opened his other eye. "Can I ask why you ever liked her?"

Jefferson snorted. "Explaining that to you will cause another delay." Not that he minded.

"I'll allow it," Blaise murmured, rolling onto his side. "I know why you don't like her *now*, but that doesn't explain the past."

Jefferson sighed, very aware that everything he was about to explain would sound exceedingly shallow to someone like Blaise. "Let me preface this by saying I was a different person back then."

"Literally or figuratively?"

"I suppose only figuratively, considering how I look at the moment." Jefferson chuckled, suddenly feeling more at ease when Blaise rested a hand on his side. "I told you before that the elite seldom marry for love."

"You did," Blaise agreed, sounding sleepy but content.

"We were betrothed in our teens. I saw nothing wrong with it —or her—at the time." Jefferson made a face. "She *is* quite beauti-ful. And as often happens with young men, I was enamored with her...ahem...*physical* features." To further illustrate, he sketched an hourglass figure in the air with his hands.

"I mean, she's pretty, but is that enough to...?" Blaise trailed off, sounding baffled.

"Past Me was quite stupid, so yes, at the time it was enough." Jefferson shook his head. "When she wants to be, she can be quite charming. And in some ways, she is *not* vile. Cinna has a soft spot for birds. She has a lovely aviary where her people nurse injured wild birds back to health." He laughed nervously. "And now I'm babbling. None of this probably makes a lick of sense."

"No, it does," Blaise said. "I only saw the woman who wants to use you, and I couldn't imagine why you would ever like her. This makes more sense." He cuddled closer to Jefferson. "Thank you for explaining. Now I won't delay you any longer."

Jefferson reached over to touch Blaise's cheek, dragging his fingers gently through the fringe of his beard. "I wouldn't *mind* if you delayed me."

The Breaker leaned into the caress. "I know. But you need to do this while she sleeps, since neither of us like the other option you proposed."

"You raise a valid point." Jefferson drew his fingers away from Blaise. He shifted beneath the sheets, easing onto his back. "Goodnight."

"It is. I'm with you," Blaise whispered, leaning over to kiss Jefferson's cheek before snugging a blanket up to his chin and shutting his eyes.

Jefferson wanted to reach out and take Blaise's hand, wanted more contact with the one he truly cared about, but that would only distract him from his task. Blaise was right: he needed to do this, and the sooner he set about it, the better. He closed his eyes, calling on his magic.

The dreamscape swirled around him, a grey void of mist. Jefferson tilted his head, considering the best way to lower Cinna's guard. He crafted a lavish bedroom, complete with candlelight to add an air of romance. He was ready to seek out Cinna and drag her to the dreamscape when he remembered one critical detail.

He looked at himself in a mirror of his own creation, shaking his head. In the dreamscape, he was *always* Jefferson. He had total control over his visage in his domain. *But Cinna won't want Jefferson.* Not if this was to be a believable dream for her, anyway. He wrinkled his nose in distaste, watching as his features melted into those of Malcolm Wells.

With the transformation complete, he sought Cinna. She wasn't difficult to locate. Because of their history and her proximity, she was in his periphery. Carefully, so as not to flaunt his magic, he pulled her into the dreamscape bedroom.

"Oh, Malcolm," she murmured with delight as soon as she laid eyes on him. Cinna stepped up against him, resting a hand on his chest. "You truly *are* the man of my dreams."

Her words sent a shock through him. Had Cinna loved him? Or had it been only lust—for power, for status, for a handsome man on her arm? But there was something genuine in her tone, as if she had let her guard down. Which she probably had. That was the whole point of this exercise. All the same, it made him a little sad to know she may have loved him, but he would never love her in return. *No wonder she slapped me.*

Jefferson gathered her up in his arms. Music played softly in the background, and he led her into an intimate dance. "Hello, Cinna. It's been a long time."

She smiled up at him, her face radiant. "It has. I missed this. Missed *you*."

I am truly the worst person ever. Jefferson met her smile with one of his own. He leaned over, taking her hand in his and trailing kisses up the length of her too-perfect arm. "You are as lovely as I remember."

Cinna shivered beneath his touch. "Malcolm," she whispered, blissful. "If only you were like this outside of my dreams. Oh." She moaned softly as he reached her shoulder. "If only you'd choose *me* over that mage. I don't know what you see in him."

Jefferson held his tongue. He had a role to play, and as much as he wanted to defend Blaise, this wasn't the time. "I'm here now," he said instead, kissing her neck.

Cinna closed her eyes. "We would be such a powerful team, Malcolm. How can I convince you? Two Quiet Ones, united. Nothing would stand in our way. Think of the romantic stories that would be told of us. How I healed you with my love from the depths of your despair."

Lies. All lies. But now, Cinna was moving closer to the topic he wanted. Just a little nudge, and maybe he could end this farce. "Perhaps so. Tell me, if we were to wed, could we hold the ceremony at the Quiet Ones' estate?"

Her eyes flashed open at the mention of marriage. "Anywhere your heart desires."

"The Quiet Ones' estate," Jefferson murmured, nuzzling her ear, kissing the tender skin beneath it. "Where is it, by the way? I've been so curious."

She sighed, relaxing into his embrace. "Not far. A few miles west of Nera. There are orange groves all around it, which have served us well to keep anyone from snooping and trying to break through the wards." Cinna twisted to look at him. "But if we wed there, it would be a private ceremony."

"Indeed," Jefferson whispered. While it wasn't an exact location, from what Blaise had told him of his plan, that would be enough for an aerial description. It seemed to check out from his memory of the carriage ride to Nera—it hadn't been as long as he'd thought it would be if the estate was further away.

Now that he had what he needed, it was time to extract himself from the dream. This was going to be more challenging than the time he'd twisted the memories of Blaise's guards, however. He had to make Cinna believe he was still there when he wasn't. Jefferson held her close as he concentrated, willing a likeness of Malcolm into existence, layered over him. Then he took a step back, satisfied when the ghost of himself remained with Cinna.

Dream-Malcolm took Cinna's hand, a roguish smile slipping across his face. He gave a gentle tug, pulling her toward the bed.

Cinna's eyes widened with surprise, then she tilted her head, coquettish. "Oh, *Malcolm*, I knew you'd come around."

CHAPTER FORTY-FIVE
Reconciliation

Blaise

Breakfast the next morning was an awkward affair. The staff who ran the household did their best, but their heart wasn't in it—they believed Jefferson, their employer, was dead. And they were probably worried about what would happen to them in the coming weeks.

Cinna's presence didn't help, either. When they came down for breakfast, she attempted to sit beside Jefferson—though Kittie must have seen it coming because she smoothly claimed the seat she was aiming for, and Blaise was already on his other side. Stymied, Cinna instead chose the seat directly across from Jefferson.

Blaise didn't like the woman, and not only because she wanted Jefferson—well, Malcolm. She seemed eager to get between him and Jefferson any way she could. But after last night, Blaise knew Jefferson wouldn't allow it. He'd been too quick to judge the situation when he'd first spied the woman walking with Malcolm. Blaise had forgotten that no matter the face he wore, he was Jefferson. *And Jefferson is mine. And I'm his.*

No one said much at breakfast except for Cinna, who seemed to enjoy the sound of her own voice. Jack hadn't come down, instead choosing to stay with Emmaline, who was still recovering from the portal spell. Blaise's mother was there, though, and he suspected she was plotting the best way to go about poisoning Cinna Smithstone. Her cutting looks at the woman almost made up for all her past hurts to him. She truly loved him and wanted to protect his heart.

When the meal was finished, Jefferson rose, getting everyone's attention. From their earlier conversation, Blaise knew what was at hand. Knew the role he had to play.

"Today is a momentous day for the Gutter. Ganland will recognize it as a nation, and at last, mages will have a land to call their own." This wasn't news to anyone at the table, but they all nodded in agreement. Then Jefferson continued, "And in celebration, we'll host a gala here this evening."

Marta, the cook who had formerly served Malcolm in Izhadell before moving to Nera at Jefferson's behest, stopped in her tracks, narrowing her eyes at her former employer. "And you're just telling us *now?*"

Jefferson momentarily withered under her question. Blaise recalled that Marta was a tough one. Jefferson cleared his throat. "Ah, yes. But I have faith that you and the others will do an admirable job."

"I can help," Mindy piped up.

"Yes, please do," Jefferson agreed. Blaise wondered if he wanted Mindy for her magic or simply to help the frazzled kitchen staff. Possibly both. "Kittie and Cinna will accompany me to Nera for the signing." He didn't mention Flora, but Blaise knew for once she wouldn't be accompanying her boss. Jefferson had called her to their suite in the grey hours before dawn, telling her their plans.

Cinna aimed a triumphant look at Jefferson as if she had won something. Maybe she thought she had since Jefferson was taking her instead of Blaise. He was fine with that. Let her think she'd won. She wasn't the one who had woken up beside Jefferson that morning.

Jefferson, Kittie, and Cinna finished their preparations and headed out. Once they were gone, Marian slipped over to him, frowning. "Is that horrible woman trying to steal Jefferson away?"

Ah, so he *had* interpreted her look correctly. "Um, she's trying. It's not going to work." Blaise shrugged.

Marian pursed her lips. "I could poison her."

"Mom, *don't*," Blaise warned. They didn't need an overzealous alchemist ruining their plans.

"I could give her warts?"

"*Mom*," he said, exasperated. Though, he appreciated her drive to protect him. He took her hand. "Walk with me. Let's talk." Blaise needed to talk to Jack, too, but that could wait. They had hours before his part of the plan needed to take action.

He led her outside, near the paddock where Emrys was grazing with Zepheus and Oberidon. It was peaceful, downright pastoral. Blaise leaned against the white fence railing. "I was going to Rainbow Flat to work through things with you. I want to understand."

Marian slouched against the rail, her eyes on the pegasi. "What part do you want to understand?"

"All of it. But mostly..." He paused, uncertain what he really wanted to know. What could heal the wounds except for time? Blaise shook his head in frustration. He had so many questions, and suddenly they were difficult to ask. "Why did you run away with me?"

She glanced at him. "I loved you from the start, even though you had to be a part of the experiment. I don't know what it was— I could think of all the other children as little more than test subjects. But you? I was the only one who could hold you and get you to calm down. To feel safe."

Blaise nodded. It was true; he'd always felt safe with his mother. *Always.* "And that changed things?"

"A little, though I obviously went forward with the experiment." Marian waved a hand to encompass him. "But then when all the children became ill and started dying..." She shook her head. "You were so sick, and it physically hurt *me* to know what I'd done to you. I did everything I could to help you pull through. And I vowed that if you lived, my days as a Confederation alchemist were over."

"So you left," Blaise whispered. *She left because she loved me.*

Marian smiled. "I did. I took you and ran as far as I could. You...I knew they would want you because of what you are. The only surviving alchemical mage, a Breaker. But you're so much more than that."

Her statement led to his next question almost too easily. He looked her in the eye. "Why alchemical mages?"

His mother traced a whorl in the wood with her index finger. "Imagine the power that comes with being able to control the variety of mage you can create. Not only that but one *superior* to natural-born mages."

Blaise wrinkled his nose at that. "*Superior?*" He'd never felt superior to anyone else, even if his brand of power did intimidate others. "How would an alchemical mage be superior?"

"You have a deeper magic reservoir than the average mage. You may not have noticed. And you..." She swallowed a lump in her throat. "Your magic is *different.*"

The old, familiar dread of being different stung Blaise, but only briefly. He frowned. The way his mother emphasized it hinted at something more. "Not only because I'm a Breaker."

"No, because you *are* a Breaker." Her voice was soft, a whisper on the wind. "There's a lot the average person doesn't know about Breakers. Things that the Confederation and the wizards of Ravance don't want to get out."

Gooseflesh crawled across his skin. The Ravanchens had

wanted him. Gregor Gaitwood, too. And the Quiet Ones. He worried at his bottom lip, thinking back to all of his conversations with Jefferson—really, Malcolm. The Doyen had connections, but there were limits to his knowledge. With his support of mages, he would no doubt have been denied crucial information.

"What do you mean?"

Marian rubbed her forehead. "I thought for years if you didn't know...if we hid...I thought no one would remember. Things are forgotten. But when it comes to power, the ones in control have a long memory." She hissed out a ragged sigh. "Words matter. Names matter. Your variety of magic is called Breaker to make it sound destructive and unpredictable."

"They're not wrong," Blaise pointed out, his tone even.

His mother locked on him with a fierce look. "They *are* wrong. Your power breaks all of the rules. *That's* what makes you a Breaker." Blaise wanted to speak, but there was something urgent etched in her expression. She leaned in closer. "Never think you're less. You're *more*. You have the potential to do things with this magic that others can only dream of. Only you could spawn an entirely new sort of mage. And that portal your friend Emmaline created? *You* could do that without breaking a sweat."

He stared at her. Emrys stopped grazing, striding over and thrusting his head over the fence to nose his rider. Blaise absently rubbed the stallion's forehead. He wanted to refute his mother's bold statement, but he couldn't. Not after what he'd done during the storm.

"Oh." It was the only thing he could think to say.

<None of this changes who you are,> Emrys reminded him, as if Blaise needed an anchor to keep him moored. He *did* need that.

"How many know all this? That I'm..." He shook his head, unable to think of how to end the sentence. *Powerful* didn't sound right, even if it was true.

"Special," Marian finished for him, fondness in her voice. Love.

"I don't know. But even if they never realize the sum of what you are, the legend of Breakers is enough to make you interesting."

He digested her words. This was a lot—more than he'd bargained for, in fact. But there was a sort of freedom in finally knowing the truth of himself.

"I'm sorry for the pain I've caused you. For all the hurt. For making you something you never wanted to be." She hesitated, turning to look at him. When she spoke, her voice was a whisper. "I can take it away if you wish. I know how to make a potion that strips magic."

He blinked, startled by the offer. Years ago, he would have accepted without a second thought. But now? He shook his head. "No. I'm okay with being...this. I wouldn't be where I am today without magic." Blaise paused. "Well, I don't mean *here.* This is a weird situation."

His mother laughed, swiping away a tear with one hand as her tension shattered. "I understand. Does this mean you forgive me?"

"I had already forgiven you," Blaise admitted. "I only wanted to understand why you would do those things. And what I am." And he had wanted to be certain that she loved him, that it hadn't been an act. "I needed to know I really had a family."

"You do. Always." Marian put an arm around him, tugging him into a sideways hug. "There was never a day when I didn't think of you as my son. That's why I got a little touchy about the idea of someone stealing your beau away."

Blaise relaxed in her embrace, a feeling of ease settling over him. As if something inside him that had been broken was repaired. He had family. He had Jefferson. Well, he had Malcolm. That was something to fix. "I have to do something that might be dangerous later."

She eyed him. "I'm honestly not surprised. Do you need anything from me?"

He thought for a moment. It wouldn't hurt to be prepared.

"Maybe some healing potions. But I'm not sure what you can make here."

"I picked up a few essentials in Thorn. If my son wants healing potions, he gets healing potions."

JACK QUIRKED A BROW. "I'M SORRY, SAY THAT AGAIN?"

Blaise sighed. "I need you and Em to come along and do outlaw things."

The barest hint of a smile tweaked the Effigest's lips. Jack had finally left Emmaline's side when the younger mage felt well enough to sit up in bed and was asking for food. Blaise had found him taking a tray from the kitchen to the room Emmaline was using.

Jack pushed open the door to the room, and Blaise followed him in. Emmaline's skin had a porcelain cast to it, and she looked exhausted, but her eyes brightened when she saw Blaise. "You're here! I didn't know you were here." She shot an annoyed look at her father. "*Someone* didn't tell me."

"You were sleeping, and things have been busy," the outlaw muttered in his defense.

Blaise smiled at her enthusiasm, moving to sit at the end of the bed while Jack settled the tray on the bedside table. "Yeah, long story, but I'm here." He watched as Emmaline frowned at the tray, clearly displeased with the selection of bland food. "Heard about your portal. Pretty impressive."

She snorted. "Yeah, but I don't think I want to do that ever again." She poked at a piece of toast. "Can't I have something else? Bacon? Eggs?"

Jack shook his head. "Not according to Mindy."

Emmaline sighed, leaning back against the pillows and picking up the toast, gnawing off a side of crust. "What did I miss?"

"Blaise wants to do outlaw things. Ain't that cute?" Jack said, unable to hide his amusement.

Blaise rolled his eyes, though he wasn't about to ruin Jack's good mood. Emmaline looked up from her food. "What are you up to?"

Emmaline didn't know any of the happenings in Ganland, so Blaise gave her a quick overview, including Jefferson's true identity. She scowled at that, probably unhappy they had left her out of the loop for so long, but didn't comment on it.

When he finished, she nodded and summarized his plan. "So, now you wanna go to this enemy's territory and get Jefferson's ring."

Jack had listened to the whole thing, a thoughtful expression on his face. "I like it. Shows they're vulnerable." He grinned, rubbing his hands together. "We'll teach 'em not to mess with outlaw mages."

Blaise nodded. He'd surprised Jefferson with his idea to get the ring back. Blaise wasn't the type to carry the fight to someone. But he'd thought more about the point Jack had made during their travels, that sometimes letting others know the sum of your strength might dissuade them in the future.

"And I get to go?" Emmaline asked, her eyes cutting to her father, as if she assumed he would immediately deny her. They all knew he would have in the old days.

"We don't know how many enemies we're likely to run across," Jack said grudgingly.

"Flora will be coming along, too," Blaise said. "I hope three outlaw mages and a half-knocker are enough." It felt strange to count himself as an outlaw mage, a fighter. But he was. He'd made that abundantly clear in Thorn.

"Do we know who has the peacock's ring?" Jack asked.

"Gregor Gaitwood."

Jack cracked his knuckles. "This reckoning is overdue."

CHAPTER FORTY-SIX
Making History

Jefferson

The huge crowd gathered to witness the historic signing didn't surprise Jefferson one bit, though he knew a fair number had come just to see *him*. The miraculous return of Malcolm Wells had made him something of a curiosity, and while once he wouldn't have minded it, he minded it *very* much now.

The gathered celebrants were no doubt curious to see how the proceedings would unfold without the presence of the Board. Jefferson knew rumors spread like wildfire through a city such as Nera, and he was certain many had come to see what Rachel would do. She had made it clear that she no longer wanted or needed a Board of any kind to oversee her, which was a sort of coup in itself. Fortunately, her popularity made a healthy portion of the populace willing to overlook her audacious move. Jefferson was glad that this, at least, was not a headache he had to concern himself with.

The Silver Sands staff had done an admirable job preparing the grounds for the ceremony. It was fitting that the rubble and soot-stained buildings served as their backdrop, a reminder of what might have been lost on the fateful day of the fire.

Jefferson scanned the crowd. Cinna sat in the front row, and she waved enthusiastically to him, blowing a kiss. He inwardly cringed, remembering only too well their time in the dreamscape. It rankled him, even though he knew nothing had happened between them. But that wasn't what she remembered. Jefferson noticed the rest of the Quiet Ones were in attendance, as he'd hoped. At least something was in their favor.

Kittie stepped onto the dais beside him, wearing a Zuzanna original and looking every bit the Pyromancer she was. It was the one Kittie had resented at first because of the flames decorating it, but now she embraced it. As she should. She was the Firebrand, after all. There was a rumble from the throng at her appearance, a combination of approval, skepticism, and outright hostility. There were still those among the population who had little love for mages, much less outlaws, and blamed Kittie for the fire.

"Are they all accounted for?" Kittie asked. Jefferson had taken the time to apprise Kittie of their situation while they saddled their pegasi that morning.

"Yes," Jefferson said, watching as Madame Boss Clayton arrived, flanked by the Bossguard.

No one was taking any chances with her safety, not after what the Board had attempted. Her children and husband filed in after her and sat in the front row, though not on the same side as Cinna. Little Romie and his sister Mary beamed and waved wildly to Kittie. The Firebrand winked at them.

Rachel nodded to Jefferson and Kittie as she took her place on the dais. An ornate wooden table separated them, a parchment squarely in the middle, along with a trio of pens. One of Rachel's aides made a quick check to ensure everything was as it should be, giving the Madame Boss a sign that all was well.

Rachel moved to the front of the platform, standing in front of the table. A pair of Bossguard stood stoically to the side, ready for action.

"People of Ganland, I thank you for joining us on a truly historic day." She paused as a few cheers surfaced from the crowd, along with murmurs. Everyone wondered how the Salt-Iron Confederation was going to react.

"I'm joined by Firebrand Kittie Dewitt of the Gutter—the very mage who saved my life."

True cheers rang out at that. Rachel was beloved by most of the populace, and they appreciated her rescue. Kittie bowed her head, accepting the accolades. The Madame Boss waited for the clamor to die down before gesturing to Jefferson. "And I'm also joined by former Doyen Malcolm Wells, who—in legendary style —returned for this historic signing."

This time, murmurs rippled through the crowd again, no doubt rumors flying around about the life and death (and life again) of Malcolm Wells. Jefferson stared straight ahead, keeping his head high and regal, playing the role of Malcolm Wells once more. If all went well for Blaise, he only had to endure this farce a little longer. Gods, he hoped Blaise was successful.

"Today, we sign a declaration recognizing the Gutter as a true nation, not only for the benefit of the mages but for ourselves," Rachel said. "We are allying with those who rooted out the evil within the very Board who should have supported me. The mages of the Gutter have proven to be worthwhile allies, and I hope that we have a long friendship and fair trade."

The crowd whooped at the mention of trade. Rachel said a few more words, then gestured for Kittie and Jefferson to join her. Kittie signed the declaration first. Then it was Jefferson's turn. He paused, taking a moment to recall his signature as Malcolm. He hadn't written it in so long.

When he finished, Rachel added hers with a flourish. Then she lifted the parchment high for all to see. "Today, on Bounty's Eve, the most fortuitous of days, we recognize the Gutter, our new ally."

The atmosphere turned to sheer revelry after that. The Boss-guard escorted Rachel, Kittie, and Jefferson off the dais. They filed into a reception room in the executive wing. Rachel was grinning, invigorated by their success.

"That could not have been more perfect," she said.

Jefferson smiled, wishing he could share her enthusiasm. But he needed to focus on what was still to come. "We're holding a celebration at the Cole estate this evening. You're welcome to attend if you like."

Rachel nodded. "I would like that. I'll be there." Then one of her staffers called her name, and she turned away. "Excuse me."

Jefferson watched her go, rubbing the back of his neck. Kittie studied him, curious. "Being Malcolm Wells really makes you itchy, doesn't it?"

"You have no idea," Jefferson said, catching his dark-haired reflection in the glass of a picture frame. *But hopefully, that will change tonight.* Cinna slipped into the room, her smile broad as she approached.

"Malcolm, you were *magnificent*." She leaned up to kiss him, and Jefferson shifted to the side, so she only caught his cheek.

He crossed his arms, taking a step back. "I thought you were going to deliver the invitations to tonight's gala."

Cinna waved a hand. "I already did. It wasn't a difficult thing." She closed the distance between them, as if she thought to win him over by sheer proximity.

He gave a sharp nod, aware of Kittie watching them. Jefferson recalled her previous words about protecting Blaise's interests. "Good. We should head back to the estate to make preparations."

CHAPTER FORTY-SEVEN
Showdown

Blaise

<I smell citrus,> Emrys announced, wings stuttering as he dropped altitude. <Reminds me of the orange meringue pies you made for Vixen's birthday. Those were good.>

Blaise shook his head at the stallion's tangent. He peered over Emrys's shoulder. The shadows of late afternoon were long, darkening the landscape, but he saw the trees dotted with oranges below. Emrys, Zepheus, Oberidon, and Tylos flew over the groves, seeking some sign of where the shrouded estate might be.

Blaise had never come up against a warded area before, but Jack had. He'd described it as feeling like an absence. Most people wouldn't think twice about it unless they knew to be aware. The pegasi flew in a pattern over the groves. Blaise spotted a few dirt roads weaving through the trees, but he supposed a theurgist might be able to hide roads as well.

Finally, Jack had luck. <We are going down,> Zepheus announced, since there was no way the riders could hear Jack with the wind whipping his words away. They followed the palomino down to the ground.

The stallions landed nimbly, tossing their heads in anticipation. Now that they were close to the ward, Blaise understood what Jack meant. It reminded him a little of the time a Dampener had muted all the sounds in the forest during an attack. An odd feeling, one that he might have otherwise ignored. That wasn't the only spell that imbued the ward, though. It tried to repel them, sending out a *wrongness* that made Blaise's stomach churn. When he took a step backward, the sensation eased.

Jack looked to be affected by it, too. His lips peeled back over his teeth, and he was armed and ready. "Get on with it. I hate this thing."

Emmaline frowned, squinting at it. "It's like the one I broke at Bitter End, but worse."

"How'd you break that?" Flora asked with interest as she fidgeted with her butterfly knife.

<Sheer stubbornness,> Oberidon commented, then pinned his ears when Emmaline swung her head to glare at him. <What? Where's the lie?>

The younger Effigest swept a loose lock of hair behind her ear. "I guess Oby's sort of right. At the time, I was tracking Mom, and my drive to find her overrode the magic of the ward." Her nose scrunched at the memory. "It wasn't pleasant, though. Be careful, Blaise."

Blaise planted his feet in a wide stance and bit his bottom lip, hoping he truly could break through the ward. *Jefferson is counting on me.* He reached out a hand, surprised when he felt very real resistance in what appeared to be empty air. The magic of the ward pushed against him, trying to force him away.

"C'mon, Blaise," Jack growled, though he took another step back as if he couldn't help it. The stallions also retreated a few paces, snorting loudly and pawing at the ground in irritation.

Well, now I know where the ward is, at least. Blaise took a deep breath, calling up his magic. Silver pooled on his skin as he sought the barrier again.

The ward pulsed with a flash of white light as soon as his magic came into contact with it. Blaise gritted his teeth, suddenly aware that the Warder had built fail-safes into it for just such a situation. Much like the protections he'd fought through on the *Retribution*.

But he was stronger than he'd been back then. His magic had grown, as had his confidence and ability to wield it. He layered his power against the ward, feeling it crack and then shatter beneath the inexorable Breaker magic. There was another brief flash, and then his shoulders sagged with relief. He no longer felt the urge to back away.

Jack heaved a sigh, coming closer. He waved a hand through the air the ward had occupied, satisfied with the lack of resistance. "That was a heavy-duty ward. Whoever made it is gonna be pissed."

"I think that's an understatement," Blaise muttered. He looked at his friends, worried about them. "You still want to do this?"

"We already knocked on the door, too late to play a game of ring and run with 'em," Flora pointed out, the most cheerful Blaise had seen her since his arrival in Ganland.

Jack grinned in agreement. "Yeah. It'll be fun." He spun his sixgun, clearly in his element now that he had free rein. "Let's see if anybody's home." They heard the baying of hounds, and the quartet of pegasi went on alert, nostrils flaring.

"Someone's home," Emmaline said as running footsteps and shouts carried to them. A line of trees blocked them from view of the buildings on the distant estate, but it was only a matter of time. She looked to Blaise. "You want one of us to stay with you?"

As much as he did, Blaise had concluded he could get into the estate house quietly on his own. Especially if his friends were providing a prominent distraction.

He shook his head. "I think I'll be okay. But be sure the pegasi let me know if someone gets hurt. I have the potions." Blaise patted the sturdy pouch at his side.

His mother hadn't been exaggerating about her stock of reagents. She'd put together three healing potions for him to carry in the event someone was wounded. Their strengths ranged from minor to a potion that would quite literally freeze the victim to give them time to reach a Healer for a life-endangering wound.

Jack shrugged. "We're gonna get some scrapes. Goes with the territory." He swung into Zepheus's saddle. "Time to stop jawing and get to business." Emmaline followed suit, though Flora stayed on the ground. The half-knocker patted Tylos and pointed to a dark grove nearby. The small white stallion wasn't prepared to fight like the others, though he'd been happy to transport Flora to the scene.

<Be careful.> Emrys bumped his nose against Blaise, his eyes full of worry.

"You, too," Blaise said with a fond smile, scratching the stallion behind the ears. "I'll be out as soon as I can."

Blaise waited as Zepheus and Oberidon vaulted into the air, only to descend on the other side of the treeline with their riders whooping and yelling to attract attention. The stallions tore across the grass, turf flying in their wake. A moment later, Emrys pushed through the trees and brush to forge a path for Blaise. He followed the black stallion's trail, glancing back to see what Flora was doing.

Her head was cocked to one side, thoughtful. "They have salt-iron in the house. Not a lot." Flora pushed her glasses up on her nose.

"Maybe to control their mages," Blaise suggested, to which Flora nodded. Jefferson had made no mention of salt-iron, but if it was a small amount and not near him, he was likely to have been unaware.

"Yeah. I'm gonna pop inside and take a look around. Holler if you need me!" Flora waved and vanished.

Emrys arched his neck as he turned to Blaise. <Call if you need me, too.>

Blaise gave a curt nod, and the stallion trotted off to join the others. The sound of fighting carried to him as Blaise kept to the late afternoon shadows, not wanting to attract attention. He had dressed in dark colors, anticipating the need for stealth.

Every few moments, the curtains in one window or another in the home twitched back, revealing a worried face peering out. Every time Blaise glimpsed the movement, he paused, hoping to recognize the person. Mostly, he saw young women dressed in what looked like formal uniforms. Household staff, he presumed.

Then, on the first floor, the curtain pulled back, and he knew the face. He'd seen it far too often in the Golden Citadel, trying to bring him under control.

Blaise froze as unexpected panic welled at the sight of Gregor Gaitwood. His heart raced, and he fought off the drive to run, to flee. Magic danced across his palms at his sudden fear. Blaise closed his eyes, swallowing as he tried to master himself. So much for thinking he'd worked through the dark memories.

But he wasn't trapped in the Golden Citadel now. Blaise clenched his jaw, strengthening his resolve. It was *good* he'd seen Gregor—he had Jefferson's ring, after all. Blaise huffed out a breath as he released the last of his anxiety. He needed to get inside, find Gregor, and reclaim the ring. It was the whole reason he'd come.

Blaise slipped through a garden and eased up to a side door. It was locked, which was sensible for a place that had found itself under attack. A locked door couldn't dissuade him, however. It was a simple matter to use his magic to break the lock and gain entry.

When Blaise slipped inside, he expected to be greeted by guards or...someone. But the corridor that stretched before him was empty, which made him think the defenders had gone to meet the threat presented by the outlaws. Anyone inside the structure was probably hiding and reluctant to fight. Blaise was glad for that since he shared the sentiment.

Now he had to figure out which room Gregor had been in. He sighed, frustrated with himself. Fear had paralyzed his brain when he'd caught sight of the Doyen, and he hadn't noticed which window Gregor had been in. All Blaise remembered was the first floor. *Maybe somewhere around the middle?* He rubbed his cheek, wishing he'd had the presence of mind to count windows.

He set about trying nearby doors. The first two rooms were empty. He had more luck in the third room. Blaise came across a trembling maid huddled in the corner; her face was burrowed against her knees. This was the part Blaise really hated: scaring innocents who had no part in this.

"Are you okay?" he asked.

She looked up, cringing at his question. Her back slammed against the wall as a reminder that she couldn't get very far. "Leave me alone! Don't hurt me!" She clutched a letter opener in her hands, probably the only nearby item she had found to defend herself.

"I'm not here to hurt you," Blaise said, which was the truth. He hoped she believed him. He held his hands up, palms open and bare of magic. "But I *am* looking for someone. Do you know which room Doyen Gaitwood is in?"

Blaise feared she wouldn't answer, locked down by her terror. But after a moment, she swallowed, nodding. "Three doors down."

Close by. That was good. "Thank you." He retreated to the threshold. "If you stay in here, you should be safe."

"Who...who are you?" she asked, her voice cracking.

This was it. He had to make it absolutely clear who had broken the Quiet Ones' defenses. Who they should think twice about crossing if they came after Jefferson again.

Blaise leaned against the doorframe, feigning ease as he answered. "The Breaker." Then he turned, shutting the door behind him and striding up the hall.

He found the door the maid had mentioned easily. Blaise wasn't at all surprised to discover it was locked. His magic took care of it once again, and he shoved the door open with his shoulder.

Gregor yelped as Blaise breached the door. But the Doyen had prepared for the inevitable. He held a revolver in his trembling hands. Gregor's eyes narrowed when he realized exactly who had forced his way into the room.

"*You!*" Gregor snarled, pulling the trigger.

Blaise was ready, too. He had his hand up, a gossamer-thin shield of Breaker magic flowing out to protect him. The first bullet struck it, the casing shattering, powder raining down. Gregor made a strangled sound, clearly not believing his eyes as he fired again.

Blaise's shield had weakened from the first hit, but it was a small matter to reinforce it. The second bullet met the same fate. The acrid scent of gunpowder bit the air, tickling Blaise's nose. "*Your* people are the ones who taught me this trick, Doyen Gaitwood."

Gregor took a step backward, glancing down at his ineffective gun. His eyes were wild. "I don't want your nightmares anymore!"

Of all the things the Doyen might have said or done, Blaise hadn't expected to be met with fear reminiscent of his own. "What?"

"Nightmares," Gregor whispered. "Your nightmares. For months, that blasted turncoat has been siphoning your nightmares to me, in a prison of dreams." He panted, as if he couldn't handle his terror. "The *bleeding*. The *pain*. The *fear*. The airship failing. I don't want any of that!"

Blaise blinked. He hadn't had nightmares for months, aside from his recent time apart from Jefferson. Had the Dreamer been feeding Blaise's trauma to Gregor as a form of torture? Blaise knew Jefferson's goal had been to make Gregor pay for his deeds, but he'd never gone into the details of *how*. Blaise only knew it involved the dreamscape. Now things fell into place, and he wasn't sure how he felt about Jefferson taking his experiences and giving them to someone else—even if that someone else was Gregor Gaitwood.

Blaise pursed his lips, thinking. He didn't want to fight the Doyen, despite all the terrible things he'd done. "I'll make you a deal. Give me Jefferson's ring, and I promise he won't torment you with my nightmares anymore."

Gregor stared at him. "Jefferson Cole is *dead*. He has no need of the ring anymore." He backed up his words with a cackle that told Blaise this man was far from well. "I *told* him. Told him he would pay for ruining my life. So I ruined *his*."

On second thought, maybe he does deserve my nightmares. Blaise clenched his fists. "Give me the ring."

"No." Gregor shook his head. "Even if I wanted to, I couldn't. I don't have it."

"Who does?"

"The Black Market. Sold it to Slocum this afternoon." Gregor bared his teeth in a too-wide smile.

The new information hit Blaise like a rock. He had to get that ring. He pivoted and headed for the door, though he paused before leaving the room.

"I'll ask Jefferson to stop giving you my nightmares on the condition that you leave us alone. If you make a move against either of us, I'll find you and show you what I can do with my magic." For emphasis, he touched a finger to the door. As he turned away, the wood groaned, spiderweb cracks forming.

"Blaise!"

Flora dove against him, knocking him down as a bullet whizzed past where Blaise had been standing only a heartbeat ago. He fell hard, his right arm wrenching beneath him in a futile effort to catch himself. There was the gut-twisting snap of bone as he landed wrong. Pain radiated through his forearm, sudden dizziness rocking him. He rolled onto his side with a whimper, tears stinging his eyes.

The half-knocker scrambled off of him, cursing as she leaped into a defensive stance with her knives out. Blaise stayed on his side. Every slight movement jostled his arm and made the pain worse. Spots swam before his eyes. *Can't black out. Not here. Not now.*

With his uninjured left hand, he fumbled for one of the small, cotton-wrapped vials in the pouch at his side. Even moving his left hand hurt. Glass rattled against his fingertips as he pulled a healing potion out.

Blaise didn't take the time to read labels—didn't think he could *read* a label at the moment, anyway. He uncorked the vial with his teeth, then poured the contents over the break with a trembling hand. An icy chill seemed to blanket the injury, and he couldn't feel his hand or the lower part of his arm anymore. At least he no longer felt as if he might black out from the pain.

Flora was staring down Gregor Gaitwood like a mouse against a rattlesnake. Though in this case, Blaise would bet on the mouse. "He's lying," Flora hissed, her eyes locked on her adversary. "He has the ring."

It took Blaise a moment to understand her words. His mind was fuzzy as the potion worked to mask the distracting pain of his injury. The Doyen had the ring. He'd hoped to distract Blaise and kill him when his back was turned. A new wave of nausea rose, and he didn't know if it was from his broken arm or the realization that he'd almost been shot with no defense against it.

"Lamar was right. You cause too much trouble to live," Gregor spat, his eyes glassy. "Every plan I make, you somehow interfere!"

Blaise rose to his feet, unsteady. His right arm felt like it was no longer connected to his body. And it was *cold*—so cold. But he would focus on that in a moment, he promised himself. Blaise shook his head, wishing that he hadn't threatened to end the devious Doyen only moments earlier. Now he had to see it through. If he didn't, Gregor wouldn't stop until Blaise was dead and Jefferson was ruined.

It was a horrible thing. Something he didn't want to do. Blaise squeezed his eyes shut as he tried to gather the courage to do something that went so far against his nature. He felt Flora's eyes on him, waiting. And Gregor's, full of malice.

Blaise's magic had killed before, but never on purpose. But for this, he had to. To protect the people he cared about. All the same, he knew this was a cliff's edge he could never come back from.

"I know you won't do it. You're too scared. *Weak*," Gregor said, then laughed his high-pitched, unhinged laugh.

The piercing *bang* of a bullet shattered the air. One moment Gregor was upright, and the next, he lurched to the ground, crimson blossoming from the center of his chest, staining his clothing. Startled, Blaise jumped aside, nearly stumbling into Jack.

The outlaw glared at the dying Doyen. "Blaise ain't *weak*. Nothing about him is weak." He spat in Gregor's direction, holstering his sixgun. "Did you get the ring?"

Blaise shook his head. In fact, he'd almost forgotten about the ring. He shivered. "No."

Jack and Flora set about searching Gregor's body for the ring. Blaise eased over and sat on a nearby chair, shaking. The cold was seeping up his arm into the rest of his body. He wanted a blanket and a warm fire.

"Got it," Jack announced, holding up a familiar cabochon ring. The outlaw glanced back at Blaise and cursed. "Gods damn it, why didn't you say you got hurt?"

Blaise wrapped his fingers around his broken arm. He couldn't feel anything aside from a weird, rubbery sensation. "We were busy. I'm okay."

"Faedra's tits, you are *not* okay," Jack swore.

"That was kind of my fault," Flora said, wiping her blood-slicked hands on Gregor's jacket. "I made him fall, and he landed wrong, but it was better than getting shot in the back."

Jack rose with a heavy sigh. "We're not gonna hear the end of this from that black stud." He moved over to Blaise, gently tucking the ring into his shirt pocket. "You hold on to that. Can you walk?"

"Yeah," Blaise whispered, getting to his feet. At least he could still feel his feet. That was a good sign, wasn't it? Jack put an arm around him to keep him upright, and he barely felt the outlaw against him.

"You're cold," Jack muttered. "What did you use?"

"Um?" was all Blaise managed through chattering teeth.

Flora picked up the empty vial and held it up. "He used something called Chill of Death. That doesn't sound foreboding or anything."

Jack huffed out a breath. "Blasted alchemy potions. You used the wrong damn one, Blaise. C'mon. We'll get you out of here and set to rights."

Oh. Blaise blinked. If he didn't feel so numb, he'd warm with embarrassment over using the most extreme potion. Chill of Death was going to slowly and inexorably freeze him until he reached a Healer. On the plus side, at least his arm didn't hurt. Nothing hurt aside from the smothering cold.

Blaise let Jack help him out of the estate, Flora guarding their backs. "Th-thank you," Blaise said. "I d-didn't want to k-kill him."

"Shut your piehole. I know." Jack whistled, and the pegasi stallions swept over to their location at a lope. Emmaline was astride Oberidon and looked none the worse for wear, though she scowled when she saw Blaise leaning on her father.

<Blaise!> Emrys snorted in alarm as soon as he saw his rider. <What happened?>

"Broken arm," Jack grumbled. "It looks worse than it is 'cause he used the wrong healing potion to stop the pain."

Emrys shook his mane, then knelt to allow Blaise to clamber into the saddle. Blaise groaned, clutching the saddlehorn with his left hand. He couldn't feel the leather, so he kept his eyes on his hand, worried that he might let go without realizing it.

"Blaise, I am *so* sorry, but I really didn't want you to get shot,"

Flora called up to him. "I'll pop ahead and try to get Jefferson's Healer to the stables."

"Do it," Jack said with a nod. The outlaw looked over at Blaise. "Hang in there. Flying ain't gonna be fun."

Jack was right. It wasn't fun at all with a broken arm, his body slowly icing over.

CHAPTER FORTY-EIGHT
The Truth Is a Weapon

Jefferson

The guests arrived at seven, including the Quiet Ones. From what Jefferson saw, most everyone invited would be in attendance, Quiet One and elite alike. He hoped Blaise was successful. This was his best chance to get what he wanted, to be *who* he wanted to be.

Cinna stood in the grand entryway, greeting guests as if she were already Malcolm Wells's wife. It grated at Jefferson, but he let it be. He only had to endure a little while longer.

Kittie was there, reprising her role of the Firebrand, along with Marian Hawthorne, though the alchemist kept to the outskirts, doing her best to remain anonymous. Jefferson had the feeling she was keeping an eye out for him, protecting Blaise's interests. He'd had mixed feelings on the topic of Marian Hawthorne. Jefferson wanted to be angry at her for hurting the man she called her son, but she truly seemed to love Blaise.

Jefferson circulated through the room, exchanging pleasantries here and there, artfully dodging questions from the curious inquiring about the faked death of Malcolm Wells. Madame Boss

Clayton arrived, which was a relief as she ended up garnering most of the attention for a while.

Although cool fury burned in Jefferson's veins, he maintained the mask of a pleasant host preparing for an evening of revelry. His steward announced it was time for food, and the guests filtered into the dining room.

Jefferson stood behind his chair, aiming a smile that he didn't feel at his guests. "What a pleasure it is to have all of you here, celebrating the historic act of the Gutter becoming a recognized nation." His gaze flicked to Phillip Dillon, and the other man gave a nearly imperceptible nod.

"In honor of this, I'm gruntled to tell you that Mindy Carman, a talented Hospitalier from the Gutter, has had a hand in preparing tonight's meal." Jefferson noted the puzzled looks of a handful of Quiet Ones and elite who weren't familiar with that strain of magic. "Hospitaliers are a sort of mage who can suggest the best sort of food for you, and they are *never* wrong."

"Interesting," Tara murmured from her seat beside Phillip, her dark eyes settling on Mindy as the smiling young woman made a loop around the room, studying the guests.

Mindy paused when she reached the end of the table near Kittie, offering a stiff half-bow to their guests. "Because of the personalized nature of the meal, there will be a brief delay in service. I hope none of you will mind."

"We'll make do," Quiet One Megan Brew said, waving a hand in obvious dismissal. The nearby elite nodded in agreement.

Jefferson turned to Phillip, who had chosen the seat beside him. "I think this will be a night to remember."

A satisfied smile settled on the older man's face. "I think it will be, Malcolm. You've done well, and I think you will be the perfect replacement for your father."

Jefferson's jaw ached from clenching it. *Bide your time. Play along.* "I'm glad to hear that my performance was satisfactory."

Conversation at the tables turned to different topics, much to

Jefferson's relief. The price of salt-iron per ounce, which was ridiculously expensive, though Tara had heard rumors of new veins discovered in the aptly named Salt-Iron Range. That pricked Jefferson and Kittie's attention—that range butted up against the Gutter. He filed it away for later—a potential reason the Quiet Ones had so much interest in the new nation. Jefferson had to catch up with the conversation when Everett Duncan waxed on about his newest racing unicorn, a colt that he claimed would sweep all the classics the next season.

"He's a certainty for the Triple Crown," Everett bragged, lifting his glass of water as if making a toast.

Megan snorted. "Only because you'll hustle the other owners to make it happen. If I had a colt or filly to aim at the classics, I'd make certain it wasn't so easy for you. Perhaps next year."

Of course, they would even rig the races in their favor. Jefferson's brow wrinkled at the new information. How far did their claws dig into everything within the Confederation? Were they like a vine clinging to the stone walls of a building, working their tendrils so deep it would be impossible to dig them out without damaging the whole structure? It was sounding more and more like that—which granted him more certainty that the plan they had come up with was the only course of action.

Mindy strode in a half-hour later, accompanied by the kitchen staff bearing the evening meal. Jefferson had to admit that it all smelled wonderful. His stomach rumbled at the first savory scent of roast chicken, which made him feel downright traitorous to think of food amid their precarious situation. *Well, best to do battle on a full stomach.*

Up and down the table, a variety of plates clattered into place before the guests. Garden-fresh salads, cuts of lamb, roast chicken, pork roast, mashed potatoes. Mindy, Marta, and the rest of the kitchen staff had truly gone all-out for their part in this. Jefferson was fiercely proud of them. None of them were powerful, but they were doing their part. He made a mental note to grant them all a considerable bonus when he was back to being himself.

Phillip eyed Jefferson's meal. "Trade with me."

Jefferson arched his brows. "Do you think we're poisoning you?" He kept his voice innocent and incredulous, though he was delighted that Phillip suspected him of treachery. Their Hospitalier was the perfect misdirection.

"Something like that."

Jefferson shrugged. Mindy stood by the door that led to the kitchen, and a muscle ticked in her cheek, though he knew it was only annoyance and nothing more severe. Jefferson reached over and lifted Dillon's plate of lamb and fresh green beans, swapping it with his former entrée of chicken breast and steamed broccoli florets.

"Just as well," Jefferson said. "I do so hate when the florets get stuck in my teeth with company over. Embarrassing."

His comment gave Dillon pause, and the other man hesitated before doubling down, lifting fork and knife to saw at the chicken only after Jefferson did the same for his lamb and took a bite.

The dinner course continued smoothly. Light chatter peppered the room, and Jefferson did his best to listen in on the surrounding conversations while maintaining his own. He watched everyone at the table closely. Midway through the course, he glimpsed a shock of pink hair in his periphery. Marian slipped out of the room, though no one else paid her any mind. Flora had called her out, but why? Jefferson hated that all he could do was sit and smile politely.

As the staff removed their plates, Seledora's mental voice tickled against his mind. <They're here. Blaise was injured, and Flora summoned your Healer to tend to it.> The mare must have sensed his sudden alarm since she continued, <It is not bad. A broken arm, nothing more. Your Healer is tending to him now, and his mother is here, too.>

That didn't matter. Knowing that Blaise was hurt sent a

tremor of guilt and worry through Jefferson. He rose from his seat, glad for all his years of practice at controlling his expressions. "I believe we have some entertainment lined up to go along with the dessert course. I'll be back in a moment." He excused himself and hurried out to the stables.

———————————

TRUE TO SELEDORA'S WORD, HE FOUND BLAISE SITTING ON A BALE of hay in the stables, his face almost as grey as Flora's skin. Jefferson's Healer, Agnes, gripped his arm in her hands as Marian Hawthorne stood on the other side, her face crinkled with worry. Jack and Emmaline were seeing to the pegasi, though they shot furtive glances at Blaise. Emrys was still tacked and in the stall across from Blaise, his attention never leaving his rider.

"Oh, Blaise," Jefferson whispered, hurrying over. He crouched in front of the Breaker, though he gave Agnes room to work. "What happened?"

Flora peered around from behind Blaise, guilt etched on her face. "It was me, but it was an accident. I'll tell you later."

"Why is he so cold?" Jefferson asked, touching Blaise's face gently. Blaise's eyes were closed, and he never stopped shivering. The Breaker hadn't even acknowledged his presence yet, which was worrisome.

"I sent along healing potions," Marian explained, voice soft. "Blaise picked the wrong one. The Chill of Death potion is intended for grievous wounds."

"It's doing its job, though," Agnes murmured, giving Jefferson an encouraging look. "I'm almost done mending the break, and he should warm up after that."

Jefferson glanced back at the house. If he lingered too long, the odds were good someone would come looking for him. Probably Cinna, and that would ruin everything. He eased over to Jack. "Did he get the ring?"

The outlaw gave a curt nod, then tapped a hand over his own shirt pocket and pointed to Blaise. Jefferson appreciated the Effigest's candor. Agnes didn't know his secrets, though he wondered at this point if it even mattered.

The Healer made a satisfied sound, rising. "He's going to be tender, but he'll be right as rain before long. Shall I help him to bed, Ms. Strop?"

Jefferson had forgotten that at the moment, Flora had command of his home. The half-knocker's lips pressed into a frown, no doubt aware that the current plan didn't include anyone convalescing. "We'll take care of him. Thanks, Agnes." The Healer nodded and headed out.

As soon as she was out of the barn, Jefferson slid in front of Blaise again. The Breaker's skin had regained a little of its color, though he still shivered. "Blaise?"

The Breaker cracked his eyes open, lifting his good hand to pull something small from his pocket. The cabochon ring gleamed up at them. "Got it."

Jefferson wanted to protest that he didn't care about the ring, that he cared about *Blaise*, but it was a lie. He needed that ring, needed it so that he could live with himself. He hoped Blaise understood that. Jefferson's need for Blaise was on a different level, but it was just as pressing. Gingerly, Jefferson reached for the ring, surprised when Blaise closed freezing fingers around his wrist.

The Breaker lifted his chin, plaintive eyes meeting Jefferson's. "No more secrets."

Jefferson's fist curled around the ring, and he was shocked by how chill both the metal and Blaise's flesh were. He reached out and cupped his beau's cheek with his free hand. "My secrets are a sort of armor."

"The truth is a weapon we can wield," Blaise whispered, and there was no doubt he was completely lucid in that moment. He squeezed Jefferson's wrist, then released it. "No more secrets. Or you'll never be free."

Jefferson swallowed. "But—"

"Go," Blaise whispered, teeth clacking with the effort. "Your guests are waiting."

Jefferson huffed with frustration. "I love you. I need you to be okay." Then he leaned in and kissed the Breaker on his freezing lips. *Please be okay.*

"We've got Blaise," Jack said, pointing toward the house. "Get in there and make your point, or this will all be for nothing."

Jack was right. Jefferson nodded, clutching the ring in his fist. Blaise didn't look like he should go anywhere except to bed, as Agnes had prescribed. The Breaker met his eyes, and Jefferson couldn't overlook the intensity in their depths. Blaise wouldn't be denied this. Jefferson swallowed. "See you soon."

He slipped the ring into his greatcoat's interior pocket and headed for the house, glad to find Flora tagging along. "I'm really, really sorry," she said, jogging to keep up with him. "I didn't mean to break your Breaker."

Jefferson couldn't help it; he had to chuckle at the absolute madness of the situation. *Gallows humor, I suppose.* "I know you didn't. What happened?"

Her expression tightened with anger. "I popped into the room where Blaise was and saw Gregor about to shoot him. Blaise didn't know—he had his back turned. I was closer to him than I was to Gregor, so I tackled him."

Jefferson drew to a stop, trembling. "Gregor tried to kill Blaise?"

"Gregor's dead now," Flora said, steel in her voice. She stared ahead of them at the house where the Quiet Ones and the rest of the elite were awaiting his return. But they could wait a few moments longer.

"Was it Blaise? Or you?" Jefferson hated to ask it, but he had to know. Not that he was unhappy to hear of Gregor's death—no, he was more concerned with the psychological weight of such an action on Blaise.

"Neither of us. It was Jack."

Jefferson relaxed at the news. He knew that if it came down to it, Blaise would do what needed to be done. But he would suffer for it. At least he shouldn't have to worry about that in this case. Jefferson buried those concerns for the time being. He needed to see this through to the end.

He paused outside the entrance to the dining room, clenching and then loosening his hands a few times to work out some of his tension. Flora patted his arm and ghosted away, as she always did. Jefferson pasted a brilliant smile onto his face and pushed the door open. The waitstaff were delivering slices of cake to each of the guests. The dessert was a delicious chocolate confection with a topping of fruit, so tempting that it had distracted most of the attendees.

Jefferson returned to his place at the table, though he wasn't hungry for the beautiful slice of cake. Phillip slid a curious glance his way, but the cake did its job, and the Quiet One was more concerned with eating it than worrying about Jefferson. But to maintain appearances, he poked at the cake with his fork, taking a few half-hearted bites while he thought about Blaise sitting in the stable, chilled to the bone.

<Blaise and Emrys are ready,> Seledora informed him. <And I'm right outside.>

Jefferson breathed a sigh of relief. Finally, something was falling into place. He waited another minute before pushing his plate away and rising from his seat. He crossed to the front of the room, which put him comfortably near the recessed entryway. It would give him the clear exit he needed.

"May I have your attention, please?" Jefferson called above the dull roar of conversation. The soft murmurs continued, most guests unaware that he had moved to speak.

A ball of flame roared up into the air, vanishing as quickly as it had come. Kittie stood across the room from him, smiling. "Sorry, but you must admit that was very effective." By the look on her face, she wasn't sorry at all. "Malcolm Wells would like to speak." She nodded to Jefferson, returning to her seat with satisfaction. He was glad that Kittie had found her way as the Firebrand.

All eyes in the room fell on him. Jefferson took a deep breath. This was it, a moment that he knew would define the rest of his life. He thought he'd done difficult things before as a politician, but this? It was overwhelming, and he knew he wouldn't have the tenacity to do it without Blaise and his friends.

"Thank you all once more for joining us this evening. Bounty's Eve is a special holiday in Ganland, a time for reflecting on the gifts granted to us by Tabris's grace." Murmurs from the crowd agreed with his sentiment. "And I'm quite glad to say that over the past months, I've been given a windfall. But it's not gold or fine goods, not the sort of thing you would expect."

Confused whispers rose at his words. Rumors taking wing. Cinna, seated a dozen yards away, beamed as if he meant her. Jefferson didn't miss her reaction, and his mouth pulled into a thin line as he plowed onward.

"By now, you have all heard the stories." Jefferson gestured to his guests, many of whom nodded. "How the distraught Doyen, overcome with grief, faked his own death. And while, as with most wild stories, there is a grain of truth to it—that's not what actually happened." He thought about Blaise, curled close beside him. Blaise astride Emrys, smiling as they went out together for a ride. "In truth, I had a second chance at life. At love."

The crowd grew noisy once more, women enchanted by the idea of such romance and men whistling in appreciation. Cinna rose from her seat, as if to accept their accolades. He almost felt bad about what was to come, aware it would crush Cinna's hopes. But not really, knowing that his own happiness was at stake.

He pulled out his ring and clutched it in his hand. "Not the way you think, though. Not at all."

Jefferson rolled the cabochon ring between his thumb and index finger before slipping it onto his customary ring finger. He felt the glamor wash over him, erasing Malcolm Wells and shifting him into the man he truly wanted to be. Cries of alarm and confusion rose from the crowd, along with a few nervous titters, as if some thought this might be an elaborate prank.

"Malcolm Wells is *dead*," Jefferson declared, his voice ringing out. "I'm Jefferson Cole, and I'm an outlaw mage. I won't be taking questions at this time."

Chaos erupted at his announcement, men and women trying to get out of their seats to accost him, to demand answers. Jefferson caught sight of Phillip trying to break free of the mass to come after him. Cinna stood in the middle of it, shock etched across her lovely face.

Jefferson caught Kittie's eye and gave her a grateful nod, then slipped out through the nearby exit.

CHAPTER FORTY-NINE
Dragons Aren't Scared of Other Dragons

Jefferson

"Are you well enough for this?" Jefferson asked, frowning at Blaise. The Breaker clung to Emrys's saddle, his skin as pale as moonlight.

"Better than I was," Blaise assured him. He sounded stronger, at any rate. "You're not leaving without me."

Jefferson nodded. In this, he knew the younger man wouldn't be dissuaded. Truth be told, Jefferson wasn't particularly inclined to argue. His world had just been turned upside-down—even more than before. If ever there was a time he needed Blaise, it was now.

<Where shall we go?> Seledora asked.

"The beach, then north. There's a little cove there where we can lie low while the ruckus dies down." Jefferson sighed, relishing the idea of peace.

The two pegasi took to the air, the stars overhead lighting their way. Seledora soared over the breaking waves once they reached the beach, and Jefferson guided her to the cove. The pegasi trotted through the surf to reach it.

Blaise and Jefferson dismounted, moving to sit on a log that had washed up in a storm and then been partially buried in sand. "What now?" Blaise asked.

"I don't know," Jefferson said softly, taking Blaise's hand. It was much warmer now. "But it's okay because I'm with you. I'm sorry you were hurt on my account."

"I was hurt because I'm the most accident-prone mage in history," Blaise pointed out. "I'm very talented at hurting myself. If I hadn't landed wrong, I would have been a little bruised and nothing more."

"Well, the fact remains that you *were* hurt, and I don't like that," Jefferson murmured, looking down at Blaise's right arm. It looked better, though. Agnes had done an excellent job. She wasn't Nadine, but she was skilled. "Flora told me what happened."

Blaise stared out at the silver-capped waves as they reflected the starlight. "Why didn't you tell me what you did to Gregor?"

Oh, not that. Jefferson didn't want to think about that right now. But Blaise deserved an answer. The Breaker's tone was neutral, but Jefferson knew it wouldn't take much to tip him over into anger. As much as Blaise disliked conflict, there were some things he would stand up for, and Jefferson suspected this was one of them.

"I was so angry about what he'd done to you. I wanted him to suffer, to understand on an intimate level every moment of pain that had been inflicted on you."

Beside him, Blaise sighed. "I know *why* you did it." His voice was so soft it was difficult to hear over the lapping waves. "But those were *my* fears. *My* experiences. *My* pain. You can't just give away those pieces of me. They're part of what's made me who I am."

Damn, Jefferson hadn't even realized he'd done the equivalent of stealing from Blaise. When he put it like that... He winced, shaking his head. "But it's *my* fault you had to suffer those things at all."

Blaise looked as if he'd been ready to say something else and paused, narrowing his eyes. "What do you mean it's your fault? Gregor was the one who held me there. Not you."

"*I'm* the reason you were captured in the first place," Jefferson said, recalling the sight of the mangled airship and destroyed fort. "If I hadn't asked you to use your magic to—"

"I would have done it anyway."

It was Jefferson's turn to look surprised. "What?"

Blaise edged closer, his shoulder brushing Jefferson's. "I would have destroyed the *Retribution* anyway. Flora told me I didn't have to. That you would understand if I didn't." He hazarded a glance before continuing, "I knew what I was getting into. Have you been blaming yourself for that all this time?"

"Obviously," Jefferson said, boggled. It had never occurred to him that it might have been *Blaise's* choice. He'd been so certain the kind-hearted Breaker had only done it at his behest.

"And you've been trying to make up for it ever since?" Blaise guessed.

"*Obviously.*" Jefferson rubbed his cheek as he considered this new information. "I made a grievous miscalculation, using my magic as I did. I should have told you."

"You should have told me," Blaise agreed. Then the Breaker reached over and took Jefferson's hand. "But we all make mistakes. Some bigger than others. I know you thought you were protecting me, but I'm tougher than I look."

You are, aren't you? Jefferson squeezed the Breaker's hand, glad for the warmth that had returned. "Did you work things out with your mother?" Jefferson asked gently.

"Yeah." Blaise was quiet for a time, leaving the only sound around them the wash of the tide and the occasional swish of a pegasus tail as they rested nearby. "I understand more about her. More about me." His words hinted at new revelations, but Jefferson didn't press. He was confident Blaise would tell him when he was ready.

"I didn't get to properly tell you, but I'm very sorry for the loss of your father," Jefferson said. "He was proud of you."

Blaise's fingers tightened on his as the Breaker turned to face him. "Wait. What do you mean? You met my father?"

"He sought me out the last time I went to Rainbow Flat." He'd been mindful of Blaise's temporarily strained relationship with his family, which had been challenging when he had to check on his interests in the other outlaw town. "I know you asked me not to speak with them, but I could hardly be rude when he was the one to find me."

"That sounds like something he'd do." Blaise nodded. He licked his lips, as if uncertain about his next words. "Why did he speak to you?"

Jefferson chuckled. "He didn't come out and say it, but I suspect he heard about me from your mother. I got the impression he wanted to see if I was worthy of his son."

Blaise glanced at him. "You are, even if you do stupid things sometimes." It seemed he wasn't going to forget about Gregor anytime soon. Fair enough. "What else did he say?" There was a hunger in his voice, as if he were seeking out a precious connection to a lost loved one. Jefferson wondered what that was like, to have such a bond with a father.

"He asked me how you were doing. He worried for you, I think. Wanted you to be okay. So, I told him about the bakery. And oh, I wish you could have seen the way his face lit up. There was so much pride in his eyes."

"I can imagine it," Blaise said. He swiped at one eye with his free hand, and Jefferson heard a soft sniffle. Then he cleared his throat. "So, that was quite an exit you made. And you sidestepped my earlier question. What's next?

Jefferson wet his lips. He'd avoided answering because, for the first time in his life, he didn't have a plan of any sort. Didn't even have another identity to fall back on. "I don't know what tomorrow will bring. But I think for now, I'd like to watch the stars with you."

Blaise squeezed his hand again. "I'd like that, too."

Jack

THE CONFUSION THE PEACOCK HAD SOWN AT HIS FANCY GALA WAS A source of endless entertainment for Jack. The gobsmacked looks on the faces of the elite as they realized Cole had pulled one over on them was satisfying. It was enough to make Jack think Jefferson Cole wasn't so bad after all.

The aftermath, though, had been a whole other mess. Many guests thought it was an elaborate joke. Others were angered, demanding that Cole pay for his treachery.

Courtesy of Flora, Jack had found a good spot to watch the crowd. He wanted to see these so-called Quiet Ones for himself, to assess the threat they might pose. Jack didn't like their interest in the Gutter. He would feel far more comfortable if they *didn't* want the Gutter to be a nation. That seemed more normal for the Confederation.

After a few minutes, he'd figured out who the Quiet Ones were among the guests. It wasn't a difficult task since he was familiar with the little rattlesnake named Cinna. She had been quick to seek out others, and Jack observed how they interacted. *Quiet Ones.*

Many of the guests went home, while others stayed to take advantage of the free-flowing alcohol. Jack waited until the Quiet One he wanted was alone, then slipped over to him as silent as a shadow.

"Phillip Dillon." He allowed a hint of a threatening growl into his voice, his favorite way to let someone know they were on his shit list.

Dillon turned, eyes wide as he took in the looming outlaw. "Who...what do you want?"

Jack stalked closer, allowing his feral smile to slide into place. "Wanted you to know we sent a message to your home, but I'm sure you didn't receive it yet." He folded his arms across his chest, meeting Dillon's gaze.

The Quiet One scowled. "What?"

Jack stepped closer until mere inches separated them. He leaned over to Dillon's ear and whispered, "Gregor Gaitwood is *dead.*"

Dillon reeled away, mouth twisting in disbelief. "But...how? Wait. *You're* the one who got the ring back to Wells!"

"Nah," Jack said with a shake of his head. "That was all the Breaker. I only settled the score." He took a step back, allowing a little more space between them.

Dillon made a whistling noise as he exhaled through his nose. "And is he the one who killed my Walker? Or was that you?"

His Walker? Jack hadn't expected the question, and it took him a moment to connect the dots. The Wallwalker. Emrys's kick must have done her in. Jack decided this man didn't deserve an answer to all of his questions. Instead, he gave a too-wide smile. "I'll let you and your buddies get going. As I understand it, there's a bit of a mess to clean up." Jack's pale eyes bored into Dillon's until the other man broke the stare.

Dillon swallowed. "We're not afraid of you."

Jack chuckled. "Dragons aren't scared of other dragons. Even when they should be." With a lazy shrug, he pivoted and ambled away, though a large part of him hoped that Dillon would either try to attack him or call him back. But the Quiet One did neither, much to his disappointment. Maybe the man had a sense of self-preservation.

He slunk back into the shadows, watching as the rest of the guests left over the next few hours. It was the middle of the night by the time only Cole's staff and the outlaws remained.

Kittie rubbed her forehead, yawning. "Can we sleep now? This has been a day."

Jack slipped alongside his wife, curling an arm around her. Yeah, he figured hitting the hay was a good idea. Even better with her at his side.

"Where did Jefferson and Blaise go?" Emmaline asked, frowning with concern.

"I have a pretty good idea where they went," Flora said. "I'll get 'em in the morning."

"Better get shut-eye now while we can," Jack agreed. "With the shitstorm Cole left behind, the next few days ain't gonna be simple."

CHAPTER FIFTY

Ambassador

Jefferson

Two days later, Madame Boss Rachel Clayton paced across the front of the assembly room, pausing occasionally to shake her head and give Jefferson a bewildered look. He had the good sense to stay quiet. Jefferson knew the only thing standing between him and a long vacation in the darkest hole of a Gannish prison was the simple fact that he'd stood up for Rachel against her Board.

"What are we going to do about this?" Rachel sputtered at last, slapping her palm against the tabletop. "We have elite out there demanding to break all ties with the Gutter because of you... because of this..." She seemed unable to decide how she wanted to end her sentence and simply shook her head, eyes narrowed with frustration.

Jefferson wet his too-dry lips. "I'm willing to take all the blame, Rachel. But don't let this destroy things with the Gutter. Please."

She frowned, pulling out a chair and dropping into it. "You've heard the Confederation is demanding we hand you over to them, right?"

He nodded. "Yes." Was her plan to trade him off to the Confederation, in order to let the declaration with the Gutter remain in place? That might be the only way to placate the Confederation in a situation like this: hand over the treasonous former Doyen.

"I've told them no."

Jefferson blinked. "What?" He was certain he'd misheard her.

Rachel braced her elbows on the table, leaning over them. "I won't pretend I agree with everything you've done. But I can see you have a good heart, and you're trying to do what you think is right." She sighed. "And besides, I have need of an Ambassador, and who better than a mage from Ganland with deep ties to the Gutter?"

His mouth dropped open in surprise. He was sure he'd lost all hope of his ambassadorship, but it had been a worthwhile loss in the grand scheme of things. "But…how?" His mind whirled, trying to figure out how she would make it work.

A hint of a smile touched her lips. "I'm being quite stubborn about the whole thing, honestly. And without a Board, no one can naysay me." Rachel shrugged. "Even if they could, who would be a better selection?"

Jefferson cocked his head. "I know for a fact you have *many* diplomats who would fit the bill." Many who would be eager to work with the Gutter, on the hunt for future profit margins.

"And none of them who have a working relationship already," Rachel reminded him. Then her expression softened. "Besides, that's the safest option for you at this point. Outside of a Gannish prison to atone for your fraud, anyway."

"I'll happily keep that off the table, thank you," Jefferson agreed, though he deflated at the reminder. It had only been two days since his announcement, but it had been a whirlwind. And during much of it, he'd kept a low profile to avoid answering questions. He was vilified in the newspapers, and he wondered at Rachel keeping him on as Ambassador.

Worst of all, though, the Quiet Ones couldn't harm him physically. They moved in another way sure to hurt him. Despite his insistence that he was Jefferson Cole, couriers had begun to deliver letter after letter declaring that his accounts were being closed and access to his funds denied. There was no proof that he existed, which Jefferson knew was false. When he'd first taken on this identity, he'd been very careful to create a trail proving his validity. The Quiet Ones were scrubbing away every trace, still intent on denying him this life.

"Are you going to be okay?" Rachel asked, her voice gentle.

Jefferson rubbed his face. "I will be, in time. I appreciate your support."

The Madame Boss nodded. "*You* supported *me*. It's high time I returned the favor."

CHAPTER FIFTY-ONE
Rich in the Only Way That Matters

Blaise

"**M**ama!"

Brody and Lucienne pelted out of the Broken Horn Saloon, throwing up clods of red dirt in their wake as they sprinted toward the group of pegasi coming in for a landing. Chester yapped in their wake, ears flapping.

Blaise pulled up his flight goggles, snapping them against his forehead as he watched his mother dismount. It had been a long road to get back to the Gutter—they hadn't dared go overland, concerned they might pose too tempting a target for the Confederation to snatch up.

Of their group, only Jack's face was on handbills, but they hadn't wanted to take any chances. Madame Boss Clayton had chartered a steamer for them, and they made the arduous journey across the Gulf of Stars and into the Jewelled Sea. None of the pegasi had enjoyed the crossing, forced to spend much of their time below decks in the hold as they trundled through late-season storms.

But they were back now, and that was what mattered. His

siblings swarmed around their mother, Brody alternately laughing and crying with delight. It wasn't long before he was babbling about the wonders of the Feast of Flight. Blaise smiled at his little brother's enthusiasm, though he was disappointed he'd missed it. They'd had to celebrate it amid a hurricane-force gale on the steamer.

Clover ambled up, watching Blaise's siblings fondly.

"Hope they weren't too much of an imposition," he called to her as he dismounted.

The Knossan shook her head, moving closer to Emrys and Blaise. "They were not a problem. I was happy to provide them with a roof over their heads and the safety they needed." Her warm brown eyes studied him. "Did you have your vengeance?"

Blaise rubbed his cheek. "Turns out that wasn't what I needed."

"That is often the way of things," Clover agreed, her hooves crunching the dirt as she shifted her weight. "Will they be staying in Fortitude?"

"Yes," Blaise answered. Even if the Hawthorne house in Rainbow Flat hadn't been in a shambles, he would have wanted it so. He didn't want so much distance between him and his family —in more ways than one.

The Knossan nodded, content. "That is good."

Emrys trotted to the stables, flicking an ear back as Blaise dismounted. More of the pegasi from their group filed in, some with riders and some without. A handful of grooms hurried out to greet them.

<Will there be celebratory cake?> the pegasus asked, nosing Blaise's shoulder. <Or, at the very least, apology cake?>

Blaise chuckled. Emrys's dream of sugary treats had sustained him during the interminable time at sea. "I'll start working on the cake tomorrow. I suspect we'll have a town celebration for our return, but you can help me sample them to see which flavor is best."

<All the flavors.>

"Not going to happen," Blaise told the stallion, giving him a fond scratch behind the ears.

He went about the business of unsaddling Emrys and rubbing him down, making sure he had fresh water and sweet feed. Blaise was happy to handle the tasks again. For the longest time, his friends had taken care of Emrys for him. Despite Agnes's effective healing, he'd been treated like a porcelain doll. Blaise had grudgingly allowed it—he was surrounded by people who *cared* about him. Family, even if he wasn't related to a single one by blood.

Emmaline walked with Oberidon to a nearby stall, then came over to hang on the partition outside Emrys's. "Same time at the bakery tomorrow?"

Blaise yawned. As much as he was looking forward to a return to normal, he needed a little rest. "You can go in whenever you want, but I may sleep in for once. Might do some baking for fun when I get up and about."

She nodded. "Sounds good. I'll tell Reuben and Hannah they're in charge tomorrow." Emmaline waved, then hurried off.

Blaise glanced up the aisle, noticing Jefferson outside Seledora's stall, murmuring to the mare. He walked over to join them.

Seledora's ears pricked in his direction, and she spoke privately to Blaise. <He's telling me I'll have to go elsewhere for work because he can no longer afford me. Your mate is oblivious.>

Blaise's mouth twitched. He really wanted to tell Seledora that Jefferson was *not* oblivious—she just refused to come out and say the obvious: that she liked Jefferson enough to claim him as her rider.

Jefferson turned at Blaise's approach, a smile sliding onto his face. But it wasn't genuine. Blaise read the worry behind it.

"Stop trying to fire your attorney," Blaise suggested.

"She told you, did she?"

"Yes."

Jefferson sighed. "I'll go into bankruptcy keeping her on retainer. Wait, I'm *already* in bankruptcy."

Blaise shook his head. "You don't owe her anything, Jefferson."

Jefferson's green eyes narrowed in confusion. "What do you mean?"

Blaise crossed his arms. "Tell him."

Seledora's sides heaved with a great breath. She raised her head as if she were going to pull away, angling it to give Blaise a nasty look. The mare raked the straw with a forehoof. <You are my rider.>

Jefferson swallowed as if he dared not believe it. He placed a hand beneath Seledora's jaw, as if he feared she was an illusion that might vanish. Then he rested his forehead against hers.

"You're only bankrupt without love," Blaise said.

Jefferson pulled away from Seledora, a smile illuminating his face. "Then I'm rich in the only way that matters."

Jack

"Seems you made a good showing for yourself, Firebrand." Jack's boots clattered against the stairs as they left Ringleader HQ. The meeting they'd just gotten out of hadn't been the most pleasant, but hadn't been the worst, either. Jack was going to be sorely glad when he didn't have to worry about meetings for a while. Kittie had presented herself and the delegation well, though. "I'm proud of you."

Kittie beamed at her husband's words. "I was with good people who helped to see it through."

Jack shook his head. "Didn't mean the delegation, though I'm proud of you for that, too. I mean your habit. It hasn't escaped my notice that you're dry as the Deadwood Forest in fire season."

"It's true for that, too," Kittie said, though she glanced away as if embarrassed. "Mindy helped figure out what works for me."

Her penchant for Caladrius root tea hadn't escaped him, either. Jack had watched her carefully since he'd arrived at the Cole estate, and he'd been surprised that, despite the cock-ups, she hadn't wavered. Whatever Mindy had figured out had been effective. "You should be proud of yourself, too."

"I am." Kittie lifted her chin, meeting his eyes. Mischief glinted in hers. "And it seems you didn't do half bad with our daughter, either."

Jack raised his brows. "Only trekked across the entire Untamed Territory with her."

"Took on the nastiest desperadoes on the continent," Kittie added, crossing her arms. She hadn't been enthused about that, though Jack wondered if it was only because she hadn't been there.

"Then portaled across half a continent." Jack didn't mean to sound so smug about it, but he couldn't help it. That was something no mage had ever done before. Then he paused, wondering if he'd misspoken. "Wait, this an ambush? You mad at me?"

Kittie eyed him. "Should I be?"

He frowned, rubbing the back of his neck. "I had an easier time fighting the Copperheads than figuring you out about this."

Kittie laughed. "No, I'm not mad at you. I'm proud that you treated Emmaline like the brilliant young woman she is."

"She's gonna be an outlaw," Jack said, his voice so low it barely carried to his wife's ears.

"Is that so bad?"

Jack pursed his lips, thinking. He liked being an outlaw. Enjoyed the danger. No two days ever the same. But was that the life for his daughter? He turned the idea over in his mind. What did he expect her to be, a townie? A woman settled down like a broody hen, only worrying about children and a household? That wasn't right, either. Kittie wasn't any of those things. Then he thought about Blaise, how the Breaker was an outlaw—and also wasn't. *Maybe Em can be like that.*

"Nah, I reckon it's not," Jack admitted, setting those thoughts aside for later.

He cocked his head. "I got something to show you."

"Jack Dewitt, did you bring me a gift?" Kittie asked, her face alight with pleasure. "And you've been sitting on it this long?"

"I needed to wait until we were in the Gutter."

She linked her arm through his. "Now you're being mysterious."

"Yep." Jack grinned, revealing a carry-sack he'd concealed in his duster. He carefully drew out the box containing the firepot. He'd hung onto it, waiting for the right moment once they were back in Fortitude and the dust had settled a little.

"What is it?" Kittie asked, studying the box.

The outlaw carefully opened the box, displaying the firepot wrapped in dragonskin. Kittie's eyes widened as Jack drew the small earthenware jar out. "Somethin' you don't see every day. And what comes of it is up to you." Something rattled within the earthenware. "Hmm, we should go to the fire pit behind the house."

Kittie regarded him with great curiosity, and together they walked from HQ to their house. There was little more than ash in the fire pit, but Jack didn't think that mattered. He held out the firepot. "For you."

Kittie accepted it, frowning uncertainly at it. "You can start explaining any moment now."

He chuckled. "Open it up and pour the contents into the pit."

Kittie did as he suggested, watching as what looked like uncut red gemstones clattered into the fire pit. A pair of gleaming black stones winked in the afternoon light. Kittie crouched down, getting a better look. "Is that fire opal? And obsidian?"

"Yep."

"*Jack*." Kittie sounded exasperated. "You forget, I only know a fraction of the arcane dragonshit you do."

He hid a smile at her frustration. "Set 'em on fire and watch."

"If you're tricking me into releasing a fiery demon from Perdition that we have to fight, so help me—"

"It's not a demon. I mean, not really."

Kittie gesticulated at him with both hands. "What do you mean *not really*? I should set *you* on fire, Jack Arthur Dewitt."

"Damn, you used my entire name," he said with a laugh. Then he grinned, stepping closer to her. "I'd never trick you. This really is something special. Promise." He followed his words by planting a kiss on her lips. She didn't reciprocate, not at first. Probably too annoyed at him playing coy. But then she relented, and he had a few sweet moments to enjoy the smoky taste of her.

Kittie pulled away first, giving him another dubious look. "Guess I'll see what ridiculousness you've gotten up to."

She stood beside the fire pit and snapped her fingers. A spark appeared in the cold ashes. She gasped as the fire—*her* fire—took on a life all its own. A brilliant flash blinded them for an instant, and Jack took a step back, wondering if he'd been mistaken. Then he heard the sharp rap of hooves on the ground and a snort.

"What?" Kittie gasped, a hand to her mouth.

A chestnut mare stood over the fire pit, her eyes shining like obsidian. She pawed at the ground, arching her lovely neck. Her long mane and tail tousled in the breeze like living flames. The mare stared at them, nostrils distended as she assessed them. She tossed her head, skittish, and tried to back away, but the invisible constraints of the fire pit bound her. The equine snorted out a fearful breath, ears flicking back and forth.

"Jack…" Kittie didn't dare look at him, her entire focus on the mare. "What in Perdition am I looking at?"

"She's an aethon," Jack said. "A horse born of fire. She was trapped in the firepot, and only arcane flame could free her."

"I freed her or trapped her again?" Kittie asked, voice sharp. She no doubt had noticed the aethon couldn't leave the pit.

"The pit is a safety measure. Couldn't exactly release a fire spirit in the middle of a flammable town." Jack watched the mare, marveling at her beauty. "Once we know she won't run off and burn down the first building she trots by, you can release her."

Kittie made a frustrated sound. "And how do I do that?"

Jack shrugged. "Touch her. Like knows like. Let her know we'll release her either way, but if she hurts this town, there'll be trouble."

His wife paused at that, glancing at him. "You brought her here so I could free her, knowing that doing so put Fortitude at risk?"

That wasn't quite it, but Jack didn't want to explain himself at the moment. "She was imprisoned, and I didn't like it. See if she'll let you touch her."

Kittie pursed her lips, then held out a hand. The aethon tossed her head, blowing out a nervous breath. Then the mare took a hesitant step closer, nostrils sucking in Kittie's scent. The fire spirit made a soft rumble. The next thing Jack knew, the aethon had shifted so that Kittie's palm pressed against the equine's broad forehead.

"Oh." Kittie's voice was breathy. "She understands. And she wants to stay."

Jefferson

"So, tense meeting, huh?" Blaise asked.

Jefferson glanced over his shoulder, watching as Blaise picked his way through the scrubby brush that sprung up around the rim of the canyon. A frigid wind whistled past them, and Jefferson tugged his greatcoat closer. He'd wandered out of town to think at the end of yet another meeting with all the stakeholders of the Gutter. "It was tense, yes, but I'm used to that."

Blaise studied him for a moment, then moved to sit down beside him. "Look, you've been pretty quiet the last few days, so I gave you some space. But quiet and introspective is *my* thing. What's wrong?"

Everything. Jefferson sighed. He wanted to tell Blaise that he was fine, but it was a lie. "I feel unmoored. The life I had..." He blew out a breath. "Everything's just *gone.*" Jefferson snapped his fingers. "Like that." Flora had stayed in Nera to salvage things, but he'd received correspondence that morning bearing word that she couldn't save his estate. He'd already lost his business assets, despite Seledora's work to find loopholes. Nothing had worked— the Quiet Ones were utterly relentless.

Blaise narrowed his eyes. "Not *everything.*"

Jefferson blinked, suddenly realizing how awful he sounded. How pathetic and ungrateful. "I said every*thing.* You're not a thing. You're in here." He tapped a hand over his heart.

"Nice recovery," Blaise said, bumping his elbow against Jefferson's side.

"It's the truth," Jefferson murmured.

"Anyway, everything's not *gone.* Just different," Blaise said, settling a hand on Jefferson's knee. "We have the bakery." He tried to keep a straight face and failed. "I'm the breadwinner now."

Jefferson snorted. "You've been waiting to say that, haven't you?"

"Maybe." Blaise grinned, and the expression was infectious. Jefferson found he couldn't resist matching it. "Anyway, I *know* you. And Jefferson Cole may be down, but he's *not* out."

Blaise's faith made Jefferson's breath hitch. "Oh? You think so?"

The Breaker continued, "You have more lives than a cat, and somehow you land on your feet. This is just one more inconvenience."

Inconvenience. Jefferson made a face. "It *is* rather inconvenient to be missing most of my wardrobe." The bank would no doubt sell everything in his Ganland house at auction. "How can I be a respectable Ambassador when I only have a choice between four different greatcoats?"

Blaise looked away, though the hint of a smirk touched his lips. "You can borrow one of mine."

Jefferson's brow furrowed at the suggestion. *How do I gently decline this offer without—wait.* "You're *teasing* me."

The Breaker turned back to him, chuckling. "Maybe. Though the offer stands if you need something from three seasons ago."

Three seasons? Blaise truly had no idea how behind on fashion he was, but Jefferson wasn't about to break it to him. Besides, he knew his beau was trying to rile him from his melancholy. He pretended to look affronted. "I would rather go naked."

Blaise laughed, the sound music to Jefferson's ears. "Somehow, I doubt that."

"Is that a challenge?" Jefferson *had* to ask.

Blaise eyed him. "I doubt that would go over well with the Ringleaders." Then he sobered. "What happened at the meeting?"

Jefferson sighed. It had been the first big meeting since the Gutter had gained nationhood, which meant that not only had the respective mayors of Asylum and Rainbow Flat attended, but anyone who might be a major stakeholder. Men and women who held the larger outlying farms and ranches were there as well, and Jefferson had become all too aware that word of his antics had spread far and wide.

"Let's see. I received a sound verbal thrashing for all of my deceptions, which has become a depressingly normal turn of events." Jefferson shook his head. "Not to say I always thought I'd avoid such a fate, but..." He shrugged. "Anyway, it seems they'll still tolerate me as Ambassador since Madame Boss Clayton already agreed to it."

Jefferson didn't dare mention that several had spoken against him, suggesting he should be banished from the Gutter for his misdeeds. To Jefferson's surprise, Jack had been the first to rise to his defense, insistent that *while the man's a righteous piss goblin, he did what had to be done.* No one seemed inclined to argue with the outlaw.

"Isn't it a relief, though?" Blaise asked, his voice little more than a whisper. "No more secrets. No more entanglements to keep straight."

Jefferson chuckled. "I don't even know what that's like anymore." He fiddled with the cabochon ring, the only bit of jewelry he wore, though he kept the ring from Blaise in his pocket. "Oddly enough, that makes me feel more like an impostor than ever."

Blaise put an arm around him. "You get to decide who you want to be now. That's what you always wanted, right?"

"Yes."

Blaise raised his brows, giving him an expectant look. "So?"

"What?"

"Tell me who you want to be. You're at rock bottom, and this is your chance."

Jefferson made a face. "I could have done without the reminder." Blaise gave him a stern look. "Right." He took a deep breath, eyes on the red stone of the opposite canyon wall. "I'm Jefferson Cole. Ambassador. Dreamer. Maybe entrepreneur again someday." He glanced at Blaise. "And outlaw mage."

The outlaw mages will return.

Stay In the Know!

Sign up for my newsletter to receive a free short story plus sneak peeks, exclusive short stories, and more!

www.amycampbell.info

And if you enjoyed *Dreamer*, please take a moment to leave a review on the platform of your choice! Reviews help indie authors like me gain a foothold in the wild world of publishing. It's a small thing that means a lot!

Did you find a typo or other error? I did my best, and even though I have a team, we can still miss things! Please email anything you catch to amy@amycampbell.info.

Soundtrack

Unstoppable - Sia
So Am I - Ava Max
That's What I Want - Lil' Nas X
When the Truth Hunts You Down - Sam Tinnesz
Heart of a Hero - Club Danger
Natural - Imagine Dragons
If Today Was Your Last Day - Nickelback
Welcome to the Show - Adam Lambert
Superpower - Adam Lambert
Take It All - Valley of Wolves
I Will Overcome - Welshly Arms
Fade Into Me - David Cook
If I Had You - Adam Lambert

Acknowledgments

I want to extend a big THANK YOU to everyone who took a chance on not only a new author, but a very unusual sort of fantasy series. I'll be the first to admit it's a strange combination—fantasy with a western flavor. But the more I write in this world with these characters, the more I love it. I hope you enjoy this journey with me!

And so many thanks to my beta reader posse: Catherine, Eline, Jen, Kat, Lindsay, Percy, Raina, Samantha, and Sumi. Your care and feedback have only made this book better.

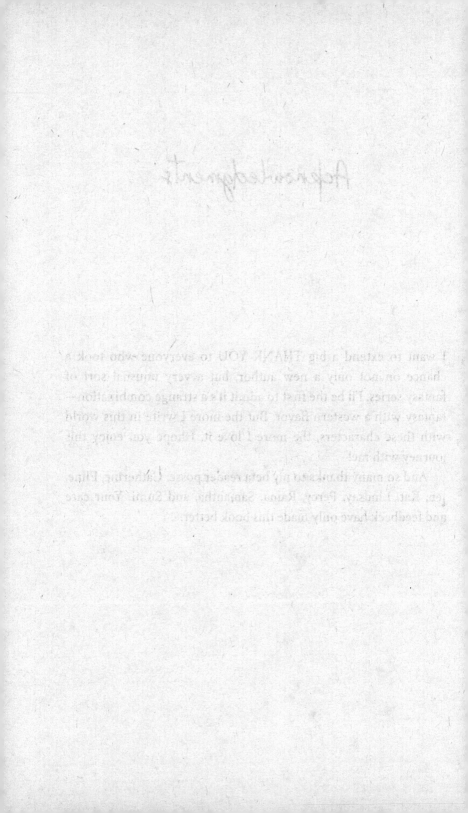

Acknowledgments

I want to extend a big THANK YOU to everyone who took a chance on not only a new author, but every unusual sort of fantasy series. I'll be the first to admit it's a strange combination—fantasy with a western flavor. But the more I write, in this world with these characters, the more I love it. I hope you enjoy this journey with me.

And so many thousand my beta readers: Catherine, Elias, Jen, Kari, Lindsey, Percy, Raaur, Samantha, and Sarah. Your care and feedback have only made this book better.

CPSIA information can be obtained
at www.ICGtesting.com
Printed in the USA
LVHW032109270722
724553LV00003B/220